I0628691

FALTER

A FALTERING SOULS NOVEL
BOOK 1

BY
HAVEN CAGE

This is a work of fiction. Any similarity between the characters and situations within its pages and places or persons, living or dead, is unintentional and coincidental.

All artwork, on the cover and within this publication, was created by Haven Cage.

Copyright © 2016 Haven Cage
All rights reserved.
ISBN: 978-0-9973811-1-5
Published by Haven Cage, LLC
United States

To the husband that stood by my side throughout my journey and still loves me, without you I'd have nothing,

To the son that inspires me to beat the resistance, may I teach you that it's okay to think outside the box and struggle in life if it means you will achieve great things in the world,

To the mother that gave me strength and a mind of my own, I hope my perseverance shows you that your trials were worth it,

To the grandmother that watered my roots and nurtured my soul, may my spirit be as steady and faithful as yours one day.

In loving memory of the father that was never my own, but was more to me than I could have ever asked for.

ACKNOWLEDGEMENTS

Through the ups and downs of my journey, and the endless waiting to see if I actually got this thing launched, these wonderful people have supported, loved, encouraged, and advised me along the way. There are a ton of faithful friends and family who have stood behind me along with those listed below, who I owe thanks to as well. Without them, you would not be reading this massive jumble of words. There is not enough gratitude in the world that could ever repay those souls for what they have given.

R. Dixon   K. Mullins   B. Olson   C. Levesque
P. Lucas   L. Grubbs   C. Gleave   C. Okey   J. Brown
A. Padgett   D. Slesinger   N. Bell   R. Lesslie

My lovely betas:
Diana Quiett   Ashley Bodette   Michelle Hughes
Dina Alexander   Tammy Becraft   Kerri Meng

I want to give special thanks to authors Renea Mason and Rissa Blakeley. They answered an abundance of ridiculous questions through this process, taking some of my newbie anxiety away. Please look them up if you are looking for more great books to read.

In appreciation of the author photos on my website, this book, and my profiles, I want to thank John Merwin.

Lastly, I want to address my editor, Jaclyn Lee. Without you, this book would still be in an insufferably passive state. Thank you for making me a better writer and fueling my dreams of becoming an author. Your help has been invaluable.

In the love of others, I have found the freedom to love myself.
—Haven Cage—

CHAPTER ONE

A Brand New Day

I sucked in a sharp lungful of oxygen. My tongue was too dry to swallow, and my teeth ached from the cold air rushing over them. An overwhelming dread yanked me from sleep too soon.

My eyelids fluttered open, but snapped shut again. The tiny bit of light sifting through my lashes was more than my senses could handle right now. My fingers twitched next to my face, but that was the only movement I could muster. The residual heaviness of a dream weighed me down against the dank pavement and left me feeling like I was tied to a cinder block, plummeting to the base of a lake.

I clenched my eyes shut tighter, willing the dream to stay fresh in my mind, but the more I tried to hold on to the fleeting shadows of my slumber, the quicker they slipped through the cracks of my flimsy memory.

"Dammit," I whispered in defeat, allowing my eyelids to relax.

The nightmarish visions were coming more often lately, yet none of them wanted to stick. My brain couldn't commit a single horrid image of the animations to memory, but they sure left an impact on my emotions. I awoke feeling like a truck hit me and my heart had been dragged to the depths of Hell…every time.

I licked my dry, rubbery lips, chasing the taste of cat shit from my mouth, and lay motionless on the cold ground with my eyes closed, listening to the city awaken. It beat its eager rhythm into the new morning like a dying heart jolted back to life.

From somewhere down the street, the shouts of a paper man broadcasting the arrival of his fresh stack of newspapers resonated against the buildings.

"What the hell does he know? I run this company!"

I jerked, startled by the woman on the street corner yelling into her cell phone.

"Taxi, taxi," she screamed while reprimanding the person on the other end of the call.

Drawing my legs closer against my chest, curling into a ball, I silently begged for just a few more moments of rest. The pungent odor of diesel, pastries, and coffee blowing down the narrow walls of my alley squashed my attempts to fall back asleep, though.

I covered my nose with the frayed sleeve of my shirt, hoping to lessen the strong mixture of aromas reminding me how hungry I was. My stomach growled and ached from the teasing undertones of food filling my nostrils. It had been two days since my last decent meal, and my body definitely felt the deprivation.

The constant patter of designer heels and children running to meet their busses drove away any chance of silence; however, it did help take my mind off my hunger—it was impossible to focus on anything but the noise.

So much noise.

I lifted my hand and pressed it over the ear that wasn't already smashed into the book bag under my head. I desperately tried to muffle the uproar, but failed. There was no getting away, considering every little sound echoed off the surfaces around me.

An obnoxious siren shrieked as it barreled past my block. My sore body cringed at the sound. It was my version of an alarm clock, and it insisted that I wake up—regardless of how hard I fought.

Releasing a frustrated growl, I slapped the pavement—because, naturally, it was the pavement's fault I couldn't sleep longer. I peeled myself off the cool, wet ground. Bits of grit abraded my skin as I rubbed the dampness from my face and yawned. I leaned back into the brick wall behind me, wincing at the stiffness in my joints, and stretched against tight muscles to massage a knot out of my left shoulder.

A cloud of smoke from last night's fire wafted down the alley toward me. "Great," I mumbled. Not only were my clothes damp, thanks to the evening drizzle, but I would smell like a campsite and the burnt steel of a fire barrel. I didn't even get to enjoy the delicious heat that radiated from the barrel the night before—and not for lack of trying. The greedy beggars from the south side of town found their way to our alley yesterday and crowded the barrels as soon as Frannie lit the fire. From what I could tell this morning, the rain dwindled the flames down to nearly extinguished during the night.

Pouting about the newcomers that stole my chance to be warm, I tugged my tattered blanket closer to my body and attempted to ward off the breeze grazing my neck and arms. I peered out over the gathered fabric covering my nose and mouth, cautiously watching the old, hopeless drunks stumbling a little too near for my comfort. They grumbled about the chill and their sad lives as they slowed to circle around the cooling fire barrel a few feet away. Thankfully, they ignored me and, instead, tried to savor the last flickers of flames lapping through the rusted holes in the steel drum.

I peeked up at the sky from under the fire escape I used as shelter and tuned out the complaining, old men. The sun shined high against a clear blue background, but the tall buildings surrounding me stopped the light from touching this end of the alley so early in the morning.

Three brick buildings joined to create the thin rectangular corridor I called home. The west wall of a museum stood as on side of the long, narrow lane, and I was leaning against the east wall of the restaurant which formed the other side.

The restaurant wasn't anything remarkable. It was a family owned business that served the usual southern fried foods. In reality, it was torture for people like us to be so close to the aroma of such comfort food, but this was the only alley that wasn't riddled with gang kids, and it was fairly secluded.

The museum, however, was remarkable to me. Funded by the state and free to the public, it supplied displays that ranged from Vincent Van Gogh's works of art to complete teachings of how the body functioned. I visited their new exhibits every week, and in the last thirteen years, they served as a solid foundation for my education.

The back wall of the library butted up against the museum and restaurant, dead-ending the alley. This wonderful building was my other source of education. Since I didn't get to attend school, I soaked up all the knowledge I could from there. I spent hours hiding in the old, musty books, determined that I wouldn't allow my mind to wither away because of my situation. The librarians watched me struggle in the beginning and then became quite eager to teach me the necessities of life once they saw my hunger to learn.

I was very fortunate that the workers of those businesses accepted me knowing I lived on the streets. They could have easily turned their heads or removed me, hindering my chance to learn. Luckily, they admired my refusal to be ignorant.

Engines whirred as morning drivers challenged each other in a race to their jobs. I squinted, directing my sleepy eyes toward the busy street-end of the alley. Subtle morning light reflected off the steam escaping the restaurant exhaust. Blurs of color from the passing cars blended with the rainbow of droplets spraying into the air. I stared at the pretty hues through the vapors and let my eyes lose focus.

I noticed a plump figure entering the alley on the other side, disrupting my hazy color show. The round man stepped into the warmth spewing from the exhaust and shivered under the abrupt temperature change. He hesitated in the heat for a moment then continued to my side where he plopped down on the ground next to me.

"It's a new day, Nevaeh. Wake up so we can get started. I need to look for a new pair of socks today." The old man took off one beaten, leather shoe and pointed to the bare pinky toe lodged through a hole in his tube sock.

I smiled at George. He seemed almost proud to have worn the pair of socks to smithereens, like it was something he needed to accomplish before feeling good about a newer pair.

"First thing's first, we need food." George jerked his chin toward the restaurant. "Jenna's workin' today, she can probably lift us something for breakfast," he said, sliding his shoe back over the holey sock.

"First of all, I've been awake." I motioned to my face and opened my eyes as big as possible to exaggerate exactly how awake I was. "Second of all, Jenna shouldn't risk her job just because we can't find one." I always felt guilty having to ask people for food.

I gathered my belongings and hoisted myself off the ground. After shoving the stray hairs from my face and straightening my shirt, I slung my dingy book bag of clothes — enough for two day's change — over my shoulder. That and the well-used pink blanket my grandmother knitted were about all I had in the world. The only other thing I owned, my most valuable possession, was the one thing I kept on me at all times.

My necklace, which once draped loosely onto my chest, pulled taut around the base of my neck now. George laughed and teased me, saying that I might as well use it as an anklet because it had grown so tight, but I refused to take it off. There was still room to breathe and swallow, so what was the big deal? I cherished the fact that I'd grown into it.

My hand found its way to the small, silver pendant, lifted it from the divot between my collarbones, and rubbed the tarnished surface as I often did. The rose engraving was barely detectable under my fingers due to years of sweat and constant fondling. I gripped my mother's locket and dragged it back and forth across the short chain as I watched George bundle up the pack he'd stowed under a broken crate.

The locket protected the last picture my mom and I took together. That day was a faded, almost nonexistent, glimpse of my past. She held me tight as she smiled and kissed a younger, giggling version of me. I stared at it every day and compared myself, as I am today, to the memories of when I was five. I'm a little rougher around the edges than I figured I should be at twenty-three.

"Come on girl!" George yanked my arm and dragged me down the alley to the grand civilization that existed around our small community of vagabonds.

I lived in this community, but I tried very hard to avoid the incriminating habits associated with street life. Stealing and lying was mostly against my nature. Unfortunately, some things were unavoidable.

George and I worked whenever we could, whether it meant cleaning store windows for a day or doing the dishes at a low-rated restaurant. Restaurants were the best, though. Sometimes they traded food for payment, especially if they were in a pinch. In the end, we always shared whatever earnings we got.

George was my only family, and I owed my life to him. He found me beneath a boat dock when I was around ten years old, while he was looking for a hiding place from the winter sting. He stumbled upon a girl under that dock, sopping wet and unaware of the world around her. I had a knot on my head, he says, the size of Texas. That was the beginning of my life as I know it.

I have some early recollections of my childhood — my mother before she died, and my grandmother who raised me after her death — but most of my memories from the time I was five until the time George found me were a blank. Five years of my life just missing, as if someone tipped me over like a teapot and poured out what they didn't want me to remember. I do remember that my father died before I was born; my mom told me stories about him all the time before I lost her too.

The tarnished necklace and a stain-ridden blanket were the only mementos of my past he'd found with me. Being so young in the memories I had, and sustaining a fair amount of trauma to my head, I didn't remember my address or much about where I came from. There was no way of getting back to where I started. I wasn't even sure if my grandmother was still alive.

Every once in a while, something sparked a flashback to a time or place I couldn't quite recall, like little breadcrumbs leaving hints about who I was before. However, they are only bits and pieces — never enough to fill in the holes.

"Come on, we'll be late gettin' the day started, and all the good work'll be taken," George called out. "Bill was talkin' bout a position opening at Joe's Café last night. Maybe it's a waitressin' job and you'll get it. You're pretty enough. You can make some good tips." I followed as he clumsily weaved his way down the streets.

George was right. I was pretty, in a girl-next-door kind of way. Smart enough, too. It's just very difficult to convince someone to hire a young woman with no past, no social security number, and no address.

"Let's make a stop at the Banquet Hall. They have nice bathrooms and those soaps that make me smell like lavender." I smiled with delight. I almost caught a whiff of the sudsy perfume just talking about it.

He looked back at me, rolled his tired eyes, and chuckled. "I really don't think it matters how you smell as long as you don't stink like ya do now, kid!"

George winced when I skipped to his side and playfully punched his arm.

"Man, I don't understand how a small little thang like you can punch like the back end of a mule." He rubbed circles over his shoulder and cowered away from my reach.

"Aw, it didn't hurt that bad. I guess I'll have to take it easier on you from now on, old man." I grinned and jogged past him backwards, provoking a race.

George's pout curved into a sly smile, then his still-spry bones kicked into gear, pounding the sidewalk in an attempt to catch up. I led us farther into the city, turning this corner and that along the way. Heavy breathing and an occasional raspy cough warned me that George wasn't too far behind.

We reached the Banquet Hall minutes later and stopped at its steep steps to take in the impressive facade. Tall, stark white pillars stood in regal contrast to the classic, red brick building. White shutters and baskets of red and blue pansies decorated each large window. To most, the Hall was the epitome of old, southern charm, and what it held within only supported those feelings.

Then, there were the signs. The Hall prohibited us from entering. It banned beggars. No Loitering signs were stationed at every corner of the building's lot. They were not so close to the entrance that it would offend those who belonged there, or appear uncouth to the true lady, but not so far away that the homeless might think we were welcome. Over the years, George and I made friends with a sympathetic guard who allowed us to bypass the Hall's policy. When he worked, we had a free pass to the spare employee bathrooms at the back entryway.

I moved to a side window out of the public's view and peered in on tip toes to search inside for our man. Through the glass, a few seconds later, I caught his eye with a small wave and smile. The guard, Dan, gave a once-down nod that meant it was safe to sneak in. I passed the message along to George using a similar nod. We hugged the wall as we crept to the back door and then waited. Our covert operation had begun.

Soon after, Dan swung the door open, placed a stick between the door and its jamb to prop it open, and stepped out onto the concrete landing. He inhaled deeply and blew a loud breath out as if it was the first fresh breath he'd had in awhile.

The guard pushed one of his thumbs under the edge of his belt and let his hand rest anchored at his waist. He strolled to the opposite end of the landing, acting unaware that we were crouched just behind him, waiting for him to signal.

With his other hand, he retrieved a soft pack of cigarettes from his pant pocket. He shook the nearly empty pack until one of the last sticks poked out of the hole and then pulled it free with his lips. After placing the crumpled package back into his pants, he dug a lighter out of his shirt pocket. Dan sparked the end of the cigarette and took a long draw while scanning the back lot for other employees. Once satisfied, his hand left the heavy utility belt and tapped the brim of his black baseball cap which read SECURITY on the front.

This was our gesture that the coast was clear.

George climbed up the stairs, opened the door, and handed me the stick. He entered before me, ducking and scoping the area with narrowed eyes like we were robbing a bank. I never liked this part of the plan, but both men agreed—against my arguing—that George always lead in case someone caught us. He and Dan wanted to give me a chance to escape.

While I waited for George to let me in, I watched Dan's back. He smoked and continued pretending not to notice the charade occurring behind him. I felt a sudden need to say thank you. There was rarely time to tell him how much we appreciated what he did while we skulked around the building.

As if reading my mind, Dan glanced at me over his shoulder and smiled before returning to take another puff from his cigarette. It was a quick gesture, but meaningful just the same. When we initially devised this plan, George and I insisted that Dan never look directly at us. We wanted him to be able to say he never saw us enter the building if questioned. Technically, it wouldn't be lying. Somehow it made me feel a little better about the whole thing.

A tug at my arm indicated it was time to move. I stepped into the hall, held the stick against the door jamb, and let the door slowly close onto the wedge of wood.

The inside of the historical building reminded me of my grandmother's home, where I lived as a child. I couldn't recall where it was exactly, but I could picture the rich surroundings of her old, colonial-style house with clarity. The aroma of history drifted from every artifact and saturated the building; the scent was a bit musty, but welcoming all the same.

The lavish adornments sprinkled around the Hall resembled the antique keepsakes my grandmother had collected over the years.

As we lurked toward the bathroom, my attention was drawn to the row of small, glass boxes sitting atop the mahogany pedestals that lined a path to the lobby. They displayed ribbons and buttons that decorated generals from battles long ago. In other cases, beautifully embellished mementos, such as hand-held mirrors and matching hair brushes, rested on burgundy, velvet pillows and gleamed under the spot lights pointed down at them.

I lifted my gaze to the shadow boxes hanging on the gray walls behind the cases and admired the dozens of recovered silver and copper coins; the light caught every pit and imperfection the little disks of metal had sustained during their years of trade and travel.

George and I eased farther along the rounded corridor, careful to stay behind the towering, gold pillars. The massive structures braced the edges of the circular lobby and did a fine job of blocking us from the view of passing employees as we headed to our destination.

A loud clamor from across the room echoed off the high ceiling. We halted mid-step, pressing our bodies against one of the giant pillars. I leaned out as far as I could without being seen and checked if it was okay to continue. No one seemed to notice, so I lingered, letting my curious eyes roam over the extravagant lobby I didn't get to see very often.

Twin marble staircases extended up to the second floor, which was gated off to visitors. Wide strips of purple satin draped in pleated half circles from the banisters as they curved down into the center of the grand room.

The place was buzzing with preparation for an event. Busy employees worked diligently at polishing an extensive set of silver plates. Another worker set the glistening dinnerware in meticulous positions atop mahogany buffets as long as the walls they lined.

Memories of eating off of grandma's special china surfaced. She told me stories about the three generations that had passed the gorgeous porcelain along. Pastel pinks and lavenders portrayed a bouquet of blooming roses at the center of each plate, accenting every flowery teacup, bowl, and vessel that went along with the collection.

"Nevaeh, never save the beautiful things in life for special occasions. Every day needs a little beauty in it," she'd chime. We'd dine on fluffy buttermilk pancakes from hand painted dishes and drench them in syrup poured from expensive gravy boats before going outside to work in the garden, just as we always did.

"Are you daydreamin' again, girl?" George whispered, interrupting my thoughts. "We don't have time to be thinkin', we need to be doin'." I turned to see the plump man put his hands on his hips and tap his foot impatiently, waiting for me to follow him.

I rushed past him, half shouting, half whispering, "You know, I *am* a woman. I was born with the ability to walk and think at the same time. Besides we're here." I knocked on the women's bathroom door and paused for a response to make sure it wasn't occupied.

"Meet you back here in fifteen," he replied, ruffling the hair on the top of my head. He pushed the men's bathroom door open on the other side of the corridor and disappeared inside.

My rough, callused hand turned the smooth doorknob and pushed it open. I stepped inside, activating the motion sensor, and the lights flickered on, illuminating the room with a soft glow. Greeted by the sweet, soothing fragrance of lilac, I inhaled and pulled the familiar scent deep into my lungs. I smiled, noticing the crystal vase standing elegantly on the gray, marble vanity, and admired its fresh display of flowers. The varying muted purples decorated the bathroom like a painting in an art gallery.

I shut the door behind me and locked it, studying the treasures hidden within the cozy room. I wondered if the people who used this restroom appreciated it as much as I did. Doubtful. It's easy to take things like this for granted. I saw this as a place of luxury, where most would see it as just a place to pee.

My fingers traced along the gold ribbon that edged the bottom of a fluffy, beige towel hanging next to the shower. Its softness tickled my fingertips. My skin tingled with excitement, knowing I was about to get an actual shower.

No sink bath today!

I unbuttoned my jeans and pulled off my shirt, letting my soiled clothes fall to the floor. I examined myself in the mirror. The image staring back at me reflected a grown woman, though strangely, I still thought of myself as a young girl with so much to learn.

I angled body parts this way and that to see better in the mirror as I took stock of the ill-effects caused by my living in the streets. A clear outline of my ribcage slid under the thin skin on my torso, and individual ribs flared and relaxed with my slow breathing. The subtle olive hue in my skin successfully hid some of the bruises and smudges of dirt I had acquired from sleeping on the ground the last few nights. They were the little...gifts...I never really wanted.

I raked my fingers through the long, dark hair spilling between my shoulder blades. Stubborn knots fought against me as I struggled to release them.

What I wouldn't give for a brush right now.

A disappointed huff escaped my mouth as my eyes lowered, grazing over the ample breasts and full hips accentuating the femininity of my shape. I frowned. Most women would be happy to have such a curvy figure. For me, it signified that I would need to be more cautious of where I lay my head at night.

Being a woman was not a good thing in my lifestyle. George looked after me, but he couldn't save me from everything. Or everyone. Unfortunately, we already verified that.

Ignoring the haunting thoughts of a bad experience, I moved toward the tub and reached for the gold faucet in the shower, turning it to scalding. Water rumbled out in a cascade of warmth. I climbed into the tub and let the water rush over me. Every hair on my body raised with anticipation as the wet heat pelted my cool skin. The stall quickly filled with steam, and I became surrounded in a wonderful cloud of mist — the hot moisture clearing my lungs of the city smog.

I grabbed the lush, white washcloth draped on the shower door and wet it.

Thank you, I thought to whoever left my favorite soap nestled in the wire toiletry rack.

I picked up the bottle and turned it upside down over my other hand. Foamy, lavender bubbles formed as I poured a generous amount onto the rag. I scrubbed the cloth over my body like I couldn't get myself clean enough. The rich lather spread over me, dousing my skin in the heavenly scent.

It felt so good to stand under the waterfall while it beat away the impurities. Today I would look—and smell—normal.

I wanted to savor the luxurious shower I rarely had the opportunity to enjoy, but my allotted time was close to an end. Soon, George would be irritated with my "need to primp", as he called it. To me, I wasn't really primping. It's not like I was putting makeup on or experimenting with some new hair style. How did he expect a girl to get ready in fifteen minutes, anyway?

When I stepped out of the stall, little eddies of steam swirled around my movements. I reached for my bag of clothes and pulled out a freshly laundered pair of jeans and a t-shirt. I stuffed the worn set back into the bag.

The soap I washed them with at the gas station the other day left the new clothes stiff, but clean. I was never one that succumbed to staying in my own filth just because I lived on the streets. George taught me how to use public restrooms to my advantage. They're not always as good as a washing machine, but it was a lot better than reeking of body odor.

I threw the well-worn clothes on in a rush and ran my fingers through the mess of soppy curls on my head.

That'll have to do.

I scanned around for something to tie my hair back. My eyes fell on the shiny ribbon wrapped around the flowers next to me. I hesitated for a moment, questioning my morals and confirming that stealing wasn't my thing. Usually, it wasn't, but I also understood you had to improvise when you had little to work with.

I wove the wet strands of my hair into a simple braid, held it tightly with one hand, and then untied the blue ribbon that bound the lilacs with the other. After looping the ribbon in a perfect bow, I glared at it in the mirror, feeling a little guilty.

No one would notice. They replaced the flowers daily, anyway. Besides, it was important to make a good impression at a potential job, right? I shrugged and tossed the braid behind my back, discouraging any more thoughts of self-persecution for my crime.

As I gathered my things, there was a knock on the door. "Ain't you done yet, girl?" the familiar voice asked from the other side.

"I'm coming," I growled, rolling my eyes at George's pushiness.

I yanked the door open, ready to blast him a new one for rushing me, but stopped, my mouth full of curses that never made it out. The brush of someone's lips and the breath of a whisper tickled my earlobe as if someone was right next to me. I gasped. A sudden eerie sensation prickled the hairs on the back of my neck.

I turned around, leaning back against the door to open it wider, and scanned the empty room, carefully considering each object's ability to make noise or change air flow. I'd left everything in its place, just as I found it when I arrived—except for the ribbon.

The damp towel was looped around its bar, properly folded and drying. My favorite soap was tucked back inside the wire basket, and the lilacs rested—slightly more scattered than before—in their crystal vase. There was nothing that could've caused any sound even close to a whisper, or make me feel so unsettled.

"Get your bony butt movin'," the old man commanded, dispelling my uneasy feeling.

I sidestepped George out of the doorway, giving him the evil-eye for his pushy comment, and headed toward the exit.

As we passed the hallway to the main lobby, I noticed Dan standing at the base of one of the curved staircases. He vigilantly skimmed over the lobby, watching visitors linger at the display cases. I cleared my throat to catch his attention. When he turned his head and smiled, I nodded with gratitude, then followed George down the hall and out the back door.

The musty dampness of the rear parking lot assaulted my nose as soon as I exited the building. City smog, rotting trash, and gas fumes stifled the hint of lavender saturating my skin. It was disappointing that I would never get away from the street stink.

George lovingly cradled my arm with his hand and ushered me toward the road.

I paused halfway across the lot as a strange rush of adrenaline flushed through me, piquing my senses. That eerie, unsettled feeling from the bathroom returned, souring my stomach. I felt the creepy sensation of being watched, being the center of a stalker's attention.

A rustling wind rolled over the parking lot like a wave and crashed into my body, flapping the loose hairs around my face. For a moment, I thought I heard my name called from the other end of the parking lot, but no one was there when I turned to look.

I glanced around at the random pieces of weathered trash and dead leaves lying unaffected on the concrete. Something — besides my hair — would have moved in a gust that forceful.

Did I just imagine it?

No, I couldn't have.

"What did you say?" I asked George, searching for an explanation to what I heard. I hoped it was him saying my name, but I was certain it wasn't.

He gawked at me, a puzzled expression on his face. "Nuthin'."

CHAPTER TWO

In The Eyes of Strangers

George and I shouldered into the rushing flow of pedestrians racing through their day. Occasionally, an elbow or knee would bump me off my path, and I'd have to catch back up with George. Four blocks down, we stopped before a tall, red door.

I studied the two-story building surrounding the eye-catching door. The bright red popped against its sizable brown and charcoal colored bricks. The same colored bricks extended onto the sidewalk, edging the windows and entryway in decorative alternating patterns. A vintage sign squeaked as it swung from wires just above the door. Swirly letters spelled out Joe's Café in red, black, and cream. Three cobble stone steps graduated in half circles beneath the entrance, inviting us in.

I climbed onto the top step and peeked in through the warped-glass windows to spy on the diners eating breakfast and chatting about their lives. What I could see of the inside appeared warm and cozy, just like the air wafting out of the door as customers came and went.

"I'm gonna go in and ask for the manager, see what he's got open. You wait here. I'll get you if it looks promising."

I held both hands up and crossed my fingers. "Good luck."

As George disappeared through the door, I hopped down to the bottom step and leaned back against the brick. I observed the people chasing taxis and running to the bus stop at the end of the block, wondering where they were headed in such a hurry.

An abundance of beautiful women in skirt suits passed me by without acknowledgement. I giggled at how awkward their professional attire, bare legs, and running shoes looked together. Where did they work that tennis shoes and business skirts were the outfit of choice?

Once in a while, a handsome man mingled in and out of the crowd. Two of them made eye contact with me as they shuffled by, talking on their cell phones, and another glanced at me from behind an open newspaper in his hand. They all smiled and nodded in my direction, but never stopped to speak to me.

My imagination ran wild as I watched the world buzz around me. I pictured what it would be like for such a man to hold me in his arms and engulf me in his love. Though I didn't mind it too much, this was a lonely way of life. Not too many guys pined after a dirty street girl, and the ones that did weren't looking for anything long term. Most of the time, they assumed I was the type that gladly accepted their money after a quick roll in the sack.

A clatter from inside the café broke my people-watching trance. I twisted and searched for George through the warped glass above me. Years of weathering had clouded and melted the old window, making it hard for me to see more than five feet or so into the building. From what I gathered, George wasn't within that five foot range. Maybe that was a good thing.

As I turned back to face the street, an uneven brick tripped me, knocking me off balance. I stumbled, almost falling off the step. My hands shot out, reaching to brace myself as an arm wrapped tightly around my waist and stood me upright.

"Oh, excuse me," I cried out, stunned.

I clutched onto the collar of a man's coat. My pulse raced, and words escaped me. I stared up into the curious eyes of my savior. They were a shade of blue-green that I'd never seen before, and so clear I could see my reflection in them. I suddenly felt very exposed, like he was diving into the depths of my soul, and he knew my deepest secrets. However, something kept me at a distance when I tried to explore his.

As I stared at him, dumbfounded and embarrassed, the heavy beat of his heart pounded against my hand. My insides tightened with excitement.

The man's full lips opened, a visible breath floating out with his words. "No problem. Are you ok?"

His calm tone settled me, but I couldn't unclench my hands from his coat. I didn't want to release him. I feared I would never see him again, that he'd disappear into the busy city. And, as I stared helplessly at him, I entertained the idea of him experiencing the same interest in me that I was feeling for him. His intense expression of concern and curiosity disappeared, and he let go of my arms.

I exhaled the breath I'd been holding. "Yes. Thanks," I answered, struggling to find something to say that would keep him there. When nothing came to mind, I gathered my wits enough to pry my fingers — and eyes — from the stranger, then straightened my clothes. He watched me shift my shirt back into place and fiddle with some loose strands of hair before turning to open the crimson door. He stepped aside politely, allowing someone to exit the café.

George shuffled out past my savior, his brow furrowed. "What are you doin', girl? Didn't you see me wavin' at ya?" he groaned.

The man nodded a goodbye to me and stepped into the café.

"No. Sorry, I was distracted." My eyes wandered after the man through the clouded window while I spoke. "What did you find out?" I lost sight of the stranger's murky form as he disappeared toward the back of the building. I reluctantly switched my focus to George.

"The manager has two openings. I told him about our situation, and that we're lookin' for the chance to make an honest livin'. Seems real nice. He's givin' us a trial period."

"What are the trial positions?" I questioned.

"I have the dishwasher's spot, and you'll get the hostess's job. Sound good?"

"Sounds great! When do we start?" I was elated. Even the smallest opportunity offered the possibility of a normal life.

"Well, you have to get interviewed too. But if all is good, we'll start today."

My gaze flickered back to the window, searching again for the man that saved me. He wasn't anywhere in sight.

"Let's go then." I reached for the cold brass of the door handle and pulled it open, moving to the side for a leaving customer. A warm gush of air tickled my face as I walked into the café.

George squeezed his round body by me and strolled toward a man in a black t-shirt and dark-washed jeans. I followed him, flashing an inviting smile to appear more personable. Presentation is everything, and when you don't have much to work with, flirting helps too.

The man wiped his wet hands on the white towel looped through his belt, glancing at George and then pinning his eyes on me. "You're right, she is pretty."

Heat surfaced in my cheeks, and I shot George a quick look of aggravation.

The dark-haired guy was handsome in a subtle way. He was clearly good looking, but not the overly sexy type with a picture-perfect face. His sharp features gave him a rugged edge that would

20

command any woman's regard.

The man offered a hand for me to shake, his lips curling into a gentle smile when I accepted it. "Hey, how are ya?" His smooth, fluid movements and polite manner hinted at the traditional, old-fashioned man he seemed to pride himself in portraying. His burly appearance paired with an obvious soft side made him very seductive.

"Good, thank you."

"Do you have any experience?" he asked, keeping his eyes glued to mine.

"I have experience as a waitress from a few jobs I've had in the past."

"Well, fortunately, hostessing isn't rocket science and doesn't require much know how." He shrugged. "If anything, you'll probably get bored with the redundancy of it."

"Sir, I can handle bored as long as it gets me a job," I responded confidently.

His lips tightened into a smirk. Shallow crow's feet surrounded his olive-green eyes, implying he was approximately thirty years old.

The guy looked me over once more, calculating his decision to hire us. "Y'all got the jobs, but like I told the George here, it's a trial period. I'll be fair, but if I catch you letting others in or stealing from me, that's it. The pay isn't much, but I'll compensate by allowing ya'll to sleep in the employee break room at night. There's a couch and a love seat in there. We've got a full bathroom in the back too." His eyes drifted between George and me. "Somehow, I don't think y'all will be as big a problem as the last people I tried to help."

I shook my head and smiled graciously.

"By the way, call me Gavyn, not sir," he insisted with a sweet wink. "Follow me. I'll show you around and get ya some clean clothes and aprons."

We trailed Gavyn, nodding and muttering replies of acknowledgment at the appropriate times throughout the tour.

The café was spacious and well laid out. Medium-sized bistro tables and chairs, currently seating happy diners, furnished the front of the cafe. A maple, hand-carved bar divided the busy eaters from the servers and prep area.

Two cooks bobbed back and forth between the large stoves and ovens hidden away in the kitchen. The small ting of a bell chimed into the noise often.

"Order up!" one of the cooks yelled, sliding a steaming order of soup and a sandwich onto the counter at the base of a huge pass-through window.

The servers behind the bar worked quickly, garnishing the steaming plates with fresh orange slices. Keen eyes investigated the meals as they arranged them on carrying trays, and on occasion, a curse word erupted from a server's mouth when they discovered an order came out wrong. None of the customers seemed to notice, though.

A dim hallway between the kitchen and the guest restrooms led to the small lounge at the back of the restaurant. This would act as our make-shift bedroom. I bypassed entering the room and strolled directly across the corridor into the employee bathroom. I ogled the amenities with excitement, daydreaming about the time I would spend in there relaxing after a long day at work. There was a large clawfoot bathtub, vintage shower head the size of a dinner plate, and a not-so-girl-friendly vanity. After promising the bathroom I would return soon, I stepped back out into the hall.

As we approached the end of the corridor, we stopped. I noticed a narrow stairwell that led upwards and looked at Gavyn curiously.

"That's my home sweet home," he informed us, nudging his chin towards the stairs. "Have a seat in the break room if you want. I'll get ya some blankets and stuff." He jerked his thumb behind him in the direction of the lounge before disappearing into the dark stairway.

George and I stood in the hall, soaking up the place's character. Paintings and signs from a different era, maybe the 1950's, hung in random spots all over the walls. It was the kind of art you found in an old five and dime store. My eyes wandered over the aged prints, studying the depictions of full-figured women beautifully splayed atop vintage cars and bizarre advertisements using fat babies and winged pigs. The old building held a sense of history with a soda shop appeal; yet, it took advantage of more modern touches like the high-tech cooking equipment and a kick-ass bar.

I put my hands on my hips and pivoted around, taking it all in while we waited.

I could get used to this.

I inhaled the sugary air drifting around me from the abundance of shakes and cherries. Laughter rumbled over the background noise from a sports game down the hall. Dishes clanked as the waitresses piled them high on serving trays.

I was already falling in love with this place.

Heavy footsteps pounded down the stairs a few feet from us. Gavyn appeared again with a smile, a mountain of blankets, and clothes draped over his arms. "These were all I could find. I kept some abandoned clothes from previous employees. Hope they fit."

George unloaded the pile off Gavyn's hands and carried it to the couch inside the lounge. "Thank you," the old man said with great appreciation in his eyes.

Gavyn and I followed George in and watched him sift through the mound, searching for something better than what we had. He chuckled and held up a clean pair of thick, white socks in front of him. His joyful eyes darted to me, knowing I would understand his excitement.

"Go ahead and change. Meet me out front afterwards." Gavyn winked at me and left the room.

I smiled at George's contentment and chose a plain, black dress from the layers of fabric. I held it up against me, contemplating its fit. The dress seemed to be my size.

As I scanned over the remaining mountain of clothes, shiny, black Mary Jane's peeked out from underneath it. I snatched them up and headed for the door. "I'll be back," I assured George.

I walked to the bathroom across the hall, the aged hardwoods creaking under my feet. I softly kicked the door shut behind me and yanked my shirt and pants off. My old clothes hit the floor with a thump.

My skin screamed with elation while I studied the quality of the new outfit. I slid the dress over my head and stared down at the long, thin strips awkwardly hanging at my sides. I struggled with the structure of the dress, stretching the ties out in front of me and crossing them over my waist in a wrinkled mess. I'd seen these dresses on women before but never needed to figure out how the "wrap" concept worked. I feared not getting it tied just right, so I fixed the sashes in a clumsy double knot. The last thing I needed was a horribly revealing clothing malfunction on my first day.

The black material draped my body a little loosely, but it would work for now. The long sleeves stopped midway down my forearms and would be out of the way while I worked. I peered down at the hemline, satisfied that it landed just below my knees. I wasn't used to wearing dresses, and this one made me a little self-conscious. My feet slid effortlessly into the Mary Jane's. They fit like a glove.

I examined myself in the mirror, straightening stray hairs and retying my blue bow. What a difference a new outfit made!

When I stepped into the hallway, George was waiting impatiently.

His expression softened as his eyes trailed over me in the dress. "Fits you well, girl," he said before rushing into the bathroom for his turn to change.

I put on my best smile and started down the corridor. A friendly-looking woman met me at the end of the hallway. She was a few years older than me and extraordinarily pretty.

"My name is Layla. Gavyn said you need help getting acquainted with our routine." Her charming smile hooked me right away.

Confidence radiated from her graceful movements as Layla grabbed my arm and playfully dragged me behind the bar. Servers pushed by us, one after another, hoisting steaming plates and colorful drinks over our heads. I seemed to be in the way everywhere, but they swerved around me like I wasn't there. I anxiously waited for someone to scold me. When no one did, I relaxed and let the feeling of home settle in my heart.

"Nevaeh, is it?" Layla picked up dishes off the bar and organized them on an empty tray next to her. "I've been here awhile, so follow me and you won't go wrong. We're very laid back here, kinda like family." She plucked a small piece of paper clipped to the order wheel in the pass-through window and set it on the tray.

"Where do I start?" I asked, ready to find my place in the cafe.

"Gavyn wants me to show you everything, so he can float you as a waitress too. There's more work if you're flexible." She held her index finger up, pointing at the sign above. "The basics first. Learn the menu, and how to prep the drinks and food."

I tilted my head back to study the large billboards nailed high on the wall over the bar area. Multicolored chalk scribbled all over the large blackboards, listing an impressive array of refreshments and entrees. It was quite an extensive menu for such a small cafe. I rambled off a few of the items in my mind: Shirley Temple, Root Beer Float, American BLT, and Eggs Bennie on Wheat. It would take some time to learn everything.

As I read the lines of food and drinks, someone bumped into me, knocking me off balance.

"Oops, sorry," the gray-haired woman murmured. She offered an apologetic smile before yelling at the cooks for messing up someone's burger. When I turned to ask Layla the lady's name, she had disappeared.

"Order up!" a familiar voice called from the kitchen. Gavyn grinned as he sat a bowl of mac and cheese on the serving counter and slid it through the window. His gaze lingered on me for a moment, then focused on the cook asking him for more olive oil.

Since Layla left me, and everyone else was flittering about their business, I decided to take a chance. My eyes landed on the table layout taped to the wall next to the drink fountain. It was a pretty simple drawing of numbers representing the twelve tables lining the walls of the café and another six that were scattered around the center floor.

"What the hell. Gotta start somewhere."

I committed as much of the chart as I could to memory and took a deep breath. Feeling confident, I moved to the end of the counter, picked up the next waiting order, and headed to the assigned seats. As I turned to walk away, I caught Gavyn's eyes watching me.

When I returned to the bar, Layla was waiting.

"Wow, you take initiative, don't you? Just be careful. We're laid back, but someone might mistake you for taking their customers for tips," she advised.

I spent the rest of the day reading order pads to memorize the food and observing the other workers prepare dishes. The rush of people around me felt exhilarating. The pace picked up during lunchtime, but I welcomed it. I enjoyed the challenge.

Layla and I were much closer by the time dinner rolled around. We'd squeezed in time during breaks to learn about each other. She obviously had much more to talk about than I did, and it was nice to hear about someone with a normal life. Behind her extreme confidence, Layla was very comforting. Her personality reeled you in, making you want to tell her everything about yourself.

After a long, busy day, it was finally closing time. I was helping roll silverware and wipe down table tops when my imagination wandered to the man I'd met at the door. His eyes were as deep as the sea. I could easily drown in them. His lips looked smoother than silk. It was silly thinking of things like that, but his image had roamed in and out of my thoughts all day.

There was something different about him. He wasn't like the men that walked by me daily, winking and smiling out of courtesy. I felt an unexplainable connection to him. It was as if he knew me without having met me before. Even now, the emotions he stirred within me were exhilarating.

Maybe he would have stayed and talked if I'd just figured out what to say. Maybe I could have snuffed this unyielding interest.

While gathering the broom and dustpan from behind the bar, exhaustion from the day started to catch up with me. George had beaten me to the shower, already finished with his work, and soon it would be my turn. Everyone was gone. The humming of the café had stopped. The only noise left was a song playing on a jukebox.

I recognized the tune and began a slow sway to the beat as I brushed the broom back and forth across the floor. Music was an escape for me, and the sweet sound of Nora Jones was one of my favorites. She sang "Come Away With Me," and I closed my eyes, dreaming of places I'd never been — of a life I could be proud of and memories I would no longer forget.

I was so distracted by my daydreaming and dancing that I didn't notice the approaching presence until a warm hand took mine. Taken completely off guard, I stumbled back into a table. The wooden legs slid, scraping against the floor. The broom dropped from my hand and smacked the hard, wooden planks with a loud pop. Stacked chairs fell from the tabletop and crashed on the ground. I felt my feet begin to lose their footing and scrunched my face with anticipation of my second clumsy fall in one day. When I didn't land on the floor as expected, I opened one cautious eye and then the other, realizing I was leaned back, securely cradled in someone's arms.

Gavyn looked down at me with regret in his eyes. "You looked like you needed a partner, and I love this song. Didn't think you would mind the company." He smiled apologetically and stood me upright. "Sorry if I scared you. I shouldn't have imposed like that." He paused for a moment before picking up the fallen chairs and placing them back on the table.

"People just don't usually get so close to me. I thought I was alone." I shook my head, suddenly embarrassed. I reached for the broom and gathered the dispersed dirt back into a pile. I couldn't bear to look him in the eyes. "I'm almost done here."

Gavyn gently laid his hand on my forearm and moved closer. "Hey, I didn't get my dance," he cooed in my ear.

I smiled and held the broom up as a barrier between us, careful not to make eye contact, "I've got work to do, maybe another time." He exhaled a breath of disappointment. "Rain check then," he promised in a soft tone, then turned and walked back toward the kitchen.

George emerged from the employee bathroom and appeared in the dining area just as I scooped the last bits of food and dirt into one large pile. "Nevaeh, the water is still hot and the towels are real soft." He grabbed the dustpan from a nearby stool and held it against the floor next to the mound. "Just don't be upset, there ain't any of that lavender junk," he chuckled.

"I'll be happy to get a second shower in one day, lavender junk or not."

CHAPTER THREE

An Eye-Opening Experience

Walking into the bathroom, I took in a deep breath and inhaled the humidity from the fog still floating in the room. I placed a folded pair of sweatpants and a t-shirt on the closed lid of the toilet, and then smoothed my hands over the fabric to push the wrinkles out. I slid my dress off and let it gather into a black puddle at my feet. Sitting on the edge of the cold tub, I reached down to unfasten the buckles of my shoes.

My thoughts turned to the incident with Gavyn. Surely, he didn't mean anything by it, but what was he thinking touching me? I hoped he wasn't one of those employers that assumed it was okay to ignore personal boundaries.

No, I couldn't see him being a creep like that.

My tired, bare feet praised the soft rug cushioning them, and I mentally shook off the thing with Gavyn. I walked to the mirror and wiped my palm across its misted surface. Reaching back, I tugged on the ribbon holding the mess of hair that hadn't escaped throughout the day. I combed my fingers through the loose braid, my curls releasing in a veil around my face.

Leaning over the sink for a closer view, I examined the fatigue induced circles under my eyes. I rubbed my hands over my sleepy face, hoping to rid my skin of the day's tension. Thankfully, my skin was still supple and, once in a while, I still saw a sparkle in my violet-blue eyes. The streets had not taken all of my youth yet.

I returned to the tub behind me, spun the knob, and waited for the water gushing out of the faucet to raise to an acceptable level. A shiver crawled over my body as I submerged one leg, then the other, and sat down in the bath. I leaned back into one curved end of the tub, holding my toes under the spray of water on the other end. The smooth porcelain consoled my aching muscles while steam rising up from the water relaxed the tension. When my shoulders were engulfed in warm fluid, I turned the water off.

There was a small window to my left. I pulled back a corner of the red tweed curtains to gaze up into the sky. The city lights outshined the stars, making it hard to see the beauty of the celestial orbs.

A chill radiated through the aged, single-pane glass and puckered my naked skin. I let go of the curtain and settled my hand on the side of the tub. The silence was wonderful. No rumbling trucks, no drunken yelling, and no worries about safety. My eyes grew heavy and closed.

Soon after, the atmosphere changed. It felt charged, like static hanging in the air. A dull vibration traveled through my limbs, and a comfortable heat flooded me. My body tightened. I ignored the strange sensation, convinced I was just tired. Rolling my shoulders, I forced the tension in my muscles to loosen once again, and the peculiar vibe retreated.

"You need to relax, that's all," I whispered to myself.

A sudden echo of fluttering bounced off the bathroom walls, too loud and vivid for me to ignore. I bolted upright, forcing water to slosh out of the tub and onto the floor. My eyes darted from one corner to another, searching for the source of the noise.

My stomach rolled, panicking over the instant change in the air.

I climbed out of the warm water and forced myself to stay calm. Each step was slow and cautious as I listened for signs of movement outside my door.

Nothing.

The fluttering stopped.

Could there be a bird stuck inside?

The sound was too heavy and forceful, though.

I tiptoed toward the door, grabbed the towel from the hook on the wall, and wrapped it around me.

"Stay," a foreign voice whispered from inside my head when I reached for the doorknob.

Stunned by the inner voice, I froze just before opening the door. I spun on the balls of my feet and scanned over the empty room again. My fear was replaced with curiosity.

Suddenly, my vision went black. Images began flashing urgently in my mind like a neon sign flickering on and off in the dark. It distracted me from any ability to think. I whimpered and frantically reached for anything familiar: the sink, the tub, the toilet. My pile of clothes slid to the floor as my hands grabbed for something that would act as my anchor. I strained to see a glimpse of my reality beyond the frenzied pictures taking over my head.

Finally, I steadied myself against the wall. I rubbed my eyes in an attempt to regain my sight, but all I could see were flashing jumbles of snapshots I couldn't make sense of. I clutched the cold sink, leaning my pelvis against the edge to keep myself standing, and begged the pictures to go away.

My skin tingled. An overwhelming ecstasy flushed out the rising fear. I'd never experienced anything so compelling. I wanted more, yet it was too much to handle. Swells of happiness, freedom, and

31

sensuality undulated into me like an ocean quenching its shore.

My useless eyes rolled back in my head. My body trembled. I moaned uncontrollably as the invisible essence overpowered me. I was in the presence of an entity greater than myself. Something of royalty, of power. It demanded respect, and I wanted to make it happy.

The urge to bow down and writhe in the beauty of these emotions threatened to drop me to the ground, but the presence held me in place. A gentle pressure kept me lifted from behind. It embraced me, firm and careful.

I wanted to let my head slump back, but the invisible force cradled it. Darkness and flickering images continued to blind me. A sweet scent, similar to honey and roses, filled my nostrils, pulling me into something of a drug-induced trance. Even though I'd lost control of my senses, my nerves grew calm. My trembling body stilled.

The pressure controlling my body guided my hand to the mirror. My finger shot out and touched the foggy glass, moving to write a message in the dampness. I was being used as a tool, but the lazy dipping and rising of my arm felt like I was composing a symphony.

I pressed my head backward into the pressure, needing to get closer. The barest hint of lips brushing over my skin sent shivers through my limp body. A lovely whisper echoed in my ear, speaking to my soul, tiny vibrations kissing my earlobe as it spoke. What I heard was beyond my comprehension, though. A language made of sound — not words — blended in beautiful harmony. I tried to tell the voice I didn't understand, but I couldn't force the syllables from my mouth, only a drunken slur.

In an instant, the pressure lightened. The air grew colder.

My sight returned to normal, but *I* wasn't back to normal.

The sorrow of everyday life drove back into my heart like a runaway train. I ached for the escape, the heaven, I had just experienced. I didn't understand the pain of human life until I was without it. The sadness inside begged for relief once again as I fell to my knees and sobbed, yearning for the phantom to hold me in its clutch forever.

"Nevaeh, don't cry. See," a deep, rich voice spoke.

Shaken, I looked up. Sloppy letters spread across the mirror. It didn't look like my handwriting, but it *was* my finger that scrawled the letters. I examined my finger for evidence. Moisture still gathered at the tip.

I don't understand what's going on. This is crazy.

Stretching out of my ball of self-pity on the floor, I stood and read the watery words running down the glass.

OPEN YOUR EYES.

"My damn eyes are open!" I screamed, wiping my tears on my forearm. "Who are you?" Desperation was clear in the high pitch of my voice.

Dew on the mirror's surface dripped through the letters. My heart skipped. What I saw may never show up again, and I would have no proof it happened.

Should I get someone?

No, Gavyn would think I was unstable.

Maybe I was, but that's beside the point. I couldn't ruin this for George — or myself. George would make a joke out of it anyway, not wanting to admit something might be wrong.

There was no one to tell.

I stared at the drying mirror. The words were only a memory now, permanently fixed in my mind. Closing my eyes, I took a deep breath to inhale any last bit of the ghostly scent.

Bang! Bang!

"Nevaeh, are you ok in there?"

I jumped. My eyes shot open at the sound of George's voice shouting through the door. "I'm fine."

"Did you fall asleep or somthin'?" he asked.

Confused, I surveyed the room. Everything was completely back to normal. Even my towel hung from its hook. I glanced down and found myself submerged in water. I didn't remember getting back in the tub.

Had I not gotten out of the bathtub?

The water was tepid, so time must have passed.

I rubbed my thumbs over my pruned forefingers, staring blankly at the raised ridges. "I...I guess I did," I replied to satisfy George — and to convince myself.

"Well, you need to hurry up. It's late, and we have a job in the a.m., thank goo'ness."

"George, I'm a big girl. It's not a crime to soak in the tub a little past my bedtime if I want. I'll be out when I get out. Go to bed you stubborn, old man."

His angry footsteps quieted as they moved farther away.

"What the hell is going on?" I whispered to myself.

If I *had* dreamt all that, it was very freakin' vivid. My head spun with theories attempting to explain what occurred.

I lifted myself out of the water, dried off, and tugged my t-shirt and sweats on. Rummaging through the small medicine cabinet, I found a brush. I worked the knots loose from my hair, staring at my reflection, and waited for the mirror to write me another message.

Nothing happened.

"Great, now I'm the queen from Snow White. Mirror, mirror on the wall who's the craziest of us all?" I slammed the brush down on the sink, and like a little girl, stormed out of the bathroom in a tantrum of confusion.

The place was dark except for the bright, blue lights of the café signs glowing into the hallway. I crossed the corridor and entered my new bedroom-slash-lounge. George was fast asleep on the couch, loudly sucking all the air out of the room.

Blankets spread out over the cushions of my loveseat. He must have made the bed for me. Guilt stung as I remembered how short I was with him. I promised to apologize in the morning.

The loveseat called me to its cushions, and I gladly accepted, hoping a good night's sleep would make sense of things tomorrow. As I drifted off, thoughts of the strange embrace from earlier comforted me. Maybe all the changes today have messed with my head—new home, a new job, and strangers that heightened my emotions in ways I wasn't used to—it was a lot to take in.

I pushed the images out of my head and put them to rest for the night. My rigid body relaxed into the firm pillows.

Time to dream about ordinary things.

HAVEN CAGE

CHAPTER FOUR

A Thin Line Between Crazy and Insane

The scent of fresh brewed coffee drifted down the hallway and through the crack in my door, beckoning me to wake up. My eyes fluttered open and squinted from the bright, yellow rays shining through the window. I remained still, appreciating the beginnings of a new day in my new home.

The raucous of clanking pans and chairs sliding off the tables reverberated from down the hall. I looked over to see George's bed was already empty. His blankets rested neatly on the arm of the couch.

I forced my tired body up and raised my arms to stretch. The slight cramp in my legs from sleeping curled up on a loveseat shorter than me was much better than the aches and dampness I usually woke up to. A new outfit lay folded on the end table next to me. I threw my legs over the edge of the cushions and pressed my toes against the floor. The cold, wooden planks sent chills up my skin, forcing me to jerk my bare feet up. I fought the urge to crawl back into the cozy bed and hoisted myself off the cushions.

I doubled my blankets over my arm and stacked them on the couch, pondering the strange events from the night before. I rubbed my fingers across my forehead then gently pinched the ridge of my nose. My nervousness grew when I considered last night might be a side effect from the head injury I sustained long ago.

Had it damaged me to the point of insanity?

What I felt was real. It couldn't have been a hallucination.

Do people who hallucinate know they're seeing things?

There was a light tap on the door frame, jarring me from my thoughts. Probably better that way for now. Any more confusion might put a damper on my ability to function normally for the day.

The door eased open.

"Ah, she's awake," Gavyn mused, stepping into the room. He placed a steaming cup of coffee on the table next to me. "The crew meets here for breakfast before we open in the mornings. Fortunately for my employees, I don't like to eat alone. Guess you could call it a perk."

"Thanks. I'll get straightened up and be right out." I fiddled with the blankets to avoid eye contact.

"Layla left the clothes for ya. She said ya'll are about the same size."

The space between us filled with a long, awkward silence. I smacked the throw pillows with my hand, pretending to be preoccupied with tidying the room.

"George has already helped himself to two plates of pancakes, so you better hurry." Gavyn smiled nervously, shoving his hands into his pockets. "See you in a minute then," he said, waiting for a response.

I smiled and nodded. I didn't know what else to say. He turned and left the uncomfortable room.

Huffing out a breath of relief, I scooped up the donated clothing off the end table. I crossed the hallway to the bathroom and pulled the door shut behind me.

When I unfolded the outfit Layla left, a pair of pink panties fell from the pile and dropped to the floor. I chuckled and picked them up, examining a set of red kissy lips printed on the back. It was more about Layla than I really wanted to know, but I was grateful for them.

I pulled on the black slacks and a plum-purple, button-down shirt. My Mary Jane's barely peeked out from under the pant legs that were almost too long. The confiscated blue ribbon from the day before matched, so I put it to good use. Watching my reflection to make sure I didn't miss any stray hairs, I tied back the giant curls that formed from laying on wet hair most of the night.

Determination to prove I wasn't crazy got the best of me. I leaned over the sink and pursed my mouth to blow on the mirror. Warm air crossed my lips, heating the glassy surface. The feeling of victory settled in my heart as faint, finger-drawn words appeared under my breath. The evidence was clear. I didn't imagine what happened. But who would believe that some phantom made me write it? I was all alone in this.

The café was full of laughter as employees traded sarcastic comments. I lurked in the background, unnoticed for a moment, and admired what a family looked like. It was thrilling to consider I might be a part of it, too.

I strolled farther into the room and searched for a familiar face. Layla waved at me in a beckoning motion.

"Hon, you fill those pants out better than I ever did. Since they fit, I'll bring more of my old outfits for ya. My closet's too full anyway," she admitted as I closed the distance between us. She hooked her arm around mine and proudly escorted me across the café like a shiny new toy.

"Thanks for all of this," I added, picking up my pace to keep up with her.

Layla nodded and continued into the kitchen. "We have eggs and pancakes on the stove. Help yourself. You've got about a half hour, and then we'll open. Plates are up there and silverware's in the drawer." She pointed to the wall opposite of us, then gracefully retreated back out into the hall.

"Good morning," George greeted somberly from the doorway.

"Morning," I returned, feeling guilty. "Hey, I'm sorry about last night. I shouldn't have yelled at you like that. Guess I'm a little overwhelmed. Can you forgive me?" I put on a sweet expression, offering my best puppy-dog eyes.

"Nev, you're like my own daughter. I could never be mad at you for long. I know you're a little hormonal and all, bein' a woman." He let out a throaty chuckle and tugged me in for a hug. I rolled my eyes as I gave his round body one tight squeeze. Ducking out of his grasp, I reached up and opened the cabinet above us then grabbed a plate.

"These people are real nice." George watched the crowd through the order window. "It'd be great if we stayed here a while. You should meet the others," he urged.

"Already planned on it." I smiled and kissed him on the cheek. "I'm going to eat. Talk to you in a bit."

George ruffled my hair in that playful way he always did then left to join the crowd. I picked up a rubber spoon and began shoveling a large serving of eggs onto my plate.

Carrying my food to the dining room, I felt the awkward fluttering of butterflies commence in my stomach. I'd never fit well in big groups of people like this. Even though a shower and new clothes made me feel like a new person, it was hard to set aside my reclusive tendencies as an outsider.

I walked the length of the four tables that the others had pushed together to form one. Before I realized it, my head bowed in an attempt to hide from the inquisitive eyes assessing the new girl. I forced my chin up, feigning confidence, and took the vacant seat near the end of the table.

A young redhead next to me dipped her chin toward me and smiled politely then continued conversing with a man across the table who was focused on buttering his bread. The dining area hummed with the gossip of the morning.

I scanned the faces creating our rectangle of friends and noticed Gavyn's gaze lingering on me from three seats down. He grinned and stood up, capturing the attention of the other workers.

"This is Nevaeh. Make sure y'all don't scare her and George off with your foolishness, please." Gavyn chuckled and ducked as a blond guy with a mohawk threw a piece of pancake at him. "Now, now. No need to get hostile, Jason."

Gavyn winked at me and began calling out names, one after another, introducing each individual with pride. I forced a timid smile and stood, shaking hands with every member of the staff until I met them all. A thankful sigh left my lips when my awkward moment in the spotlight was over. I settled back in my chair and picked up my fork eager to finish eating and get on with business.

The second day started off easier, less chaotic. When the doors opened, it didn't take long for the flow of customers to find their way inside. The café teemed with the bantering of hungry diners.

Everyone who passed through our door seemed cheery, like this was the only place they wanted to be. It was easy to revel in the constant happiness the café emitted. I was amazed with how accepted I already felt. There was a sense of unconditional belonging.

I stationed myself by the door, greeting and ushering new patrons to their tables. When I wasn't preoccupied, I enjoyed wiping down the windows. The mindless activity allowed me to gaze out into the streets and people watch—one of my favorite pastimes.

My hand guided a rag over the clear, uneven surface while I glanced outside at the figures on the sidewalk and smirked at the way the window distorted some of their features. As I skimmed over the movement outside, a breathtaking pair of eyes snared my focus.

My hand slid down the glass, causing a loud squeaking. I moved my face closer to the window to get a clearer view. The familiar aqua color remained motionless against the wandering crowd. I cursed the random heads bobbing past, interfering with my vision of him.

From behind the warped layer of glass, I focused on the face that owned the blue-jeweled eyes. It was the stranger that kept me from falling the day before.

He was as still as a picture, staring at me from across the street.

How long had this man been watching me?

I looked behind me to make sure it was in fact me he was staring at. Assured that no one else was within his line of sight, I turned again to meet his gaze.

He was gone.

Suddenly, I felt like I couldn't breathe. My ridiculous, inexplicable need to be close to this stranger was, once again, denied.

Uneasy emotions clouded my thoughts. I needed a break. I placed the spray bottle and rag in my hand on the lower shelf of the hostess desk then jogged down the hall and into the kitchen.

Layla was leaning casually against the shiny, silver counter behind her. Her long, lean legs crossed out in front of her, begging for attention. Gavyn rested a hip against the island in the center of the room. His muscular arms crossed over his chest as he spoke to Layla in a professional tone about the café's inventory.

"Hey, will you cover me for a few minutes?" I interrupted, touching Layla's elbow to catch her attention.

"Sure, hon. Are you ok? You look a little pale," she asked, straightening from her relaxed position. Concern pinched her sleek brows together.

"I'm fine, just need a minute. Thanks," I called over my shoulder and rushed toward the back door.

A stinging breeze blew over my skin as I shoved the door open, but I welcomed it. My head was swimming.

What a mysterious attraction to have for a man I've only seen twice. So powerful.

Something moved at the end of the alley, catching my attention. A silhouette leaned against the building too far away to make out a face. It didn't seem threatening, but I kept my guard up, just in case.

I stared down at my feet and tried to clear my head. I inhaled the cool, thick city air. A few deeper, lung-filling breaths and I could return to reality; I could forget him.

"Open your eyes!" an urgent whisper commanded me.

My eyes darted around the alley. I was alone. Even the figure at the end of the alley was gone. Dread amplified my muddled emotions.

Gulping a lump of fear, I spoke. "Hello? Is someone there?" Nothing but the whir of a swift breeze answered back. "There is no one here, Nevaeh," I scolded myself.

The door opened behind me. George's head peeked around the edge. "Are you ok? I heard you talkin' when I went by. Thought maybe you needed some protection." He laughed, holding up his arm and flexing to make a not-so-big muscle.

"George, I'm going crazy," I whimpered. "Something's happening. I think I need to see a doctor." My face tightened in fear, and my voice trembled.

The lines in his expression shifted into a more serious demeanor. "Nev, what are you saying?"

"Last night, when I yelled at you, I experienced something. I'm not sure what, but I heard things that might not have been there. There were strange noises...and honey, George. It smelled like honey in a bathroom with no honey. And something touched me, but I couldn't

43

see it." The pitch in my voice rose to a surprising new octave as I told George about the night before. I glanced down at my aching fingers and found a handful of George's shirt clutched in my fist. I was using him as my anchor to stay afloat.

George's brow creased, baffled by my confession, but he let me ramble on.

"A minute ago, someone whispered the same words I heard last night." I waited for him to answer, to tell me he knew exactly what was causing the hallucinations and how to fix it.

"It's because of all the change, Nevaeh," he assured, failing in his attempt to quiet my alarm.

"I don't know, George. There might be something off in my brain—from the accident." Tears breached the lower lids of my eyes.

He wiped my cheeks with his sleeve and held my face in his hands. "Let's tell Gavyn and see what he says. Maybe he knows someone who can help."

I nodded in reluctant agreement. George grabbed my arm and gently pulled me into the building.

Keeping composed while we walked through the kitchen was harder than I thought. I stared at George's heels, hoping the others wouldn't notice me crying. They rushed by us, too busy to pay attention—all except Layla.

"What's goin' on guys?" she asked in a worried, high-pitched tone.

"Nev's not feeling well. Have you seen Gavyn?" George answered for me.

"I think he's upstairs. Can I help?" Layla rubbed a small circle between my shoulder blades. "What kinda not feeling well?" She leaned forward and whispered the last question like it was a secret. "You havin' female problems?" George glanced at me with a crooked eyebrow to see if he had to answer that question for me too.

"No, it's not that, Layla. I'm sure it's nothing." I saved George the trouble.

He huffed, shaking his head, and continued. "She had an injury when she was younger and thinks it may be causin' some issues. We need to find Gavyn. Thought maybe he'd know what to do."

"I'm pretty sure Gavyn is in his apartment. Tell me what he says, and I'll go with you. They can handle it here without us for a while." Layla pulled me in for a hug. My body stiffened against hers. I wasn't used to affection from outsiders, but after a moment, I welcomed the solace her arms offered.

George and I walked out of the kitchen and into the back corridor toward Gavyn's apartment. His door was tinted with a midnight blue stain. Dark streaks from the wood grain underneath marbled the thin layer of paint, turning it into an interesting piece of art at the end of the hall.

Strangely, I felt a little intimidated as I stared at the partially open door. I told myself that I was better and didn't need to burden anyone else with this nonsense. Especially since I had no clue how Gavyn would react or how it would affect George.

I stopped a few steps from the door. "You know, I think I'm okay now that I've had a minute. This really isn't necessary."

"Girl, we *are* gonna talk to him and we *will* find some way to make sure nothing is goin' on in that noggin of yours. What you told me ain't normal." George looked down at his feet and muttered under his breath, "I should have found a way years ago to have you looked at." His expression turned to one of shame, and his eyes glossed over as if he was about to cry. This man never cried.

My heart grew heavy for him. "It's just all the change like you said. I'm sorry I made such a big deal about it." None of this was his fault, and he didn't ask to be responsible for me.

I never truly understood the depth of George's love for me until now. A special bond has always existed between the two of us, forged during all the hard times we shared. He has given me more than I could ever ask from another person: love, support, and a chance at life. George has given me a home. Not in the security of four walls and a roof, but home in the form of one person unconditionally loving another. No matter where we rested our heads, it was home as long as George was there.

"George, this is not your fault. You didn't know."

"No, but if I had money...," he answered, his apologetic voice trailing off into thought. The indentations of age lines deepened between his bushy, graying eyebrows, reflecting the pain and guilt he carried. Being the man George was—a man who made jokes of heavy situations as a coping mechanism—his expression quickly changed into the pouty puppy dog face I used often.

I let out a defeated breath. There was no point arguing with him. When George wanted me to do something, I couldn't deny him. Right now, he wanted me to get checked out.

"Old man, you drive a hard bargain. Do they teach you those guilt trips on the streets, too?" I lightheartedly sassed, pretending to be cheerful to lighten the mood, but underneath I was scared. George eyed me, surprised I mocked his persuasive attempt at getting me to do as he asked. His playful pout shifted to a stern glare that told me I had no choice in the matter.

I took another breath and peered over at the dark blue door, biting my upper lip. "Okay, but I'm going up by myself. I'll explain the situation to him the way I want. You finish up anything you can to help the others, in case we can leave soon." He nodded with a triumphant grin and disappeared back into the kitchen.

I tapped on the door and waited, but no one answered. I knocked again, then nudged the door to open the rest of the way. "Hello? Gavyn?" I called into the stairwell.

"Come on up." His distant voice was light and raspy.

"Hey, sorry to bother you, but I need to talk for a minute," I said calmly while ascending the stairs. The stairwell was dark except for the dim light at the end, barely seeping out from the apartment above me.

When I reached the top, I stepped into the welcoming space and admired the simplicity of Gavyn's home. The living area and kitchen combined, creating a large, open floor plan. A royal blue futon acted as his couch, stretching the length of the wall across from me. A low, steel-framed table squatted on a black shag rug in front of the futon. Three magazines spread haphazardly over the coffee table's glass top. One was folded backwards at the spine, open to display a Ford Mustang with a scantily clad blonde perched on its hood.

I walked farther into the apartment, running my hand along the brass-studded edging of a black club chair offering a seat just right of the futon. As I stood behind the chair with my hands resting on its back, massaging the soft leather beneath my fingers, I gazed in the opposite direction. One, beautifully plain, bay window in a stark-white frame opened the room to a view of our busy block and the building next to ours. It nearly took up the entire wall. The late afternoon sun shined in through the streak-free glass panels, illuminating the room in a pale gold. I imagined the nighttime view of twinkling lights from our neighboring businesses was probably just as wonderful.

I spun around and leaned against the chair, wondering if Gavyn wanted me to find him or if he'd come out to me. I examined the small kitchenette, smirking about the small mess Gavyn had left there. The small sink contained a few dirty dishes, and a neglected pot of coffee sat on the counter. He wasn't as meticulous up here as he was in the café.

"Gavyn?" I called out, letting my eyes wander over the little details of his home: loaded bookshelves, retro knick-knacks, and several pictures of a giggling boy playing or posing lovingly with a man in his forties.

"Hey, yeah, I'm in here. Come down the hall."

I followed his voice down a hallway that separated the wall behind the futon from the kitchen. Several feet in, on my right, I looked into a bathroom matching the one downstairs, except it had navy curtains instead of crimson. A little farther down, on the left, was another doorway.

"Gavyn?" I stepped in, and my jaw dropped. Shocked to see my boss's bare chest, I turned my head away, fighting the heat reddening my cheeks. "Oh! I'm so sorry!"

"Nevaeh, it's okay. I was just changing shirts. Jason thought it would be funny to throw a bucket of cold water on me. He's lucky I don't fire his ass."

In my peripheral, I caught Gavyn taking two quick strides toward a tall dresser in the far corner of his room. I let my gaze chase his movements, impressed with how gorgeous he looked free of the loose fabric he normally wore. My eyes widened and my pulse raced, responding to the seductive body I saw. Those few seconds were all I needed to soak in every detail. Time seemed to move in slow motion just for me.

His medium build was composed of the kind of muscle you were born with or acquired through hard, laborious work, not by spending night and day in a gym. Slight ripples undulated under his skin as he fumbled with his shirt. Each steady breath he took caused thick pectorals to bunch and stretch over his torso.

His faded jeans hung a little loose, slipping down just enough to hint at the streamlined "v" underneath and accentuate smoothly defined abs when he moved. Seemingly without thinking, he hiked them back up then opened a drawer in his dresser. The denim drifted down again. My mouth watered. Gavyn was more appealing than I ever would have thought. Even the dark-brown hair that climbed the path to his perfect belly button was alluring.

As he rummaged through a drawer, I marveled at the strong, fluid movements of his broad shoulders and muscular back. A gradual rounding of his backside began just before the edge of his pants and continued generously under the heavy fabric.

My body stiffened as I watched the hem of a fresh shirt glide over his torso and bring my peep show to an end.

I licked my lips and cleared my throat. "Um, I need your help with something," I said, finding my voice and remembering that I had a reason for being in his room — you know, other than to gawk at him.

"What's up?" He spun toward me and grinned.

Suddenly realizing how hard I was staring, I averted my gaze to the right, busying my eyes with the task of analyzing a piece of abstract art on the wall next to me. "Well, I was wondering if you knew a doctor that would help me with an old injury." I chose my words carefully, not wanting to give too much away about my possible insanity.

Gavyn closed the distance between us by a few steps. "Are you okay?"

I hollowed out one of my cheeks and trapped it between my teeth, chewing on it softly — a bad habit I indulged in when under stress. I nodded shyly and hoped he wouldn't ask for details.

"I don't know anyone, but I'll try to help you as much as I can. We can go to the emergency room. It's not far." Genuine concern showed in his expression as he rushed the words out.

"George is worried and thinks I need to be examined. I guess I do need to get this, whatever it is, checked out, but...," my cheek stung as I gnawed the inside nervously, "I really don't think that the E.R. is necessary."

He looked at me, unconvinced. His deep green eyes searched mine with uncertainty. "Nevaeh, I don't want any problems with my employees. If there is something you need to see a doctor about, then I will get you one."

My face must've relayed that I questioned his motives. He looked offended, like he knew what I was thinking. What person would do such a thing for someone he just met?

"Ya know, I'm not heartless. You *can* trust me, Nevaeh. Besides, you're my liability now that you work for me."

Not wanting to offend him more, I smiled and accepted the help; inside, I felt ashamed for having to ask.

"Thanks, Gavyn." I looked at the door and then down to my feet. Nerves knotted in my stomach. Pride told me to laugh at the whole conversation and tell him to forget about it. "George is waiting, are you okay to go now?"

"Let me grab a few things, and I'll be down in a minute. Meet me at the back door."

I nodded and then walked out of his room.

George met me as I came down the stairs. "Is he gonna help?"

"Yes. He said there's a hospital close by, and he'll help however he can." I closed the stairwell door behind me. "We'll meet him around back in a few minutes."

George followed me through the kitchen. "C'mon, Layla, we're leavin'." He waved her to come with us.

Layla untied her apron and lifted it over her head. She hung the food-stained smock on a hook next to the door and fell in line behind George and me. As we navigated around the island surrounded by employees, past two large stoves covered with boiling pots and sizzling pans, Layla barked a command at the redheaded waitress. The ginger girl glanced at me and nodded with a smile before returning to her assignment.

The door slammed behind Layla as she trailed us out of the building. The three of us waited quietly in the alley where I last heard the voice. Layla and George's rigid bodies huddled side by side, their quizzical eyes staring at me, burning with the questions they both held back to refrain from upsetting me more. I was thankful. I wasn't sure I had rational answers to give them.

I faced away from them to hide any emotion that might have shown on my face. The noise of cars and crowds at the end of the alley was calming. It grounded me, reminded me that I was still a humble street girl striving for a better life, not some crazy person cursed with hallucinations.

As I considered the many unsettling possibilities for my altered mental status, my troublesome thoughts turned into a scared plea, a prayer for help to whoever was listening.

Please, please, let this be a problem we can fix.

Tears clouded my eyes. I quickly wiped my sleeve across my face and tried to regain some courage.

The jiggling door handle startled me. I turned to see Gavyn opening the door and sliding out into the alley with us. "Are we ready?" he asked, looking up at the darkening sky.

George and Layla both answered with an eager yes.

CHAPTER FIVE

Just A Mark, or Something More

The car ride to the hospital only took twenty minutes, but it felt much longer. No one said a word. I stared out through the front passenger window, not really seeing the scenery we passed as we sped by.

Whispers of strange commands, memories of a debilitating presence, and images of haunting aqua eyes shuffled around in my head without purpose or control. I struggled to make sense of everything, to bring logic to my maddening experiences since coming to Joe's. When nothing made any more sense than it did before, I started to feel discouraged.

A soothing heat and pressure reached over my lap and surrounded my clenched fist. It was nice. I opened my hand to explore the strong, manly fingers stretching to intertwine with mine from the driver's seat.

Gavyn glanced at me and offered a reassuring smile, then focused back on the road ahead. Suddenly, my troubles vanished. His gesture quieted my world, and I welcomed it — regardless of what it meant.

When we finally arrived at the hospital, Gavyn parked the car in a spot that had just opened near the Emergency Department entrance. I followed George into the packed hospital with the others behind me.

I assessed the mass of emergent patients as we took our place in line at the admission desk. The grumbling man in front of us held a bloody rag to his temple with one hand and a clipboard of papers in his other. People groaned while they waited on gurneys lined up against the hallway walls. Many of them cried out desperately for help. Doctors and nurses hustled about, trying to tend to those they could. My ailment seemed very small and unimportant next to theirs.

The head wound man shuffled to his seat in the lobby, and we stepped forward.

"Name?" the lady behind the desk demanded impatiently.

George responded faster than me, "Nevaeh."

"Last name?" she asked in a dry, uninterested tone.

"Um, Richards," I spoke up, using George's last name since I didn't know my own.

She shoved a clipboard and pen on the counter. "These need to be filled out in entirety, and I need an I.D. with your insurance card." She eyed the four of us expectantly, annoyance clear in her disposition.

Gavyn handed her his license and a bankcard. "This will have to do for now."

I looked at him apologetically but didn't refuse. It wouldn't do any good with him. "I'll pay you back. You can take it out of my pay."

"I'm sure we'll work something out." A kind smile graced his face.

I grabbed the papers and turned to hunt for vacant seats amongst the sea of people taking over the E.R. A nurse called out a name from a set of double doors to my left, then a family of four surrendered their chairs in the center aisle of the lobby to meet her. I nearly sprinted across the room, trying to get to the seats before anyone else did. The others stayed close behind as if I would pass out at any minute and they would have to catch poor, frail me.

I sat down and began filling out the paperwork. I had to guess on most of the history questions because so much of mine was nonexistent. When I finished, Layla took my papers to the rude woman behind the counter, then returned a moment later with her lips pursed and a stern hand on her hip.

"She said they would call us back when they could. That we would have to wait our turn. Duh," Layla mocked in a grouchy imitation of the lady.

I smiled at her sarcasm and settled in for the wait.

Hours passed while I listened to George and Layla talk about anything and everything. Gavyn sat quietly beside me. This was a strangely consoling scene, considering I didn't usually have this many people worrying about me.

I think Layla enjoyed being involved in everything. She enjoyed being as close to the center of attention as possible, but not in a bad way. It was just...her. She needed to be in the picture. George undoubtedly loved me, so he would be here no matter what. But Gavyn, why does he care? I knew there were good people out there, I've come across a few of them in my day, but the number of deviant individuals far surpasses the good. Yet, when I searched Gavyn's eyes, I saw only honest intentions.

"Nevaeh Richards?" a nurse yelled from the double doors.

I stood and took a step but stopped when I noticed my crew tailgating my every move.

"I think I need to do this alone. I'll ask them to keep you updated." Their faces and shoulders drooped with disappointment, but they obeyed.

"Hi, Nevaeh. I'm Amber, your nurse." The young woman was bright and cheery with a smile that reached her caring eyes. Amber escorted me through the corridors and into a large room, longer than it was wide. She directed me toward a bed with a green curtain around it.

There were ten beds sharing the room. Other patients received treatment in their small holding areas segregated by curtains like mine. I wrinkled my nose, disgusted by a whiff of the vomit puddled at the foot of the next bed over.

A squat woman in a navy jumpsuit saw my reaction. "Sorry," she mouthed, dragging a sopping mop out of her yellow bucket and sliding it across the floor. My nausea came and went as I adjusted to the smell of puke and industrial cleaner.

Amber stretched the blood pressure cuff hanging from my section of the wall and wrapped it around my arm. She pumped and released the bulb, carefully listening to the inside of my elbow with her stethoscope. She took my temperature and oxygen then jotted the numbers down in a chart. Her small fingers pressed softly against the pulse point on my wrist. She watched the second hand on her watch make a full circle before making eye contact with me again. "The doctor will be with you soon," Amber assured, letting go of my hand. She smiled brightly and then headed for the door, scribbling more notes in my chart as she walked.

I sighed heavily and let my hands settle in my lap. Most of the other patients were here for minor things, based on the quiet conversations I overheard. But a few were not so minor. Empathy filled my heart while I listened to some of the more life-changing diagnoses. I ached for those that cried with their families after receiving detrimental news. The couple next to me heard words like "cancer" and "terminal".

"We'll be back to get the admission process started," someone said.

Unfortunately, this was a part of life and some things were

unavoidable. I remembered my own reason for being in this horrid place, and my apprehension grew.

Metal hooks screeched along the curtain rail as someone pulled back my curtain. "Hi there...Nevaeh?" he half stated, half asked, flipping through my chart. "I'm Doctor Scott. What's the reason we're here today?" He pulled a blue penlight from his pocket and stepped to my bedside where he waited for my answer.

"Well...I had a head injury a few years ago. Some strange things have been happening lately, and I want to make sure I'm okay."

He positioned himself in front of my knees and grabbed my chin gently. "What sort of things are happening?" the doctor asked as he shined a penlight into my eyes.

"Um, I've been seeing, hearing, and smelling things that aren't there." I hesitated, expecting some kind of judgmental comment.

"Are these things beeps, shapes, and colors? Or more defined? People, voices?"

The whole subject made me uneasy. "More like visions of words, a disembodied voice, and smells that are incomparable."

"Any headaches, neck pain, or blurred vision?" He traced invisible lines in the air. "Follow my finger with your eyes."

"Um, no. Like I said, this injury was years ago, and I just wanted to get it checked out." Why couldn't he skip to the important tests? "There's nothing wrong with my vision, it's my brain I'm worried about," I snapped, irritated with chasing the penlight like a cat.

Dr. Scott appeared insulted by my eagerness but continued anyway. "Well, Nevaeh, your pupil reactions are perfect. No signs of an existing concussion. We'll get you set up for a C.T. scan. The tech will come for you soon." He looked one last time over my chart, wrote something, then smiled curtly and left.

I could have told him that there wasn't a concussion, but I didn't want to piss him off. My frustration with him, and the situation, stirred up more angst. I had to concentrate on the big picture, or I would lose it.

A half an hour passed when the C.T. tech, Doug, finally came to lead me to the machine that I hoped would provide some answers. We walked in silence until we came to a door with an orange and black radiation sign on it. The tech held the door open and gestured for me to step inside.

The room was cold and sterile. I squinted at the shockingly bright lights glaring off the stark white walls. A low, steady hum surged from within the sterile room.

"Go ahead and lay on the table. It will take me a minute to set everything up. Just relax and be still," suggested the man.

I climbed on the narrow table, struggling with the need to fidget nervously. The tech remained at my side, his warm eyes urging me to relax while his hands braced my shoulders and guided me to lay down. He placed a plastic, cage-like apparatus around my head to keep me from moving during the test. The man then went into an adjoining room.

The shadow of the machine arching over my head shaded me from the bright lights above. Low knocking from the scanner and the drone of electricity pulsated around me. The energy radiated through my body and lulled me to a light trance.

Doug's voice boomed from an intercom on the machine, "Ok, Nevaeh, we are going to begin. You need to stay very still during the test. It will take about fifteen minutes."

I took a deep breath and crossed my arms over my chest, mimicking a mummy in a tomb. Shades of light shifted through the pinkish-yellow shield of my closed eyelids, and I began to move inside the mechanical ring. The table glided as smooth as the gears underneath would allow. A slight jerk indicated the end of the path before starting again in reverse. Then, the light filtered into dark purple through my lids, and a series of clicks and beeps rang loudly in my ears.

While I waited for the test to end, I called to mind the time George and I hitchhiked to the beach for our version of a vacation for a week. My muscles loosened. I eased into a restful daze, realizing how exhausted I was from the massive spurts of stress lately.

In one quick moment the air changed, yanking me away from the peace I almost found. It became thick and heavy — like mist. The odor of rotten eggs assaulted my nose. I tried to remain calm and still to finish the test, but ignoring the heightened dread I felt became impossible.

I told myself that I wasn't alone. What's the worst that could happen?

Wait...the clicking was different, less mechanical.

I opened my eyes slowly. The tunnel blocked the harsh hospital lights overhead.

"Hissss. Click. Click."

A smoky shadow hovered above me. Another hiss rang in my ears. Fear lumped in my throat. I instinctively turned my head to search the room for help, but the damn head guard stopped my movement.

"Nevaeh, are you ok?" Doug's voice bellowed over the intercom again. "We are almost done. Please don't move."

"I need to get out of here." My voice shook.

"Give me just a minute more. If we stop now, we will have to redo the test," Doug insisted.

"Please, hurry," I begged.

Tears began to trickle down my temples. My skin crawled as the eerie sensation of evil energy twirled around me. My stomach roiled as the being's ill intentions seeded in my mind. The good memories I focused on moments ago were now darkening under the phantom's attempt to infiltrate my thoughts. With each sign of weakness I let surface, the being latched onto my emotions even stronger and pried its way a little deeper.

It was clear that the thing making the noises wasn't going to leave me alone. Worse than that, the machine trapped me with it. I forced myself to ignore whatever it was and pretended I hadn't heard anything.

I squeezed my eyes shut and slowed my breathing so I wouldn't pass out from hyperventilation. No relief came. My body was so rigid that cramps developed in my limbs. I impatiently waited for the intercom to tell me I was allowed to get off the table.

A ghostly laugh startled me. It called my name in a playful, sinister tone that made me cringe.

My eyes flew open, and a face stared back at me. It wasn't human. It was something dark and morbid. I blinked hard hoping the thing would go away, but it didn't.

The phantom looked very flat and had no body, as if someone had cut the face off a skull and hung it above me. What features were discernible in its nearly translucent form contorted and shifted out of place then back again.

My stomach twisted when it smirked at me. The bile in my throat held back the scream struggling to escape.

"*Hisss. Click. Click.*" The sound erupted again from its stationary lips—almost in a questioning manner this time.

"Go away," I shouted.

The lingering haze shifted from smoky-grey to brownish-red. Its eyes sharpened. The smirk morphed into a disturbed grimace.

Suddenly, it sprung toward my face. I squeezed my eyes shut so hard it hurt. There was nowhere for me to go. The cries I held exploded out from my mouth. I thrashed my arms and legs against the table violently, shaking the machine around me.

"Get me out," I demanded. "Get me out!"

"Nevaeh, calm down. We're done...we're done. I'm coming. Hang on," the tech said, alarmed by my behavior. His heavy footsteps hurried into the room.

The table carried me out of the hole. When the brightness of the overhead lights shined through my clenched eyelids, I felt safe enough to open them. I groaned, feeling the ache that settled into my legs and arms from the beating they took. And there was a strange burning sensation on my forehead.

The tech's calming eyes came into view as he lifted the cage from around my head. "What's going on? Are you ok?" he asked, his forehead wrinkling with concern.

I jolted up, throwing my legs off the side of the hard slab beneath me. "No, I'm not ok! Do I look ok?" I answered, my voice shrill and agitated. My shaky hands reached for him, clutching his shirt and holding onto him like I was drowning. We nearly toppled over as I pulled at him to get myself off the table, unable to escape the machine fast enough. Air flooded my lungs as I sucked in breaths faster than my body could tolerate.

After a minute or two of the tech reassuringly rubbing my back and cradling my trembling shoulders, the atmosphere began to lighten. My breathing finally slowed.

I peered up at him, embarrassed by what I'm sure looked to him like a fit of insanity, and offered a thankful smile. He patted my back, then moved to open the door. "Ready to go back to your room?"

I wiped the dampness from my cheeks with my sleeve and nodded. Walking toward the door, I noticed Doug staring at me with a strange expression on his face.

"Your forehead...there's something there." He squinted and pointed above my brow.

"What are you talking about?" I raised my hand to touch my forehead. The pressure of my fingers caused the burning sensation there to intensify. I gasped. "What is it?" I asked, wincing.

"Um, I think I need to take you back to the room and let the doctor talk to you." His confused and worried tone renewed the sense of panic I was trying to suppress.

Before stepping into the hallway leading back to the Emergency Department, I scanned the room one last time for clues from the phantom. Nothing was out of place, but the faint smell of rotten eggs hadn't quite dissipated yet.

I palmed my stinging forehead and let Doug lead the way back.

Dr. Scott showed up at my bedside about forty minutes later. The stinging on my head had lessened during the excruciatingly long time lapse. All I wanted now was to be back with my family. For Gavyn to hold my hand again. For the comfort of George's cushy body against mine.

The curtain slid back, and Dr. Scott greeted me with a pleasantly confident smile. "Okay, well, the scan didn't show anything that we need to worry about."

"But it did show something?" I asked, sensing he was omitting information.

He pursed his lips in contemplation then answered, "At the end of the test an artifact appeared. The tech said that it disappeared as quickly as it came. He thinks it was a computer glitch. It wasn't on the films, so I'm not worried." His demeanor reflected his words.

"So, I'm okay? Could it be something psychological?" *Maybe I'm crazy after all.*

"I can refer you to a therapist if you want, but I think your experiences are stress related." He smiled reassuringly. "Now, the tech said you might have scratched yourself during the exam?"

"I guess." I pulled back a clump of hair covering my forehead.

His expression changed for a split second, almost unnoticeably. He was hiding his true feelings — a skill he probably learned in medical school. "It looks more like a burn to me," Dr. Scott remarked as he leaned in toward me and narrowed his eyes, scrutinizing my skin. "It's a little singed around the edges, but not deep."

I watched him closely, monitoring any variation in his manner that might seem out of place. Then, his eyes changed. He was studying the mark more intently. He'd found something odd about it.

"What is it?" I tried not to sound alarmed.

"Well, I didn't notice it at first, but it looks a little like...," he paused, seeming to second-guess what he saw. He handed me a small mirror from the supply cart beside my bed. "I'll just let you look for yourself. It's nothing, I'm sure."

I held the mirror up to examine my face. At first glance, it looked like two thin lines were burned into my head, one intersecting through the middle of the other. I rubbed at it to see if that would smooth it out. It didn't; it just hurt like hell.

"Do you see anything strange about it?" the doctor questioned, watching my face for a sign of recognition.

I stared harder, searching for what he saw. "I guess not. What's so strange about it, besides the fact it shouldn't be there?"

"Are you a religious person, Ms. Richards?"

I shook my head. Though I'd never been much on prayer and church, I had read the Bible and studied a few major religions at my library for moral and cultural direction.

"To me, it looks very similar to an inverted cross. Probably doesn't mean a thing. The precise positioning is just a little strange." The doctor penned some notes on a notepad, while I stared at the mirror.

I finally understood what he saw. I guess it depends on what you took from it. Two lines crossing each other? Or, the sign of the Devil?

It was a pretty far-fetched comparison, but the weird supernatural-like shit happening to me lately made me ponder on the symbol far longer than I was comfortable with.

"Doctor, you don't know how it got there, but I do. These are the kinds of things I was telling you about."

I was pissed. And not knowing exactly what I was mad about made me even more pissed. It wasn't his fault. He hadn't witnessed the crazy things going on in my head. I needed him to assure me that there was a reasonable explanation for my experiences even though I didn't feel there was.

"I'm sure it will be fine. Under high amounts of stress, we tend to do harm to ourselves without realizing it. I'll write you something to help you relax. If you have any more problems, let me know." He waited for me to approve the plan.

Did he just imply that I did this to myself?

I nodded and kept my anger silent. I wanted to get out of this place.

He held out his hand, palm up and open. "It was nice to meet you. The nurses will be here with your paperwork soon."

I half-heartedly shook his hand, "Thanks." *For nothing.*

Gavyn saw me sulking through the automated double doors and stood to greet me. The others did the same as I made my way through the lobby.

"Oh my gosh. Hon, are you alright?" Layla hurried toward me in a fuss.

She held me at arm's length and looked over me. Her eyes were worried as she smoothed back the tousled hair from my face. When she caught a glimpse of the singed skin on my forehead, her expression hardened and her eyes narrowed. Did Layla perceive the mark in the same manner as the doctor?

Something about her demeanor shifted during that brief moment, and then her sweet southern smile reappeared.

"I'm fine, just scratched myself. The brain is okay though." I tapped my temple with my index finger and forced a smile to ease their minds. Hopefully, they couldn't tell the difference between a scratch and a burn.

George exhaled a deep breath of relief. "What did he say it was?"

"Stress, like you said." An I-told-you-so grin replaced his fear for my insanity.

Gavyn moved to stand beside me, quiet and supportive. His closeness quickly unraveled my nervous knots. I gazed up at his wary face and smiled. He hesitated then returned the smile, but the lack of genuine happiness and the crease in his brow did nothing to convince me that all was well.

He slid his warm fingers between mine. "We're ready to go then?"

George caught our gesture and pretended not to notice as he passed Gavyn and me, heading for the door. Layla, however, fisted the hem of her jacket and rushed after George as if she was bothered by Gavyn's action.

"Definitely." My feet couldn't get me out of there fast enough.

Gavyn grazed my face with his other hand and pulled the hair off my forehead. "How did that really happen?" he whispered, observing the mark intently.

I patted his hand away. "Long story. It's not important." It wasn't long, just a bit wacko. And at this point, I didn't care to burden this man with any more of my issues. We left it at that, and I pulled him into motion, following the others through the E.R. exit doors.

CHAPTER SIX

Beware of the Changing Tides

By the time we returned to the café, it was dark and almost closing time. Only a few diners lingered quietly at their tables. One cook remained in the kitchen, and the older woman with grey hair waited on the last of the customers. Some of the chairs were already stacked on the tables and the condiments were refilled.

Slow, heavy music filled the café. Blues. An appropriate ambiance for how I felt. I was more discouraged now than before our trip to the hospital. I couldn't accept stress as a real reason for all that happened. It irritated me that I had to dump so much on the others and still didn't find the answers I needed.

George and Layla dispersed silently to check on their stations and finish up for the night. Gavyn stopped to talk with one of the patrons. I walked behind the bar and grabbed a rag, wet it, then returned to the dining area to begin cleaning the recently cleared tables. I was thankful for the busy work. It helped me ignore the matters at hand, as well as the growing snowball of questions building momentum in my mind.

"What do you think your doin'?" A hand gripped my elbow, abruptly ending my movement.

"My job?" I looked at Gavyn, surprised and unsure of why he stopped me.

"Uh, don't you think you've had enough on your plate today?"

"Look, it's helping me relax," I huffed. "I need to work on paying you back anyway."

"I really think you should take it easy for the rest of the night." He glared at me as if he could will me to surrender the rag.

"Let me do this, please," I pleaded. His grip on my arm was firm, but I could feel it wavering at my refusal to give up.

"Okay, but then you go take a bath or something—and rest."

"Whatever you say," I responded, only slightly toning down my sarcasm.

He gave me a *do it or die* sneer, then smiled and marched towards the bar.

Images of the ghostly phantom from earlier flickered into my mind. The harder I tried to forget it, the more it prevailed in haunting me. I suddenly felt the child in me want to call out for my mother, the way that children often do when they are afraid. George was nice to have, but nothing could compare to a mother's touch during hard times.

Even though my memories of my mother were limited to a few precious moments shared as a toddler, I still understood how much she could've helped me throughout my life. Every day, I missed the way her long dark curls coiled around my tiny finger as she held me. I would breathe in her scent, nestling my face perfectly against her warm neck. Hints of honeysuckle and clover always hushed my fears. Knowing she was there to sit beside me if I needed her was enough to console me during any crisis.

Enough, Nevaeh. You are a grown woman. You can't go crying to mommy now.

I shook my head to brush the feelings of self-pity aside. I would figure something out and deal with this like any other adult.

I finished tidying the tables as the last customer paid for his meal and said his goodbyes to the staff. I watched the silver-haired gentleman enclose Gavyn's hand between both of his. The gesture spoke of friendship, trust, and appreciation.

Gavyn smiled at the man and pulled him into his side, cuddling him under one arm. They slowly walked to the door.

"See you for dinner tomorrow, Tom?"

The old man confirmed with a nod.

Gavyn winked a goodnight to him before Tom stepped out of the door. Gavyn stood at the door, peering out the window until Tom was out of sight, then hurried to the kitchen.

I strolled over to the door and twisted the lock before flipping the small "Closed" sign around to signal the end of our business day. It swung back and forth in the window bringing my attention to the dozens of fingerprints smudging the glass. Spinning too quickly to grab the cleaner from the hostess's podium, I bounced off Gavyn's chest. The man had a knack for sneaking up on me. I glanced up at his face with wide eyes, relinquishing my usual unease with personal contact, and happily accepted the warmth of his body so close to mine.

He laughed and rubbed his chest, playfully feigning pain. "You should really watch where you're going."

"Excuse me. I thought you were in a different room." I bowed my head, embarrassed.

With a gentle finger under my chin, he tilted my head upward. "I was just kidding, Nevaeh. I told you to rest. Will I have to draw your bath myself?" His expression showed his joking manner, but there was a glint of hope in his eyes that begged me to say yes to the invitation.

"I'll manage just fine, thanks. I was on my way right now." I walked past him and felt the heat of his gaze on my body as I disappeared into the dark hallway.

I soaked in the tub until my fingers were pruned. After getting out and performing my nightly ritual, I padded across the hall to the lounge and set up the blankets for my bed. George's couch was empty, so I spread out his comforter as well. I felt guilty going to bed while he was still working, so I set out to check on George and make sure he didn't need help.

Gavyn and Layla's voices crept down the hall from the café area. I ignored their whispered conversation and rounded the corner into the kitchen. I passed the cold stoves and glistening countertops, then followed the back hall to where George was. When I stepped into the washroom, he was slumped over the side of the sink.

"George? Are you ok?"

He straightened quickly, startled by my voice. "I'm fine, girl." A weak smile tugged at his lips, then he continued washing the dish in his hand. "Did ya need something?"

I wandered to his side, assessing the pile of plates he had left to clean. "I was just checking on you. Will you be much longer?" I reached down and picked up a dish from the rinse sink. George offered me a towel, and I accepted. I wiped the cloth over the smooth porcelain until the water was gone, then set it on a stack of dried dishes beside me.

"No, I think I'm about done here. I'm really tired anyway." His voice was drained and heavier than usual. I studied his sluggish movements and weary disposition. There was something else, something different in his behavior, that I couldn't quite figure out. He had changed since this afternoon.

I nodded, draping the towel over his shoulder, then rubbed my hand across his back. "Okay, I'll make our beds while you finish." He leaned into the kiss I placed on his cheek. Before leaving the washroom, I scanned over him once more. He settled back into his slouch. I frowned, noticing that his breathing had deepened as if he was struggling to get enough air.

On the way back to the lounge, a slow panic started to rise in my chest, and I feared the worst for George. Thinking back on the last day or two, I realized there was an obvious change in his appearance. He looked tired. Strained. His skin was pale, and his eyes were a little more sunken and darker than normal. Consumed by my own problems, I hadn't paid much attention to the old man. Guilt tightened around my heart while I attempted to rein in my fear for George's health.

As I walked down the dark back hall, past the walk-in freezer and the pantry, I heard Gavyn's voice coming from the kitchen. Layla's soft giggle caught me off guard when it chimed through the air after Gavyn's muffled words. Not wanting to interrupt, I froze and started rethinking my route to the lounge.

"Oh, Gavyn. I don't understand why you keep fighting me?" Her voice was different. She didn't sound like her typical sweet self—she sounded playful and dangerous.

"Layla, I don't understand why you refuse to accept that we can't be together. You know how I feel about dating employees. I value our friendship and would hate for something like this to ruin it."

I peeked around the corner and saw Layla sitting on the counter with her long, beautiful legs crossed under a short skirt. Gavyn stood next to her, his strong hands working hard to fix a broken door hinge on an overhead cabinet.

She leaned toward him, her slender hand rising to touch his face. I knew it wasn't right to watch them, but curiosity was getting the best of me. I needed to see his reaction to her for some strange reason.

She gently urged his face to look at hers. Her manner was different, very aggressive and seductive. Even I could feel her intent, and I was ten feet away. He stopped what he was doing and stared at her with slight aggravation in his eyes.

She grinned. "Let go for a minute. See what you are missing." She leaned in further and slid her hand to the back of his head, guiding his lips to hers.

Gavyn tensed and pulled away from her grasp just before their lips touched. He slowly tugged her hand from his head, placing it back in her lap. "I told you that this isn't right. If you can't accept it, I'll be forced to change our working arrangements." He was polite, but stern.

Layla blew out in frustration and uncrossed her legs, her body rigid with anger. "I don't care what you do. I'm not gonna stop trying." There was fire in her eyes now. She liked the challenge. "You know we belong together." Layla hopped off the counter and sauntered to the door. She stopped and turned, resting her fists on her perfectly proportioned hips. "If you're so hell-bent on not dating employees, what are you doing with Nevaeh?"

I choked on a breath. Layla's question stunned me. I waited for him to answer, but he never did. An unpleasant silence idled between them — between all three of us.

I started to edge past the doorway, eager to escape the tension. The pang of a metal bucket, kicked by my foot, shattered the silence — and my effort to flee the uncomfortable scene. I attempted a smooth recovery and finished my noisy entrance into the kitchen, acting as if I'd just gotten there.

With them both staring at me, I felt the need to persuade them that I wasn't standing there eavesdropping. "Oh, hey guys. Sorry for making such a racket. Haven't learned my way around this place in the dark, yet." Still no response from the two, just awkwardness. "Um, I was checking on George before I went to bed. Did you need me for anythingelse?"

Good one, offer help, pretend you didn't hear a thing. Hah, right.

Gavyn's lips curled up at one corner in a smirk. "No, I think we're finished here." He looked sharply at Layla before picking up a screwdriver from his toolbox and returning to the cabinet-work.

"Yeah. For now." She glared at Gavyn and then at me. Spinning on her heels, Layla left the kitchen, every bit of her confidence intact.

"I thought we agreed that you would watch where you were going?" His lovely smile widened while he focused on the cabinet door.

"Sorry. I'm going to the lounge now. See you in the morning." I rushed to leave the kitchen before he could talk.

"Nevaeh?"

Shit, my plan didn't work.

"Hmm?" I answered innocently.

"If you want to talk about what's goin' on...," he paused, stopping his task to look at me.

The words flew out of my mouth. "Nope, I'm good. Don't need to know anything. You and Layla are none of my business."

"No...no, I meant what's going on with *you*," he quickly answered, chuckling.

I was certain my cheeks were blood red. "Thanks for the offer, but I don't think it's anything you want to hear." I smiled at him appreciatively and left the kitchen.

George's footsteps were weighty and slow coming down the hall. I listened as he went into the bathroom and shut the door behind him. The shower running provided a nice waterfall effect in the quiet café and eased my restlessness.

I lay on my little couch thinking of Layla. She seemed completely out of character tonight, and it bothered me. Maybe I was jumping to conclusions. Who am I to judge someone I barely know? She's been nothing but nice to me. So what if she likes Gavyn? It's not as if anything was happening between us. Why would it? He's just being nice, right? But the fact that he didn't answer Layla's last question sparked my interest. If given enough time, what would he have said?

A shadow blocked the faint light coming in from the hallway. I let my eyes focus on the figure and waited for it to speak.

"Hey, hon. Didn't mean to scare you. I was gonna leave you some more clothes," Layla whispered, now playing the part of the sweet woman, I thought I knew. Maybe I was analyzing things too much.

"Thanks. You really don't have to keep giving up your clothes for me."

She set them on the chair next to the door. "Oh please." She waved her hand in dismissal, "I don't mind. I always wanted a sister I could dress up. Besides, you need all the help you can get, right?" There was a cruel, stinging undertone to her words.

"Well...thanks again." I ignored her odd behavior, hoping she didn't mean anything by that.

"See you in the mornin'. Sweet dreams." Layla disappeared into the shadows, leaving me with many suspicious thoughts to sort through.

George tiptoed into the lounge about twenty minutes later, trying to be quiet in case I was sleeping. If I *were* asleep, his clumsy footsteps and deep breathing still would've woken me. I rolled over and strained to see the large shadow moving around the dark room. Under the soft moonlight filtering in through the window, I could just make out the silhouette of wet locks poking up from his head. Glints of coarse gray shined against the fading black of George's hair.

"Good shower?" I asked, letting him know I was up.

"Oh. Yeah. Much needed." He took a deep struggled breath, then coughed.

"Are you feeling okay?" My voice trembled, fearing that he might not be.

"I'm fine, don't you worry." He forced out a weak chuckle. "Think I'm comin' down with a cold or something, that's all." The couch creaked as he laid down.

"George?"

"What?" he replied with a tired voice.

"I love you."

"Love you too, Nev. Get some sleep."

I listened to his slow steady snoring for a while and then let myself fall to sleep.

I woke with the sun warming my face. George was still asleep on the couch with one arm draped over his face and a leg resting on the floor. Laughter and talking echoed down the hall as the other employees got ready for the day. I stretched out of my usual balled position and grabbed the clothes Layla left. Creeping out of the lounge, I headed toward the bathroom and leaned into the door with my hip to close it behind me.

After changing, I washed my face, brushed my teeth, and began coiling my messy hair into a loose bun. When I looked in the mirror to make sure my hair was pinned in place, I choked on the mouthwash swishing between my cheeks. The burn that had marred my face last night was gone. No redness, no scab. Nothing. The "I'm crazy" feeling returned very quickly.

The others saw it too — I couldn't have imagined it.

I tried to ignore that it somehow magically disappeared and

threaded the bobby-pin around a stubborn curl, fastening it tight to my head. I wasn't going to let that stuff ruin my day. Again. I was going to be productive, and most of all, sane.

Knock, knock.

"Are you in there, Nevaeh?" George was up.

"Uh, yeah. Almost done." I hurried, tying my blue ribbon around the base of my bun. I gathered my shoes and belongings, then opened the door.

George leaned against the wall with one hand propping him up. He coughed violently into his other hand tightened into a fist at his mouth.

"George!" I squealed, gripping his arm to help hold him upright.

"I'm...*uhah, uhah*...I'm fine. Just need something to drink. Mouth's a little dry from snoring...*uhuh, uhah*," he said in between hacks.

"I'll get you something." I ran down the hall, slipping my shoes on along the way. I rushed into the kitchen, passing the few employees that were in there, said my "good mornings" as I flew by, and snatched a juice from the refrigerator. Avoiding the questioning eyes that watched me, I ran out as swiftly as I could.

"Hey, George?" I called, sliding to a halt to bang on the door.

"Damn, Nevaeh, I just coughed a little," he answered harshly from the other side.

"Look, I'm just trying to help. Do you want the drink or not?"

He cracked the door and took the juice. "See, I'm fine. I'll be out in a minute." He shut the door in my face.

George had never acted like that before. I didn't know whether to call 911 or skulk around until he apologized for hurting my feelings. The first would only make him madder. I walked down the hallway, keeping an ear out in case he called.

The crew stared at me as I entered the kitchen, much slower this time.

"Sorry." I lowered my head, embarrassed, and moved toward the spread of breakfast foods. They resumed their conversations, unaffected by my random act of running through the building like a madwoman. I swiped a bagel from the pastry tray, a bottle of orange juice, and then proceeded into the cafe.

"Morning." Gavyn's smile greeted me when I entered the hallway.

"Hi." I held up my bagel. "Just getting something in my stomach before helping with the food prep." The words fumbled nervously out of my mouth. I didn't know how to act around him after last night.

He opened his mouth like he was about to ask a question and paused. I hurried by him, denying any chance of further conversation. Feeling guilty for dodging him, I looked over my shoulder and offered him an apologetic smile.

I found an empty table next to the window and settled into the creaky chair. The others engaged in updating one another on any events of significance happening in their lives since they last spoke. I sat in silence, staring out the window watching people pass. I wanted to take a temporary leave from my life and get lost in the crowd.

"Got room for one more?"

I glanced up to see George towering over me.

"Of course. Do you feel better?" The little bit of hurt I felt from George's harshness earlier wasn't enough to out-do my concern for him.

"A little. I can't seem to shake this cold. It came on so sudden." A small cough escaped as he finished the last word.

"Maybe we should take you to the hospital too. You really don't look that good. I'll ask Gavyn—"

"No," George cut in, "I don't wanna go to any doctor. I just need to let it run its course. It always does." His stern words broke through

77

mine.

I examined his face, noticing new lines and ridges that I hadn't seen before. Tiny crevasses added years to his already aged face. His skin looked damp and clammy. Gray undertones surrounded his eyes and lips.

"All I'm saying is that you need to at least rest. Gavyn might let you take the day off."

"We can't afford to both be sick. I'll tough it out. No big deal." George forced a smile.

"First of all, I'm not sick. Second of all, you look awful. You can't tell me you don't feel just as bad."

"She's right, George. You do look rough." Gavyn agreed, joining the argument as he approached our table. "I don't have a problem with you taking the day off. I won't fire you."

"Thanks, Gavyn, but I'd rather work. I've never been good at being sick. This'll pass."

Gavyn looked at me with remorse—like he was about to go against my wishes and wanted it to be okay. I frowned and crossed my arms disapprovingly. Staring out the window, I waited for him to make his decision.

"Alright, man. You need to stay in the back with the dirty dishes though. I don't want you coughin' on the food and getting the customers sick too. If you change your mind, let me know."

I continued staring out the window like a selfish little girl who didn't get her way. George stood and kissed my forehead, "I'll be fine, Nev." He walked away in a slow shuffle.

CHAPTER SEVEN

An Inconvenient Visitor

Layla was already cutting tomatoes when I walked into the kitchen. "Hey, Nevaeh. Ready to start something new today?"

I nodded, attempting to appear more excited about working with her than I really was. "Where do you need me?"

"Hmm." She glanced around, thinking of an assignment to give me. "You can grab the bag of onions from the pantry. Half of them need to be chopped and half of them sliced." She concentrated again on cutting the orange-red tomato in her hand.

The pantry was dark and dry. Inside were shelves that extended from the floor to the ceiling, filled with every non-perishable ingredient you could think of for an entrée, side, garnish, or topping. I retrieved the bag of onions hanging from a hook near the back and closed the door behind me. I cleared a spot on the butcher's block across from Layla and opened the bag.

The knife slid through the onion easily. My eyes stung from the released gasses. It was nice doing something that didn't required much thought. And the silence between Layla and me was not as awkward as I expected. I found myself slicing in a rhythm that slipped me into a trance.

My mind wandered to my childhood. Scents of gardenias and roses from my grandmother's garden returned to me. The memory was so vivid that the floral smell dulled the bittersweet onion. I remembered running through her garden, so young that many of the bushes hid and covered me like a fairytale jungle. The blossoms seemed to whisper my name in the breeze as I played among their branches.

One day in particular, I skipped through the colorful patches of her roses, stopping to greet and smell each beautiful bloom along the way. At the end of the aisle of bushes was a small rounded out nook of brush. Pretending to be a fairy princess, I tucked in the thicket and imagined my little fairy friends fluttering around me.

A soft wind rustled through the leaves and petals. Coolness from the shade settled on my cheeks and nose, saving me from the summer heat. Fragrant aromas of flourishing buds sweetened the air while strange, invisible whispers beckoned me to relax. I soon fell asleep listening to the magical murmurs of my fairy friends.

My grandmother's shaky voice yelled from the back door, startling me awake. "Nevaeh, where are you?"

Not ready to go in yet, I tucked even farther into the dark thicket and sat giggling, waiting for her to find me. She sounded frightened when she called to me again. "Nevaeh, please come inside. Where are you?" she cried.

My playfulness became fear. I rushed to my knees and tried to crawl out of the thicket. Something cold and rough grabbed the back of my dress. I couldn't move. It was now too dark to see what was behind me. Thorns tore at my skin more and more as I thrashed to get out. Tears blurred my vision and small whimpers escaped my lips. The cold, rough thing was slowly wrapping its limbs around my little waist like a vine lassoing me in.

Unable to move, I screamed for my grandmother. I choked on sobs in between terrified screams. I could see the red back door from where I was, but she wasn't there anymore. The air seemed to get darker. I could almost see the form of a person sitting in the thicket with me.

The sweet odors from the garden soured. I squeezed my eyes shut and curled into a ball with my head on my torn knees. I was waiting for her to save me when, suddenly, something warm from outside the thicket pulled at my arms and dragged me out. The thing that held me hostage let go with an awful screech.

Calmness replaced the chaos. I opened my eyes to look at my grandmother, but no one was there. The cool grass soothed my burning cuts while I sat on the ground confused and alone. I managed a weak whimper, "Gramma?"

"Nevaeh?" Her voice was close.

"Gramma, here I am." I hiccupped a cry. She came through an opening at the end of the path.

"Oh, thank God, Nevaeh. Don't ever get out of my sight again. You have to stay away from such places, okay? Don't hide in the dark corners." Her arms squeezed me so tight that she stifled any response.

"Damn!" Layla spat.

I woke from my daydream to see her wrapping a towel around her finger. A few drops of blood blended in with the tomato juice that puddled on the cutting board.

"Oh, my gosh! Are you okay, Layla?" I rounded the island, grabbed her arm, and pulled her to the sink. Blood poured in a steady flow from the deep laceration on the middle knuckle of her index finger. The more she moved the finger, the more her flesh pulled apart, creating a gap deep enough to see the granulated, whitish-pink tissue beneath her skin.

"Yeah, I guess I wasn't paying attention. Nicked my damn finger." She held her wound under the cool water. The bright red blood spiraled down the drain. "There are some Band-Aids in the cabinet by the door. Will you get 'em?"

"Layla, I think that needs more than a Band-Aid," I protested as I jogged over to the medical supply cabinet.

She grinned sheepishly, pulling her hand out from the water and holding it tight in the towel. "I heal fast, Nevaeh. Just get the Band-Aids."

"Okay, but I really think you need stitches," I reiterated while reaching for the Band-Aid box.

The bleeding had slowed by the time I took out the bandage. Layla snatched it from my hand and covered the deep cut on her finger. "Thanks." She winked and walked back toward the tomatoes to clean up the mess.

I went back to my station to finish the onions, but I couldn't help glancing up every few minutes to spy on Layla as she went on like nothing happened. Her reaction to the wound left me unsettled.

A few minutes later, the kitchen began to fill with bantering workers. Layla darted around, spouting off orders to everyone. We didn't speak another word about her incident, and I steered away from mindless memory wandering.

As the day went on, I found that working in the back was a lot more hectic than standing at a podium and seating people all day. I liked it. Keeping up with the fast-paced atmosphere was rewarding. I enjoyed being part of the group, feeling like people depended on me to help things run smoothly.

On my break, I went to check on George in the back. Instead, I found Tommy, another dishwasher, dancing to a song on his MP3 player in front of the wash sinks. His white shirt was drenched with water.

"Where's George?" I yelled over the music blaring from his earbuds.

He looked at me and yanked one of the buds out of his ear. "Not sure. Gavyn asked me to cover for him. He was gone before I got here." Tommy replaced the ear bud and continued washing dishes as he bobbed back and forth.

Nerves knotted in my stomach. Something was wrong—I could feel it. I searched the building for George, but couldn't find him. I ducked my head into every room, peeked into every nook, and searched every cranny, but I couldn't find him. By the time I finished scouring the lower level of the building, I couldn't ignore the burgeoning feeling of doom that was planting itself in the dark crevices of my mind. Distracted, I rounded the corner out of the lounge and ran straight into Gavyn. Again.

"Whoa, do I need to wear a bell so you know when I'm coming...or are ya bumping into me on purpose now?" A mischievous grin graced his sensually full lips.

My mind was putty for a second. I shook my head, bring my focus back where it belonged. "No, I'm not doing it on purpose. Have you seen George?"

"He wasn't lookin' too good, so I pulled out the futon in my place and told him to go lay up there. Figured it would be more comfortable...and quiet. All these goons yellin' and tramplin' down that hall can't be helpful when a person is tryin' to relax."

I sighed in relief. "Thanks for being so nice. I know it's hard to trust people like us—"

"Look," his words interrupted mine, "I don't do this because I feel sorry for you. I do this because I have been fortunate in my life and feel like I need to repay the universe when I can."

"We just...we don't have much to offer back."

He huffed out a breath and tightened his lips into a tense line.

I bit my lip, regretting what I said.

"Ya know..." He shook his head and lowered his gaze as if rethinking what he was about to say. "Are you ever gonna learn to have faith in me? Believe that I don't want anything back?"

"I'm sorry," I murmured. "I don't have faith in much of anyone or anything. It's not just you. But I'll work on it." I offered a smile, hoping it showed that I didn't mean to upset him.

"Some things are worth having faith in." He looked at me with every bit of seriousness he had and slid a curved finger softly along my jaw.

I had no idea how to respond to that. I've only ever put my faith in George. I never had anyone else that I trusted enough, yet his touch convinced me of his honesty — and I longed to believe him. "I'm going to check on George if you don't mind."

He nodded.

I heard George's nagging cough as I ascended the stairs to Gavyn's apartment. "George?"

"I'm up here. *Uhuh, uhuh*," he hacked.

His coughing sounded worse.

When I stepped into the apartment, he was lying on the futon. His face was barely visible from all the blankets piled on top of him. I dragged my feet, reluctantly approaching George's ill form. He looked really, *really* bad. Nearing the couch, I noticed his disheveled hair was sticky with sweat, and his flesh had taken on a deep, gray pallor. Almost every breath was strained; he was fighting to keep from coughing.

"Oh, George...," I tried to fend off the worry in my voice, "you look terrible."

"I don't know what's goin' on. I've always been able to bounce back from these things. I just keep feelin' shittier."

"Maybe all the change is affecting you too."

"No, I'm in one of the best places I've been in for a while. You'd think all this good food, warm bed, and steady sleep would fix it." I read the fear on his face too easily this time.

What if this was serious? He is an older man — worn from years of heartache, tragedy, and rough living. From the stories he told, I wasn't sure how he had made it this long.

"I really think you need to go to the hospital. Suck up this pride and get on with it."

He looked at me and smiled. "Nevaeh, I'll be fine. I just need to rest. Besides, I can't ask Gavyn for anything more. He has already given us so much."

"You made me go. Why won't you go for me?" I argued. My lip burned as my teeth sank in, attempting to fight back the next words. "I don't think Gavyn will have a problem. He seems like he's willing to do whatever he can to help. He *wants* to help." I hated telling him the very same thing that I was having such a problem accepting, but I hoped it would encourage George to go to a doctor.

"He's a good man. I see that. But I don't deserve what he offers. You were different. We should've checked you out a long time ago. Nothing you have done has led you to deserve this kind of life, Nevaeh." He smiled apologetically. "I'll be fine. That's the end of it."

My heart broke as I remembered how guilty he felt over his past. He'd never thought he deserved even the simplest things. I stared down at him as he lay with his eyes closed. After a few minutes of watching his heavy breathing and silently willing his sickness away, I decided to leave him resting and return to work.

When I got back downstairs, Layla was still helping in the kitchen. The cooks were joined in a rather loud, quartet version of Phil

Collins's "In the Air Tonight" as it played on the jukebox. I politely smiled and covered my ears as I walked through the kitchen, dulling the rising voices around me. I approached Layla to find out where they needed me.

"Hey. How's George?" she asked, pulling down little pieces of papers from the order wheel.

"Awful, but he won't listen to me. He refuses to go to the hospital."

She stretched and put a new piece of paper on a free clip for the cooks to see. When she brought her hand down, I noticed the Band-Aid was gone. There was no trace of the cut on her finger.

Layla turned and eyed me suspiciously when she saw me staring. "What is it?"

The shock on my face must have been obvious. "Wasn't that the hand you cut?"

"Oh…yeah, but it's fine now. It wasn't that deep after all." She dismissed my concern by casually wriggling her fingers around to show how well they worked and then walked away.

I trailed behind her. "Layla, you had a deep cut that needed stitches. You were bleeding like a stuck pig. How — "

"Look, I'm fine, Nevaeh," she interjected with a nervous giggle. "I really don't think you need to make a big deal about this. It was a little cut. That's all." Her eyes darted around the kitchen to make sure none of the other workers were paying our conversation any attention. Her tone grew serious and secretive. "I told you, I'm a fast healer. Can we just leave it at that?"

She was hiding something. I could see it in her eyes.

"Besides, I'm sure you don't really want to talk about *your* disappearing mark, do you?" She swatted the hair away from my forehead and waited for a response.

"Fine," I resigned. I could see this was going nowhere. But

nobody heals that fast. I wasn't supposed to, either. I couldn't explain my burn vanishing any more than she wanted to explain how her wound magically healed itself.

For the rest of the day, I refrained from asking Layla questions that weren't work related. Her demeanor was different now, like she was pushing me away. I did what she told me and pretended that there was nothing weird going on.

Every so often, I raced up to George and checked on him. Most of the time he was sleeping or hacking up a lung. Throughout the day, his color worsened and his breathing became more labored. I left without bothering him every time, telling myself he was a grown man, and I needed to respect his wishes — even if it hurt me to see him this way.

After the café settled from its lunch rush, I restocked the drink and prep stations. I kept to myself; bonding was the last thing on my mind with all that was happening.

Since we found this job, my life had become unbelievably complicated. I would rather go back to sleeping on the streets and being dirty than watch the one person I called family get sicker by the minute. Not to mention the added complication of hearing voices and seeing things. I tried not to think about it as I fiddled with pushing cups into the cup tube below the bar.

"Excuse me? Can you help me?"

I looked up to see a man standing on the other side of the counter watching me. My spit stuck in my throat when our eyes met, forcing me to cough.

There was something about those familiar aqua-blues that made my knees weak. Butterflies sprung to life in my belly, and then crashed and burned, somehow convinced that the man in front of me would evade my fascination and attraction for him just as he had before.

I cleared my throat. "Um, I might be able to." I stumbled to stand up straight and knocked a pile of cups to the floor. He followed my every move with an eagle's attention, his crystalline eyes glimmering under the low lights hanging above the bar. His gaze slowly shifted from my face down to my fidgety hands and then back again. The perfectly placed features of his face gave no hint of what was churning in his mind. "What can I do for you?"

He leaned in slightly, strands of gold in his dirty blonde hair shimmering to life under the light as it flowed in waves down to his shoulders. "I'm looking for someone. He's older, short." He smiled as if remembering something delightful about the person.

"Uh, I'm sorry, do you know a name? Is it someone who comes here often?"

"I believe he works here. Name is George."

"I know him, but he's not in today." I was sure that I'd met everyone George knew, and I had only seen this man in the last few days. George didn't recognize him when they passed each other on the steps the other day. "Can I leave him your name and number?"

"No. I really need to speak to him myself, Nevaeh. Can I go up and see him?"

I didn't tell him my name. And how did he know George was upstairs?

My eyes narrowed, scrutinizing the man who seemed to know more about my father-figure and friend than he ought to. My wall of defenses began to raise against the alluring stranger. I crossed my arms over my chest and leaned a hip into the bar. "What is it that you want with him?"

"I need to give him a message." He grinned again. His bewitching smile weakened my resolve in its battle to protect me from his charm. My body shivered with a surge of excitement.

I quickly averted my eyes and shoved a few more cups into the already brimming cup tube. "If I can get your name, I'll let him know you're here." I wasn't about to let him up before getting some information first. "Sorry, but I can't let you up to see him otherwise."

His muscles tightened as he shifted his weight from one foot to the other, hesitating to respond. A white t-shirt strained against his well-formed chest when he inhaled deeply in contemplation. The black duster he wore covered the majority of his body, but there was no hiding the lean muscle and bound power underneath.

His posture grew rigid and serious. "Archard," he exhaled.

"Okay, give me a minute."

I left the mysterious man and headed toward the hall. As I rounded the corner, I backed up against the wall, staying out of sight, and watched him.

Fixed in his spot, he examined his surroundings very carefully. He never made eye contact with anyone or did anything to draw attention to himself. His clothes were plain and dulled his appeal, though not very well; the drabbest of clothing couldn't take away from his cryptic magnetism. His appearance said he wanted to slide through life unnoticed, but his very nature wouldn't allow it. I experienced a special kind of torture leaving his vicinity and tearing my eyes from him, so why was it nobody else seemed to notice he was even there?

I cursed his affect and continued down the hall, peeking my head into the kitchen along the way. "Has anyone seen Gavyn?"

One of the cooks jerked his chin towards the walk-in fridge.

I crossed through the kitchen and turned right into the back corridor. I passed the pantry on the right and stopped in front of the diamond-plated metal door just next to it. Latching my fingers around the handle, I tugged, breaking the heavy, steel door free of the vacuum that sealed it closed. Frigid swirls of air drifted out into the hall, forcing a shiver to crawl up my spine. I squinted into the hazy freezer and took a step forward. Gavyn stood, with his back to me, in front of Layla. I grinded my teeth together at the sight of her delicate arms snaking around his neck.

Layla cocked her head sideways, looking past Gavyn, and flashed me a sly smile. Chills puckered my skin, and it wasn't because the freezer was cold. The intention behind her smile was clear as a bell, as well as her warming. She was marking her territory.

Gavyn grabbed her arms, untangled them from around his neck, and gently pushed her away. He spun around to find a wide-eyed statue of me, staring at them from the doorway. My heart threatened to betray me and fall to pieces.

"Sorry if I interrupted." Jealousy bubbled to my surface. "I needed to talk to you for a sec, Gavyn."

It was nearly impossible to pretend that it was normal for Layla to have him caged in her embrace. I told myself Gavyn was off limits. Yet, by Gavyn's continuous attempts to end her flirtatious actions, I could see that the man she chased didn't have the same feelings for her. Knowing that made it hard not to wonder what he might feel for me.

I didn't want things to be this way. I hoped we would be close friends, but Layla obviously felt I was a threat—and maybe I was.

Gavyn looked back at Layla and shook his head, then squeezed by me with a box in his hands. Frustration radiated from his body as he went by. I stayed in the freezer, thinking there was something I could say to Layla that might make this better, to rid the nonsense that interfered with our friendship. Nothing came to mind though. Nothing seemed right.

Layla began gathering things off the shelves, ignoring me. Her eyes were full of rage and a nasty, sarcastic smile did a lousy job of hiding her anger. There wasn't anything to mend between us, never was. She had her own agenda and no matter what, nothing with her was as it seemed.

I let the freezer door close behind me, leaving her in the cold where she belonged, and went to find Gavyn.

"What did you need, Nevaeh?" Gavyn asked, irritated when I caught up to him in the hall.

"There's a guy up front wanting to talk to George. He said he has a message for him."

His tone softened. "So, what are you asking?"

"Well, I didn't know if I should make up a story to keep him away, or if I should let him see George. It just seems very…strange. I know all of George's friends, and I've never seen him before coming to the café. I don't want to let some crazy person up into your apartment only to have him upset George."

He paused for a few seconds before responding, "Go ask George if he knows him, or if he even feels like visitors. If he wants to see him, then let him up." He walked away before I could say anything else.

I climbed the stairs and thought about Gavyn's behavior, feeling a little hurt. Why was I so upset about this? It's not like I had a thing with him. On the other hand, I felt like I could grow to trust this man— maybe as much as I trusted George.

I entered the apartment, straining to see until my eyes adjusted to the dim room. The sun's light had moved to the rear of the building, casting half the room in a fading yellow and the other half in a heavy shadow.

George was quiet and still. My stomach knotted. My chest tightened with a burst of panic. I walked over to the couch and touched his shoulder. "George?"

He didn't answer.

Gulping back a sob, I pulled the covers down to look at his face. "George, are you awake?" His complexion was pale and sheer, revealing the tiny veins spreading beneath its surface like a map of endless red rivers. The series of shallow, erratic breaths blew from his mouth. I exhaled, relieved by the strangled sound.

A voice in the back of my head kept whispering to me, telling me to take him to the hospital. And though I knew I should listen, I couldn't bring myself to do it. Maybe it was because I couldn't disobey his wishes. He hated hospitals, and I knew it would be a fight to get him there. Or maybe I was just too afraid to admit that George might not pull out of this.

I jiggled his shoulder, and his eyes fluttered open. "There's a man downstairs wanting to talk to you. His name is Archard. Do you know him?"

"Archard? No, don't know 'im," he slurred in a sleepy daze. His heavy eyelids shut, and a small puff of air blew out of his mouth in a light snore, signaling that he was dozing off again.

I gave him another gentle shake. "He said he has a message. Do you want me to send him up?"

With his eyes remaining closed, George mumbled, "Sure."

Watching him fade in and out so easily was difficult. It was so unlike him. I was still a little unsure about letting a stranger up, considering George didn't exactly seem lucid enough to make logical decisions, but it wasn't my choice to make.

I let him fall back to sleep and hurried out of Gavyn's apartment, taking two steps at a time as I descended his stairwell. I set into a slow jog down the hallway, my heart racing at the thought of seeing Archard, again. My skin tingled when I neared the end to the hall. My body reacted so strongly to him, and there wasn't a thing I could do about it.

I slowed my pace and sauntered back into the café, finding Archard right where I left him.

"Is he ready for me?" He moved gracefully across the floor in my direction.

"Look, Mister, I don't know who you are or what business you have with my father, but I'm willing to let you speak with him. Just understand that he is very sick right now, and I don't want you upsetting him. If you do, I will personally remove you myself."

He didn't know that George *wasn't* my father, and it gave me an edge. Unfortunately, we both knew he was too strong for me to remove him from anything, but I let him think it over anyway.

"Nevaeh, I come as a friend and wouldn't do anything to upset him —"

"And how the hell do you know my name?" I interrupted, agitated by his creepy know-all ability.

"Does it matter?" The cool, collected stranger arched an eyebrow and waited expectantly for me to answer.

"Yeah. Kinda," I spat back with the cockiest attitude I could muster.

"It won't change anything. Will you take me to him now?" His tone was too quiet, too gentle.

He peered into my eyes and smiled as he side-stepped me, gliding towards the hall. A surge of electricity flowed through my body for the split second our paths crossed. I gasped, stunned by the sensation that didn't appear to affect him in any way. Gathering my wits, I jogged ahead and ushered him toward Gavyn's apartment — even though he had completely pissed me off with his dismissive answers and calm attitude; even though he did unexplainable things to me just by being near.

When we reached the stairwell leading up to Gavyn's apartment, I looked over my shoulder to make sure he was still following. In the darkness, I saw a faint glow radiating from his eyes. They had become a soft neon blue.

Completely captivated by the unusual orbs staring back at me, I misjudged the first step. The tip of my shoe hit the ledge, causing me to stumble forward. Archard's hand shot out to grab my arm before I could brace myself against the railing.

Too engrossed to be distracted by the incident, I righted myself and continued gawking at his eyes, fascinated by their reflective radiance. "Are your eyes...?" I let my ridiculous question trail off and shook my head, dismissing what I was about to ask. There was no way his eyes were glowing.

Archard slid his hand slowly down my arm, skimming his fingers over my skin with a feather-light touch, and let go.

I pictured in my head what my less than graceful movements must have looked like, and a deep flush heated my cheeks.

It was almost impossible to focus on anything other than the man behind me. He followed without saying a word as we climbed the last few steps, but I was more than aware of his proximity; I could feel the energy flowing from his body. His presence felt wrong and right at the same time. Something familiar lingered between us, but I couldn't put my finger on it.

My mind raced with new questions about Archard, so much that I'd forgotten George's condition. When we entered the apartment, George's appearance harshly reminded me.

"George? This is the man I was telling you about."

His breathing deepened, but he didn't acknowledge that he heard me.

I looked back at Archard and tried to read his expression. That was useless. No surprise, no sympathy, no worry. Nothing.

I glanced out the bay window and took in a beautiful view of the four o'clock sun next to us. Pale blues, bright pinks, and deep purples were creeping into thick, cotton clouds that seemed low enough I could reach beyond the glass and touch them.

Archard interrupted my thoughts of running away on those clouds when I caught him moving across the apartment from the corner of my eye.

I shuffled toward the last beams of sunrays sweeping over the front of Gavyn's apartment before evening set in. There was a plain, square end table with a small, white lamp sitting on top, hiding in the shadows next to George's feet. I approached the table and leaned over, reaching under the shade and twisting the knob. The room's late afternoon haze brightened under the little bit of light shining from the lamp, but at the same time, it made the shadows on George's face appear more severe. I approached the other end of the futon and gently nudged his shoulder.

Archard kneeled down beside me at George's head and gazed at the sleeping man with such empathy and respect that it seemed they had known each other for ages. He whispered in George's ear, and then leaned back and waited. A smile graced George's face, and his heavy eyes pulled open.

Happy surprise lit up his face when he looked at the man stooped beside him. "It's you," he said in a tone that implied he was seeing someone long ago lost to him.

Archard brushed a sweaty curl off George's forehead. "I have a message for you, my friend."

George's happy expression faded to concern. He looked at Archard for a moment, then at me. Struggling with the words, he asked, "Nevaeh, would you let us talk awhile?"

I felt a little offended. Why couldn't I stay? He never kept things from me. "George, I really don't think — "

He stopped me. "Nevaeh, this man came to tell me somethin', and I think it's best if I hear it in private." When I didn't budge, he added, "Please."

Archard never took his eyes off George. I gave a short nod, then walked out with my lips pressed together in a hard line and my arms crossed over my chest. I stopped a few steps down from Gavyn's apartment door.

In the silence, I hoped to hear just one word exchanged between the two men, but not even a whisper echoed from the open doorway. Defeated by the inability to hear what they said, I decided to give them their privacy.

CHAPTER EIGHT

Where In The Hell Is Archard?

The café was filled for dinnertime, and the atmosphere was alive with chatter. I struggled to focus on my job and prepare drinks for the servers, but my mind continuously drifted to Archard.

His very essence left an imprint on me. I felt a pull to him, like gravity wanted us together. Uncontrollable, unwanted, and unrelenting. It seemed crazy to think about him with such familiarity and need. Frankly, it was scary. I'd guarded my emotions over the years for a reason. I refused to let myself get hurt. This attraction was too strong and would only lead to certain vulnerability. That was unacceptable.

A woman's loud, guttural laugh shattered my distracting thoughts of Archard, and I realized how ridiculous I was being. The most important man in my life was upstairs, sicker than ever, and I'm thinking about some stranger like a silly, daydreaming school girl.

The rush of customers had come and gone within a couple of hours. Time ticked by so quickly that I'd forgotten how long Archard was upstairs. A twinge of anxiety tightened my chest. I didn't want to interrupt them, but I felt the need to check on George.

I approached Gavyn from behind, my fingers aching to smooth over his back and steal his attention. He was working behind the serving bar with his head down, chopping away at something I couldn't see, oblivious to my presence.

"Gavyn?" I called, leaning a hip against the steel cabinet next to him.

He looked up at me with indifference. "Yeah?"

The lack of interest in his tone was hurtful, but I continued. "I finished stocking, and we're kind of slow now. Do you think it's okay if I check on George? That guy's been up there a long time."

"He's still up there?" His indifference turned to worry, and a soft wrinkle appeared between his brows as he glanced back down at what he was chopping. "Yeah, I think it'd be a good idea." Deep, green eyes shot back up to mine. "Do you need me to come up with you?"

I shook my head, trying to show strength and fearlessness. I untied my apron, slid it over my head, and set it neatly under the counter. Gavyn watched my movements, his gaze sliding over my frame. When I turned, and he realized I saw him watching, he quickly returned to his state of indifference and bowed his head, slicing his knife into a strawberry. I rolled my eyes, maddened by the mixed signals, and stomped off.

I rounded the corner into the hallway and flattened myself against the wall, letting two customers pass as they exited the guest bathrooms.

"Excuse us," the man said, glancing at me for a second before returning to his conversation with a young woman about what store they would go to next.

I ignored the clatter of a pan crashing to the floor in the kitchen—along with the colorful spray of curse words that followed—and jogged by, heading straight for the stairs at the end of the hall. I pulled the dark, blue door closed behind me and climbed up the steps.

Stopping just before entering Gavyn's apartment, I knocked on the doorframe and waited for a response. No answer. I rushed through the doorway half expecting the worst, but George was still lying on the futon. Alone.

"George," I whispered, quietly padding across the room. "Where's Archard?" His skin heated my fingers as I touched his wet forehead. Wiping the sweat from his brow, I asked again.

He grumbled and opened his eyes slowly. "Huh?"

"George, can you hear me?"

"Of course I can hear you, girl. I'm sick, not deaf." A weak smile curved his lips.

"Where did Archard go?" I asked, scanning the room for any signs of change or something missing. It would be my luck he was a thief. Nothing looked out of place though.

"He left a while ago."

Hearing George's feeble voice deepened my fear for him, but I didn't want him to know it; so, instead of dropping to my knees and wallowing until he surrendered his stubborn pride and went to a hospital, I kept my composure, carrying on as if little was wrong. "Well, what did he say?"

His eyes closed, again. "He brought me a message of peace. Said my sins were forgiven." He coughed, struggling to catch a decent breath. "Said I would be better soon—better than ever."

I lowered to the edge of the chair behind me. Tears welled in my eyes. My vision blurred. What was he talking about, sins? I did not consider George to be a very sinful man. Neither of us were big on faith, but if we were, I'm fairly certain he didn't believe some strange man could grant him forgiveness. Why would Archard tell him something like that? George must've misunderstood.

I eased back into the cushy, black leather chair at his side and stared out the massive, clear pane of glass opposite me, searching for a way to escape the fears that were making my head throb. A cool breeze whistled in through a crack around the slightly ajar window. I narrowed my eyes and leaned forward. I didn't remember it being open before I left.

George's teeth chattered next to me, drawing my attentive gaze away from the opening. Below the pile of blankets, his body shook around shuddering breaths.

I pushed myself out of the chair, sneering at his discomfort, and marched over to close the window. As I approached the pane, a shiver from the sharp sting of the cold air bit into my skin. My hand reached out to pull the gap closed, but I stopped with my fingers resting on the latch. Easing it open further, I leaned out into the chilly evening. The breeze ruffled my hair, but did nothing to clear my head.

I surveyed the narrow alley filled with eerie shadows and dampness below me. My nose scrunched at the occasional sour smell of mold and stray animals drifting on an updraft. I assumed that this building and the one next to it were pretty old considering they didn't have any fire escapes. My heart skipped a few beats when I glanced down and became overwhelmed by a disorienting sensation of falling.

The second floor was higher off of the ground than it seemed. No one would make that fall uninjured; if someone decided to jump...good luck. But, for just a moment, I let my mind ponder the freedom one might find in the brief descent. There had been many nights of my life, during my rather hellish times on the street, I'd considered ending it all. And what about now? If George died, what would be left for me?

A nip at my nose reminded me how cold it was and that I'd been hanging out of the window long enough. I pulled the glass panel in, latched the lock, and looked around for anything broken that could explain who opened it, and why.

Dismissing the thought of a break-in due to a lack of evidence—besides the fact that no one could have possibly scaled the wall to get in from the outside—and George being far too ill to get up and do it himself, I realized there was only one person who could have opened the window. Archard.

Irritation dug into my nerves.

How could he do that after seeing how sick George was?

I cursed under my breath and turned to walk away. My movement reflecting on the glass revealed a smudge on the smooth, translucent surface. I'd almost missed it. The smudge shimmered under the last sliver of sunlight inching its way out of Gavyn's apartment. Its opalescent glimmer had a touch of gold, like mother of pearl on a seashell. The small, imperfect oval of film resembled a single fingerprint, yet there was no distinguishable print pattern.

I bent over to examine it closer, spotting a single fuzzy fiber sticking out from the center. It was creamy-white and soft as silk. I plucked the fiber from the spot and rolled it between my thumb and index finger. A familiar odor rose from the fuzz, pulling me into a vague memory. The smell was fainter than I remembered. It was intoxicating, indescribable, and invoked feelings that heated my cheeks to a rosy red.

I breathed in deeply, the vagueness of my memory clearing like rippling waters smoothing to expose the depths below. It was the same aroma from the bathroom on the first night of my stay here.

I closed my fist around the fuzz trying to place where it might have come from and how it got here. I opened my hand and lifted it closer to stare down at the small white strand, waiting for an answer to pop into my head. Finally, an "Aha!" moment. Down—the fuzz resembled down feathers. A bird must have flown to the sill and left the smudge and strand of feather.

I was happy to find a logical answer to at least one of my questions, though it didn't render a reasonable connection to the familiar smell. I held up my palm and pursed my lips to blow the tiny feather away, but before the breath left my lips, the fuzz began to disintegrate. It crumbled into pieces so small I could barely see them, then drifted from my palm.

I stared at my hand in disbelief, flipping it over and back again, surprised by what I just saw. How does something just fall to pieces like that? It was solid when I held it—I was sure of that. This couldn't be another trick.

I gulped, forcing saliva down my anxiety constricted throat. "George, do you remember a bird flying in? Did you hear any wings or rustling?" My voice trembled, afraid that I could be imagining this. I glanced over at the window. The smudge was still there. Not imagining.

"No, Nevaeh. What's wrong with you?" He squinted, looking me up and down. Worry shadowed his face when he saw me standing by the window gawking down at my open hands, flipping them back and forth like I was losing my mind. I stopped flip-flopping the second I realized he was watching me and slowly lowered my arms to my sides. I forced a small smile to ease the stress I saw growing in the tight wrinkles on his forehead.

"Nevaeh…are…are you ok?" A wheezing came from under his gruff words.

"Do you remember when Archard left?"

"No, I think I had fallen back asleep before he went. Why?"

"You don't remember him opening the window either?" My tone was as soft and calm as I could manage.

He coughed after every other word he spoke. "Dammit, Nevaeh, what is your problem with Archard, and what the hell is going on with the window?" His voice was louder and raspier than before, emphasizing that he would yell if he could.

"Nothing. Never mind. You need to relax. You're using too much energy talking." I tried to settle him back down and get his coughing under control.

"Well, quit asking me so many dag-blamit questions, and quit *not* telling me what they're about." The coughing subsided when his tone lowered.

I returned my shamed gaze back to the window, scanning the roof of the building across the alley, the narrow opening leading to the street, and the ground below. I was hoping to see something that could offer even the slightest clue of what left the evidence on the window. There was nothing. No animals, no people. There wasn't even the empty boxes or trash you would normally see in an alley.

My eyes pulled back to the filmy smudge. The subtle shifting hues of the darkening sky outside brought the shimmering print to life. The faint afterglow from the dying day shined through the print and carried the colors out into a funnel of rainbows, flickering to the floor. Dust specks twinkled like tiny sparks as they swam in the air, swirling inside the light path.

My angst and confusion stilled while I stared at the beautiful colors. It was breathtaking. Warmth caressed my hand as I held it in the beam of light and let the colors reflect off my skin. Then, I noticed that the amount of flickering colors was quickly depleting. My eyes bolted back to the glass pane. The smudge was shrinking. Something invisible was wiping it off the surface of the window. Within seconds, the smear was gone. I touched the glass to feel for anything, any sign of the beauty that was just there. The surface was smooth and dry.

All evidence was gone without a trace, just as the fuzz had gone.

What the hell just happened?

This—the little insane things—made me feel alien in my own mind. I dropped to my knees to catch my breath and keep from hyperventilating—and for God sake, stop the room from spinning.

I thought about everything that happened over the past few days: the strange dream I couldn't remember, the hallucinations, the vivid odors, the fast-healing burn, Layla's cut, and the strange little things that just disappeared for no reason. They had to mean something.

Then there was Archard. In the instability of my mind, he drew me in.

My insides grew numb. I realized how much energy I had recently wasted trying to understand everything. Maybe I wouldn't ever understand. I slumped against the wall, too exhausted to hold myself up anymore.

God, why is this happening? Haven't I had enough confusion and humiliation in my life already? Am I even supposed to figure this out? Or, is this some sick joke you're playing to teach a lesson to someone who doubts you so much?

Shame clouded my heart as I silently scolded God. But how can I have faith in a being that allows a person to suffer, then offers no answers when asked for help?

"Dammit, Nevaeh, you are an adult, and you have learned to take care of yourself. Don't be such a pity-party."

I crawled across the floor to George and laid my head against his side. Each of his forced breaths raised my head up and down slowly. The rhythm was soothing. It reminded me that he was still alive. His face was more serene than I had ever seen, even when he was well. He looked relaxed, in spite of his pale, gaunt skin and the constant shaking from his sickness.

What could Archard have said to George that gave him such peace?

Climbing back into the leather chair, I clutched my mother's locket and unconsciously polished the metal between my fingers, its smoothness comforting me. My eyes closed to think of her, and I drifted away.

"Nevaeh…Nevaeh."

My whispered name came with a soft touch sweeping the hair out of my mouth. My eyes fluttered open, and I saw Gavyn's outline leaning over me in the faint glow of moonlight spilling into the room.

"Yeah?" I answered lazily. "Oh no, Gavyn I'm so sorry." I straightened myself up, throwing my legs over the edge of the seat. "I meant to check on George and head back down, but I sat down and…" I had fallen asleep. "What time is it?" I asked, rubbing the sleep from my eyes.

"It's nine. You wanna come down and get something to eat before I finish closing the kitchen?" He flashed that caring smile of his. "Then you can get to work helping us close up." He glanced at George with sympathy softening his rugged features. "There's nothing you can do by just sitting here. You need to do something to take your mind off of things…and we could use the help."

When he looked back at me, his eyes showed the softness I'd seen since the beginning. I didn't sense any of the coldness that occurred over the last day or so.

"Yeah, of course. I should've been down there helping out a while ago. I'm so, so sorry." I started pulling myself out of the crevices of the chair. "I don't mean to constantly take advantage of your kindness…"

His hand grabbed mine, stopping me mid-movement.

He slowly lifted me up, peering down into my eyes. "I told you before, I don't mind. I get that you have a lot going on. You can't help that it all came with a new job. I'm just glad that it happened with you here." He paused, his gaze moving to my mouth and lingering there for a moment. I watched his beautifully full lips move in the shadows as he continued whispering to me, "Nevaeh, I see that you are relentless in your ways, but I am *offering* help. You don't have to do this alone. No one should." His warm hands slipped around my waist, pulling me closer to him. We hesitated for a second in our closeness, and I could feel the alluring heat emitting from his body, warming me and warming my soul.

He inched his lips down to meet mine. I drew in a long, deep breath. His breath smelled of sweet strawberries from the café. The gleam in his beautiful, green eyes was confident but wanting. As much as I wanted to taste his lips, my nervousness won. This was not the right time for me to explore our affections.

I gently pulled his hands from my waist and broke our connection, then turned towards George. I tucked George's blankets under his sides, ignoring the yearning in my chest begging me to wrap myself in Gavyn and whatever he offered. "I should get something to eat and get to work."

I smiled at Gavyn one last time before walking out of his apartment.

Gavyn's actions were a mystery to me. I had a hard time adjusting to the thought of love and tenderness coming from a man without a cost. My lack of experience wasn't helping in this matter, either.

I hadn't dealt with the gentler side of men. The side of men that I'd seen romantically was not romantic at all, but acts of loneliness and despair forced upon me in the shadows of a dark abandoned warehouse while George was away hunting us food. I shuddered at the memory of the man's nearly black eyes and days-old body odor that soaked into my skin wherever his dirty, bare hands touched me.

Thankfully, George found us before it was too late and saved me from the thralls of such a monster. He would've left me there to die when he finished — or killed me. The scene of George beating the man unconscious with a steel beam and dragging me from beneath him plays in my mind often.

I'm not so naïve regarding affection between men and women that I don't know the positive effects of real love. I know that not everyone's intentions are driven by lust. It was just difficult for me to trust anyone in general, let alone the whimsical feelings I have when I'm close to Gavyn.

My emotions stir when I'm near him. I want to let go and let him take care of me. I can't, though, not without knowing where the future will lead George and me.

I stepped down the stairwell slowly, taking time to clear my head before leaping back into work. When I reached the bottom, I took solace in the darkness, staying there for a second. I closed my eyes and inhaled one more deep, cleansing breath.

As I touched the doorknob, I was blinded by a white light more luminous than the sun. I covered my eyes and squeezed them shut, trying to correct my sight. The brightness continued to saturate my vision with my eyes closed, until moments later, pitch blackness closed in around it like a curtain. A panicked whimper escaped my mouth, my hands slapping against the walls I was no longer able to see. Jumbled pictures began to cycle swiftly behind my eyelids like a movie fast-forwarding in my head. My body went limp, and I fell to my knees with a painful thud.

CHAPTER NINE

Premonition

Hiding with anticipation behind the heavy, wooden door, sweat dripped along the hard ridge of my nose and into the tightened corners of my mouth. The saltiness stung as it dampened a healing cut on my lip. I fought the urge to wipe the beading moisture from my face, afraid that they would find me if I made any sudden movement.

My insides churned as an awful odor from outside the confessional crept around the door. Heaviness grew around me. The air racing in and out of my lungs thickened.

Sulfur, burnt skin, and evil was a smell I'd grown familiar with, but I don't know that you ever really adapt to such a repulsive stench. Something about being near the stinky demons seemed to instantly trigger my vomit reflex. Luckily, in my recent exposure to them, my gag control had improved.

They spoke in mind-numbing screeches and clicks, forcing me to forget my nausea and refocus. I eased over and peeked through the crack, hoping that a big, ugly face wouldn't be staring back at me.

Dim candlelight and the radiance of a full moon spilled into the cathedral. I'm sure, at one time, it had been a beautiful place of worship. Now, it was a rundown, forgotten ruin.

My eyes wandered over the old building, examining its weak but elegant beauty. Stressed and splintered hardwood floors stretched beneath lines of broken pews. Remnants of frayed, red velvet rippled down the center aisle. Green ivy twirled up massive, chipped marble pillars that used to brace a high, domed roof. Sparkling stars drew my attention to the large holes in the ceiling where faded pastels portrayed Jesus' ascension.

I glanced at the front of the church, watching a mouse scurry across the raised platform. A huge, stone altar stood alone on the elevated floor, longing to hold the fruits of Jesus again. And a single golden chalice lay on its side atop the altar collecting dust; the only remains of the blessed wine it held before was a deep-red ring staining its cup.

Something moved at the rear of the church. I leaned into the door and pressed my face against the crack for a better view. Scattered among the last few rows of pews, the demons maneuvered between the benches, carefully scanning over the cathedral for any enemies. Their large, hideous forms barely fit between the rows.

I watched the hell-bound creatures creep through the building, and my curiosity spiked. Just looking at them invoked evil urges hidden within my soul.

Lie, cheat, betray the good you know to be right, and kill by our side, they seemed to whisper.

The darkness calling to me begged for acknowledgement.

I wondered if the effect they had over me was because I'm different. Or did the bad in everyone flare in their presence?

I shoved my wandering thoughts away. This wasn't the time to question their abilities. The important thing was to remember that they had an effect on me, and I needed to fight it.

They moved, unorganized, among the aisles. Even the small vermin infesting the vacant church piqued the demons' suspicion as they scurried under their feet. They hadn't located us—yet.

My worried gaze swept over the dark corners of the church, searching for those with me, but I didn't see any of them. Panic and loneliness rushed through me. I had to remind myself they were close, whether I could see them or not.

The monsters stopped, inhaling deeply through bare, skeletal noses, like predators tracking prey. I stilled, hoping that the sweet incense drifting through the air stifled the fragrance of my battle-mates.

An angel's scent was unlike any other. They emitted the perfume of home, comfort, and the fulfillment of any desire imaginable. Each aroma was different, and very personal, for anyone given the chance to experience it. For the demons, it was a silent alarm. As putrid to them as they were to us. The demons' distraction from the angels wouldn't last long.

A low hum of feathery wings rustled through the cathedral balconies. The demons stopped, turning their faces upward. Something had changed. An unseen flux in power strained against the atmosphere.

My instincts sharpened. Anxiety intensified. It was nearly time.

His familiar warmth wrapped around me like a blanket, calming my nerves. It was only his energy that surrounded me though, not him. I closed my eyes, disappointed that he was so far away. I pictured his face and pretended his soft skin caressed mine.

A soft voice spoke to me—his voice—from someplace inside my mind.

Prepare yourself, Nevaeh, the time has come. They are here, and we are ready.

His influence overpowered me. I couldn't fight the distraction. I consumed every heavenly sensation imprinted on his message. Happiness, love, lust, and satisfaction pulsated through me.

The intensity was almost too much for my senses to bear, but I yielded to his influence anyway. A need to be near him, kneeling at his beauty, fluttered in my heart. Even after all my training, keeping control with him was difficult. I hated myself for it.

I opened my eyes, frantically searching through the crack around the confessional door. I hungered for just one look. Maybe it would give me peace.

Beautiful, shimmering eyes darted my direction. He was perched in a darkened corner on the other side of the dilapidated church, deep concern shrouding his face. His energy jerked away as he shouted into my mind.

Focus, Nevaeh!

The demons' sickening stench was closing in on me. The instantaneous nausea settling in my stomach awakened me from my needy trance. Bile saturated my mouth. My saliva thickened. With one big gulp, I swallowed the puke rising in my throat and strengthened my resolve.

They found me.

I sensed the monsters outside the door, waiting for me just as I waited for them in my wooden sinner's box. A confessional was a perfect place to get the sudden urge to ask for forgiveness — to pray for supernatural strength — right? Yet, out of pure spite, I didn't want to. I accepted this fate, but that didn't mean I was happy about it.

The atmosphere grew heavier and thicker. My chest tightened with each breath of foul air. A haunting silence quieted my mind like the calm before a storm — an omen of the struggle about to begin.

I chanted words of repentance, only half believing God would actually accept them as atonement. I wasn't even sure my heart regretted anything I had done. I liked to think it did — that my confession meant something — in case the battle didn't end well.

My head cleared. An instant rush of strength empowered my body like never before. The door flung open. I leapt into the air higher than gravity should have allowed and landed in a crouch on the hard ground. I was energized, fearless.

Maybe God *was* listening.

I slowly rose and gauged my surroundings. The demons confined me within a circle, pure hate and evil rolling between them like a poisonous fog. The pain they conveyed made me want to scream from the bottom of my soul.

They hadn't sensed my heavenly soldiers, yet. There focus was entirely on me. I grinned. Everything was going as planned. Perhaps, they were too intrigued by the human waiting in the shadows for them to notice the horde of angels watching them from above.

The few seconds of hesitation that passed while they assessed me as a threat allowed me to study them closer. Nothing could ever subdue the terror that choked your throat when in a demon's presence. Their heads, twice as big as mine, resembled a human corpse after severe decomposition. Charred eyes, sunk deep into their skulls, glared back at me — measuring my worth as an opponent. Sharp jawbones protruded and moved as they communicated. Screeches seemed to resound from under the seamless stretches of skin beneath their noses.

My eyebrows pulled together in disgust, my gaze lingering on the thin layer of melted flesh fused together into a wrinkly area of skin where lips should've opened.

Where the fuck are their mouths?

Rotten folds of meat melded to the sides of their heads instead of ears. I couldn't understand how they heard the high-pitched screeches they made.

Snorting and huffing, the monsters stared me up and down.

Ragged breaths extended and contracted the jagged ribs bulging awkwardly out from their strange chest cavities. It was as if something pressurized their torsos from the outside, forcing the front ribs to buckle inward against the curvature of their back ribs.

The demons' brows angled up at the ends, worsening the malicious intent in their expressions. I got the notion they would smirk if they could. Apparently, they decided I wasn't much of a threat.

My petite five-foot-four frame was no match. Brownish-red flesh clung tight to lean builds, which stood at least six feet tall. Their muscles flexed in wiry, long patterns around thin rotted masses.

My body tensed as I watched them bend their large, boney knees and curve their wide shoulders in, hunching into attack positions. I would've been more intimidating if the angels stood beside me, but I needed to be alone for the first part of this battle. It was important that they challenged me.

The demons closed in around me. I grabbed for the cold metal strapped to my back and wrapped my fingers tight around the hilt, the sword sliding easily from its sheath. I raised it in preparation.

Sweat dripped from my brow. I cursed the urge to vomit. Settling into a squat, I impatiently awaited their move. Traces of satisfaction showed on their marred faces as they observed me.

The anticipation burned an ulcer in my gut. I just wanted to get started already.

Come on assholes, what's one little human? No one will know, right?

It took all I had to hold my mark.

Be patient, I reminded myself.

The time that lapsed made me wonder if the battle would ever begin. Did they think I was too meek to bother with, or were they making me wait on purpose?

Then it happened, a ripple in the energy.

Behind me, the whooshing of a claw swiping through the air

caught my attention. That was enough of a move for me. I pivoted and faced the attacker. Its razor-edged fingers scraped the skin on my shoulder. Goose bumps formed on my cool skin as warm blood trickled down my arm from a burning laceration. Without a second thought, I reacted and sliced the sword through the space between us.

Damn. I missed.

The demon ran. It jumped, clinging to the nearest wall with a force that buckled the stone façade, boney claws digging into rock and mortar. Its strong legs flexed and used the wall as leverage to hurdle over my head. I spun to locate the monster and saw that the rest had flocked around me again.

My heart skipped a beat. This was a disappointing start.

I retreated until my back was flat against the cool wall. Scanning the rafters, I prayed that the angels would join me soon.

The demon to my right barreled closer, ramming his shoulder into my head before I could react. My body scraped along the stone a few feet, and I almost toppled over from the sudden dizziness spinning my surroundings into a blur. The clatter of my sword falling to the ground, leaving my hand empty of defense, registered in my ears. I pressed my body into the wall and shook my head, shifting the cathedral back into its proper place and stillness. After a few seconds, my equilibrium recovered enough I could move without feeling drunk.

I raised my hands up and curled my fingers around the ledge of a stone sconce above me, lifting my body weight off the ground. A pained groan pushed from my throat. My brain throbbed from the stabbing pain that came every time I moved. Swinging my tired legs back and forth through the air in front of me, my body built momentum until I let go of the sconce and hurled myself toward the demons. I landed on two of them, toppling them like dominoes. The others filed in to snatch me from the dogpile.

I crawled over the corpse-like lumps and scurried across the dusty floor on my belly. My eyes landed on the bejeweled sword shining in the moonlight a few feet away. Stumbling to my feet, I pushed off the ground into a clumsy sprint toward my weapon.

One of the monsters snagged my shirt as I ran. My body jerked to an abrupt stop, heels digging into the ground when it started to drag me backwards. Its grip on my shirt bound me so tight around my chest I could barely breathe. Focusing on the sword only inches from my feet, I held my breath and lunged toward the weapon as hard as I could. Sharp claws tore through the fabric, freeing me from the demon's grasp.

Inhaling deeply, I reached a shaky arm out and closed my hand around the hilt. I spun around and charged, unsure if I would make contact. The tip of the sword met a hard surface then slid smoothly forward, piercing the demon's stomach. There wasn't any blood. Instead, harsh smoke and ash puffed out from the wound, filling my eyes and nose.

I sucked a quick, involuntary breath and choked on the cloud of ash and death. The vomit I'd been holding back made its way out, splattering at my feet and clumping with the mess of debris and dirt on the ground in front of me. Straining to find a sufficient breath of air in the puff of filth floating around me, I sputtered, cough after cough, until the cloud finally settled.

Through a clearing swirl of smut, the silhouette of a lifeless mass became clear. Its rotted flesh and hollowed form made the body on the ground look as if it had been dead for centuries.

Another monster rammed into my side, lifting me off the ground and carrying me at least ten feet before slamming me onto a pew seat. My back cracked against the wood, knocking the air from my lungs. I rolled off the bench, a sharp sting riding the length of my spine, and slumped down onto my hands and knees between the rows of seats, dazed and breathless. Instinct forced me to set into motion and crawl away like my life depended on it. And, truthfully, it did. I was getting my ass kicked.

The demon smashed through the aisle after me, shoving the pews aside in a path of destruction. It stumbled forward, reaching for me. I dodged its grimy hands, rolling under the next pew over, confusing the big, dumb monster.

I clutched the bottom of the seat above me and slid myself along the floor on my back until I reached the end of the row. A glint of silver flashed like a beacon beneath the pile of broken wood the demon had tossed aside. I climbed out from under the seat and dove for the mound, hoisting the broken plank off the top. I shoved my hand into the splintered pieces of pew, wincing at the new cuts opening on my skin. My fingers wrapped around the heavy metal and pulled it free.

Glancing over my shoulder, I found the demon closing in on me. Surrender was beginning to look like a valid option. The aching in my bones and muscles grew to unbearable heights, threatening to dominate my will to continue the battle. I shook my head and drew in a deep breath. Fighting the pain, I sprinted toward the front of the holy ruins. I leaped on top of the altar, gripping the sword with white-knuckled force — awaiting the evil that was sure to follow.

The demons' mangled forms blasted through their obstacles, plowing down more pews, lit candelabras, and empty offering tables. They smashed dried fonts and toppled every statue of a saint in their path before finally crowding around me and the altar. Their horrid bodies emanated sheer ire and frustration. Every pair of black orbs focused on me and, through the darkness, I glimpsed the frightening deeds they intended to enact upon me.

I closed my eyes and spun in a circle on the balls of my feet, swiping the sword through the air as I turned — determined to exterminate any monsters standing within range. Two loud thuds satisfied my ears. The giant mutated bodies collapsed on the ground.

Puffs of ash billowed upward from the open-ended necks of the beheaded corpses lying next to the altar. I pinched my nostrils closed with my thumb and forefinger, squinting to see beyond the clouds of dust. The massive bodies of those still thriving joined in a new circle and drove toward me.

They came from all directions, seizing my legs, yanking on my clothes, and knocking me off of the platform. More pain seared my skull when I smacked against the marble floor. I fell so forcefully I couldn't regain focus this time. Mountains of evil bodies stacked on top of me, heavy and suffocating.

Sweet metallic blood drained from somewhere in my sinuses and trickled down the back of my throat. The pressure in my head was nearly enough to make my head explode.

Screeching and deep, throaty grunts rang in my ears. Covetous hunger flared in their black eyes as they sunk knobby claws into my skin and gnawed on me through sealed mouths. Even without the ability to open their lips and take a bite, their ravenous jaws crushed down on my arms and legs through the layer of skin blocking their teeth and tried their damnedest, intent on tearing into my limbs. My body jerked and convulsed as they attempted to eat me, aching numbness filling the bits of flesh pressed too tightly.

Groans of exasperation reverberated above my broken body. They stopped; I assumed because they weren't getting any satisfaction from gnashing me to death without results. My eyes, swollen nearly shut by the beating I took, cracked opened to see the creatures ripping the membrane over their jaws. They pulled and picked the burnt flesh with their sharp, bloody nails, desperate to create the mouths they were denied.

The monsters knelt over me, starving, with holes in their leathery skin, yielding glimpses of rotted teeth. One of them pushed an awkward tongue-like muscle through a gash in its flesh. It slowly leaned down on all fours, hovering over me, and trailed its sticky, foul-smelling tongue over the blood oozing from my cheek. The monster sat back on its heels, its evil expression shifting to one of demented ecstasy as it rolled its black tongue against the roof of its mouth and savored every last taste of me. Tremors rolled down my spine at the sight, knowing that the demon would come back for more.

My chest tightened, anticipating them all diving in at once to feast on me, but instead piercing screams sounded in unison. A territorial riot broke out over which fiend would get my body first. The massive forms pommeled and threw each other, kicking and trampling me in the process. I attempted to move but didn't have the strength. My broken body was too weak from the pain and abuse.

A warm puddle spread around me, soaking into my hair, warming the back of my head as it lay on the hard floor.

All I could think was, *Where are you? You should be by my side.*

My eyelids grew heavier by the second. I fought to stay awake, but the pull was too much. The heartbeat ringing in my ears slowed and was becoming more distant.

I grew angry and enraged at the circumstances, yet I couldn't find the means to voice even the tiniest curse.

He could have stopped this. *God* could still save me. If he wanted to.

What was the point of so many trials if I wasn't going to make it any farther than this?

I shivered on the cold floor, helpless and limp, the agonizing pain and relentless bleeding dulling my light. Shallow, irregular gasps rushed from my diminishing body.

From some place on the outskirts of the cathedral, floating on the wings I longed to touch, I inhaled his essence, his taste sweetening the copper on my tongue. The familiar sugary fragrance comforted me, beckoning me away from the evil warfare reducing me to ruins. I let go and focused on the peace promised by his energy, fleeing to a safe place within my memories.

A smoldering hand pulled at my leg, yanking me from the group of monsters. The rough fingers burned into my flesh like hot coals, distracting me from my happy musings. My skull banged against uneven slats of marble as the lone demon lugged me away from the protesting horde behind us.

After several feet, the dragging stopped. A moment of relief came in the dark corner, away from the brawling demons, but I knew it wouldn't last long. I slowly rolled my throbbing head toward the rogue monster, wondering why it hadn't dragged me to my death yet.

Teeth gnawed behind its torn, gnarled flesh, preparing for the meal of a lifetime. Coal-colored eyes landed on the banquet at its feet — me.

The demon's concentration wavered, its head jerking toward the ceiling in search of something unseen. It sucked deep breaths in through its bony nose and exhaled puffs of smoke through the rips in its disfigured face. Finally, it noticed the odor that wasn't native to the church, the incense no longer masking the divine scent of the angels.

My leg dropped from the monster's hand and crashed to the floor. A fresh surge of pain filled my lower body. Clicking and screeching began again, undoubtedly warning the others that they were not alone. Then, sudden silence saturated the air.

The pause before the big show.

The demons' heavy frames stomped toward each other, abandoning me to reunite against the greater threat.

A low rumble pulsated through the church, rebounding off the stone like the drone of thousands of hummingbirds amplified. The cathedral's walls and floor shuddered under the intense power emitted by the angels' beating wings. A gust of wind rushed through the building, stirring dirt and debris into little eddies around me. I choked on the mouthfuls of grime and dust thickening the blood pooling in my throat.

Majestic roars sang out from the vaulted ceiling as the heavenly soldiers flew out of the shadows. The high-pitched blend of musical notes was beautiful but unbearably sharp. I gritted my teeth as the echoes of their yells built pressure in my head, forcing warm liquid to trickle from my ears.

Fiendish screeches from the demons interjected, signaling the start of the other-worldly battle.

My eyelids closed. Booms from massive bodies colliding and dropping from above sent shivers down my spine. I hoped that it was the monsters falling, not the angels.

The pungent odor of ash and soot wafted into my nose. A good sign I thought, until the occasional wet, sticky fluid spattered against my skin and sunk me back into unease.

A soft breeze traced over my body, soothing the heat of dozens of open wounds. I clung to the breeze like it was my first gasp of oxygen after almost drowning. The heavy, smoke and ash laden air that filled my chest lightened, permitting his honeyed fragrance to permeate each audible gasp.

He hovered over my broken body and brush his fingers across my cheek, assuring me that he heard my prayers of desperation. The gentleness of his touch pulled me back from my impending oblivion. His beautiful face beamed down on mine, careful not to hint at how bad the situation was. A quick shimmer of his aqua-blue eyes gave him away though. Sympathy, love, and defeat hid in their depths, his hardened expression doing little to disguise the sorrow and concern he was trying to bury deep inside.

I wanted to tell him how I felt, but it was too late for sharing feelings. Many times had passed in our moments together when I should have said something, made my confession and not been so stubborn. Now we'd never know what might have been.

I struggled to keep sight of him, but couldn't stay awake any longer. Visions of him holding me in his arms enticed me away from reality and lulled me to an endless sleep.

I thought I heard a whisper of endearment drifting on the breeze of his wings as he left me for battle. The words, "I love you, Nevaeh," replayed over and over in my fading thoughts.

Whether it was real or not, I wasn't sure, but it would carry me into my last moments of this life, and hopefully into the next.

Surrender came swift to the unbeatable power pulling me under. My heart was satisfied enough to rest.

CHAPTER TEN

A Moment of Weakness

"Nevaeh? Nevaeh!" Gavyn frantically shouted, stumbling down the stairwell.

His knee hit my back when he knelt behind me. Strong, worried hands grasped my shoulders like they were keeping me from floating away. He shook me and yelled my name, but I was unable to answer. I was paralyzed. My ability to feel and hear everything around me was crystal clear, yet I couldn't speak, see, or move. Gavyn spun me around and laid me across his legs, cradling me in his arms. Quick, shallow breaths warmed my cheek, but the comfort of that wasn't enough to stop the chaos in my mind.

My head swam with mysterious tableaus of the vision I'd just experienced, yet my failing memory dissipated the images as if my brain was rejecting them. The few scenes that remained faded under a foggy mask, rendering it impossible for me to make out exactly what they were. Momentary flashes of bright lights followed a second's worth of clear shot, but nothing made sense.

Jumbled voices and sounds narrated the tableaus, similar to a busy street with everyone talking at once from every direction. I couldn't recognize a single person or thing. The noise, like the vision, faded too, forgotten along with the countless nightmares I'd recently had. My head throbbed from the constant shifting, and I felt drunk with dizziness. I waited for the last of the effects to subside, helpless and comatose.

"Heeeelp!" Gavyn cried out next to me. "Somebody, help! We're in the stairwell!" The last few words trailed off as he realized no one would hear over the chattering café. He rocked us back and forth, waiting for me to return to him.

The passing minutes felt like forever, but slowly Gavyn's handsome face materialized. I watched for a moment to make sure what I saw was actually him and not another image flashing before my eyes.

He held me with his eyes closed, his head turned up toward the ceiling. Panic struck when I saw his mouth moving and no sound coming from it. Maybe this *was* another flash photo.

Suddenly, I could feel my arms working to reach for Gavyn, reaching for some minute of grip on reality. He jerked his head down to look at me. His worried eyes filled with relief and he smiled. His strong, protective hand covered my cheek, pressing my head into his chest.

"I thought I was imagining you. I couldn't hear you talking," I explained through relentless tears.

"I was asking someone else for help." He reached up and smoothed my tousled hair. "You might want to try it sometime." A forced grin curved his lips.

I clung to him and wept until my tear ducts were dry as a bone. My life had become too much for me to handle. I was losing the only man I considered family, my mind was turning into mush, I couldn't trust my senses anymore, and I certainly couldn't trust my heart. This release was a long time coming.

With his arms tight around me and his chin resting on top of my head, Gavyn sat in silence, allowing me to finish my breakdown. It was so comfortable with him. I didn't want to pull myself away. However, the time came when I was drained, and we had to move out of the moment.

I looked up at him through my puffy, swollen eyes and took a couple of deep, shuddering breaths to calm my nerves. I hiccupped between gasps, struggling to gain control of my breathing. "I can't take this anymore." My voice was low and shaky. "I don't understand what I'm supposed to do. I keep seeing things, but not in a way I can make any sense of them. What am I supposed to do, Gavyn?" I opened myself to him. There was no one else to help me and, hey, maybe there's a chance he won't think I'm a complete nut and run.

"I don't know what to do any more than you do, but I'll be here for you however I can while you try to figure it out." He quickly looked away like he didn't want me to see something hiding in his eyes, like he had an answer but wasn't ready to share it. "When you're ready to talk about what you've seen, let me know and I'll listen." He looked back down at me with a smile that didn't extend to his eyes.

His fingers combed through my hair, stopping at the back of my head. His expression softened, and our eyes fixed on each other. The pressure of his hand on my head hardened just enough to guide me toward him.

There was no urge to resist. I wanted to kiss him. A bundle of emotions and flutters whirled inside me as he lowered his mouth to my forehead. He pulled back and slid his other hand under my chin. The gentle nudge of his fingertips on my jaw brought our mouths to alignment. He closed his eyes, lips slightly parted, and waited for me to touch my lips to his. I fully intended to accept the invitation this time. I moved in and paused to enjoy the warmth of his strawberry breath on me.

The door flew open with a bang next to us, and we jerked away from each other.

"What are you doing?" Layla's eyes sparked with hate and jealousy when she saw us.

I glanced at Gavyn, hoping he wouldn't mention anything that had happened in the last fifteen minutes. Layla didn't need to know any more about me than she did. Who knows what she'd do with the right information.

His gaze roamed over my apprehensive expression while answering Layla, "Nevaeh fell off the last few steps, and I ran to make sure she was okay. We were letting her rest a bit longer before trying to get her up."

Her face was shrouded in suspicion and disbelief. "Uh huh... well, you have a phone call at the front. Some guy says he wants to talk to the manager." She scanned me over, examining me for threats to her ego more than for injuries.

I clumsily scooted off Gavyn's lap and stood up with a minor twinge in my knee where I'd hit the floor. I grimaced and inhaled sharply, letting the pain show to help Layla quiet any assumptions.

Gavyn reached for the handrail and pulled himself up in one quick sweep. "Are you coming to get something to eat?" His lovely, green eyes asked me to follow him more than his question did.

I glanced at the top of the stairs, thinking of George. "Yeah. I think I'll get something for George too—some soup maybe."

Layla rolled her disapproving eyes and locked her arms across her chest. "Whatever," she answered before turning on her heel with a flair of attitude and heading toward the café. I followed her out limping for effect.

Just as I started to pass the kitchen door, Gavyn's hand tugged softly at my side and directed me out of the hall. He skipped past me to pick up the phone, then nudged his chin towards some big copper pots on the stove.

I moved to a cupboard and pulled two bowls out, then ladled a heaping portion of soup into each bowl. Arranging the food on a tray I retrieved from the drying rack, I remembered to grab some crackers and hot tea.

I walked toward the pantry around the corner, stalling at the door for a moment, and stared into the darkness. A developing fear of the unknown coaxed the hairs on my neck to stand up. Putting on my "big-girl panties", I swallowed and went in anyway.

It took me a minute to find the light string hanging from the ceiling. I cringed at the unease stirring around me. The light flickered on and I jumped back, choking on a gasp. A face was glowering at me.

My heart returned to its usual rhythm when I recognized who it was.

Layla.

She scowled at me with disdain. Again, my heart quivered from the pure anger that hovered around her like a black cloud. I wasn't exactly sure what to say to her anymore. She was like Dr. Jekyll and Ms. Hyde. The unsettling silence between us lasted long enough to make me fidget.

Just as I was about to say something, though I wasn't sure what, she spoke. "I know what you're doing. I get it. He's a sexy, successful man. His gift helps, too. But I want him, and I'm willing to fight for him." She looked down at her feet, almost like she was questioning her next words, but she continued, "They want him really bad. They told me if I get him to join us, I can have him as my partner." She looked back at me with such ice in her eyes that I wanted to cower under a rock. Her long, thin fingers wrapped around a tomato on the shelf next to us, picked it up, and held it in front of my face. "So, leave him alone," she commanded, squashing the fruit in her hand. She opened her fist, dropped the mess of skin on the floor, and licked the red, runny juice sliding down her fingers.

Layla's lips curled into a deviant smirk as she pushed past me, ramming her shoulder into mine as she left the pantry.

My rigid body was anchored in place by the shock of Layla's threat. I massaged the sore spot where she shoved me with one hand and slowly reached for the tea bags and crackers with the other.

Composing myself, I headed into the kitchen. I grabbed two mugs from a stack on the counter, filled them with hot water, and then dunked the tea bags in the steaming liquid. I had to get back to George. Layla's actions were not my top priority right now. Even if they did make me think twice about Gavyn. And what the hell was she talking about? What gift did he have? Who wanted him?

I was almost to the stairs when I heard footsteps behind me.

"Nevaeh."

I turned slowly, gripping the edges of the tray tightly so I didn't spill hot tea and soup all over me. Gavyn slowed as he approached my side.

"Look, don't worry about coming back down to help. It's already closing time, and you need to tend to George. We'll be okay without you for tonight." He looked at the tray I was holding and started rearranging the items on it. "If you put the heavier things closer to you, it'll be easier to carry."

I couldn't help but smile at his obsessive-compulsive type actions. "Yes, boss."

He grinned. "Oh, Nevaeh?...Try not to fall down the stairs again," Gavyn joked, jogging toward the cafe.

I climbed the stairs, crept into the apartment, and inched over to the coffee table. I sat the tray down, eyeing George's sleeping form. A pile of fresh blankets lay on the leather chair. I assumed Gavyn left them before he came to my rescue.

I went to Gavyn's bathroom, retrieved a washcloth from the

cabinet, and then to the kitchenette where I filled a bowl with warm water. Sitting my gathered items on the edge of the coffee table beside George, I sighed and stifled back the tears stinging my eyes.

The layers of blankets were drenched with sweat. I peeled them off him and dipped the rag into the water, then wrung it out. Blotting the ick from George's face, neck, and arms, I prayed he would suddenly get better. The old man moaned under my touch and smiled with appreciation, but never fully woke up.

I gently placed the clean blankets on him, one by one. Episodes of coughs and gasps for air came and went as he drifted in and out of sleep. I finished cleaning him the best I could without moving him too much.

Kneeling on the floor at his side, I watched his sick body work double time to keep him alive. "George?" I whispered.

"Yeah?" He responded wearily with his eyes closed.

"George, I think it's time we get you to a hospital. Or maybe I can find a doctor who makes house calls."

"Honey, I ain't goin' to no hospital. And I ain't havin' a doctor come here." He wasn't yelling or getting defensive like I expected he would. His answer was final, yet gentle. He simply stated that he didn't want help.

"But, George, you're not getting any better. You can't keep thinking you're going to get well because of what Archard said." My hands balled into a fist, wanting to pound my anger and fears away on Archard's chest. My shoulders drooped in defeat, knowing that he wouldn't change his mind—no matter what I said or did. "I need you to get well for me, and that requires going to the hospital," I whined.

His exhausted eyes opened and focused on mine. He smiled lovingly, "Nevaeh, I taught you everything I know, which ain't much. I know in my heart you'll be taken care of. Besides, you are a grown woman now." George exhaled a frail breath. "I'm tired of living this life, baby girl. I was shown a whole new life, one where I wouldn't have to struggle to live. With the daughter and wife I lost a long time ago. The guilt that I've carried for years has been taken from me, and I'm okay accepting the forgiveness given to me now." He lifted his weak hand up and caressed my face tenderly, as a father would a daughter.

I held his hand to my cheek and nestled into it, not wanting him to let go. I sat silent in my defeat, trying to think of ways to make him go to a doctor.

"I can move on now. I can see my family. You don't need me anymore."

"What do you mean? I do need you, George. Please don't leave me." My eyes squeezed shut, denying that any of this was happening, willing me to wake up from the nightmare. The tears broke through. I couldn't imagine my life without this man. "Stay," I begged. His hand eased back down against his body, and he fell back asleep with an apologetic smile.

I thought about what he said, feeling confused and abandoned. Leaning back on my heels, I wiped my arm across my face and sniffled back the tears. There had to be a way to fix this.

I was surprised to hear him talk of his family from before. He didn't mention them very often, it was too painful. There was never a need to push the subject. Over the years, I learned he once had a nasty drinking habit that was attributed to horrible things he experienced as a child.

George tried to straighten up when he met his wife and was successful for the most part. He told me that they had a young girl, seven I think, and they were a picture-perfect family. Occasionally, though, he would have a drink or two without his wife knowing.

One day was a particularly rough day for him. He had a few whiskey and cokes before heading home to pick up his girls for dinner. On the way to the restaurant, it started raining heavily. Because he'd been drinking, his reflexes were slow to react when he hydroplaned. George lost control of the car and ran off the road. The car slid into a tree with such impact that his wife hit her head on the dashboard, and his kid was thrown from the car. By the time he woke up, they were both dead.

After that, the drinking consumed him again. He lost his job, his belongings, and he didn't have any of his own family to rely on for help. That was the beginning of his life on the streets.

I watched George sleep as I played his horrible story in my head, imagining the hurt he carried inside for so long. I wished that we'd talked about that part of his life more. Maybe the guilt wouldn't have been so bad for him.

He'd always told me I was his second chance. He quit drinking the day he found me under the dock. He believed an angel led him to me, so he could repent for what he'd done by taking care of me. For whatever reason, he found me, and I'm glad he did. George *is* my family, blood or not.

Nausea soured my stomach at the thought of losing him, of living without him. I stood and stretched my legs, pulling the blankets up to his chin before sinking into the leather chair next to him. My eyes wandered around the dimly lit apartment, noticing how the blue glow of the moon and stars emphasized the heavy shadows extending from the darker corners.

I watched, feeling unsettled, expecting one of the eerie shadows to move or shift shapes. The uncomfortable silence around me didn't help my distress. I kept waiting to hear some nonexistent, strange voice in my head give me crazy demands.

My stomach broke the silence, growling insistently. I picked up the soup and sipped from the side of the bowl. *Drinking* soup was strange for most people, but for me, it was habit—and would remind me of George when he was gone.

The first time he showed me how to drink soup, I was young and my mouth was too little for the bowl. The soup leaked from around my lips and dripped down my chin. George laughed with delight and did the same to mock me, spilling his soup onto a thick beard. We giggled at our messes over a rare warm meal. Memories like that would forever stay with me.

A small replica of a grandfather clock chimed from Gavyn's bookshelf. It was only ten, but it felt like one in the morning. Fatigue settled over me when I saw the time as if my exhaustion was in sync with the clock. I listened for music coming from the jukebox in the café but couldn't hear any. I figured Gavyn would be up soon.

Not sure that I wanted to be awake when he came up, I set the bowl down and closed my eyes, forcing my body to relax. It just didn't seem like the right time for us to talk about whatever was going on between us. And frankly, I didn't have the energy to deal with it.

I wanted to escape into a deep sleep and pretend nothing was out of the ordinary in my life, that all was well in my little reality. I pictured George happy and healthy, sitting with me in our usual alley. I pictured my life without voices and scary faces, and I imagined meeting Gavyn in another time and place as I fell asleep.

I woke with a sudden jolt. The table lamp was off. Through hazy eyes, I scanned the dark room. My attention focused on the yellow, back-lit face of the grandfather clock across the apartment. The small pendulum swung back and forth, ticking with the passing seconds. It said 2:20 in the morning.

Dammit.

I rubbed my face and groaned, pissed that I could only get three or four hours of solid escape at a time. Not nearly enough.

I leaned forward, listening intently to make sure George was still breathing. They were short, shallow breaths, but they were breaths nonetheless. Satisfied that he was still hanging on, I stretched myself out of the chair that had swallowed me during my nap and tottered toward the bathroom.

I entered the hallway and noticed a light shining out into the hall from the cracked bathroom door. I smiled, mentally thanking Gavyn for leaving it on to guide me through the apartment at night. Slowly, I eased the door open and stepped inside.

There he was.

My pulse raced, and my breath quickened. I watched him step out of the tub and pull the shower curtain closed. He hadn't realized I was in the room, yet. With his back toward me, he slid a black towel off of the rod next to him and dragged it over the wet ripples of his torso. My eyes drifted down to his toned ass which was incessantly begging me to go over and squeeze it.

Billows of swirling steam dampened my face. The scent of him, freshly bathed, dampened other areas of my body.

I was unable to move or find the courage to say something. Beads of water rode happily down his back, moistening the gullies between each muscle. His tempting body flexed as he wrapped the towel tight around his waist and tucked one end under the other at the front, hiding him from my hungry gaze.

He turned, picked up a comb from the counter, and leaned in toward the mirror. The heel of his palm made a squeaking noise as it slid over the glass. His olive-green eyes lingered over the reflection of himself for a moment and then jetted up to meet my gaze.

I gasped in surprise and quickly spun, setting into a speed-walk back towards the living room as I floundered with embarrassment. Not only had I completely invaded his privacy by staring at him like a lion ready to pounce on its prey, but I ran away, pretending he hadn't noticed me salivating over him. I got about halfway down the hall when I heard his raspy, surprised voice behind me.

"Nevaeh?"

I pivoted around sheepishly, noting how good he looked with the towel draped around his gorgeous, sculpted hips. "Yeah?" My voice cracked.

I knew there was no getting around what happened. God, why couldn't he have put some pants and a shirt on before coming out after me? I averted my eyes as much as possible, but it was hard not to notice that his hair was still shiny and wet. His body glistened under the tiny droplets of water trailing over it. I was practically drooling at the sight of him.

"Did you need something?" he asked.

"Um, yeah, I needed to use the restroom...but I can wait." *Oh and, by the way, I need you too.* I fidgeted, harnessing my urge to run from the humiliation.

"Well, I'm finished in there. You can go in."

I darted my eyes to the ceiling, but not before seeing his enticing smile.

"Are you okay?" he asked, folding his arms over the bunched muscles of his chest, still smirking as if he could read my thoughts.

"Yep, just gotta pee." I flinched at the comment that gave him more information than he needed to know.

"It's all yours." He stepped away from the door, making room for me to pass, and bowed with a permitting outstretched hand. The towel slit opened at the side as he bent, exposing a thick upper thigh.

I swallowed hard and walked to him. "I'm *so* sorry." The guilt in my voice was obvious. "I didn't mean to walk in on you...I thought you were in the bedroom."

His head bowed, his eyes gravitating to the floor in a moment of thought. He boyishly peeked up under his brow, gauging my reaction. "Did you mean to watch me?" Another slow, sexy grin pulled at his lips. The anticipation on his face satisfied me as I thought about the proper response.

"Yes, but I'm sorry for that, too," I answered shyly. No use in denying that it happened. He saw me.

In one quick movement, Gavyn closed the gap between us, crashing our mouths together. That instant, I completely forgot everything except how much I enjoyed feeling his lips on mine. One of his hands grasped the side of my neck keeping me from resisting—not that I could manage such a thing—while his other hand scooped around the small of my back, forcing my small frame to succumb under his much larger frame. His grip tightened and lifted me up to my tippy toes. An unavoidable moan crept from my throat as he gently pushed me against the wall, trapping me in an envelope of heat. His warm lips brushed, inch by inch, from my mouth down to the nape of my neck, stopping only to tickle my skin with soft kisses. Moisture from his wet body soaked into my shirt, pasting the light fabric to my over-sensitive skin.

Something inside me was tense and tingling with the need to get even closer to him. It begged for a more intimate connection. Touching him was not enough for the greedy animal in me. It wanted to swallow him in its passion. This feeling was way too intoxicating to stop.

Is this what I've been missing? What a shame.

A switch had flipped. I was ready to give in, to let him be the one to love me and take care of me. I was ready to love him, to trust him, and to be the object of his adoration.

Gladly accepting these emotions, I wrapped my arms around his neck and fingered through his smooth, glossy hair. My fingers lightly grazed down the muscles on his shoulders and upper back. I couldn't help but smile between kisses at the sweet goose bumps forming on his skin. With every deep, uncontrolled breath, I savored the cedar fragrance drifting from his skin.

To my surprise, his hand drifted around my thigh and pulled my leg up to brace it around his waist. I felt what the towel was hiding, engorged between my thighs. My body reacted with my own kind of excitement at his arousal — slick and chaotic.

He pulled his mouth away and licked his lips, staring tenderly at me.

"What is it?" I asked, disappointed he'd stopped.

"I'm sorry," he exhaled, dropping his forehead and resting it on mine. His restrained grip eased my leg back down to the floor.

"About what?" His chin was smooth and clean-shaven against my hand as I lifted his face, forcing him to meet my gaze. "I know what I'm doing. You're not taking advantage of me if that's what you're worried about." I glanced down the hall in the direction of the living room and remembered the ill man sleeping there.

My guilt reared its ugly head. I'd forgotten about George in the heat of it all. "Oh my God," I breathed. "How careless of me." My focus remained on the end of the hallway, not wanting to see the disapproval in Gavyn's eyes. "I should be the one who is sorry. I just got so caught up with you and..." I could feel the shame reddening my cheeks, "this isn't really a good time, I know."

"No, Nevaeh, it's not that. I...," his forehead creased with concern, "I have some stuff I think I need to tell you. It's about what's been going on with you." He shook his head, leaning his head back to look at the ceiling with frustration. When his eyes returned to me, the lines on his face displayed his own shame and pleading, as if asking *me* for forgiveness. "I wasn't sure if it was what I thought...and I'm still not sure, but there's a possibility. If we're going to be like this with each other," he shuffled his hands back and forth between us, "I have to be honest with you."

"What are you talking about, Gavyn?" I chuckled nervously, confused by his vague admission.

"Why don't you check on George and let me get dressed. Come to my room when you're done, and I'll tell you all about my theory." He brushed a strand of hair from my eyes and smiled. "Okay?"

Unhappy that he wanted to get dressed, but glad that he seemed to have a theory, I nodded. He planted a sweet kiss on my forehead, then turned to enter his room.

I headed into the bathroom to straighten myself up before checking on George. The motions between Gavyn and me replayed in my head like a slow, steamy movie as I ran my fingers through my hair and adjusted my damp shirt. My body tingled all over thinking about how he held me, how he kissed me.

God, how he kissed me!

A loud bang from the living room startled me, jerking me back to reality.

George cried out to me, the pain in his voice alarming. I rushed out of the bathroom, yelled to Gavyn, and ran down the hallway. A sudden knot in my stomach told me I wouldn't be prepared for what I might find when I reached George.

CHAPTER ELEVEN

Death As You Know It

I rushed into the living room. George was laying on the floor, wedged between the futon and the coffee table. A thin, red line of blood trickled down his temple. His shaky hand reached up, grabbed the edge of the table, and tried to lift himself off the ground. His weakened body slumped down, unable to muster enough strength.

I ran to him and shoved the coffee table out of the way. Kneeling at his side, I saw a panic in his eyes that I'd never seen. George thrashed around, clutching the leg of the futon beside him while I fought to get him off the floor. Sheer terror strained his face as he focused on one spot on the wall across the room—a dark, blurry shadow.

"George, look at me. You need to look at me," I yelled over his distraught muttering. George glanced around the room, searching for someone who understood his wild ranting. I turned my head and noticed Gavyn lowering to his knees next to George's head. My wide eyes gawked at Gavyn, begging for help, but he only looked past me— staring at the wall, too.

"This isn't how it's supposed to end. That bastard lied!" George cried out. "He lied to me. He lied to me," he repeated, over and over again.

The peace I'd seen in George's expression after Archard disappeared was gone now. His eyes were almost black, and his skin was so thin I could see every tiny vein forcing blood through his body.

"They ain't the right ones to take me. He lied. Get 'em away. Don't let 'em take me," he screamed, latching onto Gavyn's arm as if he was about to be yanked from the room at any moment. Gavyn tried to calm him, but nothing seemed to help.

I yelled over George's senseless mumbling, demanding that he focus on me and concentrate. Again, I tugged on his arm, struggling with his heaviness and erratic movements. I glared at Gavyn for not helping me, but it didn't matter. He just sat there, staring at the damn wall, engrossed by the same stupid shadow George was screaming about.

Finally, I stopped pulling on George and watched the man who acted as my father for so long slip farther away from me. Tears began to pour down my cheeks like a faucet had opened. I couldn't restrain the overwhelming emotions anymore. I slumped helplessly on the floor and waited for his end to come. Time seemed to stand still as I experienced the pain of losing George—deepening the grief unraveling in the pit of my stomach, prolonging that heartbreaking moment when I realized how close his death was. My heart pounded in my ears, muffling George's words. I clutched my chest, trying to slow my rapid breathing.

He shouldn't leave the world like this. His death is supposed to happen quietly and peacefully, years from now.

Gavyn's hand moved to my thigh and lightly squeezed, drawing my attention to him.

"You can't see it?" Bewilderment settled across his face as he realized I had no idea what he was talking about.

I wiped the tears from my cheeks, knowing more would only

follow. "What are you talking about? See what?"

He raised one of his hands and raked it through his hair. "I thought you were one of us. Are you sure you can't see?" He looked so confused.

I took two strained breaths, my chest too tight for them to be very deep. "Gavyn, I can't do this right now. I don't understand what you're saying." I shook my head, dismissing his nonsense. "We need to get him help. We have to get him back on the couch and call a doctor." I tugged at George's shoulders again with no avail.

Gavyn grabbed my wrist tightly, holding me still. "Just stop," he shouted. "I need you to focus. Let everything in your mind fade away, and focus on seeing what's *not* there." His gaze returned to the shadow on the corner. "Nevaeh, I know you are one of us. You have to be. I can feel your energy. You just have to open your eyes." He let go of my arm and slowly pushed himself up.

I chuckled deliriously at his words until I realized none of this was a joke. He was serious.

"Nevaeh, open your eyes. Now!" he commanded me in a low urgent voice.

"They are open, dammit!" I squealed back, stunned that he was repeating the same phrase I was forced to write in the bathroom only nights before.

"Spiritually — not literally."

Rising up next to him, I wiped more tears away with the heels of my hands and took a deep breath. I directed my attention to the corner and tried to focus on the shadow. It felt completely stupid and inappropriate at such a time, but if that was what it would take to get Gavyn to help me with George, then I'd do it.

I attempted to clear my mind, which seemed unfathomable. Surprisingly, though, the blob of darkness began to waver in its shape. It began to reach a solid black tendril out across the wall, stretching its dark limb onto the floor. Inch by inch, it slithered towards George.

Stunned, my mouth gaped open. My soppy eyes followed the phantom's movement across the hardwoods.

"No, No...Get me away from it," George pleaded in terror, breaking my concentration.

I jerked back to coherence, realizing how close the thing was getting to George. "I can't do this! Help me get him out of here, please," I begged Gavyn.

"They will come no matter where he is. We can't stop them. Now focus!" he demanded again.

I closed my eyes and cupped my ears to muffle the sound of George's whimpering. Numbness spread through my heart, deadening the too soft emotions I had exposed. When I was ready, I opened my eyes.

A red glow radiated from the corner. It illuminated the entire room. The light ebbed and flowed in its intensity. Tinges of orange and yellow flickered through the red like electric currents. I looked at Gavyn in disbelief.

He nodded, knowing that I now saw what he saw.

An awful odor filled the room, smacking me in the face as my awareness of this alternate reality grew. I gagged and leaned over the table, my fingers curling tight around the edges, trying to get my bearings. My stomach swam with waves of nausea.

Gavyn stepped closer and clasped my hand in his, raising me out of my bent position. His presence calmed me, unexplainably relieving the nausea and dizziness I felt.

"They are coming. You need to focus just a little longer." The sympathy lingering in his voice did little to release the coil of dread twisting in my gut.

"What is this? Who's coming?"

"I can't explain it right now. You have to be ready for what's about to happen. Whatever you see, understand that I can't do anything to change it, and if I could, I would."

My fear and worry heightened to a new level as he spoke. He let me go then knelt back down, placing one hand on George's chest, and whispered, "I'm sorry, friend. I can't keep this from happening. All I have to offer is a little comfort while we wait."

George looked at him gratefully and relaxed against the hard floor. Instant peace smoothed the creases of terror contorting his features. "Thank you," he muttered to Gavyn with relief. He reached a tired hand out to me, and I gladly took it. "I love you, Nevaeh, no matter what you choose."

George closed his eyes and exhaled a soft, shallow breath. His last breath.

Gavyn removed his hand from George's chest and leaned back on his heels. I couldn't move. The shock of everything was too overwhelming.

George was dead.

I barely felt my knees hit the floor when I fell beside his limp body. I latched onto his hand, my knuckles turning white, my thumb mindlessly rubbing back and forth over the smooth band of gold encircling his left ring finger.

Loud screeches and moans echoed from the center of the red glow, diverting our attention from George. The wall appeared to weaken and stretch against something pushing from behind it. The plaster groaned and creaked as it bent around what looked like the shape of a long leg pressing out from the other side. A torso and two arms appeared above the leg, straining to break through. The figure shoved and pushed violently, determined to puncture the barrier keeping it wherever it was, manipulating the wall as if it were nothing more than a thin sheet of latex.

With panic wrapping a tight fist around my throat, I observed the once solid surface giving and stretching like rubber. How was this possible? Whatever was trying to get through was large and determined.

There was an abrupt tear in the wall and the dark figure erupted out into Gavyn's apartment. It's wickedly intent gaze scanned over the room, a predator hunting its prey.

It was there for one thing and one thing only.

I pushed myself up, weak-kneed, and studied the dark head slowly swiveling around, casing the room for its victim.

The monster reeked so badly I could taste it. This time there was no stopping the vomit climbing to my throat. I doubled over and retched on the floor. My legs couldn't hold my weight any longer. My eyes rolled back, then blackness came.

I woke up moments later seated between Gavyn's legs, my back snuggly pressed into his chest, secured in his embrace. He had dragged us into the end of the hallway, away from the monster exploring his apartment, away from George's body. I looked over at the troubled face resting on my shoulder, watching the scene playing out in his living room.

I cringed when a loud screech bounced off the walls and pierced my ears. My eyes shifted to the corpse on the floor and the monster closing in on it. The disabling heartbreak flooded back in when I recalled the moments before my black-out.

I shoved forward, fully intending to protect George, but Gavyn's fingertips dug into my biceps, gripping me so tight it hurt. My legs kicked in front of me, and I thrashed from side to side, struggling to gain some leverage against his restraints. I didn't care what that thing was, I just wanted to save George from it.

"Why aren't you doing something?!" I screamed at Gavyn, pounding my fists into his thighs. Hot tears flowed from my eyes.

The being lowered onto its knobby knees and prowled toward George. Its hungry eyes zoned in on me and the ruckus I was creating, daring me to come closer—to invade its precious territory. I stopped fighting Gavyn's hold on me and retreated back against his body, winded by my failed attempts to reach George. I scowled at the monster from afar, relaying the hate I caged for it.

Gavyn cautiously loosened his grip on me and whispered in my ear, "Don't move."

I couldn't move if I wanted to; I was frozen in a haze of fear and anger. My thoughts suddenly connected, and I realized the monster staring at me now was familiar.

Impossible.

I saw this demon in the vision I had in Gavyn's stairwell. Every burnt piece of flesh and melded feature shuffled forward from the forgotten place in the back of my mind. The mouthless face, the black eyes, and the lean skeletal body. It was all the same.

I should be happy to know I'm not insane, that Gavyn was experiencing this too, but instead terror sunk its fangs deeper into my emotions. My entire existence was only part of a greater, scarier, and more complicated truth that refused to stay hidden from me anymore.

The demon lowered, its marred, angular face less than an inch from George's skin, and sniffed. It grunted and moaned with each inhalation. I was disgusted, yet I couldn't bring myself to do anything about it.

My jaw clamped down in anger. My fists clenched against my thighs. Every muscle in my body tightened, eager to hurl me towards this thing and take it down fighting. I couldn't let the evil of such a creature contaminate George. Yet, shock, or maybe fear, wouldn't allow me to satisfy my urges.

"What is it going to do?" I asked quietly. Even a whisper couldn't hide the fright and grief in my voice.

"I don't know. I think it's here for George's soul," Gavyn explained, waiting for me to react. "It's an Animus Demon. That's what it does. It harvests souls." He leaned his head against the wall, evading my scared eyes, and stared at the ceiling. He knew that whatever was about to occur wasn't going to be good. The regret was clear in his pinched brow, tight lips, and twitching jaw.

"Harvests them for what, Gavyn?" I whined, forcing the words out. Somehow, I already knew the answer, but I needed him to say it.

"It harvests for him. The King of Hell." His head dropped down and he fixed his gaze to where my hand was flattened over his leg.

Instinct kicked in. Before I realized it, I was sprinting towards George—and toward the demon. Gavyn yelled my name as he lunged up and chased after me. Even if I knew how, there was nothing around to fend this thing off. I didn't care though. My focus was on George. He didn't deserve damnation. I wasn't about to let him go without some sort of battle, no matter how little competition I was for the monster.

Before I reached George's lifeless body, Gavyn's arms hooked around me, yanking me to a halt. My vision blurred from the tears welling in my eyes. "No. Don't," I screamed. I dug my nails into Gavyn's arm, clawing for freedom from his grasp and crying uncontrollably.

"We can't change this part, Nevaeh. I'm so sorry." He hugged me from behind and kissed the back of my head while I wrestled to get away, my hands and legs fisting and kicking the air.

A strange sense of serenity overtook my emotions, and that wave of numbness magically rolled in again. I didn't want to be numb from this. I needed the pain to help me defend George.

The monster's black eyes homed in on me. I sensed the demented satisfaction it experienced from my anger. It climbed over George's body like a wolf guarding its meal and begged me to engage. There was an almost recognizable disappointment in its unnatural expression when I finally quit resisting Gavyn.

We stood powerless and defeated, allowing this thing to hover over George. It sluggishly lowered its face to his, hesitating so it could savor the moment. Everything went stale. The red glow faded, its screeches muted, and the room felt empty—void of anything human. The monster's crooked ribs expanded under its burnt flesh, inhaling a deep breath. It snorted the breath back out its bony nostrils, choking on the air it had unrightfully stolen from the room.

It breathed in again, deeper this time. Then, I saw it. A translucent substance snaked upward, streaming from George's mouth into the demon's boney nose. The substance leaving George resembled fluid, but it moved like smoke—weightless against gravity.

The demon continued to inhale and exhale deeply, choking between extractions, stealing more of George's essence each time. George's body began to tremble and convulse beneath the monster, but the animation of his corpse was still unmistakably lifeless and empty.

An unnerving bundle of emotions lashed at me again. "Is he okay? I thought he couldn't feel anything anymore," I questioned Gavyn, sobbing around my words.

"His body is dead, Nevaeh, but his soul isn't. He's resisting. The soul struggles with the demons when they come. And the demons struggle with the fact that they have to transport a human's soul inside them."

"So, George is hurting?" I whimpered.

Gavyn nodded. "This way is not an easy way to go. It's not what God intended." He spoke the words in a sad whisper. "The human soul is a pollutant to their kind. That's why they look like that. What they really want is to devour human flesh, not the souls they are forced to gather and carry into Hell for their master. He has taken their mouths to deprive them of what they want most. They've become the epitome of envy and desperation." Gavyn's tone was almost sad for the demon feasting before us. "Their once human form has burned and melted away from the evil they have binged on over such long periods of time. They are the worst of the worst."

"George doesn't deserve this," I pleaded. I was mad at myself for accepting defeat so readily, but I didn't understand what was going on. I wasn't sure how to change it. I had to trust Gavyn. The outcome of this couldn't change, regardless of my heart breaking into a million pieces.

The demon emptied George of any last essence it could muster, his precious vapor lessening with each breath the demon took. His body's convulsions quieted to shivers.

"I can't watch this anymore." I spun around and buried my face into Gavyn's chest, listening for the last wheezy inhalation from the demon.

A loud rumble shook the room. When I jerked my head up to see if the "taking" was finished, I noticed Gavyn staring at the ceiling instead. A grin, so slight that it was barely there, showed an ounce of new hope on his face. My heart beat faster in response to Gavyn's change of expression. Anticipation exploded within me. Maybe he saw something that could stop this. The few seconds that passed were unbearable as I waited for him to let me in on his secret.

"What's going on? Can we free George?"

"Look." He nudged his chin upwards.

The walls began to ripple around us like jelly. The rumble echoed throughout the apartment, growing steadily louder and more intense; even my bones vibrated. A gust of wind swirled through the room, propelling my hair in every direction. My skin puckered, and a shiver rose up my spine from the coolness of the wind whipping around us. The strength of the gust increased in speed and strength, carrying Gavyn's magazines into the air and lifting George's blankets off the futon, nearly sending them into flight.

The ceiling's smooth plaster surface blurred and began to shine like a watery reflection above us. Small waves undulated from a center point outward, pulsing from the thunderous booms. I searched Gavyn for any sign or gesture that could explain the pool developing in his living room, but he stood calm and confident with a knowing smile tugging at his mouth.

I glanced down to see if the demon had finished prying George's soul from his body. His corpse was alone on the floor, lifeless.

I would never get that last moment back with him. No more jokes traded between us or hugs shared during hard times. George wasn't there anymore; only a shell of wear and tear—not the father I loved for so many years. There was no intervening at this point—no miracle to save him.

I found the demon crouched against the end of the futon, gawking up in fear at the expanding whirlpool on the ceiling. It lurched, choking through its bony nose as if there was food lodged in its throat that it couldn't get out—couldn't *let* out. The monster hunched over, gagging on the soul it had taken, desperately trying to vomit it up.

Some gratification came with knowing that George's soul was toxic to the being. Even if the demon wanted to let his soul go, its lips were literally sealed, forcing it to contain the excruciating essence.

I latched onto what little enjoyment I could while the demon suffered. The wind slapped at my ears so hard that it drowned out Gavyn calling my name. He clutched my arm, getting my attention, and pointed to the ceiling.

The whirling water churned more viciously now; the small swells escalated to large crashing waves, circling an inverted funnel. The need to run for cover surged through me. I wasn't sure how, but a hurricane rearing its ugly face in the center of the room seemed entirely possible.

The mysterious waters were angry above us. However, the swirling fluid seemed to retain itself enough to keep us safe from its impending destruction. Controlled disorder. With my eyes closed, I took a cleansing breath to clear my head in case this was one of those "focus, Nevaeh" kind of moments.

I opened my eyes to see cool droplets of water trickling down toward us. A listless mist with big globules the size of pebbles floated from the ceiling. The repugnant odor from the demon subsided, and a more appealing aroma filled the room—a refreshing smell that sent chills of exhilaration through my body.

The faded, red glow retracted, returning the colors of the apartment to their original hues. I let my head fall back and escaped in the sense of peace the new commotion brought. The cleansing moisture dampened my hair, sticking it against my face and neck. Tranquility engulfed my pain and caution. Surely, another devastating event was about to happen, but I took refuge in the glorious flow of power infiltrating the room.

A final gust of wind sucked the water off my face like a vacuum, and all movement ceased. The floating droplets of water stilled, suspended without motion, just above my head; thousands of smooth, glassy beads of wetness strung up by invisible line.

The beads held their positions, stuck in the air, anticipating a command that would allow them to continue in their intended paths to the floor. Small puddles on the hardwoods froze in mid-splash, yearning for the droplets to finish crashing into them, as was the natural sequence of these things.

All was quiet. No rumbling noise and no rippling walls. Only the circular motion of the pool on the ceiling and the shuddering of the demon continued.

Gavyn was at my side, his body rigid with expectation. "Wait," he whispered.

So much was running through my mind that it was difficult to keep a clear perception. I battled the constant notion to surrender to a much-needed mental breakdown. Hysteria was creeping out from the corner of my mind, but I forced myself to rein it in for a later time.

The room suddenly flexed against a flare of amazing energy that knocked me off my feet. Breathing became harder as the air rushed out from the center of the opening above us and thickened, turning the room into a balloon almost ready to pop. Walls creaked from the pressure, and the static droplets began to quiver where they hung.

Gavyn scrambled to help me stand again and started searching my body for injuries. I pushed the damp hair out of my face then swatted his hands away. But, when he grabbed my arm in an offer of support, I gave in. I needed him. I couldn't go through this on my own.

The monster groaned louder than I'd heard so far. My eyes darted to where I'd seen it last and found the fiend hunched over in pain, clawing the floor, heaving itself closer to the hole in the wall it had entered through.

"He senses them coming. It won't be long." His face lit up with excitement.

"Who is coming?" I wasn't ready for any more surprises, especially the otherworldly kind. I grew irritated with his lack of explanations, but forced myself to trust Gavyn.

The whirling pond over our heads, waking with movement moments before, was now motionless. The fluid appeared smooth and silver like mercury.

Curiosity urged me closer to the pool, needing to see what was in it. I saw a reflection of myself with a puzzled expression. However, the longer I studied the liquid, the thinner the consistency got, becoming more and more transparent by the second.

Gavyn tugged on my arm. "I think it's time to move back."

I ignored his advice and leaned away from him, staring up into the center of the reflection. "Wait I...I think I see something." I shoved his hands off me as I squinted up at the shiny surface, detecting an object moving on the other side. "I just want to see."

The movement resembled a bird diving for fish. Only, I saw what it must look like from the fish's point of view; the blurry shape of something higher on the food chain jetting toward me.

CHAPTER TWELVE

From Fire Below To Water Above

"LOOK OUT!" Gavyn screamed, yanking on me hard enough to drag me down to my butt. I hit the floor just as a sharp, energy-packed bang rang into the atmosphere.

Another, more intense pressure blasted outward from the center of the water. The walls buckled and splintered around us. Books toppled off the bookshelves, pictures jumped from their nails, and the furniture skid along the floor.

The force flung me backward across the room in a seated position, my legs dragging in front of me as I slid. My body collided with Gavyn's coffee table, the edge stabbing into the center of my back and expelling the breath from my lungs. I came to an abrupt stop when the table crashed into a wall, breaking my slide but shoving the corner harder into my spine.

I gasped as a spike of pain drove up my vertebrae. My eyes moistened from the tears I was determined to hold back. I tried to move again but decided against it when the jolting ache in my back radiated to my legs.

The pressure continued to build in the room at an unbearable pace. My lungs seemed to deflate more and more each time I gasped for air, preventing me from taking a sufficient breath. My lack of oxygen began to alter my vision, casting a foggy blur everywhere I looked.

Planted on the floor, slouched against the bent, metal frame of the coffee table, I rolled my head around to hunt for Gavyn—and some sign that he was still conscious. My sight was fading, but I was able to recognize the body slumped against a distant wall. He wasn't lucid, but I could see his chest rising and falling. He was alive.

My weak limbs stopped me from going to him, and with my lungs suffocating, I couldn't even say his name. Panic set in. I was trapped inside the prison of my own brain, my body failing me.

I attempted to rock myself off the floor, but what little movement I did manage only slid my torso sideways, landing me on the floor with my left arm pinned under my side and my legs twisted out in front of me.

With my lungs nearly empty of air, each breath just a tiny hiccup of oxygen, thinking was becoming a chore. I lay immobile, expecting the end like a dying fish trapped ashore.

The hard, wooden planks chilled my cheek as my head rested against the floor. I thought about how alone I was. George was gone, Gavyn was unconscious, and things were happening around me that I didn't understand.

My gaze flicked over the hardwoods, but a hazy mind, and a small puddle of water inches from my face, obscured my view from Gavyn and the monster. Tiny peaks from the splash extended up from the little patch of water and froze in position like statues, waiting for the world to resume movement.

As the last bit of air left my body, blackness seeped in around the image of the small splash of water.

I welcomed the ending. I begged for it to be quick, to take me away from this life. I accepted my fate, knowing that there was nothing left for me here. Painful yet loving memories of George surfaced, making me eager to leave. There would be no more happy times in my life without George, so why stay?

Cool moisture sprinkled my face as a bead of water plopped into the puddle next to me. Fresh air whooshed back into the room. I sucked in an audible lungful of air, allowing it to infiltrate every asphyxiated part of my body. My muscles relaxed and tingled with the return of the oxygen they craved. I could, somewhat, focus again.

Droplets of water all over the room crashed to the floor, freed from their static state, and gathered into winding streams that rolled along the floor then disappeared between the floorboards.

Finding the courage and strength to move, I slowly eased up on my elbows, grimacing at the pain that remained in my back. My eyes darted across the room where Gavyn was propped up against the bar stool behind him, peering up into the pool above. The demon crouched on the floor convulsing, stalking me with its black eyes. George's corpse lay motionless, pinned between the futon and the leather chair that smash against each other during the chaos.

The room was eerily quiet. No painful moaning, no screeching, no whistling wind. Nothing. The invisible power was harnessed for the moment, but a building tension in the atmosphere indicated it would not be contained for much longer.

Through the silvery water above, I saw the blurry figure on the other side growing larger. It was almost here. I crawled across the floor towards Gavyn, realizing that I didn't really want to be that close when the thing came through after all.

My eyes settled on Gavyn's mouth when I reached his side. He was yelling at me, but I couldn't hear him. Had I gone deaf from the noise? He repeated something again, but finally gave up when he realized I wasn't getting it.

The moment I tucked myself against Gavyn's side, something broke through the glassy surface on the ceiling. My eyes focused on the object, and my mouth fell open.

The water gave way to large, bare feet. Ten toes, high arches, solid heels. They were human—not at all what I expected. Then, toned calves and strong muscular thighs slipped through. The figure lowered one section at a time from beyond the shiny liquid, each part as human looking as the last.

The being wore a tightly fitted, brown leather shirt with the front laced up by a leather cord, barely covering the chiseled blocks of muscle beneath the fabric. His bulging arms strained though the sleeveless openings of his shirt and twitched as he tightened his fingers into powerful fists at his sides. Wide strips of leather, reaching from his waist to his knees, fastened to one another with metal studs in a skirt-like pattern. Hints of soft, red fabric peeked through the slits of the heavy leather when he spread his legs slightly, anticipating the landing.

My gaze drifted to the gleaming sword fastened to his right hip. It was heavily jeweled with a gold-plated hilt that looked worn in some spots where his fingers likely rubbed during use. He wore a short dagger on his other hip, plainly decorated on the handle but ornately beveled along its sharp, waved edge. He reminded me of a Trojan warrior, down to the protective clothing he squeezed himself into, the weapons on his belt, and the fierce confidence he conveyed.

When the descent was complete, a dangerously masculine and unnaturally attractive man stood in the middle of Gavyn's living room, studying his surroundings carefully. Surprisingly enough, I wasn't afraid—I wanted to get closer. I wanted to touch him.

A strange serenity radiated throughout the room and masked the fear I probably should have felt. I could feel the weight of Gavyn's eyes on me as I began to crawl toward the man, but I needed to get closer.

The sight of the warrior conjured a heat that raced through my veins. The smell wafting from his skin was intoxicating. I gulped tasting the dense, bittersweet odor on my tongue while my eyes feasted on the alluring details of his physique.

I was irrefutably attracted to the form in front of me, but I couldn't help feeling like I was being deceived by my emotions. He was just a man I assured myself—a man from another world. But, there were other things I sensed that made him much more.

My body pined for him. His very presence drew me in. It was lustful, but on a far different level than I'd ever experienced. There was another emotion blending with the lust, something more pure.

My heart and body wanted him—yearned for him to want *me* and accept *me*. My soul, however, hungered for the man to praise, love, and protect *me*. Through all of these emotions, though, my brain was caging fits of rebellion against the figure invading our home. In my mind, I knew the man was not mine for the taking. I knew something was off with the whole situation, but I couldn't resist.

My head tilted back, my eyes tracing a line from his bare feet upwards. When my gaze roamed over the chestnut hair resting upon his shoulders and the stern features of his face, I noticed what made him more than human. His tall frame stretched about six feet, four inches tall, but there was a portion of him that reached even higher and was still concealed by the pool.

Are those...? No, they can't be.

Wings.

The being squatted down, dragging the remainder of two large, white masses out of the water. He rolled his shoulders once, readjusting the weight hanging from his back.

An angel? He's a freakin' angel.

Massive, billowy limbs flicked out around his shoulders then reached for opposite ends of the room before neatly folding against his back as if he were a bird resettling its graceful wings to their proper places.

The angel turned and glared down at the demon cowering in a dark corner. He marched toward the monster, trailing long feathers along the floor behind him. The city lights shined in from the window and glinted off thin, golden plates heavily dispersed throughout the white of his wings. I squinted, eyeing the intricate gold pieces. They mimicked his other plumes, but seemed to offer a kind of armor woven in with the rest of his silky down.

Clawing and scraping at the floor, the demon hefted its charred body toward the wall, eager to escape. The angel confidently claimed the last few steps separating him from the monster, lifted his foot, and then stomped down on the demon's throat, pinning it to the floor. He leaned over, wrapping one strong hand around the underside of its bony jaw. In one sudden motion, too fast for me to register, the angel hoisted the tall demon into the air, dangling it from an out-stretched arm above him.

The winged being stared up into the evil, mouthless face and spoke, but I couldn't make out anything he said. The eerie silence still filled the room, stifling my ability to hear.

Frustrated, I looked over my shoulder at Gavyn. His eyes darted from the angel to me. Understanding my questioning expression, he held out his hand, coaxing me back to him. The calm look on his face said he would explain and that everything would be okay. As my hand reached his, he pulled me to his side and huddled me under his arm. Then, we waited.

The angel shook the beast violently and slammed it against the wall. Dust and pieces of plaster fell around the two large bodies as they wrestled for what seemed like an eternity. He leaned his shoulder into the monster, pressing it harder into the wall while punching it in the abdomen. The surface dented and cracked under their pressure.

Trembling and jerking, the demon slapped its decomposing hand against the plaster. Beams of light erupted from behind its long fingers and morphed into a pulsing, red glow. The angel's bicep and forearm muscles strained as he struggled to wrench the demon onto the floor, but the monster sunk its talons into the plaster, refusing to budge.

The wall weakened to the same rubbery state it was when the demon entered Gavyn's apartment, stretching from the demon's attempt to push itself back through. Its evil face glared at me over the angel's shoulder with a hint of satisfaction just beyond the pain it endured from harvesting George's soul. Fragments of white-hot light shot out from rips in the thin surface, and the new hole swallowed the monster's body, yanking it from the angel's grip.

The opening slammed shut. The glow ceased.

It was gone at last; but so was the spirit of the only father I knew.

Gavyn's hand slipped under my arms and tightened around my waist. He tugged on me twice to get my attention. When I looked up at him, he dragged me over his leg so I sat between his thighs and scrunched his face up, squeezing his eyes closed with urgency.

The angel spun around to study us. All I could do was peer back into the peridot-green eyes measuring me. His once fierce and determined features were now soft and inquisitive. Deeply bowed lips spread over his pearly teeth into a wide, charming smile. He winked at me.

What the hell? A cocky wink...that's what he's giving me in response to this whole situation?

With the clap of his hands, an echo of energy exploded from the winged warrior, rippling out towards us.

Gavyn hugged me to him suffocatingly tight. We smashed backwards into the barstool which crashed into the bar. I clenched Gavyn's pant legs and pulled, trying to pry myself off his chest, but the force was too strong. His hands gripped my hips and pushed but failed to alleviate the weight of my body against his. The overbearing energy kept us glued together.

Walls creaked around us from the shift of buckled drywall retracting to its usual smoothness. Dust that had fallen during the scuffle trickled in reverse through the air, sealing the cracked surfaces. Gavyn's furniture skid across the floorboards to their original spots, scraping the floor like nails on a chalkboard. I grimaced from the uncomfortable sound, suddenly able to hear again.

The pulsating pressure was subsiding. The room was clean and intact like nothing happened. Our bodies relaxed, and we both jerked forward, heaving breaths of relief. Gavyn's hands slid to my waist and rested there, maintaining our connection. I was thankful for the comfort he offered, no matter how little it actually helped.

A low rumble of laughter started from across the room. The angel placed his fists on his narrow hips and took two strides in our direction.

"Gavyn, it's been a long time." The angel's voice was smooth as butter with a velvety tone that sent a shiver through my body.

"Ten years, Malach," Gavyn replied coolly.

I stayed silent, shifting my focus back and forth between the two, expecting one of them to throw in an explanation of what in the hell happened.

"So...she can see." The angel nudged his sculpted chin in my direction, his steel gaze settling on my confused expression.

"Yeah, but it's all very new to her," Gavyn said, rubbing his thumb in soothing circles on my stomach as he spoke to the angel. "We're not sure what gift, yet."

I glanced over my shoulder at Gavyn, searching for an answer to any of the millions of questions sweeping through my mind. Of course, he didn't respond to a single one.

"She doesn't know anything."

Irritation outweighed my patience as the two of them observed my every reaction and talked about me as if I weren't in the room. I'm sure I relayed about twenty different expressions portraying what I felt on the inside, but apparently my annoyance was lost on them.

"How about one of you clue me the fuck in." I flinched, realizing the harshness of my words, and wished I'd chosen a kinder vocabulary in the presence of an angel.

They laughed at me. How could they laugh at a time like this?

"Nevaeh, I'll explain as much as I can. I think this is why you were brought to me." Gavyn glanced at the being striding towards the futon for confirmation.

The angel shrugged then flexed his wings to the side and sat down. They ruffled a bit before lying neatly along the back of the seat.

I snorted at the ridiculous sight before me.

The tall, heavenly being sprawled on the futon with his long legs tucked awkwardly against the edge of the cushions, and his bent knees opened wide. The leather skirt-thing draping over his lap barely hid the enticing parts beneath it, but he didn't seem to care. And his freakin' *wings*, they stretched beyond the ends of the futon by almost a foot in each direction.

I never actually believed in angels before, but if I had, this would not have been how I pictured meeting one. Most people, I think, imagined them standing majestically on a mountaintop, towering over demons—not lounging on a damn couch as if he were on vacation.

My eyes dropped to his feet, and to the right lay George's vacant body. I could sense Gavyn tensing behind me. He was probably waiting for me to have a complete panic attack.

I was devastated that George was gone. But I also accepted the fact that the corpse lying on the floor wasn't George anymore. Nothing was going to change that.

"Why don't you go down to the kitchen and get something to drink. I need to talk to Malach for a minute...get some things straightened out." A soft smile curled at Gavyn's lips, but it didn't hide the concern in his voice.

I couldn't believe he was asking me to leave. Especially when this seemed to have everything to do with George and me.

Shoving my angry temper tantrum aside for another time, I swallowed my pride and pain. "Alright. But when I get back, I want answers." I was surprised to hear the firmness of my demand; on the inside I was sniffling like a child. I took one last glance at the angel and headed towards the door, shaking my head.

After surviving every pain-inducing step down the stairs, I paused at the bottom of the stairwell and stared into the black hallway leading to the cafe. Shadows remained unwavering in the faint neon glow of the cafe lights, but I couldn't help feeling like I should run right back upstairs and beg someone to come hold my hand in the dark.

I laughed off my reluctance to enter the hall and forced my feet to carry me forward. After a few snail-paced strides, I felt confident that nothing was lurking in the shadows and padded into the kitchen, flipping the switch on before I crossed the threshold.

The bright kitchen light stung my sensitive eyes, strengthening the nagging headache I'd recently acquired. I pulled a glass from the cupboard, filled it with water, and leaned my hip into the counter next to the sink. I ignored the cup in my hand and instead contemplated what was left of my life. So much had changed in the blink of an eye that it was hard to wrap my head around it. My goals of getting a good job, maybe one day going to school, and having a normal life seemed so unimportant now. I couldn't even plan my next twenty-four hours because I hadn't the faintest idea of what was real anymore.

I dumped the entire cup of water into the sink and slammed the glass down on the counter. They had enough time to figure out what they were going to tell me, and I had enough of the waiting.

I marched toward the kitchen door and turned off the light. As I stepped into the hallway, something moved in the café.

"Hello?"

No one answered.

A shadow darted across the floor, drawing my attention to a silhouette peering in through the window. I edged along the wall towards the front of the building, straining to see who lurked outside. The amber glow of the street light shined on her golden hair like a halo, but I knew better.

My body stiffened when I saw the face on the other side of the window was Layla's.

What was she doing out there?

Her emotionless gaze beamed in my direction. The emptiness in her stare made me feel as transparent as the window she was pressing her nose against. I waved to let her know I saw her. Then, something in her eyes changed, darkened. Her hand rose to mimic my wave, and her perfect pink lips curled into a mischievous grin, tainting her innocent beauty.

Though the woman outside looked like Layla, she was no longer the Layla I knew. The ill-intent oozing from her rattled my bones. I immediately ran for the light switch a few feet ahead, flipped it on, and then looked back at the window.

She was gone.

I entered Gavyn's apartment, once again amazed at the sight of the angel's human-like actions. His oversized frame glided through the kitchenette. His wings twitched behind him while he rummaged through the cupboards. Gavyn ignored Malach's invasion of his home and sat on one of the bar stools, sipping from a beer bottle.

I observed quietly as the two acted like nothing out of the ordinary had occurred. At least, I was quiet until I sneezed from the dust still swirling through the air. They stopped in their tracks, their eyes locking on me.

"God bless you," Malach said, grinning.

I crossed my arms over my chest and glared at the angel for a moment. "So, who's ready to give me some insight about tonight?"

Gavyn crooked an eyebrow and peered over at Malach expectantly.

"Dammit, just tell me already!"

"Guess I should be going, then." The angel reached for a box of Twinkies in the cabinet. He popped open the end of the cardboard, pulled out the yellow treat inside, ripped off the wrapper, and then stuffed the cake into his mouth. He sucked in his well-defined gut and shoved the Twinkie box behind his leather belt as he chewed. "Mm, you guys really know how to indulge in good food down here." He held up one last bite of cream-filled cake in a toasting motion, then crammed it in his mouth. "Thanks, Gav."

Gavyn rolled his eyes and drank his last sip of beer. "You're gonna make me fill her in by myself, then," he dead-panned.

"I have every bit of faith in you. Have fun." He patted Gavyn's back then strolled toward George's body.

Malach bent down and gently picked up the corpse that lay on the floor. The being cradled the body in one arm like it was weightless and lovingly caressed its cheek with his other hand. The angel's eyes searched the hollow face for a moment and mumbled some words in a low foreign language. Then, as quickly as his tender demeanor came, it left—reverting to the somewhat comical version of a heavenly soldier.

"What do you think you're doing with George's body?" I demanded, stomping across the room to stop the angel.

He winked arrogantly, unfazed by the clear anger in my eyes. "I'm taking it with me."

"You can't do that!" I protested, stopping just a short distance from the angel. I became very aware that the fewer steps between me and the winged man, the more my body wanted to bow down and praise him.

George deserved a proper burial. That was for me to do. I needed to take care of him — or, at least, his body.

"Relax, Nevaeh. I will take it to the Heavens with me for safekeeping," he responded, I think a little intrigued by my brashness toward him.

In spite of my protective reaction, I was sure he sensed that I desperately wanted him. I could feel my body involuntarily leaning in to get closer to the angel. My breath was deep and heady, and there was a lack of conviction behind my words. It was incredibly hard to deny the fact that I wanted nothing more than his arms to embrace me and to feel his massive hands sweep across *my* cheek.

"Why does it matter now? I thought the demon took his soul."

Gavyn approached me from behind, softly grabbed my forearm, and slid his hand down to mine. "Let him go. I will explain. George's body is safer with them."

The sincerity in his tone begged me to trust him.

Staring into his kind eyes, I remembered my developing feelings for him. My real emotions bubbled to the surface and erased the lust and need pulling my soul toward Malach. It wasn't the pining for the angel I felt anymore, but a growing infatuation for the man in front of me. I made a quick mental note not to trust myself, or what I felt, around the heavenly being. I smiled sadly at Gavyn and nodded with assurance that I would let whatever happened happen and trust his judgment.

Just then, a warm breeze floated through the room, twirling my hair around my neck as tiny raindrops began to fall around us. I looked to the ceiling and found a growing puddle softening the surface above me once again. The sides stretched farther and farther with each swirl of circulating water. It was tamer this time.

"Guess I'll see you guys later." Malach widened his stance and stiffened his back, pulling George's shell closer against his body. His massive shimmering wings unfolded behind him and took my breath away. He was beautiful. It almost hurt to see him leave. I wanted to kneel and weep at his pureness.

As if by cue, tears flooded my eyes when he flexed the masses of white feathers up. The angel was leaving me here with my misery.

"Wait," I demanded. I ran to George and gently took his left hand in mine. The thin, gold band slipped off his finger with ease.

I pushed the dulled circle of metal onto my thumb, spinning it around a few times as I thought about the hope that George had to see his family again and how he'd been denied that chance.

I squeezed George's hand one last time and lowered it, planting a kiss on his cold, gaunt cheek. Stepping backward, I stared down at the bare strip of skin on his ring finger. The flesh where his ring used to be was paler than the rest of his hand. I continued spinning the band on my thumb as the weight of grief constricted my chest. This hunk of dented gold would be all I have left of him now.

I tore my eyes from George's shell and looked up at Malach. I nodded. Malach silently returned the nod and bowed his head, acknowledging my unspoken permission to take George. In one vigorous motion downward, the angel's powerful wings rocketed him and the corpse up through the watery vortex. The ceiling smoothed and hardened, assuming its true form.

I stopped sobbing for the angel's departure the moment the portal closed, yet, a single tear trickled down my cheek after they departed. It carried only a drop of the sorrow shredding my heart to pieces, but that one fell solely for George.

CHAPTER THIRTEEN

A Whole New World

Silently, I said my goodbyes to the last of George and turned toward Gavyn, wrapping my arms tight around his waist. Inhaling his cedar scent, I tried desperately to lose myself in his warmth. He held me in a gentle embrace and kissed the top of my head. With my ear to his chest, I heard him breathe me in.

I lifted my gaze to meet his and searched for some hint of his thoughts. His eyes clouded with regret and worry.

Did he regret welcoming me into his life?

I averted my eyes so I wouldn't have to see any more signs of disappointment. He lifted his hands to either side of my head, urging me to look back at him. His strong fingers threaded through my hair and stopped when his palms reached my temples. He traced his thumbs over my brows, smoothing the creases I had unconsciously created there. I closed my eyes and savored his consoling touch.

The warmth of his breath intensified when he lowered his face to mine. Even with my eyes closed, I could sense him smiling as he hovered just above me. I smiled too, thinking about how much I wanted him to kiss me, to *love* my pain away.

Though it seemed like centuries, only a few seconds passed before I finally felt the dampness of his lips. Every cell in my body jolted to life. One small kiss, then another and another—increasing in passion and pressure; the next one more engaging than the last. His tongue gently slid between my lips, persuading my mouth to open under his.

I traced my hands up his back and neck, then tangled my fingers in his hair. Pulling his mouth harder against mine, I deepened the kiss, welcoming him into my soul.

A surge of adrenaline charged through my body. Tiny moans escaped my mouth, making apparent the growing need inside me. His breath became heavy and fast with each stroke of our tongues. He pressed me into him, grinding our bodies together, digging his fingertips into my flesh. My mind focused on the raw intensity of our connection and almost forgot about the world around us, about the devastation of losing George.

Gavyn growled, lightening his kisses before reluctantly breaking away. I groaned from the loss of connection and opened my eyes. He smiled and lowered his forehead to rest against mine. "I'll make us some tea. We have a lot to talk about," he panted.

Of course. Now that I didn't want to talk—I just wanted to get lost in him and forget—he was all up for a conversation.

I tugged the wrinkles out of my shirt and tucked my hair back behind my ears. "Ok."

I padded to the bathroom to straighten my disheveled emotions while Gavyn made tea. Feelings of apprehension surfaced. Even though I needed answers, I wanted to pretend that nothing life changing had happened and move on. With Gavyn. I wanted to discuss how we felt about each other, not monsters and angels, or death and afterlife. It was selfish of me, I know, but it hurt too much to think about the recent events. It felt easier to deny them.

The whistle of a teapot screamed down the hall as I stared into the mirror, searching for the girl I once was. Dark circles of sadness and exhaustion underlined my eyes. I sighed and rubbed my palms over my face, attempting to wipe away the signs of tragedy—with no success. I marched out of the bathroom disgusted with the embodiment of sorrow and confusion I had become.

Gavyn met me at the end, holding a steaming mug of earthy, amber-colored liquid. I accepted the tea, inhaling the alleviating aroma into my sinuses, and took a sip. He watched me closely, gauging my demeanor.

I shuffled to the futon and sat down, taking notice of the pinkish hues sluggishly gliding into the room from the bay window. A new day was dawning.

Gavyn disappeared down the hall and returned with a throw blanket. He wrapped it snuggly around my shoulders. I looked up at him, smiling with appreciation, and tugged it tighter to me. Sitting beside me, he opened his mouth as if to say something then closed it again. His lips curved in a tender smile. "Where would you like to start?"

I didn't know where to start. I didn't even quite understand where my reality ended and the new one began. I kept expecting to wake up in the leather chair and see George lying on the futon, feeling better after a nasty virus.

Gavyn must've sensed the anxiety clawing at my chest. "How about we start with what you *do* know." He cupped his hand over my thigh and lightly squeezed. That strange, uncontrollable calmness waved through me again, pushing the anxiety back into its hiding place.

"How do you do that? Make me calm down so easily?"

"It's my gift."

I chuckled. "Uh…a little sure of yourself, aren't you?"

He grinned. "No, Nevaeh, what I mean is that it's a gift given to me by God."

"By God?" I asked in disbelief, breaking out into hysterical laughter.

Why was that so hard to believe? In the past six hours, I witnessed a soul-sucking demon who emerged through—and back into—a solid wall as if it were paper, after it took the spirit of the only father I could remember. I'd also been graced by the influential presence of an angel who descended through an upside-down rain puddle, scooped up George's body, and ascended back into the puddle to enter the Heavens. But this—Gavyn having a God given gift—was hard to believe?

He patiently waited for me to work it out, nodding with reassurance when he saw the light bulb of acceptance turn on in my eyes.

"When did you get this gift, and what exactly is it?" I questioned quietly, not sure if I really wanted to know.

"I have the gift of emotional influence, but I'm also considered an Inductor—someone who sets out to recruit Celata to our side before they are tempted to join the Dark. My influence is a tool for my actual vocation, so to speak." He observed me closely, speaking in slow sentences so as not to lose me in the details. "I have known what I am for about ten years now."

I interrupted him to clear a passing thought. "Around the same time you last saw Malach?"

"Yes. Malach was the angel that explained to me what I am." He sighed and fixed his gaze on the colorful view out the window. "I'd lost my last living relative—my father. I was desperate, alone, and angry. Strange things were happening to those who came around me. I noticed that everyone I physically got close to was as angry as I was for no reason—violent at times even. I would see a person on the street laughing and joking with a friend, and as soon as I came within three feet of them…it was like throwing a switch. They immediately became maddened. Sometimes the feeling they got from me only amplified their own anger."

His glossy eyes lowered to his lap.

"One person, in particular, went into a deep rage. I was sitting on a bench, waiting for the next bus to come. Despair toyed with my emotions, made me obsess over my dad's murder. The pure hatred I held onto was unreal.

"I got so worked up, I started crying and hyperventilating. I turned to the man next to me and grabbed his arm for help, but I couldn't catch my breath to ask. The man's happy expression morphed into this dark, deceitful sneer. He stood up, gripped his umbrella, and walked to the woman passing us on the sidewalk. I was frozen to the bench, unable to do anything but watch as he stabbed the umbrella into the woman's chest."

Sadness clouded his face as he went silent for a moment, replaying the memories in his mind.

"She was twenty. So young." He took a deep breath and turned his eyes to me. "It was chaos. People ran to help her, mothers shrouded their children from the scene, and the man with the umbrella...he fell to his knees and wept while begging for forgiveness for what he'd done. I can still picture his face and pinpoint the exact moment when he understood what happened—the disbelief in his frightened eyes when he realized it was his hand that took the woman's life. Only it really wasn't him. It was me."

"So, because you were in so much pain, it transferred to that man and caused him to react to it?" My heart ached for him—and the poor woman who died.

"Yeah, pretty much. I ran when the police and rescue showed up. It was dark and cold by then. Malach found me at an abandoned playground miles away from the bus-stop, huddled in a ball on the ground." A smile crept across his mouth. "He was giving off a glow so bright that I had to squint to look at him. When I asked what he was, he told me he was an Archangel." Gavyn paused, scrutinizing my expression—probably waiting for me to question his confession.

I nodded my head, urging him to continue. There was no way I could deny the claim that Malach was an angel.

"He told me about a race of people on earth that were born with gifts. Malach called them *Celatum*—The Hidden. These people come into their gifts at different ages, usually around a tragic time in their lives. Each individual can do different things... has different powers. So, it's almost impossible to know who is a Celata until right before they are aware themselves."

Sensing the change in my demeanor when I glanced at the floor, he allowed me to soak it in and waited for the questions he knew I was forming.

"So that's why you weren't sure if I was one of these Celatum or not?" Gavyn gave a quick nod and let me piece more of the puzzle together. "But you *did* know that something terrible was going to happen...and you didn't warn me?" Anger tore through me like a hot blade. He could have told me something bad was coming, even if he didn't know exactly what, but he didn't.

"I didn't know this would happen, Nevaeh. I swear. I was hopin' that you livin' on the streets was tragedy enough." Regret flared in his eyes. He really had hoped the tragedy of my upbringing had been a sufficient torture for my initiation.

"But what about my gift? Wouldn't it have shown by now if that was the case?"

"I thought maybe you just didn't recognize it, yet."

I cradled my face in the refuge of my hands and continued processing while he went on.

"Just like we all come into the gifts at different times, the intensity is different, too. These powers are personalized to our souls. Some come into them all at once, others take years to develop. Malach says

174

we vary so much to signify God's love for the things inside us that make us unique — the pieces of our souls that make us special to him."

"But I've never had a relationship with God. Why would I be given such a gift? Hell, up until now, I wasn't convinced there was a God…and I'm still not sure I'm on His side." I let the last few words trail in a whisper, almost ashamed of my lacking faith.

"Just because you don't believe in Him, doesn't mean He turns His back on you. He is there whether you accept Him or not, waiting for your soul's return to its maker."

"And if I don't want to accept Him, or this gift?" I asked smugly, showing the doubt I harbored for Gavyn's Lord.

"Why wouldn't you, Nevaeh? You've seen a glimpse of the players in this game. Why would you choose not to be one of us?"

"Is it really a choice? I don't remember anyone asking me if I wanted to give up George for some damn power. I didn't even know all this existed until he got ripped from my life," I yelled, twisting the edges of the blanket into a bunch. Seeing the surprise in Gavyn's expression made me realize how close I was to losing it. This wasn't his fault. I couldn't blame him.

I lowered my voice, composing myself. "Just tell me the rest of what you know. I don't want to talk about the personal side of it all, yet. I just need the information…*please*." I drew in a deep, slow breath. Gavyn reached out to offer a consoling touch, but I leaned away, retreating into the crook of the armrest behind me. Could I still trust him?

He sighed and lowered his hand, looking a little offended, but he continued. "All humans are born with purpose — even if it's only to produce more humans and teach them God's way. *We* were fashioned to help in the Heavenly War. Our innocent souls are kissed to life. The plans of our lives are laid out on a map, so to speak. God knows the destination of every path we might take, but it's our choice which path we walk. If we take the path not meant for us, we can direct our lives back towards the original plan. However, we have to suffer the consequences that formed from the decisions we previously made. The plan is always predestined, but never certain. With each new conflict and new choice, the rest of our life's path can shift."

"I don't understand. What does this have to do with the gifts and the Celatum?" I shook my head, attempting to rattle things into place.

"Like every other choice we come across, to accept the gift and how we use it is in our hands. You can deny the gift and move on with your life, but you will never forget what happened. You won't stop seeing this world of ours. You just kinda float through life dormant, but aware." He looked to the ceiling suggestively, then back at me, grinning. "Or you can choose sides and be part of a battle that is bigger than anything most will ever fathom."

"Choose sides?"

Gavyn nodded. "He wants us to *choose* him, so he gives us the option instead of forcin' us. The gift stays with us in the hope that if we join the Dark Celatum, it might remind us of his love every day we are away from him." He exhaled a heavy breath then slouched back into the cushions, resting his head on the back of the futon. "I guess we are so important that He will let His own weapons be used against Him if it means one day they might return to Him."

We hushed for a minute, contemplating the grand gesture of God's sacrifice. Then, I realized that we somehow wandered away from Gavyn's story. "So...after Malach explained about the free will thing and the Celatum, what happened?"

Gavyn's expression relaxed. The fact that I was asking questions must have assured him that I wasn't going to run — yet.

"Malach only came to me because the pain eating away at me was harming others. You see, Archangels don't usually deal with us on a personal level. Their duties are on a much higher scale than dealing with humans individually, but I was becoming too dangerous to leave unchecked.

"He explained that my gift was very useful when controlled but could be disastrous in the wrong hands. To the heavenly beings, it was important enough that they broke their cover and told me about my gift before I came into it completely—and before one of the Dark recruiters got to me. I learned that I had to let go of the pain and channel it into what it was meant for, before I unintentionally killed anyone else." His gaze flickered with a hint of the guilt buried deep in his heart.

"So, do you always control other people's emotions?" I asked, refocusing the conversation away from his troubled thoughts.

He chuckled softly. "No. And it's not really controlling. I call it swaying. A little more subtle than a push, but more forceful than an urge." A playfulness lightened his tone.

"How often have you used it on me?" Images of him kissing me in the hallway danced before me. Did I really like it as much as I did, or was that him *swaying* me?

"Not often. I've only used it on you to relieve some of the anxiety during what's happened in the past few days. It was a very low intensity. I didn't want to numb you. Just wanted to help you cope a little better." He looked down at his hands. "Does it help?" he asked timidly.

"I don't know. How can I tell when it's you?"

"The times you were angry or anxious then felt calm without explanation—that was me." His voice was soft and thoughtful. I understood what he meant to do, but I wasn't sure how I felt about getting my emotions hijacked.

"And the pull I felt with Malach? Was that you?"

Gavyn huffed and rolled his eyes. "No, that was all Malach. They all do that. I felt it too in the beginning." He finally looked up from his hands and scanned the room as he spoke. "It's not them that you are attracted to. It's the Grace. The traits of Heaven they carry with them.

The smells, the lust, the yearning...it's all because, deep down, our souls hunger, on a very primitive level, for anything that offers us even a glimpse of God. Our system can't handle their pureness and kinda goes haywire. It gets easier though."

"I thought lust was bad."

He shrugged. "On a human basis, it's the initial foundation that leads to genuine attraction. Before two people get to know each other, there's something that sparks between them, something that reaches out and smacks us in the face. It doesn't come from a little list of requirements you think that person might meet; it stems from the carnal need to have that person's body close to yours—the smell of them, the heat, even the thought of them touching you can drive you wild before a word is ever spoken." He licked his lip, and his eyes drifted to my mouth for a moment. "In a demented, evolved way, lust fuels our motivation to love."

I was speechless. Our eyes met, and the intensity in his gaze wouldn't allow me to ignore the suggestiveness behind his words. A shiver quaked my body. The notion of "love" floated steadily between us with implication.

"Yoo-hoo?"

We both jumped at the intruding voice coming from the bottom of the stairwell.

"Anyone up there?" Layla called in a sickly-sweet tone as her footsteps approached Gavyn's apartment door.

He lifted his wrist up, glancing at his watch. "Shit, it's breakfast time already." Shooting a quick look to the door, he whispered, "There's more I have to tell you. We'll talk tonight. You stay and get some sleep. I'll take care of the rest."

I grabbed his arm as he stood. "There is no way I can sleep right now. I have to work."

Gavyn nodded his head, approving my plea to keep busy.

Seconds later, Layla strolled into the living room like she belonged here. "Hey, Gav—oh, I didn't know you had company." She stopped abruptly just inside the door, her icy gaze locking on me. She threw her hand up to cover her mouth, feigning surprise. The hand dropped from her smirking, apple-red lips and rested on a cocked hip as she eyed me with disapproval. She absolutely knew I was up here.

"Relax, Layla. We were talking about George," Gavyn said, hurrying down the hall toward his room and then back out with a fresh shirt in his hand. I stared at Layla suspiciously while she ogled Gavyn.

"Hah, whatever, Gavyn. Not my business." She stretched her arm out in front of her, examining the perfectly manicured nails on her fingertips. "Just didn't want to interrupt anything," she added, cutting a sideways glance in my direction.

If eyeballs were laser beams, I'd have a hole in my head from the glare she blasted my way. Her fake kindness wasn't fooling anybody.

"Right," he responded, clearly not convinced by her innocent act either. "So then, what did you need?"

"I got here a little early. Figured I'd see if you needed any help makin' breakfast." Layla's meddlesome eyes roamed over the room and settled on the vacant pile of blankets. "Uh, what happened to George?"

I kept silent, mostly because I had no clue how to answer her. I couldn't really come out with the reality of things and say, *Well Layla, to tell you the truth a demon ate his soul, and his body now resides at P.O. Box Heaven.* I pursed my lips at the sarcasm she brought out in me; even in thought I was snarky with her.

"We took him to the hospital late last night. He's not doing so well." Gavyn said, subtle worry lines forming on his brow.

She gasped, clutching her hands over her heart. "Why didn't you call me? I could've gone for moral support." Her shoddy attempt at concern made me want to gag.

"I'm going later to check on him. I'll let him know you asked about him," I said with the most appreciative smile I could fake. I could play her game too.

Gavyn interrupted our little banter of dishonesty. "Layla, why don't you go down and unlock the back door. I'm sure Mick will be here soon. You guys can get some prep ready." He tossed her the keys and took his shirt off to change it.

She blatantly stared at him, focusing on every ounce of muscle she could see. He, of course, paid her no attention. I don't think he even realized she was screwing him with her eyes. I, on the other hand, *did* realize it and cleared my throat to distract her.

She grinned—obviously pleased with herself—and ignored my gesture while gawking at Gavyn until the hem of his shirt finished trailing down his rippled muscles. I don't know if I was in more disbelief that he could be so completely oblivious to her, or that I was getting so damn territorial over a man I, as of yet, had no claim on.

Without a single look my direction, Layla turned towards the door and jingled the keys in her hand. "See you in a bit," she sang.

We waited until her clunky steps reached the bottom of the stairwell and the apartment door closed before we both sighed in relief. "Now what?" I asked, needing some sort of actual plan to get through the rest of the day.

"I don't know. I guess we just stick to the story that George is sick at the hospital and answer any questions with as little explanation as possible."

"Especially, Layla's," I spat under my breath.

He smirked. "Let's go get something to eat. I still have a business to run."

"How do you do it? Put up with the normalcy of life knowing what you know?" I could barely accomplish daily functions, let alone run a café and pretend to be normal.

"Nevaeh, I've had ten years to learn to deal with living two lives. You've had less than twenty-four hours. If I *didn't* have a piece of what a normal life is meant to be, I would be so overwhelmed by the angel-demon stuff that I'd forget what I was fighting for." He leaned over and pressed his soft lips to my forehead. "Come on. Time to put on a happy face."

His mouth arched into an over-exaggerated, teeth-showing grin. The silliness of his expression forced me to giggle, and I followed suit with my own cheesy grin.

I couldn't leave the pictures of George and the demon behind though. Thoughts of Malach and his white billowy wings drifted in and out of my thoughts. And Gavyn—I'd never look at him the same. He was my safe-hold in all of this. He was the only one I could trust. Yet, something twisted in my gut, something that told me to be careful.

Was there anyone I could really trust anymore?

CHAPTER FOURTEEN

Friend or Foe?

Thankfully, the morning hustle and bustle started early at Joe's. The restaurant's chaos eased the constant shuffling in my mind and kept me from breaking down about George every waking second.

The majority of the staff asked how George was within fifteen minutes of Gavyn and me coming downstairs.

Mental note: Layla could spread news quicker than lightning.

I'm *so* sure she did it out of the goodness of her heart too.

Gavyn had assigned me to do prep with him in the kitchen for most of the day. It was soothing to look up and know he was there. That, maybe, we were sharing the same thoughts when we caught a glimpse of each other. Then, at other times, I found him staring at me from across the island and experienced a gentle flush of tranquility wander through my body. In those moments, I felt like my problems had washed away. My psyche was clear and serene. I knew it was Gavyn swaying me when affectionate, satisfied smiles spread across his kissable lips.

Layla and I traded glares through the pass-through window now and again. She didn't say anything, but the "Don't mess with me, bitch" look she gave me said enough.

The more I thought about her, the more something she said picked at me. "They want him really bad...if I get him to join us...I can have him as my partner." *Could she know? Wouldn't Gavyn know if she was one of the Celatum?* I reminded myself to ask him about her possible involvement in this whole thing later.

Lunchtime zoomed by, and then the café slowed to a snail's pace. This allowed my brain excessive time to zone in on the painful things I was attempting so hard to escape. With less need of me in the kitchen, I decided to keep occupied bussing the few tables recently emptied in the cafe.

The sun had shifted to the rear of the building during the rush hours. The low glow of pendent lights and a kaleidoscope of colors, dancing across the floor through the warped glassy panes like a prism, painted the room.

I stopped at a table next to one of the tall, aged windows and admired the breathtaking rainbows seeping in. Beyond the ripples, I saw him studying me. The wavy glass distorted his features, but I knew it was Archard. No one had eyes that beautiful. No one stirred those uncharted places in me like he did.

Anger churned deep in my belly, even as he drew me in.

What did he tell George that had him convinced everything would be okay, and why wasn't it okay?

He had to know answers or, at least, where I could find them.

The urge to tell him off took over, and I bolted out of the café. The heavy door slammed behind me with a bang that echoed through the crowded street. I jogged to where I saw him standing, but he was gone. I placed my hands on my hips, biting the inside of my cheek while I impatiently searched for Archard in the hordes of people moving down both ends of the street.

I had every curse word in the book ready to blast at him, as well as those I'd made up. For some reason, I felt like he could connect so many pieces of the puzzle. He knew things—I was sure of it. And, though the magnetism I held towards him was uninvited, I had to know why it was there. Not because I wanted to, but because it would be devastating to my very core if I didn't find out what it meant.

I inspected the faces racing by me, but none of them were Archard. My heart throbbed from the constant distance that seemed to always come between us. I was mad as hell, yet the thought of never getting close to him made me crazy.

As the overwhelming and unexplainable pain of his elusiveness weighed me down, I turned to walk back to the café. It would only be a matter of minutes before I fell to the ground and started weeping like a baby. I refused to let that happen.

"Looking for me?" His voice was deep and barely above a whisper next to my ear. His chest pressed firmly against my back.

I gasped, partly because he surprised me and partly because I buzzed with electricity when he was this close. "As a matter of fact, I was," I breathed, spinning around to face him. In my head, I ripped through all the awful things I wanted to say. I was surprisingly disappointed when I found myself unable to tell him what I really thought. With every passing second, my will wavered. I wanted him to hurt like I hurt, but the strange need to love him was stronger. The need for him to hold me—to comfort me—became too much.

Only one word came to mind now. "Why?" I whispered. A tear trickled down my cheek.

"Why what?" he asked with a calm, unknowing expression. His endless eyes burned into mine, full of the knowledge he was hiding behind that impenetrable demeanor.

I knew he saw the pain on my face. I knew he understood what I was asking. How could he stand there so composed without even the tiniest offer of solace?

"*Why what*? That's it? *Why what*?" I scoffed. Flashes of anger crackled inside me. "I know you had something to do with George's death, I just don't know what. I deserve some answers—no, I demand them! He was fine before you left and then..." I stopped myself, afraid that if I continued I wouldn't hold back any of the gory details. The sidewalk, with dozens of people around, was not the place for that.

His cool, solid manner became visibly rattled. "You have no idea what you are talking about. You have no understanding of these matters, so don't get so judgmental, little girl," he growled, leaning down an inch from my face.

"I'm not a little girl," I yelled at him, puffing my ample chest out to prove my point, "and how do you know what I—"

My ranting came to a halt when a feather floated out from under his long, black duster. My wide eyes trailed the white softness as it glided along the crisp breeze between us. I looked back at Archard. He stared at me intently, his brows pinched together and jaw twitching, gauging my reaction.

A few of the puzzle pieces clicked into place. I rewound to the day before and remembered the fuzzy down stuck to the window. His bronze skin shimmered in the slightest way as he swiped at the feather. The picture of golden, glistening residue on the glass reappeared in my thoughts.

"You're...you're one of them." A gratified smirk tugged at the corners of my mouth. *He* had left the eerie evidence. He was an angel.

"You have no idea what you're talking about." The anger behind his words and the aggravation in his manner definitely implied that I'd struck a nerve. I couldn't figure out if it was my accusation that upset him, or that I discovered some sort of truth about him. Really, it didn't matter to me. All that mattered was that I had an answer, something to grasp in the whirlwind of my ever-changing reality.

Before I could respond, he was gone, the black duster flapping behind him as he turned a corner into the alley beside Joe's.

I took a deep, contented breath and returned to the café.

I had a hunch he would come back around.

He may not have confirmed it, but for now, I was totally okay with thinking he was an angel. Maybe that would also explain the attraction. It felt different from Malach's pull, but I was willing to believe that they all had different intensities like the Celatum—for the time being.

"Hey. Where did you go?" Gavyn met me at the door, holding it open as I stepped inside. The instant I saw his face, a twinge of guilt soured my happiness. Feelings for Gavyn were flourishing in my heart, but there was something in my soul that reached out for Archard against my will—and the lines were beginning to blur.

"Uh...I went outside for a minute. Thought I saw someone I knew."

"Uh huh," he responded doubtfully. "Layla said you were looking for me."

"What? No." Grinding my teeth, I bit back the irritation boiling in my blood. I didn't know what game she was playing, but I could see her attempts to beat me every chance she got. "Speaking of Layla, I have a few things I want to talk to you about."

"Alright. We can add it to the list of things I already planned on telling you later." His eyes probed mine like I was a book of secrets for him to read.

I bent to pick up the tray of dirty dishes I had left on the table beside us. "What time did you want to go up?"

He looked around the café, assessing how busy it was. "I can get Johnny to close up tonight. So, I guess...eight-ish. Is that okay?"

"Yeah. I just wanted to let some of our old friends know that George is gone." Tears stung my eyes as his name rolled off my tongue. "He had a few buddies in the old abandoned warehouse we used to hide in."

"Okay…please be careful." Gavyn's warm hands cupped both sides of my face and gently pulled me closer. Butterflies tickled my belly as he softly kissed my lips. "I don't like you goin' by yourself, but I can't go with you right now."

I shook my head, waving my hand through the air in dismissal. "I'll be fine. Besides, I need to get out of here and spend some time by myself." A reassuring smile convinced him not to push the subject any further.

Gavyn smiled and nodded then walked back towards the server's window. A figure moved in the hallway to the right of him, catching my attention. Layla emerged from a shaded area of the corridor, crossing her arms over her chest and winking at me before she slinked back into the shadow and disappeared from view.

Oh, the bitch was definitely up to something, with all her stalking and skulking around, but I wouldn't let that ruin my life. Besides, what was the worst she could do? Pull my hair and smack me? I knew how to defend myself against that.

It was around six when I finally left Joe's. The streets were almost clear of the rush hour traffic, and the moon was drowning out the fading sun. Bright streetlights flickered on in unison, lighting my path down the sidewalk beneath them. I loved the beauty of the night. Sparkling stars and the blue radiance of a lazy moon always seemed to lull my emotions.

I roamed slowly through the gloomy side streets, finding my way back to an old warehouse. Orange flames flickered out of steel barrels and small fire pits, lighting my pathway between the tall city structures. I passed by the clusters of homeless people gathered around the fires with my head down and my hands shoved in my pockets, avoiding any chance of drawing attention to myself.

Memories of my old life returned, bringing tears to the corners of my eyes. Memories of George reading me stories and teaching me while *we* warmed by those fires surfaced. Memories of cold winters and hot summers spent searching for food and jobs. We were happy together, even if we struggled for the necessities.

There was a sense of remorse eating at my heart for these people. I felt guilty because I was able to leave this life, and for whatever reason these people were stuck. Tonight, I would eat a warm meal and lay in a warm bed while they suffered.

Most of all, I felt guilty for George's death. Maybe if he hadn't found me under the dock, he wouldn't have been destined to die such an early and awful death. Surely, the demon wouldn't have taken his soul.

I approached the boarded-up door of the warehouse and wiped the tears from my cheek, letting the numbness fill my heart again.

I knocked on the wooden planks, using a rhythm designated as our "secret code". A long pause followed while I gave George's friend time to answer.

"Who is it?" a voice asked from the other side of the door moments later.

"It's me, Vinney. It's Nevaeh."

"Is anyone with you?" Vinney was paranoid from being robbed one too many times.

I rolled my eyes and answered, "No."

"Where's George?" The shake in his voice was a telltale sign of the tremors he'd acquired in the last three years.

"Too much drinking," George would say. I guess that was why they were such close friends. Vinney was about fifteen years older than George, but their drinking problems kept them tied to each other.

Since he'd managed to control his need for liquor, I think George kind of assumed the role of his sponsor, constantly dragging Vinney out of his binges.

"Well, where is he?" Vinney probed again impatiently.

"Are you gonna let me in, or do I have to discuss this standing out here in the dark?"

Chains rattled on the other side of the door. A few seconds later, Vinney pushed it open and poked his head around, lips curved in a toothless smile. He grabbed my elbow and hastily pulled me in, his jaundiced eyes searching behind me for any stalkers. His trembling hands took a minute to replace the chain, but I knew better than to offer help. In his mind, he was the only one that could do it correctly. I wouldn't dare interfere with his sense of security.

We walked in silence as I tailed him into the lower level of the huge factory. This was his mansion. He moved here years ago when the business closed. He'd worked in the building as a machine operator before he was laid off, so I guess he always felt at home here. Soon after they let him go, the company flopped belly up and shut its doors. Vinney caught wind of the owner's demise and decided, since they were the reason he'd lost everything he'd owned, it was only right that he took the warehouse as his home. I couldn't blame him. The beggars hadn't taken over it yet, it was warm and secure, and he knew the layout enough to keep it that way.

Vinney limped ahead of me, his cane tapping against the floor when he stepped. My eyes brushed over the rigged piece of pipe in his hand and remembered when George helped craft it into something that would help brace Vinney's bum leg.

I gulped back my overwhelming emotions and shook the memory from my mind, focusing on a frayed hole in Vinney's jacket.

Never really a big man, he looked even frailer than he did the time I saw him just a few months ago. A musty-sweet smell oozed from his knotty pores. "How's the drinking going, Vinney?"

"Pssh," he swiped his hand through the air in rejection, "we haven't visited in months, and you want to ask me about my demons?" I knew he wasn't offended; he just didn't want to fess up to the recent binge I sensed he had.

"I'm concerned for you. That's all." I dropped the subject there, hoping that my mentioning it was enough for now.

We made it to an old janitor's quarters in the basement; this was Vinney's favorite place to hide. Fortunately, whoever stayed there before left a decent cot and blankets. He motioned for me to sit on a stack of crates as he shuffled to a little metal trashcan in the center of the floor and stoked the struggling flames inside with a hollow pipe.

"So, where is that old dog of yours?" His raspy chuckle played in the air, attempting to coax a smile from me.

"Vinney," I huffed, pinching the ring on my thumb and spinning it in fast circles. "I'm sorry to tell you this, but...," the words felt thick and acidic on my tongue, "George died."

He laughed in disbelief. "Naw, really, where is he? I know how he likes to play jokes, but ya ain't gonna git me this time."

I peered down at the gold band I couldn't stop fidgeting with, quietly waiting for it to sink in. I don't think he was the only one it was sinking into though. When he saw the trail of wetness run down my cheek, he finally accepted what I said.

"My God in Heaven." He stumbled down onto the cot, mindlessly slid his ratty cap down off his head, and clutched it against his chest. A quiver in his lower lip led to a mass of tears flooding the aged valleys of his face.

I left my stack of crates and sat beside him, wrapping my arms around his shuddering shoulders. Any restraint on my own tears let loose, turning into sobs that stole the very breath from my lungs. We wept for our lost loved-one in the comfort of each other's arms.

This would be the only memorial George would get.

Thankfully, Vinney never asked how. I didn't think I had the strength to lie, but I didn't want him to know the terrifying truth either. It was enough to know George was gone. Nothing else mattered.

Eventually, I helped him lay down on the cot and covered him with the ragged blankets piled at his feet. "I'll be back in a few days to check on you, Vinney. I'll try to bring some clean clothes and food," I whispered in his ear as he drifted to sleep.

I roamed through the huge building in no immediate rush to leave, soaking up the solitude and listening to loose gravel and dirt crunching on the concrete under my feet. Having a good cry brought me a small token of peace—for now, anyway. After days of being smothered with craziness, I finally had a chance to come up for air.

After I entered the cavernous upper level, I noticed a quick shuffling noise scraping against the dirt floor behind me. I stopped and examined my surroundings. It was just me and a lot of broken, rusty machines to the rear of the large room.

Probably just some brittle nuts and bolts giving out.

Yeah, that had to be it. Just keep telling yourself that, Nev.

I ignored the angst burning an ulcer in my stomach and moved on.

After a few more steps, a rock skipped across the floor to my right. I paused, listening closely while I scanned the area with my peripheral vision. No sudden movements. The only thing on that side of the warehouse was the smudged industrial windows hanging close to twenty-five feet over my head and the beam of moonlight filtering through them.

The urge to scream lumped in my throat. My muscles tensed, and my feet planted firmly to the ground as I listened for more movement. "Hello?" I called out, attempting to sound as fearless as possible.

Childlike giggling echoed against the steel walls.

Dreadful recognition forced her name from my lips. "Layla."

I turned slowly, searching for her. Instead, I witnessed black, wispy forms stretch from the shadows and break away like sentient, sooty smoke floating along the walls and floor with an agenda I wasn't quite sure of yet.

The instant reflex to run triggered in my legs, but I refused. I had to be strong and stand up to her—and the demons haunting me.

"What are you doing here?" I struggled to grasp my waning self-assurance. Bile scalded the back of my throat. The putrid odor wafting from the floating demons made my stomach toss and turn. "Answer me!" I shouted as vomit threatened to rise to my mouth.

"Tsk, tsk, tsk. What's the rush, Nevaeh?" Another smug giggle bounced off the high ceiling. "Got a hot date?"

I couldn't find her in the silvery hues of moonlight streaking the factory. The swimming blackness lurched closer, intensifying the sick feeling in my stomach. "What do you want?" I yelled, grabbing my roiling abdomen.

"I already told you what I want. You're not listening."

The black masses hissed as they slowly slithered toward me like snakes, preparing to strike.

"It's not my fault Gavyn doesn't want you. Ever think you're just too much of a bitch for him?" As the last words came from my mouth, Layla stepped out from behind the conveyer machine I passed by a minute before. Ire emanated from her porcelain skin, making her look perilously pretty.

I couldn't contain the puke stuck in my chest any longer. I

doubled over and threw up. I felt defenseless.

She sauntered in my direction, laughing. "Awe, poor baby. Can't handle the evil inside yourself?"

"What are you talking about?" I huffed, wiping the remains of stomach fluids from my mouth.

"Ah...no one's told you yet." She chortled arrogantly. "You've been marked, honey. They want you, too — though, I can't understand why."

"Marked?" I forced myself to stand straight and slow my breathing, resisting the urge to puke again.

"I knew they wanted you the moment I saw the brand on your forehead."

"The inverted cross?" I rubbed my fingers over the healed skin on my forehead and narrowed my eyes at her incredulously.

Now only two feet away from me, I could see her baby-blue eyes had changed. A very subtle crimson ring outlined her crystalline irises. They were void of the personality I'd met my first day at the cafe. There was a corruption behind them now, one that gave way to a dangerous power flaring in her soul.

She groaned and rolled her eyes. "Cliché, I know, but it works. It's easily recognizable when we're looking for recruits but indistinct enough that the denser idiots won't think twice about it and cause problems." She took off her denim jacket and dropped it on the ground, then rolled up the pink, silky sleeve on her left arm. There was an inverted cross on her forearm. It seemed to glow red-hot under her smooth skin, lighting her flesh like a flashlight was shining through it. "You see, baby cakes, we *are* sisters. Whether we like it or not," she added with distaste in her tone, "And once you choose to be one of us, we can all live happily ever after."

"I am *not* your sister," I snarled. "Don't ever forget that."

From the corner of my eye, I noticed the black silhouette of her body moving on the floor behind her, but she wasn't moving at all. Several of the wispy, shapeless figures broke free of her shadow and began creeping across the ground toward me, expanding and multiplying as they floated closer.

In an instant, I kicked my legs into gear and ran faster than I ever ran before.

"Get her!" Layla shouted to the shapeless clouds. The smoky clumps slithered off the wall and joined the forms on the floor chasing me. I glance over my shoulder to see them forming one big mass of pitch-black wind. They rushed in from all sides and encircled me, spinning around me as I ran. My hair lashed and stung my face. The demon storm grew stronger and faster, trapping me in its center.

"You can't run forever, Nevaeh. Eventually, you'll have to make a choice. No point in putting it off," she bellowed over the whirring winds.

The smoky beings surrounding me amplified my sickly urges. My stomach knotted and cramped, rejecting their presence. I fought to keep the sour bile down. I only remembered seeing five of the demons crawl from the shadows, but together, their cyclone of fury extended all the way to the ceiling.

Layla's voice pierced through the whirling monsters. "Just make a choice, and this could all be over."

Paralyzed by sickness and absolute disgust of the things spiraling around me, I fell to my knees and retched uncontrollably.

"I don't know what you are talking about," I panted between yaks, "but I do know that I'll never choose the side that you're on."

The bitterness and utter rage radiating from the ghostly demons closed around my throat like a fist. An invisible, evil weight pressed down on me, grinding my knees into the rough gravel.

"Go ahead. Fight it. You will change your mind." Layla's snooty tone dared me to protest. It was almost as if she wanted me to suffer the consequences of denying whoever wanted me so badly.

Layla mumbled something in a language I couldn't understand. The demon cyclone replied with sharp hisses and sniggers. Deformed, ghostly faces, resembling the one I'd seen at the hospital, darted out of the funnel and shot through me like arrows.

They entered and exited my body relentlessly. My bones creaked and ached, yielding as much as they could from the invasion of the large masses without shattering to bits. I screamed from the intolerable pressure of them shifting my organs around and threatening to gut me where I kneeled.

Morbid visions of my broken corpse, lying bloody and scattered on the warehouse floor, stunned me into focus. I had to get out of here.

Rigid and dizzy from the abuse, I tensed my muscles, forcing myself upright, and leaned back on my feet. With my hands fisted at my sides, I held my breath and bared down against the floor, using what little strength I had left in an attempt to expel the demons inside me.

My heart pounded, pumping blood hard through my veins, vying to keep me alive. I sucked in a gulp of air and lunged back down on all fours with no success at stopping the demons.

Agonized groans erupted from my mouth. My limbs shook and wavered under my weight as I tried to regain the will to fight. It would be so easy to give up at this point.

They jerked me back and forth like a piece of meat in a tug-of-war game between starving dogs. I fixed my blurry eyes on one spot ahead of me, barely able to see the wall beyond their murky forms. I waited for the moment I could make a move but wasn't sure how much more I could take.

Finally, an opening.

A path to the door was clear for about two seconds. That was all I needed. I figured, if they can get through me, then I could get through them. I heaved myself off the floor, stumbling from side to side as they attacked my weak body.

Once I got enough footing under me, I ran like hell. A resistance, similar to a film of Jell-O with thorns in it slowed my escape as I propelled through the storm of demons, but I endured the pain and shoved through.

Bursting out, my eyes landed on the exit, and I sprinted forward.

Nearing the emergency door, I slowed to a clumsy jog and squinted. There was something in front of the chained boards; a sparking, transparent film hanging between me and my freedom. If it hadn't been for the thin, orange bolts of electricity snapping within the substance every few seconds, I doubt I would have noticed it.

I glanced back at the ghostly demons gliding across the floor after me. They were gaining fast. No other doors were close enough. I'd never make it in time. I didn't know what was in front of the exit, and I really didn't want to find out, but my options were limited.

I tried to veer in the direction of the front entrance, but instead fell on my side and slid uncontrollably across the ground. Skid marks trailed in the dirt behind me. Gravel and dust tore my palms open as I dug my hands into the floor, hoping to stop myself before slamming into the sparking substance in front of the door.

I tumbled ass over elbow, finally coming to a stop, but I was already too close to the mysterious film. It was too late.

A deep fire began to consume me, charring my core from the inside out. I tried to scuttle backwards but couldn't. The unseen tendrils of a wicked and hungry power wrapped around my ankles, raking me closer to the flickering wall.

The heat inside heightened as it spilled from my center, surging into every available space in my body. My blood boiled, and muscles contracted mercilessly around my already aching bones. I coughed and sputtered, my chest blazing as if I could exhale flames like a dragon.

I rolled and clawed at the ground, trying to loosen the force's hold on me, but the movement only deepened the searing sensation beneath my flesh.

Screams exploded from my mouth so intense that my voice sounded alien. I glanced at my hands, expecting to see blisters forming from the smoldering inside, but my skin was intact and smooth.

Was this all an illusion, one of those things I needed to "see" my way through?

Bound by the torment of solar flares igniting within me, my brain refused to let me think about anything other than the agony ripping through my nerve endings. I was losing focus fast.

As I lay on the ground, completely immobilized, Layla's frame edged into my vision. She leaned closer to examine me. The confusion on her face was not what I'd expected. I assumed she would be thrilled to witness the slow death I was experiencing.

She considered the demons starting to float over my body like a deadly smog with pursed lips, then mumbled another command in their language. The creatures instantly scurried away.

The expression on her face softened, a glint of concern creasing her brow. "What the hell, Nevaeh?" She had no idea what was going on either.

Shock flooded my emotions. I had no idea where my fate would end. At least when Layla was a possible cause of...whatever this was...I knew she could stop this. But she wasn't. There was no telling when I might find release from this agony—if there was release.

With all hope drained from me, and Layla staring at me curiously, I accepted that this might be my end. If I couldn't beat the invisible energy sucking me in, the sheer torture of it would kill me soon.

Ideas of a future with Gavyn teased my heart while I drifted closer to unconsciousness. Would he end up with Layla, clueless to her true nature and intentions? Would the demons take my soul as they did George's?

I forced my gaze to the electric film again and watched the murky forms that had chased me disappear around the edges of the substance like smoke rolling under a door. A quick flash of the Animus demon coming out of the wall in Gavyn's living room popped into my head.

Oh shit, this thing is a portal!

Where would it take me? Besides that, if I could even muster enough strength to pull myself away from its grip, how would I get past Layla?

I'd have to choose the less threatening of the two evils. Layla's sudden conscience couldn't be trusted. Who knew when she would get the urge to call the demons back to finish me off?

I tried to work through the raging blaze inside my body one last time. I gritted my teeth and forced myself up onto my elbows, then plopped over on my side, managing to roll a few inches closer to the portal. Red-hot tingling surged through my hand as I lifted it and reached into the sparking façade to grab the doorknob beyond.

A loud crackle rang in my ears. The hand that entered the sticky, hot goo stung like a million amps electrified me to the bone, and then it disintegrated. I couldn't pull away.

Oh my God, what have I done?

The sound of Layla shouting over my own screams reverberated through my skull. "NO! Nevaeh, you'll never make it!"

A rough force yanked the rest of my body through the portal.

CHAPTER FIFTEEN

The Devil Is In the Details

An earthy, woodsy odor tickled my nose, waking me from a deep sleep. My groggy eyes would not open though. I lay still, allowing my other senses to awaken. The alluring smell filled my nostrils, calling to me, arousing me. I couldn't help the moan of pleasure escaping from my lips. A bead of sweat dribbled along my collarbone, causing goosebumps to pucker on my skin, and I shivered. The atmosphere was thick and dewy — welcoming like a warm, tropical day.

Something silky glided against my body as I shifted on a cushioned surface. I stretched and arched my back, exploring the smooth fabric swaddling me.

Suddenly, I realized that I didn't know where I was. I couldn't remember how I'd gotten here. An eerie haze shrouded my mind, making it impossible to recall what happened after I'd left the café. I scrunched my face, willing the memories forward, but nothing happened.

My eyes snapped wide open in a panic, and I lifted up on my elbows, searching for familiarity. Instead, I was astonished by the wistful beauty of my surroundings. A tranquility floated through the room like a fog, kneading the unease from my shoulders. Somehow, it felt as though I belonged here.

I glanced down at the cushy surface supporting my body and saw that it was an oversized mattress. The chamber was large, but the bed, with its curling wrought iron frame, took up most of it. A strange sensation brushed away my instinct to flee, convincing me that I was destined to lay here for eternity.

Mountains of soft pillows were piled at the head of the bed while a lake of smooth, lustrous, crimson sheets wrinkled around me and poured over the edges in a cascade of rich silk. Such fancy things were beyond anything I had ever enjoyed.

Tiny dots of light beamed down on the silky sheets, accentuating the sheen of the fabric, drawing my eyes upward. Thousands of glittering stars floated above me, trapped against an onyx ceiling. The little orbs bunched together, creating puddle-sized galaxies that radiated the only light in the room. I watched with an open mouth as shades of purple, pink, and blue swirled through the black atmosphere and exploded into tiny nebulae. It was as if someone scooped a room-sized portion out of space and let it loose within these four walls.

The miniature night sky hovered so low that I could almost touch it, yet it seemed unbound by the room's height. Curious, I pushed myself up to stand on the bed and examined the vastness caught above me. I reached out to pluck one of the orbs from the air, but it retracted away from my touch—like little fairies afraid of a human hand.

A faint breeze blew through the tropical atmosphere, grazing my skin, and I suddenly became aware of how naked I was. I couldn't bring myself to care, though. I had bigger things to worry about.

I spun in a slow circle, examining the four intimidatingly solid walls constructing the approximately twelve feet tall cube surrounding me. Their black, glossy marble gleamed with the reflection of the little trapped stars. Each wall seamed fluidly into the sparkling canopy of night above.

While admiring the magic of my chamber, I experienced the unexpected flux of another life force's energy entering the room. Feelings of uncertainty and trepidation spawned from my heightened emotions. I quickly yanked the sheet up to cover my body and searched the room. My skin tingled in its presence. I couldn't see anyone, but clearly I wasn't alone. It was aggressive yet protective— masculine in every meaning of the word.

The new energy did something, lessened its dominance perhaps, and soothed my angst, settling the knot forming in my gut. Relaxing, even though my senses begged me not to, I eased into the safety and well-being promised by the presence.

I felt loved, embraced, and wanted by this thing. My brain questioned the secretive intentions I detected from the energy, but my heart craved it. The invisible creature was gentle and enticing, but at the same time harbored a rough and careless way. It absorbed my fear and anxiety, then infused me with notions of erotic pleasures.

I dropped to my knees on the soft mattress and closed my eyes, imagining the being seducing me. Visions of a faceless man with waist-length raven hair and godlike muscles toyed with the intimacy of my mind. He stood at my bedside, towering over my needy body. I eased down, lying on my back in waiting.

As I envisioned what he might look like, his greedy, invisible hand caressed my skin from head to knee, then parted my thighs demandingly. The hunger in his touch, slightly raking into my flesh, was far more delicious than anything I could ever imagine. And, while his fingers traveled up and down my body, he whispered the raw, ravenous things he could do—if only I'd give in.

Undulating ecstasy ebbed and flowed against my body like ocean waves rocking me into submission. I implored his darkness to conquer me—to make me blissfully high like the beautiful poison of a mind-numbing drug.

The woodsy scent spiraled around me again, and I knew it was coming from my dangerous lover. The natural, piney musk—strong and manly in tone—dulled my inhibitions. I drew my head back, arching my neck and chest up for him, then focused my closed eyes on the image of him alone. I abandoned my doubt, my fears, and the feeling in my gut telling me to run. Every bit of my senses overloaded under his seduction.

I sucked in a deep breath through my mouth, tasting his fragrance this time. Saltiness with a hint of molasses saturated my taste buds. Immediately, my body stiffened with arousal.

The rise and fall of my chest quickened. My moans became raspier. Beads of moisture from the humid air trickled down my neck and traced the underline of my breasts, leaving goosebumps where they touched, teasing my sensitive skin along the way. I longed to see the true body of the being making me yearn for him so badly, but my lover's touch disappeared the second I opened my eyes to search for him; only a distant hum of his energy lingered in the room.

I whimpered, feeling cold from his abandonment. Everything was so elusive here.

My eyes darted around the room, hoping to catch just one glimpse of him. There was nowhere to hide. There was, however, a large ornate door opposite of the bed. I crawled toward the edge of the mattress to examine the door closer, but hesitated when I glanced down at the floor. Beyond the crimson silk, lay an exact likeness of the ceiling above. Nausea and disorientation came with the idea that nothing was beneath the bed—that it might be floating on some starry oblivion.

Gripping the edge, I carefully settled on my stomach at the foot of the mattress. I reached out my hand, clearing the hem of fabric that spilled off the side, and found solid ground.

The floor *was* there. It was a smooth, glassy surface. A mirror, I guessed, or an illusion to make a person stay put. The hairs on my neck stood up.

Someone's trying to keep me in this cage.

The persuasion of the man in my vision faded more. He was backing away from me. Loneliness dragged my high spirit down as I sensed his energy waning, but I could think a little clearer now.

I have to find a way out.

I wrapped one of the oversized sheets around me and stepped a cautious foot onto the floor. My imagination continued to play tricks on me, convincing me that I should fall into the abyss below. Thankfully, the cold surface pushing up against my bare feet reassured me. I continued walking and refused to look down.

I neared the arched door and noticed elaborate carvings etched into the wood. I looked closer and saw bodies positioned upon each other.

My cheeks flushed as my gaze slowly roamed over each smoothly etched line, studying the forms with a morbid interest. Some were couples, or groups, performing various sexual acts for one another. Others were humans and beasts together. Some were submissive to their dominants with fear and agony marring their faces, yet their bodies stretched toward their masters, begging for more punishment. It's a fine line between the things we do out of lust and the things we do with love, however, none of these had a hint of love involved. That's what made them so unnatural, so devious.

Random acts of violence were mingled with the many daring sexual encounters. Smooth surfaces of wood raised and lowered, depicting scenes of murder and brutality: a blade neatly opening an exposed neck, a boulder bludgeoning a turned head, and spears impaling helpless bodies.

Living on the streets had granted me an unwanted taste of the worst in people, but the amused expressions portrayed on the violators sent chills up my spine. True satisfaction and enjoyment fixed on their features as they delivered nightmare after nightmare to their victims.

My belly churned at the vile nature of the carvings, but I couldn't turn away. There was something strangely appealing about them. I skimmed my fingers over the bold edges of wood and wondered what it would be like to render myself to those situations, to really lose myself under the emotionless, base need to cause pain in others. What pleasures could come from such abhorrent experiences? Could I bring myself to do such dirty deeds? Submit to them?

As I stood there, dazed and staring at the door. Muffled sounds penetrated from the other side, distracting me from my wandering thoughts. I pressed an ear against the wood and held my breath to listen. Excited moans reverberated through the door. It sounded like more than one person—a large group, maybe.

I stepped back and eyed the door suspiciously, unsure if I really wanted to see what was beyond my room. It was obvious that I couldn't stay here forever, even as enticing as it was. Maybe the people on the other side would be able to help me get home.

The knob was warm against my palm as I turned it and pulled the heavy door open. A blast of sweltering air rushed into the room, blowing my hair behind my shoulders. My eyes began to water, blurring my vision of what waited outside. I gulped in a deep breath to resist the heat smothering my lungs. Slowly, I let it out and inhaled another hot breath. As my body adjusted to the steamy new climate, breathing became easier. I wiped the sweat off my forehead, rubbed the moisture from my eyes, and planted one bare foot over the threshold, then the other.

The presence that came to me inside the room, accompanied me out. It was barely there, but I could still feel the gauzy shroud of it sticking to me like a spider web.

I was surrounded by a tunnel of rock and dirt walls. I trekked along the dirt floor, soil collecting between my toes in brown clumps. I moved through the tunnel at a snail's pace, dodging boulders and small rocks that had fallen from the jagged walls and ceiling.

Endless black iron doors lined either side of the long, dim passageway. My eyes bounced back and forth between the small windows at the top of each door. Different colors of light flashed out of the windows, throwing a strobe of rainbows into the corridor.

The length of the tunnel was deceiving. Large torches lit the path ahead of me, looking as if it ended only a short distance away, yet when I approached what I thought was the end, more torches appeared and the path continued on.

Sensual moans bled from the metal doors I passed. The stone walls echoed with the sounds of hundreds of people in the thralls of passion. Feverish and heady, they all chimed together, but something troubling in the guttural sounds made me uncomfortable—even scared. I had to move.

There has to be an exit somewhere.

Unease crept back into my bones, and I noticed that the protection of my elusive dark lover had changed. My heart started to ache with guilt, sensing that I angered him for not staying. With each sluggish step forward into the passageway, his anger mutated into something more evil and violent, something that would bridle my will and use me however it wanted. I trembled as the notions of love and bliss he had placed in my mind transformed into disturbing implications of rape and torture.

I wrapped my arms around my middle and edged past the first room.

He's not real. His threats are just a figment of your imagination, Nev.

I eased by the next five doors with averted eyes—feeling like they were closed for a reason. I wasn't meant to see what hid behind them, like I wasn't meant to see my lover.

By the time I closed in on the seventh door, though, delicious purrs resonating into my ears made the temptation too great. I wanted to peek inside just one room.

A sly voice whispered to me, telling me I might want to stay—that I might like what I found. "Look inside," the whisper coerced.

Electric green lights flickered from the seventh window like a firefly calling to its mate. I rose to my tippy toes and leaned into the metal door.

Through the blinking, lime-colored illumination, I saw a gorgeous woman with movie star confidence perched on a high-backed, Victorian chair in the center of an empty room. Pretty, paisley fabric covered the cushions beneath her, adding to her timeless beauty like a frame surrounding a priceless piece of art. And that dress—silk draping delicately off her milky shoulders and cutting sharply across her bare thighs—only enhanced her statuesque frame. She was the kind of beautiful that evoked instant envy and implied insatiable vanity.

Long, husky moans escaped her heart shaped mouth, sounding as if a skilled lover was servicing her well. But, her face told of a very different experience. Her model-like features were hardened with an endless terror.

Confused by how the lady sounded and what I saw on her face, I lowered and put my ear against the door jamb. Movement rustled on the other side.

Hissing. I heard hissing.

When I popped up to look in again, a shadow paced along the wall behind her. The woman's eyes widened and darted around the room frantically. Her slender legs kicked and fought to escape the chair she was bound to—a detail I hadn't noticed before.

The blinking green light flashed on, and I saw a horribly disfigured creature appear from a shadowy corner and approach the frail woman in tense, shuddering strides.

Darkness.

A flash of green light.

Facing away from me now, I could see that this was not an Animus demon. This was an entirely different demon with an evil all its own.

Darkness.

Flash of green.

The demon's body shuffled awkwardly toward the woman. My eyes trailed down its back and I gasped. The over-exaggerated curvature of its spine forced nubs of yellow bone to poke through broken skin at each vertebra like spikes. Small trickles of blood oozed from deep festered holes scattered over its dying flesh and then dripped to the floor. It dragged a booted foot through a dark droplet on the dirty ground, smearing the blood as it stopped in front of the woman.

Darkness.

Flash of green.

Its sharply angled head struggled to look down at the woman, restricted by a short, nearly nonexistent, neck. I held my breath, afraid the demon could hear me from the other side.

Its bulky arms worked eagerly at the woman in clumsy, messy movements, performing some torture I couldn't see from behind its wide, stocky frame.

Darkness again, then a flash of green flickered on.

Fibrous muscles pushed and tugged against its decaying skin as it moved. Every few minutes, I jumped, startled by the demon's unnatural shaking; it was as if a jolt of electricity ran through its massive body and reset its vile purpose.

Why isn't she screaming?

I was scared for the woman. She would die at the hands of this demon if I didn't act now.

Darkness.

I reached to open the door, but there was no knob or handle.

What the hell kind of door doesn't have a knob?

I frantically slid my hands over every inch of the metal slab, pressing any notch I felt, digging my fingertips into every crack. Nothing happened. I peered back into the window, hoping that the lady was still alive, but all I could see was the deformed back of the monster standing in front of her, bathed in a neon lime glow. Helplessly watching the tragedy behind the door almost had me wishing for her death — for mercy.

Darkness.

Green flooded the room once more. The demon's arm was stretched high above it, a gleam of light reflecting off a long, thin blade in its hand. Slicing through the air with no effort, the knife slashed down to the woman. The fiend slowly shuffled from in front of the woman, circling around her in bumbling steps.

Darkness.

I cried out when the light returned. Her cheeks gaped open and hung along her jawbone. The monster had slashed the woman's face, beginning at her left ear and slitting through the corner of her lips. Red gushed from her filleted flesh and soaked into her gown. Her eyes begged for a release that she knew would not come.

My fists mindlessly pounded against the door until the pain in my hand started traveling to my elbow. "Why aren't you moving? YOU HAVE TO TRY!" I yelled, sliding my limp hand down the door. Her head never lifted to see me, but the demon's did.

Hard cheekbones covered in patches of charred, red and black skin stretched out from under the fiend's sunken charcoal eyes. Its thin lips reared back into a tight, horrifying smile. The pure hatred and satisfaction in its expression seared into my eyes as I helplessly waited for what would happen next. Tipping its head back, the demon began the siren, belting out a piercing screech.

I fell to the floor, covering my aching ears. The earthen structures around me rumbled and began to shift, splitting open into deep crevices. A streak of fire flared from one of the torches and sparked along the ceiling, riding the plains of the tunnel farther than I could see. The surface of the corridor turned to ash as easily as a piece of paper scorching from one corner to the other. The tunnel quaked, splintering the ground and walls. I crouched against the large boulder next to me for protection. White-hot cinders rained down from above and stung bits of my uncovered flesh.

The once tempting odor that I'd found so alluring when I first woke here evolved into a putrid sourness. Blissful moans, which playfully called to me before, morphed into loud desperate screams praying for help.

My stomach cramped and rolled, straining to rid itself of the bitterness closing in on me. What was a beautiful and mysterious paradise unfolded into an evil, terrifying prison.

As the transformation ended, I leaned against the hot slab of stone and wondered what power could make me forget how I'd gotten here and where I'd come from. What could've changed my surroundings so abruptly? Would it ever let me go?

I cautiously looked around the edge of the boulder and stared down the endless corridor, begging for a savior to magically appear. Instead, I found countless doors. They were still the same impenetrable cages that trapped the poor people whose pain never seemed to end. Even after all that chaos, after the tunnel cracked and burned, the prisons remained intact.

This was all a game, I realized. They were toying with me. Showing me what they wanted me to see. The lush fabrics, the beautiful surroundings — it was all an illusion. The miles of rocky cave with endless holding cells was reality here.

I turned my head to look behind me, my eyes following the path back to *my* room. Lumps of red, singed fabric lay in a pile on the dirt, the magical mirrored floor gone. The chamber was dark—the starry light snuffed out like a candle. All its mystical appeal had faded, allowing the truth to be known. There were only promises of a bleak solitude waiting there, now.

A sad whimper escaped from the door next to me. I rushed to stand and chanced another peek. Everything had changed inside the gorgeous woman's room, too. Her cheekbones pushed out harshly against her hollow face. Grime and blood painted black spots on her pale skin, emphasizing the existing shadows there. She was alarmingly frail and withered—not the Hollywood beauty I saw before.

Stuffing poked out of holes in the dingy fabric covering her chair. It looked soiled and distressed like she had been tied to that seat for years. The pretty dress that hugged her voluptuous curves now hung too loose for her bony figure. Rips in the blood-stained silk allowed glimpses of thin skin lying over faint blue veins that struggled to keep the woman alive.

As my eyes lingered over the woman's true form, I realized she screamed because she couldn't help it, not because she hoped someone might save her. She was far from salvation. Her forlorn eyes told me that she knew there was no help for her. She was weary and hopeless from a lifetime of reliving episodes of the same punishment over and over, for who knows how long.

The demon inside continued to slash at her body, ignoring me to focus on his task at hand. Seconds after her flesh was filleted open, it healed only to be slit again. The demon didn't miss a beat when it came to dicing her to shreds. Infinite practice had developed a precision of its art.

I could never stop it. I would never be able to help her.

Refusing to witness anymore abuse, I sprinted down the

cavernous tunnel. I didn't know where it would lead, but I had to move. I ran past door after door, forcing myself to ignore the screams reaching out to me. I knew I would be just as useless to them as I was to the woman I abandoned behind door number seven.

Just as my feet began to bleed on the harsh, rocky floor, I was yanked into a dark alcove. I grumbled and fought against the arms binding me. A large hand covered my mouth, stifling my protests.

"What are you doing here?" The voice was gruff and low—a male. He panted heavily against my neck. "You're not supposed to be here. How did you get in here, Nevaeh?" He wasn't scolding me or trying to murder me; he spoke out of concern. He addressed me as if he knew me, but I couldn't see him with my back pressed against his chest and his hold keeping me still.

Puffs of steam rolled off his feverish skin, and the unpleasant smell of smoldering flesh rolled into my nostrils. I swallowed down the vomit lurching up into my throat.

I jabbed my elbow backwards into the man's stomach as hard as I could. His grip loosened, and I spun to look at the only other person in the vicinity not screaming or being tortured.

He appeared perfectly normal, aside from the tendrils of smoke rising off his skin. Dark matted curls stuck to his sweaty face. He was older, maybe fifty-something, but in very good shape. I opened my mouth to interrogate the man, but paused when I looked into his eyes. They were violet-blue like mine.

The same color. The same shape.

"Who are you?" I whispered, searching his face for anything that would spur a memory of how I might know him. Perhaps, he was an uncle or cousin I hadn't known about.

He hesitated. His forehead wrinkled as he struggled with what he was about to say. When his mouth opened to answer, someone shouted for me from a distance.

"Nevaeh, where are you?" the man bellowed.

My heart skipped. It was strained and desperate, but I'd recognize the voice anywhere. Tears stung my eyes, and my interest in the stranger was no longer important.

"George?" I ran from the alcove, leaving the stranger behind. "George, I'm here! Where are you?" My feet couldn't carry me fast enough toward his cries. The agony in his voice tore at my heart. He needed me.

There was no end to the hallway, so I began looking in the doors, thinking that maybe he was in a room.

Oh God, what if he was being tortured by one of those demons, and I couldn't get to him?

Every room containing another person that wasn't George brought relief. Then my name echoed against the rocky tunnel followed by a shrill scream, and I was reminded that he couldn't possibly be safe in this horrid place.

By my estimation, twenty minutes passed before my body slowed against my internal fight to find George. George's voice seemed to float farther away with every step I took, sucking the hope right out of me.

I stumbled to a stop, leaning over to catch my breath. My hands kneaded the muscles contracting in my thighs. I hung my head, glancing at my feet and the bloody footprints I was leaving behind. I grimaced, realizing how bad the gashes on the bottoms of my feet stung.

I would never find him here, not this way.

I slouched back, leaning against the hot stone wall. My breathing steadied, and I noticed a disturbing silence in the tunnel. No more screams or cries. No more flickering lights or torches either. Blackness had swallowed the path behind me and was fast approaching from the direction ahead.

An unnerving solitude gathered around me like water filling a pipe, drowning me in isolation. At least, if I could hear the screaming, I knew I wasn't alone in this awful place. Fear was wrapping its nasty hands around my throat and squeezing tight.

Wait, was that…?

I strained to see something moving in the dark. My body tensed at attention, preparing to fend off my enemies the best I could.

Ominous whispering fluttered in my ears, startling me from the bleak silence I was focusing on. The whispers grew louder, like someone turned up the volume in my head. The mutated voices became thunderous. I clamped my hands over my ears to prevent my eardrums from bursting.

Moments later, it all stopped. Nothing but silence again. Then, a deep, booming laugh rattled the tunnel.

"Ah, Nevaeh. Are you having fun yet?"

I fought back the feeling of defeat that was crashing down on my will to survive. "What do you want with me?" I yelled.

Another growling laugh rumbled the ground beneath me. "You know what I want," it responded.

"I don't even know where I am, or who you are, or how I got here. How the hell could I know what you want?" I was quivering inside while trying to maintain some sort of strong front.

"'How the hell?'" it repeated my words playfully. "Funny that you use that phrasing. You see, Nevaeh, I'm the dark side that you hunger to devour. The freedom that you seek. I'm offering you a life beyond what you could ever imagine. You only have to accept me. I will make you happier than you could ever dream."

My thoughts raced, working to decode what was said. "Are the people trapped in the rooms here supposed to be happy? If that's happiness, I don't want it." The words left my mouth with less confidence than they held in my head. "Please, I just want to go home," I whimpered.

"Those maggots in the rooms are getting what they deserve. They disobeyed and have to pay. Everything has a consequence, they are reaping theirs," the voice snarled. A deep sigh stirred the stagnant air in the tunnel, and then the voice settled to a calmer, more caring tone. "You were never meant to see that, Nevaeh. I did not want to scare you. You are special. You carry gifts that no Earth-bound has ever possessed." Excitement lightened its words as it continued. "You, my pet, are far more powerful than your brothers and sisters."

"What are you talking about? I have no brothers or sisters."

"Oh, but you do, my pet. You belong to those that live with the knowledge of a world far more superior than that of ordinary humans. Why He didn't make them all as interesting as you, I'll never understand. Humans are so weak."

"We are not weak," I argued through gritted teeth.

"No, my dear, *you* are not." A low chuckle sounded from the darkness. "But you are not human. You are something entirely different. You are the best of both worlds. That, I think, is why you, my child, were able to traverse into our realm and live." A long pause of eerie silence drifted about as it let the information sink in. "You chose to come here when you put your hand through the portal."

"No. I didn't choose any of this. I just wanted to get away. I don't want any of this! I will never choose this. NEVER! Do you hear me?"

The ground beneath me vibrated, and fragments of rocks and dirt plummeted from the ceiling. The whispers began their angry chants again, humming in my ears at an unbearable intensity. "You may not want this, but we will have you. One way or another, Nevaeh. Our army is many, and we are eager. We *will* have you. We will make you choose us," they spoke, their strangled voices synchronized as one.

What little confidence I'd managed to dredge up moments before faltered, convinced they would achieve the sinister promises they made at any cost. Somehow, they would find a way to pull me over. A billow of smoke puffed from the dark, and hot steam burst from the cracked rocks. Sulfuric odors soured the tunnel, triggering the recurring nausea in my stomach. "You will join us, child," the mutated voices demanded.

The ground trembled in a rhythmic pattern as if a giant was taking slow steps toward me, its heavy feet pounding closer and closer. I waited for the thing with the booming voice to leave the shadows and force me to obey.

"I will not be one of you!" I shouted, determined to hold my ground.

In the haze of steam, I saw a silhouette so large that it had to stoop to fit in the cavernous tunnel. Black, feathery wings dragged uncomfortably against the walls. My eyes focused on the two large, blood-red eyes beaming back at me. The figure lunged down onto one knee. Enormous fists, nearly half my height, smashed into the ground as the giant leaned forward to close the distance between us. Vile breath blew into my face while the beast stared me down.

Its rubbery, matte-black skin wrapped dense muscles, bunching to attain a smaller mass so the beast's enormous frame could fit inside the tunnel. Shiny, onyx horns curled out from the top of its skull and coiled down towards its face. The two slick crests bracketed my shoulders on either side as the beast's head lowered to mere inches from my face.

I waited for it to mumble some sort of impending doom, but it seemed to enjoy staring at me with conceited disregard; this was a very effective way of scaring the shit out of me.

The giant opened its mouth to speak and white pointed teeth threatened to cut the flesh of its lips. "Come with us, Nevaeh," it commanded. The massive human-like body hunched back, anticipating my answer—like a lion preparing for a kill.

"I...Said...NO."

Before I could brace for the beast's impending attack, a sudden glimmer sparked to life on the wall to my left. There was a pang in my right side as someone barreled into me and shoved me into the shimmering surface. The familiar sting and shock of electrocution invaded my body. The fire from within burned at my core; the pain of a portal, once again, paralyzing me.

I watched the massive, black being hurl itself forward, barely missing me, and clobber the man pushing me into the portal. The agony intensified.

Seconds later, I was unconscious.

CHAPTER SIXTEEN

I Don't Need No Stinking Babysitter

The sucker punch of an aching body startled me awake with a gasp. Fresh scratches from the rocks beneath me stung my cheek. Something warm trickled from above my lip.

I pushed myself up with weak arms and wiped grit from my face. Red smeared my palms from what, I could only guess, was my first bloody nose—ever. My head swam with a dizzying array of images, but slowly my memory returned. Unlike entering whatever plain that was, exiting it allowed me the vague recollection of what happened from the time I left the cafe until now.

Remembering that I was naked when I landed on the other side of the evil opening, I checked myself to make sure I was covered. Though dirty and a little gooey, all of my clothes were in place.

I slowly turned my head, my neck too stiff to move faster, and scanned my surroundings. I was back in Vinney's warehouse. An artificial light shined through the high windows, so it must've still been nighttime. Hard shadows stretched across most of the floor, but I didn't have the eerie feeling that I had moments before Layla and the demons made themselves known. I exhaled a sigh of relief and enjoyed the completely unthreatening silence for a moment as I regained the last of my bearings.

I stood up and dusted the filth from my clothes. I limped, taking a few steps to work out the charlie-horses forming in my thighs.

This must be what it feels like to be hit by a truck.

It didn't hurt this bad coming out of the portal on the other side, but I guess that's not to be trusted since almost everything on the other side was an illusion.

Bending over to shake my pants down, I noticed a shadow sweep across an illuminated spot on the floor next to me. I looked up at the window above, expecting someone to be there spying on me. The feeling of wanting and happiness flooded me so fast that I should've toppled over in my weakened state. The familiar sweet smell of love and passion wafted richly around me.

An overwhelming urge to scream in frustration lumped in my throat. Why did the otherworldly beings always overtake my emotions? Tears tumbled down my cheeks, and I gave up resisting the notions that filled my body.

"What do you want from me?" I whined to what I assumed was an angel lingering near. "Can I not have a moment to myself anymore? Don't I deserve that?"

A voice invaded my head, kindly but sternly responding with *Of course you do. But unfortunately, your circumstance demands constant watching.*

I knew I should be surprised by the intruding person in my brain, but it felt so natural, like he'd staked his claim there long ago.

There was no questioning who it was anymore. I recognized it right away and loved the comfort it brought, but I was angry at the same time. Angry for the control he had over me, for the lack of answers he'd given me, and for the constant pulling me in and then pushing me away.

"If I need a babysitter so badly, why weren't you here before when I was getting my ass ran through by demons?" I waited for him to respond and became enraged when he didn't. "Answer me, Archard!" I demanded.

I can't, he thought into my mind. Hints of his regret mingled with my own emotions.

"You can't—or don't want to?" My words came quiet and without the expectation of an actual answer. I fell to my knees. I surrendered to the urges he brought, to the controlling powers taking over my life, to defeat, and to the mental destruction of it all.

A rhythmic wind stirred at the other end of the warehouse and moved toward me, lifting puffs of debris off the ground and then dropping them with a patter along the way.

Thrum…thrum. Thrum…thrum.

Like the beat of a resting heart. Such a simple sound, yet so full of wonder.

My gaze scoured the ceiling for him, tracing every metal rafter and beam. I squinted into the shadows, trying to force my eyes to adjust. Finally, I saw him soaring in from the western portion of the building. The radiance of his smooth skin and the sheen of his aqua eyes created its own faint glow in the dark.

Archard's wings resembled Malach's in size and softness, but his were slightly more tattered and had inches of gorgeous deep purple tipping each of his long feathers. The small amount of light shining into the building reflected off gold, metallic pieces staggered throughout the milky-white.

The pulsing of his wings continued to slow until he finally glided the rest of the way down. His bare feet landed on the ground a few feet in front of me with the controlled ease of a dancer. In one fluid motion, he kneeled on a knee before me. His expansive wings stretched out beside him, draping the floor in a blanket of gleaming

221

feathers. They were so mesmerizing; I couldn't take my eyes away.

"Why me?" I cried, dropping my head and refusing to look him in the eyes.

His warm hand reached out, caressing a finger under my chin, urging me to meet his gaze. My head lifted, submitting to his touch, but I still couldn't bring myself to look into such holiness.

"Look at me, Nevaeh," he whispered in a gentle plea.

The allure was too great. I longed to stare at him. I yearned to memorize every valley and rise of his heavenly face. And to kiss him — that would surely destroy my humanly standards of kissing for the rest of my days. It would be worth the risk though.

My eyes traced the hard outlines of his jaw, moving to his deliciously red, parted lips. I swallowed hard, tempted by the redemption I saw waiting there. His sharp, regal nose was next. My gaze hesitated there a moment, afraid to see what was lying in the eyes just above.

I sucked in a deep breath, gathered my courage, and looked up. I was pleasantly surprised by the sympathy and concern staring back from the depths of his jewel-like eyes.

"I'm so sorry," he said.

With movement that was so fast and smooth I could barely keep up, his hand moved to the back of my head and pulled me to him. He dropped his other knee and pivoted forward, bringing our bodies together. The second we were close enough, the heated slickness of his mouth crashed into mine. The sensation was unbearable. Supple. Fierce. Urgent.

For once, it felt as if he desired me the way I did him. Jolts of power ignited between us, sending a welcomed wooziness straight to my brain. The freedom and serenity bound within our intimacy was intoxicating.

I found my hands running up his lean rippled chest, bare and hot under my fingertips. I stroked a trail up his strong neck, and then entangled my fingers in silky ribbons of his hair, tugging slightly to keep him near.

Heavy breaths fled our open mouths as they moved against each other. His arms hooked around my waist, saving me from any chance of separation. I closed my eyes, allowing my other senses to relish the moment.

A soothing, warm pressure wrapped around me, supporting my back and engulfing my torso like a cocoon. Curious, I peeked out from my lazy eyelids, careful not to leave his lips, and saw that his wings were enveloping me in a cradle of lush feathers.

I moaned, the desire too much on my senses. His eyes flew open, widening in surprise. We melted into each other, searching one another's soul, enjoying the sweet-salty mix we made as our tongues danced.

All of my anger swept away.

A muffled sound came from outside the warehouse. I paid it no attention, but Archard broke from me and glared at the door. I felt as if he snatched away a piece of me that I couldn't live without. Tightening his grip around my waist and flexing his wings behind him, he waited and listened.

Nothing.

His face relaxed, and his ocean eyes returned to me.

"What is it?" Nothing could be so important that it required him stealing his lips from mine.

"Someone's coming for you," he said quietly.

"What? Who is it?" My insides twisted, anxiously anticipating an attack—and the feeling that our time together was finished.

This was probably a lapse in his judgment anyway. Pity for a sullen girl. But I experienced something far more potent tonight than the other times we were near each other. What I felt for him was different from the lust I had for Malach. Something about Archard made me want to abandon everything for him.

"I have to go." His hands lingered at my waist.

"No, don't go. I need you. I need answers." My hands locked behind his neck, determined to keep him captive. I needed him more than I needed to breathe.

He smiled, kissed my cheek, and tugged my hands down. With a forceful, forward, swoosh of his wings, he stood up effortlessly.

Another sound of something scraping against the door caught his attention. "I'll see you soon," he whispered. Archard turned and swept the great white masses of feathers downward, launching him into the air.

The moment he flew away, my soul crumbled. My chest ached, and tears stung my eyes. I didn't want this dependency on him, but it was out of my control.

Would this happen every time I saw him? Would I give in to him and then be left broken a little more each time?

I managed one last plea for him to stay with me. "Archard, please." The whimper sounded pitiful and ridiculous. I couldn't let him have this power over me. He darted to the ledge of one of the windows above me, perched on it, and glanced down at me. I stared after him as he pushed the window open and ducked through it.

Though it felt like I did, I *didn't* die.

As the seconds passed, I became a little more whole without him again. Forcing myself to harden my emotions, I stood and slid into a shadow.

A moment later, the ragged, wooden door scraped against the ground. Still fastened with the chain, it only opened a few inches.

"Nevaeh? Are you in there?" The man sounded tired and worried.

"Gavyn." I ran from the shadows to let him in. "Gavyn, I'm here."

Slowing just before reaching him, I turned back and scanned the line of windows, wondering if Archard was still watching me from outside.

What now? What do I tell Gavyn?

Go to him. He can offer you more guidance than I can. Archard's words echoed painfully in my head. My heart ached as if someone had stabbed me. He was pushing me away — again.

Tell him what you must, he thought, reluctance straining his thoughts.

"Nevaeh, are you coming? What are you doing here?" Gavyn pushed against the chained door again and shoved it open enough to squeeze his upper body through the crack. He looked distraught, but every bit of his distress eased when he saw me.

"I'm here." I stepped closer. He grabbed my arm and yanked me against his upper body, sandwiching the edge of the door between us. He hugged me so tightly that I couldn't breathe.

"Oh my God, Nevaeh." He examined my face, kissed me, and then hugged me some more.

"I'm ok. Really." I tried to convince myself more than him. Was I okay? I felt a reconnection to the man holding me, and I liked it. But the link I had with Archard was deeper. Something that was there whether I wanted it or not.

"You didn't show up last night. I've been up all night and all day looking for you." He stepped back, maneuvering me under the chain and through the slight opening he had wedged himself in. "I almost went home, and then I thought I should check here one last time."

"You've been here before?" I asked as the last of my body shimmied between the door and warehouse wall. I hugged my chest and shivered as the cool, fresh air outside sent chills over my skin.

"Yeah, a few times in the last twenty-four hours. One of the homeless people saw you come in here." He shrugged off his jacket and draped it around me.

"I've been missing for that long?" It seemed like only hours in the portal.

"What happened, Nevaeh? Where did you go?" He gripped my shoulders, focusing on my reaction.

"Right now, I just want to go home and clean up. I'll tell you everything when we get back. Let's get out of here." I couldn't tell him about Archard though. Not until my emotions calmed. Though our connection was strong, I needed to discern how much was what I truly felt and how much was the bogus angel-attraction crap.

He nudged me into his body and cupped my cheeks softly, warming my skin in the heat of his hands. He pressed his lips to mine. His kiss grounded me, brought me back to earth. His touch leveled some of my confusion. I pressed into the fullness of his mouth and invited the composure that he brought. This felt right—stable.

Don't do this to me, I begged my heart, *Don't let me fall for both of them, then make me choose.*

When he parted from me, I noticed his eyes were glossy and his expression full of peace. "Come on, let's get you home." Gavyn took my hand and led me back into the city.

Gavyn unlocked the door to Joe's and held it open for me. I squeezed by him, stepping inside the quiet space. I breathed deeply, inhaling the never-fading scent of strawberries and ice cream. The café's warmth stung my cold cheeks but calmed my chattering teeth.

He locked the door behind us, placed a careful hand on the small of my back, and led me to the stairwell, leading to his apartment. "I think it's safe to say you'll be staying with me from now on?" An enticing smile tugged at his lips.

"Gavyn, I don't want you to feel like you have to—"

He interrupted me with a wave of his hand. "I don't feel like I *have* to do anything. I *want* you to be close. I can't lose you again, Nevaeh."

He waited for me to take the first step onto the stairs—waited for me to accept his invitation.

Still unsure about my feelings for Archard, but not wanting to end things with Gavyn either, I accepted and climbed the stairs. Gavyn followed close behind.

About halfway up, his hand found my right hip, and he closed the gap between us. The heat of his body beside me washed away the uncertainty in my heart. He offered a coupling that would survive any future with me—no matter which way I chose to go. A chance of a life full of love and support, of steadiness and stability. As stable as it could be, given the circumstances. Not the constant thrusting into loneliness, after only a taste of affection, that Archard seemed to put me through.

Gavyn followed me as I wandered through the apartment toward the bathroom. He scooted around me and removed a towel from the small corner cabinet.

"I'll go find ya some clothes." He paused next to the sink for a moment as if fighting the need to leave.

"Okay." I took the towel from his hand and waited for him to decide on his next move.

"Kay, then." He left, tugging the door closed behind him.

I sat the towel on the counter and looked myself over in the mirror.

What a mess. I was covered in dirt, blood from my nose, and... *what the hell was that goo?* Bruises and a few burn marks marred my skin, bringing fresh pain when I accidently brushed against them. *And I thought the streets were rough on me.*

I shuffled out of my disgusting clothes, careful not to cause myself more pain, and turned the faucet on. My hand thawed as I held it under the heating rush of water to find a tolerable temperature. I pulled the shower lever into place and slid the navy-blue curtain closed to trap the glorious heat inside the tub.

Gavyn tapped lightly the door. I yanked the towel from the counter, wrapped it around me, and then let him in. "All I could find were some old sweats and a t-shirt of mine." He neatly set the clothes on the edge of the sink and rested a hand on top of them. His shy eyes grazed over me through the mirror. "Hope these'll be alright."

"They're fine." I couldn't care less about what I was wearing at this point, but I smiled appreciatively.

"Need anything else?" The tension between us grew with every second he stayed. His tongue ran across his plump lips, leaving a pretty, wet sheen.

I wanted to get lost in him. I wanted to surrender myself to the somewhat normal life he represented. I *needed* him.

"Yes," I breathed, a little shocked that I actually said it. Butterflies flittered in my belly at the notion of making a move on him, but I had to follow through. I had to see where our attraction might lead. Stepping closer to Gavyn, I slid my fingers along his sharp jaw and coaxed his face down to kiss me. He didn't resist.

I detected that undeniable aroma again, the one that called to me when Archard was around, drifting on the puffs of steam escaping the shower curtain. I refused to break from Gavyn. I refused to let Archard distract me whenever he felt like it.

You only come when it's convenient for you. I can't rely on the feelings I have when you're around. I need someone that wants me wholeheartedly and won't make me feel your emotional lies. You can't keep doing this to me, I thought, begging for a reprieve from the angel.

Nevaeh, I do not want to cause you torment. I will leave you with him if that's what you want, but you can't deny your feelings. You know they are true. You cannot hide from the many choices you need to make, either. Remember that.

His voice in my head, along with the fragrance he emitted, vanished as quickly as they had manifested.

I relaxed into Gavyn's embrace, our tongues softly twisting around one another. His lightly callused thumbs brushed my back just above the edge of the towel clinging to my body. It felt good. It felt real. Something I could grasp onto without the chance of it fleeing.

Gavyn trailed his hands slowly down my sides, then broke our kiss to look into my eyes. His brow furrowed as he searched my face.

Without a word, he walked to the shower and held out his hand, inviting me closer. I wasn't sure what would happen, but I accepted the invitation anyway. I trusted him and how I felt with him.

My feelings *were* betraying me. I was falling fast for Gavyn.

A thankful smile formed on his mouth when my palm covered his. He gently squeezed my hand then let go of it. Strong chest and stomach muscles flexed and stretched as he pulled his shirt up over his head. Then there was a moment of delay. Everything he did was slow and begged for my approval.

Pleased with his need for assurance—and where things seemed to be going—I moved my trembling hands to his pants and clumsily unbuttoned them. He released a deep, raspy groan as my fingers brushed his lower abdomen while I worked.

The quickness of his breath excited me. Silky moisture gathered between my thighs.

Finally, I pushed his jeans and briefs down, sliding them over his thick thighs and letting them drop to the floor. I bit the inside of my cheek and kept my gaze fixated on his sexy lips, too nervous to look at the lower half of his body. He watched my expression curiously and grinned when I stilled.

Gavyn lifted his hands to unfasten the towel tucked at my breasts. I quickly knocked his hands away, blocking his action—a reflex from years of having to fend off sexually depraved goons. Realizing what I'd done, I yanked my arms back down.

"Sorry," I said, my cheeks heating with shame and embarrassment. He was standing naked in front of me, completely vulnerable, and I automatically denied him the same from myself.

Gavyn leaned in close to my face. "Relax," he whispered next to my temple, "we can say stop at any time." Catching a matted piece of my hair between his fingers, he pushed it back behind my ear and kissed my cheek. Before his lips left my skin, I turned and entrapped his mouth with mine. Kissing him relentlessly, I made my intentions clear. I most certainly did not want to stop.

Suddenly, the terry cloth that was separating us fell to the floor. My nipples hardened, prodding against his panting chest. He grinded into me and the trail of hair along his bare stomach tickled my navel. I moaned into his mouth, my legs weakening from the pressure of his bulge teasing the delicate mound of skin at the apex of my thighs.

His strong hands reached around my hips and cupped the base of my rear, lifting me off the ground. Impulsively, I wrapped my legs around him for a better grip. Another gruff growl escaped him, and a gentle squeeze braced my bottom. I beseeched his hands to explore farther and find where I was most sensitized—for him to feel how slick and excited I was.

He stumbled out of the pants bunched around his ankles and carried us into the shower. Little droplets of hot water sprinkled down my back, puckering my chilled skin. Gavyn carefully lowered me down and guided me under the showerhead.

His attentive hands wet my long, tangled hair and directed the water over my body. Every caress made me want him more, but I held tight reigns on my desire and enjoyed the moment. There was no need to rush. I was safe with him.

He lathered soap into a washcloth and started at my shoulders, rubbing leisurely circles while working his way down. I quivered as he washed away the filth. Tortured whimpers vibrated from my lips when he slid the washcloth over the throbbing areas I wanted him to explore so badly, but he remained mindful not to touch me with his bare hands and not for too long. The gentle pressure of his fingers was just as effective through the soapy cloth as it would have been without it though. The sensation of his hand rubbing over my hardened nipples, palming the plump curves of my breasts, dragging the rag down my trembling stomach and slipping between my folds — it was just as tantalizing as I imagined.

The strain in his expression hinted that if he touched me — flesh to flesh — it would all be over. The gentleman in him would not be in control anymore. Something more feral would take over.

Oh, how I wished he would let loose. My insides spasmed with an eager hunger for him. I wasn't sure how much more I could handle. I leaned back into his chest and looked up over my shoulder at the beautiful, olive eyes exploring my naked body.

I could tell he was thinking of the intimate things he wanted to do with me by the passion in his eyes and the quickening change in his breath; not to mention, the swelling length of flesh between his legs, pressing against my ass.

His need to respect and ask permission was becoming a bit frustrating. I wanted him to overtake me, to lose control and do what he wanted. However, the fact that he kept his composure let me know he wasn't the type to get what he wanted then leave, as was my experience in the past. He respected me, and he appreciated me. For that, I was thankful. If only I could control *myself* a little better.

When he was done with me, he washed himself. I'd reached out for the rag, intending to return the favor, but he backed away shaking his head, refusing to let me have it. He had just washed every part of my tightly wound body. I was going to, at least, see what he was denying me. Abandoning shyness, I let my eyes follow the soapy water as it trickled down rope after rope of delightful muscle.

Warmth swirled in my veins as I watched. My body reacted with arousal, swelling here and tightening there all over again. Dewy moisture slickened my thighs, eagerly readying for such a man. He was stunning.

He turned away to let the water rinse his dark hair, and I couldn't stop myself from gliding my hand down his sudsy neck and wide shoulders. His body stiffened as I traced my fingers from the toned ridges between his shoulder-blades to the underside of his perfectly rounded, muscular ass. I grinned, feeling dozens of goosebumps raise under my touch.

He gasped as I slowly pressed myself into his back—flesh to flesh. He continued to wash, permitting my hands to wind around his torso from behind and wander along the ripples on his chest. I would have to be content with just touching him. For now.

As I let my hands wander farther down, circling his navel with my finger and venturing below the tiny divot, he grabbed my wrist and gently pulled free from my hold. He turned around and smiled sheepishly, stepping under the shower's waterfall to rinse his front side. I licked my lips, watching the suds slide down his masculine form. He leaned in close, teasing me further, and reached to turn off the cooling water.

"If we start, I won't be able to stop."

"So don't," I permitted with a mischievous grin.

He froze, debating some internal battle as he eyed my wet body. Apparently coming to an answer, he reached for the towel outside of the shower and gently patted the droplets from my skin. Gavyn wrapped the fabric snugly around my chest and waited for me to climb out of the tub.

Confused, I leaned a hip against the sink, watching him dry and step out onto the floor. His brow furrowed again when he shot a glance my way. Was he really holding back to be a gentleman, or was there something else?

"I'll make ya something to eat. Go 'head and get dressed." He bent down to kiss my forehead as he fastened the towel around his waist. Shutting the door behind him, he left me cold and alone in the bathroom.

CHAPTER SEVENTEEN

A Choice to Be Made

I opened the bathroom door and stepped into the hallway. The mouthwatering odors of pancakes and coffee wafted through the apartment. I couldn't remember the last time I ate. I gladly let my feet carry me toward the kitchen.

Every few steps, I stumbled over the too-long legs of Gavyn's sweatpants and attempted to roll them up—only to have them unroll with the next step. I had to admit, there was something erotic about being in his clothing. I loved knowing his body had stretched against the threads covering my skin. Even after laundering, I could still smell faint hints of his cologne embedded in the fibers.

"Are you sure?" I heard Gavyn ask as I neared the end of the hallway.

"Not exactly, but we think so." I stopped in my tracks when Malach's voice answered.

"Alright, then. I'll figure out what to tell her."

My stomach soured at Gavyn's response. Was he going to lie about something? What was he hiding? His words planted a seed of distrust in my heart, a seed that threatened to take root and abolish any faith I'd finally instilled in him.

"Okay." There was a pause, then a noisy chewing sound. "Man, these pancakes are awesome. Glad you made them for me."

"I didn't make 'em for you, but help yourself, asshole." Obvious sarcasm and irritation flared in Gavyn's tone.

"Now, now. Is that anyway to talk to an all holy being of the Heavens?" Malach pouted, feigning sadness and shock.

"Yeah, well, I'm not so sure how holy your intentions are. You keep giving me more bad news and expecting me to do the dirty work."

The angel chuckled.

"Are you gonna stay and eat everything I'm cooking for her, or are you leavin' sometime soon?" Pans banged, and grease sizzled as Gavyn scolded Malach.

"I'm leaving, don't worry. You have much to tell her, that is your job after all. Unless you've changed your mind as to what side you're on now."

"Not yet, but if you keep pushing me, I may reconsider."

"Hey, I'm just the messenger." A frenzy of wind kicked up in the apartment, blowing my hair in every direction. "Hello, Nevaeh." Malach's deep, knowing voice startled me from my eavesdropping.

"Hi." Embarrassed, I emerged from the shadows of the hall just in time to see him and his glory crash through the ceiling. The pressure temporarily took my breath, and the thunderous crash of his exit rang in my ears. It wasn't as bad as the first time he blasted through Gavyn's roof, but it was definitely noticeable. Hopefully in time, this would all get easier.

After his dramatic departure, the ceiling mended quickly, erasing any evidence that he'd barreled through it seconds before.

Gavyn faced the stove, continuing what he was doing without a glitch. "Hungry?" he asked, spooning some scrambled eggs onto a plate.

"Um, yeah. Listen, I'm sorry about the eavesdropping."

Look at me. Tell me you're not mad at me for listening in. Tell me you're not going to lie to me.

I couldn't bear it if he lied to me now.

"It's ok. I wasn't expecting him to drop in like he did." He flipped a pancake effortlessly in the air. "Ya know, it's been ten years since he's been around—and then you showed up." He finally looked at me and grinned. "He must like you."

I smiled faintly. "What is it you need to tell me?" I slid onto a stool at the small bar across from him and waited, staring at the fork and knife he had placed neatly on a napkin to my right.

We had to get it out sometime, why not now?

"Here, eat up." He sat the plate on the counter in front of me and ignored my question.

"Thanks," I answered curtly, unfolding the napkin and resting it on my lap. I grabbed the knife and fork and cut into a syrup-drenched pancake, taking a bite and glaring at him expectantly while I chewed. I sat the knife and fork down, refusing another bite until he answered.

"Ugh." He sighed and rolled his eyes, frustrated with my stubbornness. "Nevaeh, we have a lot to talk about. I know something that might answer some of your questions, but I can't promise you won't have more by the time we're done. There is a lot I don't know. Malach can only give me bits and pieces, which doesn't help." His gaze dropped, and he turned back to the stove to make another batch of pancakes. "So, eat for now. When you're done, I'll explain what I can." He glanced over his shoulder to make sure I was putting food in my mouth.

I observed him in silence as I picked up my fork and took another bite. Quiet and thankful, I devoured my meal, agreeing to suspend the interrogation a little longer. Many thoughts raced through my head, but I came to realize how difficult it must be for Gavyn—having to introduce a person to something that was way more real and more complicated than most could even fathom.

Gavyn carried his own plate, stacked high with pancakes and eggs, to the spot at my left and straddled the stool, taking a seat next to me. Every so often, we exchanged a smile, or he tucked a fallen piece of hair behind my ear. Side by side, we finished our meal and coffee. We were comfortable in each other's presence, but the room was charged with the loaded issues we needed to discuss.

Once we were filled to the brim with breakfast, we left our cleaned plates and empty cups on the counter. Gavyn took my hand and lead me into the bedroom.

My eyes scanned over his room, appreciating the simple details. I hadn't noticed how nice it was in there before, probably because I was only noticing him.

Gavyn walked to the other side of the room and tied back the charcoal-colored curtains framing a small window opposite the door. I turned my head, examining the abstract painting I had seen before and admired the many shades of red brush strokes on the canvas.

Gavyn's quick movement caught my attention as he turned around and leaned over his bed. His busy hands worked to unravel the twisted, cranberry-tinted blanket at the foot of his mattress, then dragged it to the headboard. His dark-green eyes glanced up and saw me watching. His lips curved up into an apologetic smile. "Sorry about the mess," he said, his hands sliding over the cover to smooth out the wrinkles.

The yellow glow of a rising sun spilled into the room, contributing a soft ambience to the atmosphere. I felt at ease here with him—safe.

"We'll be here awhile, so I figured we better get comfortable." He laid down on the bed, propping his head up against the pine headboard, and crossed his ankles. Opening his arms, he invited me to lay with him.

I crawled onto the bed, cuddled into his warm side, and settled my head on his chest. For a moment, I wanted to give in to the strong beat of his heart against my temple and fall asleep, but too much was about to be revealed.

Gavyn's arms held me tight against him, and a regretful sigh left his lungs. "Where to begin?"

"Can't help you there, sorry." I giggled, trying to alleviate the edge for him.

"Okay..." He paused, contemplating what he was about to say. "There is a story in the Heavens about a child. This child is special. It's said to be Celatum, but more than that because it's a half breed of some kind."

"Half breed? What do you mean?" I interrupted, already confused.

"Well, they say it's half Celata and half demon." He stopped, possibly waiting for another question.

My insides knotted as I held back the hundreds of questions forming in my head.

He continued, "The story is old, and more like a prophecy. Nobody thinks it has actually happened, yet. They're not even sure it will. Malach believes the story, though, so he's bringing it up again — as he's done a few times in the past." He rolled his eyes. "From what I've heard, he does every time a Celata with unusual powers is initiated."

"The angels talk about a female Celata that fell in love with a demon male. This is the only instance where the two came together willingly. It's not unheard of for demons to mate with a human or Celatum, but usually the demons rape them.

"This demon...rumor says that he is the only one who chose to renounce his evil ways. He was so in love with this woman that he chose to surrender to God and relinquish the power he'd gotten from

Satan when he took sides long before that. Somewhere along the way, they had a child. The Clavis. The Key.

"Satan heard about the demon's choice and became furious. He, being the father of deceit, refused to allow the demon to leave. He forbade the demon from realm-jumping anymore, keeping him in Hell to rot.

"The woman was heartbroken and angry at God for not doing anything to save the demon, and that's where the stories become different. Some say she killed the child, others say she ran away to find her lover. Only God knows the truth about what happened, or has yet to happen." Gavyn's caring hand smoothed my hair over and over again as I listened.

"The angels think that a being created by such strong races would be truly magnificent. It would hold powers beyond those ever seen before. Both realms would hunt the child and would sacrifice a lot to get it." He paused, seeming to mull over something in his head.

I peered up into his eyes. "What are you saying, Gavyn? I mean, it's a great story and all, but I don't see what it has to do with me."

Please don't have anything to do with me.

"I don't know, yet," he said, his lips pressing together in a thin line.

I released the breath I was holding, relieved.

"But Malach seems to think it has everything to do with you. He thinks you are the child, Nevaeh."

That familiar sour feeling crept back into my stomach and burned a path to my throat.

"No. That's not possible." I sat up, abandoning the safe, warm place next to Gavyn, and stared down at the ring on my thumb. I nervously spun it with my other hand.

"Why not?"

"You said you didn't think it was me." My voice was becoming more agitated and worried by the syllable.

"No. I said I don't know." His hand reached for my face and directed my gaze toward him, "Why not, Nevaeh?"

"Why would Malach think it's me? I haven't done anything special or extraordinary." Panic wrapped around my throat. I waited for him to come up with some flimsy reason based on nothing.

"He said you would know the reason. He wouldn't tell me though." His soulful green eyes stared down into mine, reaching for the answer I hadn't voiced, yet.

The light clicked on in my head. *The warehouse.*

"I hardly think seeing demons and angels, or having funky visions makes me any more special than the next person."

I wasn't ready to tell him about Vinney's. What if it changes how he feels about me? What if Layla was right and we are some sort of sisters — as much as I'm against the idea?

"Nevaeh, I don't think that's what he is talking about. Did something else happen?"

Ugh, he's gonna make me do it. I'm going to have to tell him if I want to get more answers.

"Okay. Layla and some demons might have chased me through the warehouse," I confessed, sheepishly.

Start small, good thinking.

"Layla?" His eyes widened in surprise. "What was she doing chasing you?"

"She's with them. The Dark ones, I guess?" I don't even know what the hell to call her. She isn't a demon, but she definitely isn't good.

"She was with the demons?" He looked at me intently, hints of denial in his eyes. "I mean…I know she can be a bitch, but I didn't think she was with *them*."

"Well, she is, and she wanted me to join them. When I said no, she got mad and sent the demons to chase me down." I watched as his face harden, and his eyes narrowed. "She wants you, too. Didn't you know?"

"Of course, I knew she liked me. She was always very flirty with me. I just assumed she was a girl with a crush. I guess I couldn't sense her because she had already chosen sides." He turned his head away, looking out the window to hide his disappointment.

Even though he didn't want to be with her, I hadn't even considered that they were friends. This would change things for them now.

"I just feel like I should've done something. Maybe I could've swayed her back to our side. I could have saved her." He gazed at the floor, still pondering over what I'd said. "I wonder how long she's been Dark."

"I don't know, but she looked pretty decided to me. What could you have possibly done?"

"I can't believe the past few years of her working for me...I just can't believe that she's been Dark the whole time." Reluctant acceptance began to shadow over his eyes. "Usually, I sense the undecided ones. If I'd sensed her, I could've swayed her, maybe," Gavyn shook his head in defeat. "I can't believe she played me all this time. She was Dark, and I didn't even know it. I'm such an idiot." He leaned forward and raked his hands through his hair, then down his face.

I expected the disbelief and surprise in his voice, but he almost sounded as if he'd lost a lover, not a friend. I held my tongue and tried to rid my feelings of jealousy. It was too soon for that, and I had no idea what their history was before I came.

I changed the subject. "So, I'm not quite getting how this all works. You make the choice, then what?"

His attention finally focused back on me. "When God feels it's time, you come into your gifts. Unfortunately, I think the initiation time's relativity to tragic events happens in order to spark our faith,

242

making us desperate enough to face our spirituality. Perhaps, our gifts develop from that desperation." Gavyn hesitated for a moment.

"The free-will is the bitch of it though. One option is to do nothing with them, as I've said before, and accept the constant reminders and consequences. For example, if I had refused to hone my gifts and make a choice, then I could have hurt or killed a lot more people. My gift could have gotten even more out of control." Sadness and guilt crossed his face, undoubtedly for the woman who died from his rage.

His features hardened, quickly. "You can choose Light and work among the angels, battling for the fall of evil. You'd think this would be the obvious choice, but the sacrifices in this life are sometimes too much. One sacrifice you've already made is an example of that. Those you love are constantly in danger. Evil will stop at nothing to persuade you to their side. They know that at any moment, all you have to do is utter the words, and you can renounce God. Many have been taken from their families in situations like what happened to George."

Just the sound of his name made me long to hug him one more time.

"Too many people get caught in the crossfire." Gavyn put a consoling hand on my shoulder. "Then there are the angels, which aren't always pleasant to deal with. They fight for the same cause, but they don't always see us as strong enough to help, or deserving of the gifts God gave us. This path is probably the most difficult to follow out of all the options, but the endgame is worth it.

"The other option—you can go into the Dark and fall under the control of Satan. Sometimes his power seems to offer more. It's more appealing. Sometimes he can threaten you into feeling obligated to choose him to save another. Many have strayed from us this way. I believe this is the game he is playing with you.

"If you choose the Light, you can always change your mind. God respects your will to choose. But, as said in the story about The Clavis,

Satan doesn't give up so easily. From what I understand, once he is done with your gifts and you've worn out your welcome, you begin to evolve into demon forms. What form of demon, depends on your usefulness and sins."

"Wait, like the demon from your living room? That was a person before?" My stomach churned at the idea of becoming one of those beasts. Was the demon torturing the woman in the chair a person once, too?

He shrugged. "Maybe. Some demons fell from the Heavens with Satan. Others, he spawned. Those that change into demons, do so over years and years of paying for their decisions regarding their master. What they did to please him, or to piss him off."

"So…if Layla doesn't do what is asked of her, she could be turned into one of those monsters?" Never would I wish that on someone, no matter what they do to me.

Gavyn nodded his head once, confirming my question, and leaned back against the headboard again. "It can take centuries of torture on a soul to get them the way he wants."

Silence hung in the air around us as we thought about those that had fallen under Satan's grasp and the fate they may come to.

Gavyn cleared his throat, breaking the heavy silence, and returned to the original topic. "What happened after she chased you?"

Obviously, he wasn't going to let this go. "Well, the demons had me trapped until I saw a door and tried running for it. Then, when I got closer, I realized it was a portal. It was similar to the one I saw here. I had no other choice than to try to get away, so I reached through it and was sucked in before—"

"Whoa, wait, back up! You got sucked into a portal?" He sat up surprised, nearly toppling me off the bed. His hands grasped my shoulders, twisting me to face him. He asked again with urgency, "You said sucked into a portal, right?"

"Uh, yeah," I responded dryly. All my muscles tensed, anticipating Gavyn's next action.

"Nevaeh, that's why Malach thinks you're the one. Humans and Celatum can't cross realms. They can't handle what it takes to push through portals — let alone what is on the other side." Excitement grew in his voice. "Demons can though."

I chuckled lightly trying to hide my confusion, and the fear of what he was implying. "Gavyn, it sounds like you think I'm a demon. That's impossible."

"Nevaeh, stop saying that. You should know by now that anything is possible. And, yes, I'm saying you might be half demon. No one has ever gotten within two feet of a portal and lived to see the next day. Most people kind of do this internal combustion thing."

"Well, maybe that is my gift. I can't be a demon, Gavyn." I struggled to calm the sudden trembling in my words. "Wouldn't that make me evil or something? I mean, I'm not a nun by any means, but I don't think I'm evil. Am I?"

Take it back. Say the words — "No Nevaeh, you're not evil."

"No, I don't think you're evil, but none of us have ever come across anything like this. There are very few things in this life that have rules or protocols, Nevaeh. They just...are. This though — the crossing realms thing — that is only for the otherworldly beings." He offered a comforting smile. "We have to tell Malach."

"I thought he already knew. And why do you keep smiling? This isn't a good thing, Gavyn." The urge to completely hyperventilate and freak out was closing in on me fast.

"He knew something happened, but he wasn't sure what. He's not your angel, so he can't lock in on you completely. He just knew something very important happened to you. I think once you went into the portal, you fell off their radar."

"Wait, you said he's not my angel. I have an angel? They can track me?"

"Yeah, we all do. We don't usually see them, but they keep tabs on us. Especially Celatum. We are more at risk, so they stay close in case we need help."

"Well, who's my angel? I think I've definitely needed some major help in the past few days."

"I don't know."

"Well, how do you know Malach isn't my angel?"

"He's not a Guardian, he's an Arch. He only comes to interfere when the demons have crossed their boundaries. For instance, when the demon took George, that wasn't supposed to happen. The angels should have lifted him. Unfortunately, Malach told me that once the demon harvested George's soul, he was powerless to do anything about it. Malach would've had to cross *his* boundaries. The devastation of that would be far beyond the loss of one soul."

I started crying, my chest shuddering in between ragged breaths. Gavyn wiped the tears streaming down my cheeks with his knuckle.

"Malach is sorry, Nevaeh," he whispered.

"He's sorry? Oh, well, that fixes everything." My words lashed back at him. "So, before I could even 'make a decision'," I said snarkily, "George got caught in the crossfire. Now, Malach is sorry. Well, I can't accept that. Why didn't he come sooner? Why did he wait until the last of George's soul was sucked into that monster?" Gavyn sat patiently on the bed beside me, trying to hug the hurt and anger away, letting me get it all out. "If I'm the only one who can cross realms, then I'll do it again. If that's what it takes to free George. I heard him when I was there. I know I can find him."

"No, Nevaeh. Just wait until we can talk to Malach. Maybe he can talk to your Guardian and get more answers. We can't be sure that going to the other side won't pull you over. They have Celatum like me that can sway you. You are very vulnerable right now. Without you choosing sides, you are up for grabs so to speak. And, if you are part demon, I'm sure it will be harder to resist them. Your spirit is at its weakest right now."

I reached up and entangled my right index finger in a curl dangling over my shoulder while contemplating his words. "I'm thinking maybe I don't want to choose. I don't want to be under the power of Satan, but right now, I can't see agreeing to work under angels and a God that isn't much interested in helping me when I need them."

"You'll leave your gifts and your soul to be fed on by the demons, then. If they figure out that there is even a chance that you are The Clavis, I can't imagine what they will do to get you. They won't leave you alone. They won't let you live out the rest of your life in peace, Nevaeh."

The fear I saw in his eyes shocked me. It was like he was picturing what would happen to me if that occurred. I couldn't bear looking at him and lowered my head.

"Besides, without knowing exactly what you can do, none of us have any clue what that might mean for those around you. Your gifts will be way stronger than mine."

Gavyn guided my hand away from the curl I wrapped around my finger and engulfed it in his.

"I'm not ready to make a decision, Gavyn. If there is a chance to save George's soul, I *will* sacrifice whatever it is I have to." I sighed, regretting my next agreement. "But, I'll wait long enough to talk to Malach."

CHAPTER EIGHTEEN

Who Am I?

"So, I'm right this time." The warrior angel leaned back, pinning his glimmering wings between his body and the futon. Superiority and contentment lit his majestic face upon finding out that his hunch may be correct.

I watched Malach smile proudly and devour a bowl of sugary cereal from the other side of the room. Keeping my distance, I found, was a necessity when around him. It helped dull the incessant need to jump on the angel and make love to him—to smother him, and weep at his feet. The ever-shifting emotions he evoked were overwhelming. Even with me at the other end of the room, I felt the urge to bow down, crawl to him, and graciously suck on his toes in order to touch his magnificence. Thankfully, my compulsion to slap the smug-ass look off his face, as well as my anger towards him for the robbery of George's soul, counteracted the call to love him.

"We don't know for sure, but she's done something I've never heard of before. That's why we're coming to you." Gavyn spoke to the angel while he monitored the strain that must've been apparent on my face.

"Ah. So, what is it that happened when your connection to us went dark, darling? Did you go Dark, too?" His arrogant grin said he'd made up his mind about what had happened. He was already accusing me and judging me for taking the other side.

A rush of hate blazed inside me. I clenched the edge of the counter I was sitting on. Bruises would form on the pads of my fingers from the pressure, but the pain of it helped me overcome my yearning enough to function and communicate with the being I was growing to despise.

"No, I didn't go Dark. *Yet.*" I snarled the last word as a threat. "However, I did go somewhere dark. I guess I crossed into Hell. Unless there are other realms that you haven't told me about? You seem to be good at keeping important details to yourself." I snapped, waiting for him to respond — hoping he felt the anger I was shooting at him with my eyes.

"Well, to my knowledge, there are four. Heaven, Hell, Human, and Spirit." He smirked, again. I was sure he was thrilled to have so much information hanging over my head. "Only one would cause our link to you to sever."

"Then you already knew the answer, why bother asking?" I retorted.

His expression softened. "Until now, we didn't think it was possible."

"Why didn't *He* tell you?" I jerked my chin toward the ceiling, implying the All-Knowing-One.

"God," he said, insisting the respect I hadn't given Him, "only tells us what we need to know. If He doesn't want us to know, then we don't. We are just as human as you when it comes to the intellect of God." A moment of humiliation and modesty lessened his harsh demeanor for the blink of an eye before his cockiness returned. "We knew you left somehow. We weren't sure if you had chosen the other side, or if you were taken."

"So, if I choose to go Dark, you can't see me anymore?"

"No," he growled. "Make sure that is not the incentive you use to make your decision, Nevaeh. You will pay for your freedom from us dearly if you do."

"Don't worry. I won't even consider you when it comes time. If the circumstances call me to the other side, you will be the last thing I consider." Nobody mattered more than George.

"So, you are still toying with the idea, then?" Malach raised an eyebrow, expecting an answer.

"I thought we were gonna talk about the possibility that she's The Clavis." Gavyn interrupted, redirecting the conversation.

"As we shall," Malach replied, not breaking his intense stare from mine. He searched my soul for an answer that wasn't there. Refusing to allow him time to find the answer before I did, my sight settled on Gavyn and the unease he seemed to be experiencing.

"What do we know so far?" he asked Malach, possibly as ready to get this over with as I was.

"She can see demons, not just when they take a soul, but any time they are near her. Her father is unknown to the angels. She has crossed portals. She has visions, another gift not given to just anyone. Oh, and her Guardian seems to be M.I.A." His lovely face turned to Gavyn, relaying something I didn't understand.

"What does that mean? I have a Guardian, right?" I gulped down the panic rising in my throat. "I don't know exactly what difference that makes, but I should have one, right? Everybody has one, don't they?" My words tumbled out, scared and rushed.

Guardians kept us safe and watched over us. If I don't have one...I don't even want to think what that might mean.

The concern on Gavyn's face didn't help alleviate my worry. "Apparently, your Guardian has chosen to take a leave of absence from the Good Graces." Disappointment flickered in Malach's eyes.

"Leave of absence?" My voice squeaked like a preteen boy in puberty.

"Yes. He's not completely fallen, but has chosen to break ties with us." Again, he looked at Gavyn. "You see, God gave us the same choice as the Celatum. We too can choose sides. Seems your Guardian has chosen to become neutral. He is static — as are you at the moment." Distaste layered Malach's words. Gavyn sat on the bar stool next to me heavy in thought, offering no response.

"Where does that leave me then?" I felt lost. Even living on the streets with George, I never felt truly lost the way I do now.

"That means you're the closest thing to The Key so far, and you no longer have someone to spiritually guide you into your gifts or through life." He spat the words through clenched teeth. Surprisingly, Malach didn't direct his anger at me; he appeared upset with my Guardian, or lack thereof.

"And if I have no spiritual guidance — "

Gavyn cut me off, "Your inherent conscience will begin to fail."

"And that would be bad." If I had no control of my conscience, if I chose the Dark, and if I was this Clavis they say I am — with so much power — I could be disastrous in any realm. The meaning of what they said began to weigh on my soul, drowning me in regret for thinking so selfishly. If that was the case, I couldn't pick George over the Light.

Just then, I understood Malach and his choice not to take George's soul back from the demon. I understood that sometimes, one soul is not worth that which might be lost in the outcome. A sharp pang in my chest forced tears from my eyes. My heart would forever ache for George if I didn't at least try to redeem him, but how could I, knowing what I know now?

"Why would my Guardian choose to be neutral?" I asked as I fought back sobs.

"I don't know." For the first time, I saw the warrior angel's gaze fall to the floor, his expression confused and sad. "I have told you all that I know, Nevaeh. The fact that I'm not being given more information is another reason why I suspect you're The Clavis."

"I don't understand. You know things, but then you don't?"

"Look, I'm an Arch. My duty is in battle and worldly concerns. I don't meddle in individual matters. That is what Guardians do. They are the beings that carry humans through life, guiding, inspiring, consoling, and tending to their souls. That is their job, to whisper in the ears of a human, to steer them to righteousness without forcing or overcoming free will...," his stern eyes filled with pain for his brethren, "just to have those ears turn the other way. Constant disappointment and sorrow come to those beings. In the end, the sin you humans are born with usually gets the best of you and betrays the bonds the Guardians have strived to nurture for so much of their lives."

His expression steeled, straining to hide the painful emotions he truly felt. "This is not what I was made for. So, no, I don't know much about you. And it's not my job to feed your bratty need for answers."

I decided not to push his temper and sat in silence.

He set the empty bowl down on the coffee table in front of him and leaned back against his wings, crossing his ripped arms over a muscled chest. "All angels are connected in a way. We can feel when another is hurt, happy, needing help or missing. However, we share our knowledge the same way as yours, word of mouth. We are not all-knowing as He. The information I've gotten, my dear, is from talking to the Guardians. The only reason I intervened here the other night was because I was given orders to."

"What orders?" I asked quietly.

His teeth clenched, and his jaw twitched with superiority. "The Lord wanted me involved. For some unknown reason, He sent me to tend to this matter — whatever it is."

"But why would *you* be sent if it's an individual matter?" My brain screamed from overload, struggling to connect the dots.

"I don't question—I do what I'm told. All I can think is that the outcome of whatever happens with you will be of grave importance to all realms." A sly smile lifted at one corner of his mouth.

"So, how can we know if I am this 'Clavis' for sure?"

"I don't know, yet."

I was flipping-the-fuck-out inside. My heart pounded, my breath rushed in and out, and my mind raced with jumbled questions. "Why would God hold these things from you? I mean, you'd think He would want me on his side and would do whatever was necessary to get me there," I whined.

"He has reasons for what He does. We don't always see the logic in it." Watching me roll my eyes at his cliché response, he continued, "Think about it. If a child accepts Him freely on their own, aren't they more likely to stay with Him? Their love stronger and more adamant than if they were persuaded or forced? He strives for true love. He accepts the choices made against Him, no matter the pain. But remember, just because He forgives you and loves you when you stray, doesn't mean there won't be consequences from your own accord."

His words burned through my heart. I knew the right thing to do, but was it in me to do it? Did I have the strength to leave George to suffer the torture I saw in the portal? At this very second, he could be experiencing unimaginable agony. The possibility of one of those demons harming him made my chest constrict.

"What's the next move?" Gavyn chimed in after a moment of silence between Malach and I.

The angel tore his eyes away from me. I know he could see the battle inside me. The fact that I even had to think about it seemed to intrigue him. "Right now, there is nothing more to do. Not until I find out more—or she declares herself," he answered Gavyn, then directed his accusing glare back toward me. "It would be nice if we could find your Guardian."

"Sure, I'll just charge up the angel tracker strapped to my back." I snorted at the ridiculous thought and rolled my eyes.

"You will know when you find them. You will have a bond that is unlike any other."

As the words left his smiling lips, only one face flashed into my mind. I inhaled the whisper of his name. "Archard." When I forced his image from my thoughts, I realized I was clenching the counter even harder now, and Gavyn and Malach were watching me intently.

"Nevaeh, do you know who it is?" Hope laced Gavyn's tone.

"No," I lied. I couldn't tell him, yet. I cared for him too much. If Archard was my Guardian, it would explain the strength of my feelings when I was near him. Maybe, I could stop it. Maybe, I could control the bond, now that I knew why it was there. But I couldn't tell Gavyn until I knew my feelings for Archard were nothing more than a pesky side effect of our supernatural tie to each other. And there wasn't a chance in Hell I was going to give Malach any more insight than I had to.

My eyes followed along one of the Archangel's soft wings. He lifted an overconfident eyebrow at me. Could he know that I might have an idea of who my Guardian is?

Knock, knock.

A light tapping at the door made us all jump. Before I could even get off the counter, Malach was up and blasting through the ceiling. The pressure was a mere gust of energy now. A beautiful mixture of colors beamed down from the silvery opening of his portal. The sight was mesmerizing—like a rainbow of warped, wavy reflections. I could almost enjoy his portals opening and closing now.

Gavyn passed under the puddle on the ceiling as it shrunk down to one tiny drop of water and disappeared. "I'm comin'," he called to the door.

I moved into the hallway in case it was Layla.

"Hey, man, I just wanted to know if you needed me to open up. We're all ready down there." The voice was male. I released my breath. "Oh…and Layla left a note for you." A white envelope crossed over the threshold as Gavyn reached for it.

"Yeah. Can you go ahead and unlock the doors?" He glanced back at me and then again to the person at the door. "I'll be down in a few." Gavyn gently pressed the door shut and walked towards me, tossing the envelope onto the bar.

"Aren't you gonna open it?" I tried to hold back my surprise at his gesture.

"Nah." He made the last few steps and wrapped his arms around my waist, "Nothing to worry about now. You have enough to deal with." He smiled then intersected my beginnings of a protest with a kiss, soft and sweet. "Now, get ready. I have human duties to take care of, and you're going to the library. See if you can find anything about the Guardian Angels and The Clavis there."

"First of all," I pulled at the droopy sweats I had on, implying that I didn't have any clothes. "Second of all, do you really think there will be anything in the library about the *story*?" I wasn't about to admit that it might be a prophecy.

"Yes, I do. Other Celatum have jobs, too. Some of them are authors, and I'm willing to bet that they documented stuff about this life. Besides, you need to learn as much as you can."

One of his fingers dipped inside the loose waistband of my sweats and traced along my bare waist. Heat radiated from his hand and warmed my cool skin, sending a shiver through my body. "I'll see if I can find some girl clothes for ya." He smiled at my reaction to his touch and kissed my forehead.

As he left, my eyes settled on the unopened envelope lying on the bar. Something urged me to peek. Jealousy or deceit—I could feel the ill intentions creeping out of the corner of my mind. I quickly shoved them away and decided against any snooping.

The icy morning air helped perk me up since I was seriously lacking some sleep lately. I strolled through the crowded streets, happily blending in with the ordinary people passing by. There was comfort in the strangers. It felt…normal.

Pulling the brown, bomber-jacket Gavyn found tight against me, I enjoyed the prickly sensations the wind left in my lungs. Memories of George and me, cuddling next to a small fire and telling folktales, surfaced. With those memories came that impatient ache in my heart, longing to save the father I lost. I shook my head to dismiss the thoughts, carefully putting George in a safe place at the back of my conscience.

I focused on where I was going and noticed that almost every person I passed was grinning directly at me; the grins were not friendly by nature, but strange smirks. Hard shoulders shoved into me as they strolled by. The space around me filled with more and more people, elbowing and pounding into me.

"*Hisss*," I heard from one of them, then another. "*Hisss*." A foul, sickening smell polluted the air. My gut rolled on itself, threatening to vomit.

I searched the crowd for anyone that didn't look like a grinning zombie, anyone that could offer help if my internal demon radar was accurate. Everyone just stared right through me with their eerie smirks. There was no one to help.

Suddenly, someone stepped in front of me, blocking my path.

Be strong. Don't show fear. They might just want to ask me directions.

As we silently glared at each other, the woman's face began to distort. The skin around her mouth loosened as if there were no muscles holding it in place. Her lower eyelids drooped until I could see the thin, red membranes behind them. Some features sharpened as others slackened against her bones. Her color paled to an ash-gray. The whites of her eyes filled with inky black and swirling blood-red. She smiled at me impishly through the mess of sagging skin.

Cackling erupted from her throat. Panic cut through my nerves sharper than a knife.

My eyes searched desperately for help again in the mass of bodies, but no one acted as if they saw me or the woman.

"What do you want?" I shouted at the lady.

A blend of voices hissed from her mouth. "We are always watching you, Nevaeh. Come, join usss."

"I have not decided yet, demon."

I can do this. Be strong. Be strong.

"Yesss, we know. Time is running out. The Master wants you to decide. If you want to sssave your precious George, make a decision, little one." Another sickly cackle rumbled out of her droopy mouth. "You have one week, child."

I almost hurled at the sight of the red, raw flesh showing beneath her sagging eyelids and the thick drool stringing from her lips, but I swallowed it back.

You can't show weakness, Nevaeh.

"I'll think about the offer." My words trembled.

The demon-woman's head began to turn away from me. It didn't stop. Bones crackled and popped against the torsion as her skull rotated on a stationary frame.

She continued laughing. However, the laugh was now full of agony and gurgling. Silence followed when her airway collapsed against the three-hundred-and-sixty-degree rotation of her head.

Puke filled my mouth and exploded like a volcano onto the sidewalk. I couldn't decide whether it was because she was a demon, or because of the terrifying dislocation of her head.

In between heaves, I caught glimpses of the demon stumbling backwards off the sidewalk. People moved around her oblivious to what was happening. They just glided to the side as if she were merely a road sign in the way.

The possessed woman stepped into the street and collapsed on the ground. No screams, no gasps. No creepy grins focused on me. Only the chatter of uninterrupted conversations filled the air when a truck rolled over the lump of skin and bones lying on the roadway. The driver didn't even stop to see what they hit after the axles lifted and bounced over her corpse.

I sucked in a lungful of air, finally done emptying my stomach. I stared at my surroundings, unsure of what was real and what was in my mind. Do I see if the woman she was still lived, or do I ignore what just happened and hope the demon was dead?

Just then, white and blue flames engulfed the body, burning it to ash in a matter of seconds. I couldn't stop the tears that started pouring from my eyes. Should I feel sorry for the human she might have been? Or was it demon the entire time? The human instinct inside of me, the person I was before exposed to demons and angels, wanted to mourn for the woman. Another part of me knew better.

I ran through the crowd and into an alley. I leaned against the cold stone of the building behind me. A shiver snaked up my back. Gasping for oxygen, I fell to the ground. My body shook with uncontrollable sobs. The remorse I had for the soul that might have died in the street quickly turned into dread. The message given echoed off the walls of my head.

"Save your precious father…one week, child."

Tired, weak, and emotionally defeated, I closed my eyes and whispered his name, the sound of it warming my lips.

"Archard."

He was the only thing that could save me now. I couldn't make this decision on my own. I was afraid I wouldn't make the right one.

I lay, raw and broken, in the cold alley with tears pooling beneath me. Pieces of my soul were unraveling in the dark while insanity toyed with my conscience.

"Archard," I whispered again, just before sleep and pure exhaustion carried me away.

CHAPTER NINETEEN

The Big Guy Upstairs

The serenity of sleep sank into my bones, lulling my scrambled thoughts. Still and silent, I waited for a dream to begin. I waited patiently for my soul to escape to a happier place. Yet, the quiet sanctuary of my imagination stayed distant for some time.

Walking through the in-between of reality and sleep, I found bleakness at each step. Was I already dreaming? Had my brain overloaded so much that I couldn't dream anymore? Or was this a sign of my failing conscience?

Echoes of my own voice answered when I called out. The claws of desperation and loneliness sunk into me. Moving farther into the bleak reverie, my unconscious body became light and airy—a mist floating through the dark.

The feeling that another presence was watching me from the vast, empty space sent a surge of unease through my nerves. Each breath became louder and faster, drumming in my ears so loudly that I barely heard the voice calling to me from a distance.

My vaporous hands reached for an anchor to hold me in place and keep me safe, but they only found more air. Then I propelled forward, tumbling in all directions.

"Relax, my dear," someone gently urged.

Something about the entity brought instant calm. My heavy erratic breaths quieted, and I surrendered my need to know where I was going, allowing myself to be whisked away on the invisible current carrying me. It was peaceful—like floating on warm water in the middle of a hot summer night.

"Why are you so tense?"

I laughed. "With everything that's happened, I've learned to be cautious all the time."

"Do you not know me, child?" The question, I realized, had no tone and no pitch. It just...was. Voiceless words and loving emotions that swirled among my own thoughts. Each expression induced feelings of joy and empathy—emotions that morphed into conversation and nurtured my very soul.

"Why do you call me child?" My heart skipped, remembering that the demons had called me that.

"Because you are mine. Always will be."

For some reason, I didn't want to protest as I had when The Dark One called me child. "Who are you? The only father I've known now resides in Hell. No other father has been there."

"I am truly sorry for what happened to George. He was a child of mine as well." Sadness drifted into the atmosphere, then cleared like a wave riding the tide. "I am the one that gave you to him. I have been there far longer than he has. And will remain afterwards." I sensed the presence's smile, and it lifted my spirit.

"But he found me by himself," I protested.

"No, Nevaeh, I was there. I brought him to you. I gave him a chance at redemption. He was given the chance to achieve greatness with his wasting life, and he has redeemed himself." Another invisible smile softened the air.

"I don't understand." Just as the words passed my lips, murky visions of a drunken George appeared against the black backdrop and played as if they were on a movie projector. A bright white mass of light was holding him upright while he walked. George's eyes were closed like he was sleepwalking. He stumbled around the jagged rocks under the dock, guided by the light which kept him standing.

"You are Him, aren't you?" I whispered in amazement. It was strange to think I was talking to God. I'd barely acknowledged him even existing before, but now I couldn't deny it. He was opening my eyes — and my heart.

"I am," He answered, pleased that I understood. His love filled the air, cradling my troubled spirit.

I didn't want to feel His love. I was angry at Him.

Why now? Why is He coming to me now?

"So, you are God." Fire burned beneath my words.

"I know that you are angry with me, child — "

"Don't call me child," I interjected, cutting into the tenderness working to calm me. "You may be the 'Almighty', but to me..." I hesitated. I couldn't bring myself to say what I was really thinking. This wasn't the deity I wanted. "You have left me alone! You gave them George. He's being tortured, and his soul tossed around as a bargaining tool. Why didn't you send Malach sooner?"

"Understand this — I have never left you alone. Whether you chose to acknowledge it or not, I have always been there for you... and for George. I have been beside you, as I am now."

"Beside me now? Lurking in the dark ruins of my dreams?"

"I'm only in the dark because you put me there, Nevaeh." His demeanor never showed any hint of anger. Just concern. Had I locked Him in the darkest parts of my soul? Or was it the hypothetical demon half of me that insisted on keeping Him hidden?

"Am I the Clavis?" I asked directly, pleading for an answer — for direction.

"It is too soon for you to know. I have things planned for you, for your world. Things have to fall into place at the right time. Like a puzzle, the big picture will be revealed when all the pieces are put together correctly." A moment of silence passed before He spoke again. "I will remind you of one bit of information that you have forgotten. George was not your birth father, Nevaeh."

"My real father died. How am I supposed to find someone who's been dead for over twenty years?" Subtle amusement ebbed and flowed against me.

Is He laughing at me?

Answering me as soon as the thought occurred, he said, "Yes, I am laughing at you. I love your tenacity. It gives you character. As for your questions, I'm sure you'll figure it out. I have placed help in your path, but only according to your need. It will not be easy, but I'll be with you, my child." The last of His words seemed to drift away too soon.

"Wait, are you leaving?" I was angry, but I also felt a connection I never had with Him before. Surprisingly enough, I actually didn't want Him to leave.

"Trust me...," the words were barely audible, "I will always be by your side, Nevaeh. Whether you want me or not." Whispers of His love trailed on the dying affirmation.

His presence vanished, and my vaporous body began sweeping backwards toward the physical plane it came from. I tried to enjoy the journey, but in the end, I knew I would have to confront my dreaded reality again.

The loud babbling of people rushing by the alley assaulted my ears. I drew in a deep breath, and my nose filled with the honeyed scent I could recognize anywhere; I knew that Archard was near. His enticing aroma overwhelmed my senses with love and protection. I could feel the heat of his aqua eyes staring at me.

"You came." A grateful smile tugged at my lips as I lay on the cement with my eyes still closed. I couldn't look at him. My strength would fail me in the presence of his beauty. "I need to talk to you." I waited, but no response followed. "Are you my Guardian?"

In an instant, his scent dissipated. My eyes shot open, searching the alley as I rose from the dirty ground. No trace of my angel lingered. I was alone—my heart shredding, again, from Archard's abandonment.

Hobbling onto the busy sidewalk, I dodged people laughing at funny jokes, lovers holding hands, and determined individuals shifting eagerly around those in their way. I headed toward the library, assessing my life and all that it had become. I acknowledged how different it would be from now on, even if I continued to be neutral and live my life pretending nothing had happened.

I could never have a simple love, or an ordinary career. I'll never know what it's like to go to my nine to five in the morning, come home to a house full of kids at night, and repeat the day over and over again until I die at a peaceful, old age. The whispers of demons and angels would always haunt me. I understood that now. Look at all that had taken place so far, and in such a short time. They would yank at my spirit, begging me to take their side. The guilt of refusing a responsibility that was ingrained within me would eat at my conscience.

It was my duty to help fight for those who stand strong in their faith, as well as the souls that falter like mine. Even if I don't have the power Malach claims I have, even if I'm not The Clavis he and Gavyn seem to think I am, I *am* a Celata. There is no doubt now, with all that I've seen, that I am different.

The question remains, though, was I different for the right reasons? Am I meant to fight for the virtuous things in this life, and in the afterlife? Or will the inherent evil in my soul overpower what I think is right?

The sweet darkness that called to me in the portal had latched onto my heart like a cancer deteriorating what virtue I was born with. Regardless of which way I chose, there's definitely no going back to the humble life of living on the streets.

CHAPTER TWENTY

Book-Keeping Is Hard Work

I shouldered into the heavy door and entered the library. Everything was quiet. I inhaled the odor of old books that had soaked into the walls and the orange carpet from 1970 and smiled. Even though the building had a rather large, open, double-level foyer, cozy memories of the hours I spent there made the walls feel close and comforting. I walked to the dingy, Formica covered counter and leaned my back against it, inspecting the empty library while I waited for a staff member to help me.

"Oh, sweet Nevaeh!" a high-pitched voice chimed from my right. Margie, the librarian, rushed toward me with a stack of books in her arms. She hoisted the heavy pile onto the counter and greeted me with open arms.

"Hey," I said, bending over to hug the petite lady in return. It had been a while since I saw her. The aging lines of her face creased a little deeper, her hair shimmered with a tad more gray. We chatted about the usual conversational topics: the weather, her grandchildren, and her husband. I couldn't tell her anything about my new life, but there was a welcome sense of normalcy in pretending all was well. I missed the ordinary interaction — as ordinary as I'd ever had anyway.

"So, what are you looking for, missy?" she asked, trying to control the shake in her elderly vocals.

"Well, I'm looking for books about angels and demons." I expected her to ask why and attempted to think of ways to get around explaining the details.

"Oh," she exclaimed, slightly surprised. "You know, I saw an angel once." Margie smiled, wagging a crooked finger at me, and ushered me down the tight aisles of books.

"Really?" I asked, skimming my eyes over the hundreds of titles we passed as I followed her. I don't know why, but my first thought was the usual reaction when someone says they've seen something supernatural. *Yeah, right.* Then I felt bad. Who am I to say that she hadn't seen one? I've seen them, why couldn't she?

"Yep. It was long ago, but as sure as I'm breathing, it was there." She turned between two tall, overlooked bookcases at the back of the library and stopped midway down the aisle. "Right here, actually. Funny, huh?" Margie exhaled a giggle as she seemed to recall the experience.

"Funny?" Before she answered, I scanned the books she'd led me to and realized what she meant. Decaying leather peeled away from the binding of books centuries older than the librarian herself. I read the imprinted spines while taking in the intriguing fragrance of eras long ago. Lettering in golden, ancient script spelled out things like "Angelus", "Demonic Possessions", and "Heavenly Wars on Earth." Yeah, it was somewhat comical that an angel showed up in the section of books about angels. "Margie, what did it say to you?"

"Oh, nothing much really. Its mouth moved, but I couldn't understand a single word it said. I only heard what sounded like wordless music playing in my head. Then it handed me this." Her knobby fingers reached toward an empty section. Whatever book she intended to show me was missing.

"Oh, my. Well...it *was* here." I watched as she frantically searched the titles to see if the book was misplaced. "I never let anyone check these out because they are so old." Her wrinkled brow deepened, panic sparking in her eyes. "Nevaeh, I'm not sure what happened to it."

"It's okay, Margie. No big deal." I assured her, but it was a big deal. What if it held the answers I'd been looking for? I placed a comforting hand on her shoulder and smiled. It wasn't her fault the book disappeared, nor was it her responsibility to be involved in this anymore than she had to.

"But...but I feel like it was the one I was supposed to show you. I'm not sure why, but it was important to you for some reason." Tears trickled down her cheeks. "I...I just know I was supposed to show you that one book." She nervously tugged at her sweater, crossing it tight over her chest like she was trying to hide her suddenly naked body. Her glossy eyes flicked back and forth over the shelves.

Why was she getting so upset over this? She didn't have any clue as to what was really happening. Did she? "Do you remember what the title was? Maybe we can see if it's at another library."

She stared through me in thought, her thin eyebrows pinching together. "The binding was smooth, red velvet with silver lettering on the front." She continued with absolute certainty as if trying to convince herself that she'd really seen it — that it wasn't a figment of her imagination. "This book was different. It was special. The knowledge it held radiated from the pages like sunbeams. There were secrets in that book. Secrets only meant for you. It vibrated with them," she said softly, her words fading as she became lost in the memory. Her eyes darted down to the floor while she roughly massaged her forehead.

My heart sank to my stomach. "Margie, how do you know you were supposed to show *me* that book? Why not anyone else?"

"I don't know how, I just know," she answered, pulling a crumpled tissue from her pocket and dabbing tears off her cheeks.

"Why didn't you give this to me when you saw the angel?" My words sounded harsher than I'd meant.

She blinked a few times, confused by my question. "Honestly, Nevaeh, I'm not sure. It's as if everything has been wiped from my memory save for a few fragments. Just enough to know that this could be disastrous."

Disastrous? What the hell did this book have in it?

"Do you remember what the angel looked like?"

"I can't remember. I can picture the being, but not any specific features. It's just a jumble of faces all at once. I'm so sorry, Nevaeh." A short groan escaped her lips as she tried her damnedest to hold back a deluge of sobs.

"No, I'm sorry." This stupid curse had touched even those who are distant in my life. I smoothed out the wrinkles on her sleeves and hugged her reassuringly. "It's fine. I'll just search these books." I said, hiding the concern underlying my words.

Before I could say anything else, Margie raced past me and disappeared beyond the end of the aisle. I pushed aside the frustration and slid a book off of the shelf next to me, impatiently thumbing through the pages as soon as I opened the cover. I shoved the useless book back in its spot and yanked out another, searching for one that might reveal some sort of secret that would instantly speak to me.

Bits and pieces of information about the different kinds of angels and their duties filled the pages. Drawings of humans morphing into demons illustrated others. This was all very informative, but it wasn't what I was looking for.

I leaned against the shelf behind me and sighed. Margie's reaction replayed in my head. Who—or what—did she see? Two angels came to mind, but realistically there were likely more heavenly beings than I could count. I couldn't assume it was Malach or Archard.

A dreadful thud from the lobby echoed through the shelves.

"Margie?" A sinking feeling knotted in my stomach. "Margie?" She didn't answer.

Sprinting between the bookcases, I feared something bad would be waiting when I found her. My heart pounded heavier and faster as I neared the front of the building. Sour bile rose to my throat, and I recognized the symptom well by now. A demon was near.

I rounded the last corner leading to the lobby, bracing myself for what I might find. Pungent air choked the breath from me. My feet stopped abruptly the second I saw her, causing my shoes to squeak against the smooth floor. I gasped in shock, covering my open mouth with a trembling hand. The sad sight of Margie lying on the crimson splashed marble floor scarred my cheerful memories of her for life. She lay motionless and damaged, coughing on her own blood, looking at me through lightless eyes. The sweet, carefree woman she used to be was diminishing fast.

The steady patter of something dripping on the floor pulled my eyes upward to the loft banister above us. Red smeared along the railing, beading into little droplets of life that plummeted next to Margie's dying body.

She must have fallen, I thought, glancing back at Margie.

Then, I saw the monster skittering down the stairs. It had pushed her over the railing.

An Animus demon crept over from the bottom step, crouching on its haunches beside my librarian. It wasn't taking her soul, but clutching onto something in Margie's right hand. Rotted talons ripped and scratched at her flesh as it struggled to pull the object from her grasp. Somehow her frail, arthritic hand kept a determined grip on whatever it was.

"Nevaeh, it stole it before I could give it to you…I tried to get it back," she gurgled, death overpowering her life.

271

"I'm so sorry," I cried to Margie, hoping that she would forgive me.

The muscles in her agonized face relaxed, and her eyes went blank. With her last breath, she released the object.

The demon scrambled backwards, clenching onto what it had stolen from Margie. The monster stopped to watch my movement, glaring at me with deep, dark orbs. It didn't appear to be scared, but rather curious about me.

The more I looked into its horrid eyes, the more I felt a burning inside. The demon's gaze was like acid to my soul. I averted my attention from the monster's stare and found what Margie had died for. The object had a reddish sheen to it, but I couldn't tell if it was blood or something else. The monster hid the treasure within long, boney fingers, grasping it as if life depended on it.

"I'm tired of your games," I yelled, surprised by the confidence I suddenly acquired. That wasn't so bad. I could stand up to this evil fiend. I'd seen it before and knew what this monster was about. But why did he want the object? Why didn't it steal Margie's soul like they'd done to George?

"Give it to me." I held out my hand and eased toward it.

If I didn't know better, I would've sworn it laughed at me from that hideous, mouthless face. The wall behind it began to shimmer and waver in solidity, like fumes in a hot desert. Streaks of red-hot electricity bolted from the wall. That ever-growing pull to the darkness called to me.

"Oh, no you don't!"

The demon's atrophied muscles twitched with anticipation. Energy hummed from the shimmering wall, beckoning to the demon as it did me. The portal begged me to enter.

"Don't do it," I commanded the demon.

Dammit, the demon was definitely going to do it. It slowly

retreated backwards, keeping its gaze fixed on me. Was it testing me—teasing me? Did it want me to chase after it?

A white, crackling bolt whipped out from the opening and illuminated the object in the monster's hands. It was a book. *The* book. Erratic sparks of light shined along the deep, red velvet binding. The fiend hugged the book close and sped up its retreat toward the wall.

I leaped for the Animus without thinking. My stomach cramped in excruciating pain. My skin singed from the inside out. That tell-tale taste of stomach juices leaked into my mouth, letting me know I'd ventured too close to Hell's danger.

I locked onto the demon's leg. Bits of rotted flesh slid like jelly beneath the pressure of my fingers and peeled off the monster's muscles. "I'm not letting go, you bastard. I'll latch onto bare bone if I have to." I tightened my grip, digging my nails into rubbery strands of tendons on its ankle.

The demon arched into the air and screeched.

Oh, so it does feel pain, I silently mused as the monster dragged my agonized, frozen body into the portal behind it.

This journey into Hell seemed more painful than the last—maybe because I didn't pass out. This time I actually begged to be unconscious. My body burned from an inferno within that was unreachable and unstoppable. Blood boiled in my veins, threatening to melt the very fibers of my being.

Time seemed to stop while we traveled the space between Earth and Hell. Willowy black figures reached their desperate hands out of the darkness and tugged at my legs, screaming for redemption. I held onto the Animus and ignored the wretched spirits.

Every surface, even the air, felt like saw blades shearing my skin. The demon screeched, hefting me along with each slow step. It never once tried to detach me. It wanted me to ride along into the hopeless pit of Hell.

Finally, after an unfathomable time lapse, a humid orange glow brightened the space around us.

We had crossed the threshold.

The limping demon halted and scowled down at me. My pain subsided to a dull sting; at least until a blow to my ribs stole the breath from my lungs. I grunted and coughed from the pain, curling into a ball on the ground, but I kept a tight grip on the demon's leg. It lifted its free leg and positioned it over my head in anticipation of smashing my face in. As it thrust its foot downward, I quickly rolled out of the way, keeping my hands clasped around its other ankle.

I gulped back the nausea and yanked on the putrid limb as hard as I could. Brittle bone grinded against brittle bone. The creature fell to its knees, squealing.

The book, where is it?

I pushed myself up and searched the ground. Under a mound of chalky, yellow dirt, I was able to see the faint sheen of red velvet.

I dealt the demon one good kick in its rigid spine and dove for the book. Clouds of the yellow, sulfuric dust puffed up from the ground, sticking to my face and eyelashes, shielding my view. I gasped uncontrollably, my nose and lungs coated in the foul-smelling granules. I was winded, blinded, and disoriented.

That was a stupid move, Nev. No more leaping for anything in this sulfur pit.

The bastard grabbed a fistful of my hair and pulled up, lifting me high off the ground, leaving my feet to dangle in the air. My scalp stung with a sharp, ripping sensation. I sunk my fingers into the demon's wrist, struggling to lessen the tension on my head.

Another high-pitched squeal sounded from the demon's head. Swinging from my hair, I kicked and punched at the monster. Distant screeches reverberated against the rocks, answering my monster's call. My chest tightened, and my heart skipped when I realized they were getting closer.

What have I done?

"LET ME GO!" I yelled at the fiend, tugging against its grip. Its large hand swung around and punched me in the face, catching me off guard. My fingers pressed against the stinging spot on my cheek bone. The scenery around me became blurry, my head swimming from the impact.

Oh no, don't pass out, don't pass out.

My equilibrium teetered back and forth, keeping me guessing at which way was up and which was down. Black spots speckled my vision.

Oh, no.

Heavy steps skittered toward us, then alarming screeches rang in my ears.

This is it.

My body gave up and hung limp from the demon's vise-like hands.

The sudden smell of ash filled my nostrils. I fell to the ground with a thud. My legs ached from the crash, but my scalp praised the release. Slowly opening my eyes, I saw the demon lying beside me, black orbs staring into mine. Its gaze was hollow now. No evil, no dread—nothing. It was completely vacant.

"Come on!" A nervous voice yelled from above me.

The awful odor of burning flesh triggered my nausea, again.

"Get up! You have to get out of here!" Strong, steady arms raised me off the ground, cradling my body against a heaving chest. "Nevaeh?" The man kept saying my name, trying to wake me from the fog. My head throbbed more and more as he set into a jog. "Nevaeh, you've got to wake up! You can't stay here!" My body bobbed limply in his arms as he increased speed.

I wiggled in his arms, wanting to get down, but his grip held me too tight. Beads of sweat dripped from my pores and mixed with his, our clothes sticking together along my left side. The putrid odor of this world made it hard to inhale. I sucked in long, slow breaths, cringing as the dense, sour air passed over my tongue and entered my throat.

Tortured screams drifted through the hot, stagnant air.

My groggy eyes shot in the direction we were running. Through the orange, dim glow, I saw a vast desert with mountains of boulders extending high into a treacherous landscape.

The suffering screams grew louder. We were running toward them. "Where are you taking me?" My voice sounded scratchy and weak.

"That's a good girl. You have to wake up," the man urged in a tender tone.

I focused on the face of the man carrying me. "It's *you*." His violet-blue eyes captivated my attention.

"I'm Kenet. Right now, that's all you need to know." The man's dry, cracked lips curved into a soft smile.

"Where are you taking me?" I repeated.

"Can you run?" Kenet ignored my question as he scoped our surroundings.

"I can try."

"Then, try now." He slid me to the ground and tugged me along before I could even tell my feet to move. I stumbled at first, but my legs finally steadied and established a poor excuse for a jog. We weaved around towering rocks and ducked in and out of coves that were almost invisible until we were right next to them. Blood-curdling roars boomed like thunder across the orange sky, some so sinister I wouldn't be able to sleep without hearing them in my dreams.

Kenet's eyes constantly searched and assessed the area for threats. "We've got to get you out of here," he mumbled again, partly to himself.

I shook my head. "No. There's someone I'm looking for, and I don't want to leave until I know where he is."

Why did this man always show up? Not that I was upset. He seemed to come at times that I needed him. But, why was he helping me? Why did I trust that he would take care of me?

"Nevaeh, the longer you stay, the more you will be influenced. And the influences you feel here are not pure." He stopped and yanked me into a rocky crevice. One of his smoldering hands covered my mouth while the other pressed a finger to his dry lips, gesturing for me to keep quiet. The smell of his burning skin made me gag, but I didn't fight him.

Seconds later, three demons, like the one that slashed the woman's face, straggled by our hiding spot. They shuddered and shook, moving in short, choppy steps. I stiffened with terror, recalling their capabilities; I knew that if they found us, they might do the same to me or worse.

"I will not be able to save you every time you come here. I know who you seek, and I know where he is. He is okay…for now. You cannot continue to look for him. You only put him in more danger," he whispered as his decaying hand left my face. He was begging me to stay out of this place, and the concern in his eyes nearly had me convinced.

"How do you know where George is? How can I trust you when I don't even know who you are?"

"I have been appointed his keeper. But, every time you enter the portal, I have to leave him to save you." Kenet leaned against the wall across from me and tilted his head just enough to see around the edge of our crevice. He nodded letting me know the demons were gone.

"Wait. You left him?" I yelled. "How could you leave him?"

"Shut up!" he said in a strained whisper, glancing toward the demons to make sure they didn't hear me. "I will always choose you over that man. You are more important than you realize." He smiled and brushed a strand of hair behind my ear.

"Please take me to him," I whimpered. "I need to see him. It's my fault he's here."

Kenet hesitated, arguing my request in his head.

"No. I'm sorry, I can't." Without further discussion, he turned, pulled me out of the cove, and led me to a drop off a few feet away.

He lowered onto his belly and scooted over the ledge. He stopped just before his head disappeared beyond the cliff's edge and stared at me expectantly. "Well, c'mon."

Rolling my eyes and huffing to cover the sudden fear of heights I was experiencing, I lowered to my knees, threw one leg over the side, and then the other once I found footing along the steep wall.

"Just don't look down," Kenet advised me from below.

"Easier said than done," I whispered, gripping the handful of rock keeping me on the side of the cliff.

We slowly climbed down one hundred feet or so of steep wall, descending toward the floor of a dry, yellow ravine. Demon screeches echoed against the craggy plains from above; they were getting louder. Soon, I suspected they'd be close enough to peer down at us from the cliff's ledge. We picked up the pace, scaling the last of the wall within a couple of minutes.

Kenet jumped off backwards, landing safely on the soft, sand-like bottom, and wiped the sulfur dust coating his palms on his black, military grade pant legs. "That's it. You're almost here," he encouraged, looking up at me as he rested his fists on his hips.

I stopped two feet from the bottom, glaring back at him. He smiled then wrapped his hands around my waist, guiding me down until my feet touched the ground.

"Okay, Nevaeh. Are you ready?"

"Ready for what?" I squeaked nervously.

"Ready to go home." He jerked me into his chest and hooked his arm around my neck so I couldn't escape.

"No, I don't want to leave yet. What about the book? And I need to see George!" I thrashed against his body with no success of loosening his hold. We shuffled around a huge, protruding boulder, and I stopped fighting him. An Animus demon was only a few short paces ahead of us, entering a portal. Crackles of electricity charged the shimmering air and lit the barren valley with bright, white zaps.

Twinges of that burning pain bubbled in my blood as he pushed me closer to the opening. I settled on the fact that this would not be my last visit to the dark place. There were too many answers here.

My muscles stiffened against Kenet's body, expecting the pain to ignite any second. He lifted me off the ground and whispered something in another language as we moved. Finally, he stopped in front of the shimmering portal and looked down at me with a saddened expression. It was, almost, as if he didn't want me to go.

"Nevaeh, please don't come back here again." His jaw clenched together. Bolts of electricity sparked from the portal and pierced his torso as if he was some kind of conductor, then radiated into me. He continued to hold on despite the turmoil I saw on his face.

My body began to convulse and react to the portal's punishment. I was amazed that I was alive after experiencing it so many times now. But I knew that I would make it through somehow.

I had no choice if I wanted to save George.

Struggling against the agonizing current electrocuting us, Kenet set me down gently. His hand cradled my head as he dipped my paralyzed body backwards into the opening. He roared when his hand entered the opening with me. Then, I was ripped from his grasp, taken out of his realm, while he was forced to stay.

CHAPTER TWENTY-ONE

So That's How It's Going To Be?

The portal closed behind me. I lifted my weak and exhausted self from the ground, flinging off some of the other-realm's goo sticking to my skin. I looked around to figure out where the opening had spat me out this time, but I didn't recognize the area. It appeared to be a small rear parking lot behind some sort of movie theater.

I jumped, startled by a young guy and girl exiting the door next to me. One second they were laughing and carrying on, the next they were walking away from me as fast as they could in silence, their eyes cautiously keeping track of my movements.

I'd gotten used to seeing those reactions when I was a filthy, homeless girl living on the streets. People were never sure if they should stop to offer help or run away pretending they didn't see me.

I made my way to the front of the building, sticking to the parts of the sidewalk lit by streetlights. Dusk had fallen while I was gone. Gavyn was probably worried sick about me. I hoped I hadn't lost too many days in Hell. Time was too precious to squander away between worlds now that I had a deadline to consider.

I followed the lines of familiar buildings and found my way back to the café. The neon "Open" lights were off, so it must've been later than ten o'clock. Tiny butterflies filled my belly as I neared Joe's. It was exciting to come home to Gavyn, to have at least one solid pillar in my life, and to know that he cared for me. There was so much I needed to tell him. Hopefully, he could help me figure out some things about the book and the man that's been saving me on the other side.

I wrapped my hand around the brass handle and pushed the door open. A blanket of protection and safety wrapped around me the second I stepped inside the cafe. I gladly accepted the sensation and hugged it tight against my heart.

The tables were already cleaned and prepped for the next day. Brightly colored lights from the jukebox lit the room in a lovely rainbow glow. A satisfied smile stretched across my lips. I hadn't been this happy or felt this at ease with a place since I could remember. I strolled down the hall toward the bright light spilling out from the kitchen.

Two steps short of the doorway, I heard voices carrying into the hall. I stopped, recognizing Layla and Gavyn. My breath hitched. She mumbled an answer, responding to a question Gavyn asked.

What is she doing here? Why is he talking to her?

Something stirred in my belly, and it wasn't the butterflies this time. Something was changing. I felt a dangerous shadow stretching its sinful arms and awakening inside me.

How could she even show her face, knowing that I might be here?

"C'mon Gavyn, do you really think I would do something like that? How long have we been friends?" Layla mused.

"I know we've been friends for a long time, but why would she lie to me?" Gavyn's voice was layered with doubt.

"I would never hurt her. I'm sorry to say it, but I think she's crazy. I saw what she did in the warehouse. Why would anyone try to enter a portal?" She made a solid attempt at sounding concerned for my sanity, but I didn't buy it.

"So you *were* there? Why Layla? What were you doing there?"

There was a pause while Layla undoubtedly thought of a lie to tell him. "I saw her leaving the café and wondered where she was going. That's all. I followed her and saw her talking with some angel, Gavyn. She is with him. I saw her. She kissed him. She is with *him*, Gavyn."

NO!

My stomach plummeted, and my heart broke for Gavyn. Oh, how he must've felt. I fought the need to run in screaming, *I choose you, Gavyn.*

What a bitch.

How could I fix this?

"I don't know what they have going on or what they are up to, but it's just not right for her to keep it a secret." She waited a few seconds allowing the words to settle in his mind. "Seems awful distrustful to me."

Gavyn's whisper clipped in, full of uncertainty. "No, she cares for me."

The guilt was shattering, drawing shame-filled tears to my eyes. I never meant to hurt him.

I will get her. I'll wait and follow her — make her pay.

It scared me how badly I wanted to hurt her. I never dreamed of harming another person like that before. Suddenly, my forehead began to sting. My fingers found their way above my brow and massaged the sting away as I leaned closer to the door.

"I care for you, Gavyn. I always have. Why can't you see that?" She was doing a damn good job pretending to be meek, but it only made me want to hurt her even more. I would find a knife, follow her home, and gut her.

Look at the pain she is causing. She is turning everything around just to get him on her side, my inner voice pointed out.

The burning on my forehead intensified. I glanced at the mirror hanging across the hall from me and saw the inverted cross glowing bright orange beneath my skin.

I rubbed hard at the disturbing patch of skin but became distracted when Gavyn spoke.

"I don't know who to trust anymore. Why are you doing this, Layla? Why couldn't you just stay gone?" Gavyn's sadness cast a heavy gloom on the rest of the café as if the building felt his pain.

"Because I want you, love. We belong together. Now you know my secret. I am Celatum too, my love. Let's fight these battles together." Slow heels clicked across the floor. "You can trust me," she whispered.

The wet, smacking sounds of kissing assaulted my ears. Soft suckling of flesh and tiny moans filled the air. Their murmurs grew deeper and more urgent while I hid in the hall quietly begging him to push her away.

I wanted to run in and break them up, but I couldn't. Guilt and shame weighed me down like cement shoes in a lake.

How could he trust her? How could he dismiss me so easily?

Not knowing what else to do, I fled the café, stomping my feet against the wooden floorboards as I ran for the exit. I grabbed the doorknob and twisted it, fantasizing that it was Layla's neck I was wringing. I leaned into the door, shoving it open, and stumbled onto the brick steps outside.

Navigating my way into the alley beside Joe's, I crouched beside a large, metal trash can and folded myself into a tight ball. There was no one to comfort me; there was no one to help me think this through.

It's simple, just go back in and fight for him, Nevaeh.

My guilty heart wanted to, but my faltering trust wanted nothing more to do with Gavyn. If he can turn on me that effortlessly, why should I trust him only to have him leave me when things get worse? Sounds of Layla kissing Gavyn resonated in my head. Tears welled in my eyes. I pounded my fists against my temples, trying to dispel the taunting noises.

She doesn't deserve him. She was wrong.

It was so easy for the twisted words to slip from her tongue. She's definitely capable of doing whatever it takes to get what she wants.

Why should she get away with it?

There's nothing Layla wouldn't do to get her way.

I can play that game, too.

As my thoughts stirred, the darkness inside me emerged, bringing me new strength. It felt...good. I could do this.

It wouldn't be wrong if I got rid of her since she is one of the Dark Celatum, right? I might even be doing the world a favor.

Tendrils of sweet temptation twisted around me.

I'm going to kill her.

That became my comfort. I sniffled back the tears, happily accepting my plot of revenge, and began working out the details in my mind.

Hours later, the pitter-patter of high heels clacking between the buildings woke me from a light sleep. I shifted forward onto my hands and knees behind the trashcan, leaning out just enough to see the sidewalk. I stared at the yellow halo of light illuminating the cement under the streetlamp. Bitterness dug into my emotions when Layla strolled past the alley.

Now is your time, my inner voice urged with a wicked giggle.

I took off my shoes and ventured out of the alley, following Layla's route along the sidewalk, silently stalking my prey.

The burning on my forehead flared. This time, I ignored it. I didn't care what it meant anymore.

Damp gravel and concrete pressed into the pads of my feet as I stuck to the buildings' shadows and observed Layla. My hate grew with every step she took. She was so happy and carefree, humming as she went. Her joy was unacceptable.

We walked four short blocks and stopped at a chic apartment building. Layla typed her pass code into the security box, pulled the gate open, and stepped into the courtyard. I scurried to the entrance, wrapping my hand around the iron rod before the gate latched behind her. Hidden under the shade of overhanging trees and vines, I peered through the wrought-iron fence, studying Layla's every move—anger boiling just beneath my skin.

I hated her even more for looking as pretty as she did in the hazy, blue moonlight—her flawless blonde hair and smooth skin glistening from the radiance. She beamed with delight. What had she and Gavyn done together? The possibilities were unbearable.

Layla sat on the edge of a stone fountain in the center of the courtyard, dipping her fingers in the water and then flicking the moisture off. She leaned over and slid her designer pumps off, then gathered them by the straps. A small cat pounced up beside her, hungry for attention. She muttered something to the fluffy feline rubbing against her arm, then grabbed it by the neck and threw it against a tree ten feet away.

I gasped and covered my mouth with my hand to stop from yelling at her.

Heartless bitch!

She stood up, grimacing at the cat with disgust, and sauntered to her ground-level apartment. Her keys jingled as she unlocked her door and pushed inside. Once she entered her home, I snuck through the courtyard, careful to keep my body pressed against the shadowy walls.

I approached her black door and looked up at the large, silver number six nailed to it.

How appropriate.

I reached my hand out and slowly turned the knob. The latch clicked, and the door swung away from me, practically opening itself. I was grateful she didn't lock it since I had no experience picking a lock. My hand slid over the recesses of the wood and around the edge of the door, controlling its movements as I guided it open farther.

I poked my head into the apartment and searched for Layla. All was still. Adrenaline pumped through my veins, fast and steady, as I entered.

The apartment was dark. Only a sliver of light spilled into the den from what I assumed was her bedroom. Layla moved around, opening and closing drawers, in the adjoining room. I tiptoed into the kitchen and took cover behind the bar. My eyes roamed over the counter and found a butcher's block stocked with knives conveniently sitting beside the microwave.

The biggest blade suited me just fine.

I wrapped my fingers around the handle and smiled, gratified by the scraping sound the smooth blade made as I slid it out of the narrow slot. It was heavy but well balanced. I jabbed the knife through the air a few times to get a feel for the weight of it. My weapon of choice. I thought about dragging the sharp blade across Layla's perfect skin and grinned.

The bedroom door opened. My stomach sank, and I dropped to the floor. Layla pranced into the den, grabbed a bag off the dining table, and returned to the bedroom, pulling the door mostly shut behind her. I waited and listened with wild anticipation. The timing had to be just right.

A few minutes later, water splattered into a bathtub. She was going to take a shower. This might be easier than I hoped.

A sudden sensation of snakes slithering over my skin alarmed me.

I swiped my hands over my arms and legs to get them off, but nothing was there. I stiffened, scooting into the corner cabinet. Invisible tendrils of wickedness wound their way up my body.

My breathing sped up, and I held the knife out in front of me with both hands, ready to defend myself against the unseen presence easing its way into the atmosphere. I squinted into the dark, desperately searching for the outline of a body.

"Who are you?" I whispered.

Delicious desire blossomed in my belly. Unable to deny the demanding manifestation, I succumbed to its power. I sat forward, kneeling in submission, licking my lips as the black sweetness of the presence's power flourished and fueled my reason for being there. It directed my focus back to Layla, urging me to fulfill my plan.

I crawled to the wall next to her door and peeked into the bedroom. Her naked body passed by the cracked door. I leaned in closer for a better look, focusing on the inverted cross scarring her forearm as she stopped at the foot of the bed and pinned her hair into a messy bun on top of her head. I was suddenly more aware of my own mark than I wanted to be. I grinded my teeth and balled my fists, my hatred for her expanding to a new level.

Layla disappeared into the bathroom, humming a happy tune. The door creaked as she shut it behind her.

I am nothing like her.

You are so much more, Nevaeh, the dominating presence agreed as it sent a caressing ripple of energy over my hypersensitive skin. My body and soul were lost to the being's seduction.

You can do this. We can do it together, my love, it crooned in my thoughts.

Part of me didn't understand what was going on. I couldn't believe I was capable of the vengeful plan in my head. I didn't want this presence controlling my actions—or my emotions. However, a bigger part of me begged to experience the power that would unfurl if I gave in to him.

I relaxed into the devilish charm and welcomed him to join me in my revenge.

The muffled scrapes of curtain hooks sliding across a shower rod filtered through the bathroom door. I stood and crept into Layla's room.

The sound of water beating relentlessly against the plastic and Layla's incessant humming echoed off the bathroom walls while my eyes scanned over the room. Her white furniture was decorated in shades of pale pink and cream. Not the black and red fabrics and dead chickens I expected.

My mysterious companion gently guided me toward the bathroom, his invisible body pressing into mine.

I will help you, my love, he assured.

The very essence flowing in my veins heated with hunger for him, and for the blood we would spill together.

He will help me, I thought, drunk on temptation.

I inched slowly to the bathroom door and placed my hand on the cold, silver knob, my knife heavy in the other. I eased the door open, only a little, to make sure the opportunity was right. Steam billowed out around me and stuck to my skin. His disembodied breath, hotter than the steam, skimmed over my neck.

That's right, baby. Go in and take her. Take what she has, like she has taken from you.

Oh, the wickedness. Images of my strong faceless man flashed in my mind, mesmerizing me. Thoughts of how happy we would be when we finished this bitch excited both of us. Visions of us lying in her blood, entangled around each other, making love next to her lifeless carcass, danced before me.

"Nevaeh, what are you doing?" Someone whispered urgently

from the bedroom door.

I snapped back from my wicked reverie, the dark hold loosening from my soul. Instantly, I was drowning in remorse.

"Oh my God, what *am* I doing?" I breathed to myself in disgust and disbelief. The visions disappeared. I blinked through my confusion and glanced over my shoulder, exploring the room with unclouded sight.

Archard's gorgeous face stared at me, his ocean eyes filled with concern and pleading. "Don't do this," he whispered, cautiously approaching my side with his hands held up open-palmed in front of him.

An intense charge sparked through the air behind me, anger riding its vicious current. The hostile force blasted into me, possessing me. My left hand raised the knife against my will, while my right hand opened the bathroom door completely.

"Please, help me!" I begged Archard.

"Nevaeh, don't!" His hands grasped mine, slowing my movements but not stopping them. "Why are you doing this?"

"I can't stop it," I squealed. I was not in control of myself anymore. The dark force was strong and determined, willing my limbs to do its bidding.

"STOP!" my angel commanded, snatching me away from the door. Archard dragged me toward the exit while the invisible presence planted my feet to the floor and leaned against his grip.

The invisible one recited a disembodied chant and laughed wickedly in my ear. My hand shot out, slicing the blade across Archard's wrist.

"Fuck," he cursed angrily, his grasp slipping from my arm.

"I'm so sorry," I cried.

My back suddenly slammed into a wall, knocking the breath from my lungs. I slid to the floor, struggling to find air again. Something grabbed my arm, yanking me off the floor and hurling me into the dresser. I slouched against the drawers, screaming as sharp pains shot through my shoulder and down the arm dangling at my side. The dark force had cast me aside to fight with my angel.

The two forgot about me for the moment and battled each other, tearing the room apart in the process. Through my tears, I watched Archard dance around the room…alone. His arms jabbed and grabbed at nothing while his legs jumped and kicked the air. The only evidence that Archard's attacks reached the invisible force was the occasional dent that appeared in the wall.

In the background, the water turned off. Soon, Layla would come out with her temper blazing.

"Archard," I yelled, failing to get his attention.

The blonde home-wrecker crashed into the bedroom naked and dripping wet. "What the hell are you doing here?" she spat with fire in her eyes.

"We've got to go." Archard kneeled beside me and draped my good arm around his neck. In one quick motion, he gripped my waist and lifted me off the floor. I screamed, pain shooting from my dislocated shoulder straight to my hand. "Hold on tight."

Archard stood at attention, cradling me against his chest, and spread his wings out behind him. They were breath-taking. With one flex of his shoulders, his massive appendages stretched from wall to wall. A sudden, brilliant light burst from his body, whiting out everything in the room. My eyes burned, and I became blinded by the power he emitted; it was like looking at the sun from space.

Layla shrieked, and the dark presence dissipated from the atmosphere. No more malicious temptations clouded my emotions. I still felt the immense hatred toward Layla though. Maybe not enough to kill her now, but definitely enough to hurt her.

Archard propelled us into the air. My head swam. The world spun.

Shit, not again. I fought to stay alert.

"It will be okay," my angel breathed in my ear just before I passed out.

CHAPTER TWENTY-TWO

Against My Will

Menacing shades of gray and red whirled around me like blood-tinged smoke. The unsteady motion was disorienting. I couldn't gather my bearings.

Where the hell was I now?

"Hello?" I shouted. The colors shifted directions, seemingly angry at the sound of my voice. I squeezed my eyes shut and massaged my forehead; I was sure that at any moment my skull would split. "Someone, please help me," I sniveled.

The new stab of pain accompanying my last plea convinced me that it wasn't a good idea to talk anymore.

How do I get out of here? Was there a freakin' portal I have to go through here, too?

"Nevaeh...," a female voice called out to me, sounding warped like a damaged cassette tape playing.

Desperate to leave this place, I chanced the pain again. "Hello?"

I pressed my fingers against my closed eyelids, trying to alleviate the pressure squeezing my brain like a vise grip.

"Nevaeh, I'm so sorry, baby," the woman apologized. "I was only trying to help." The words were barely discernable.

Quick flashes of a little girl, dark hair with ringlets, bombarded my thoughts. They moved so fast, I could hardly keep up. Flashes of a boat, blue maybe, speeding against a rough wake. A mental rush kicked the images to an old woman hurrying the little girl into the boat under a starless, night sky. I couldn't see their faces. They moved with such urgency it was as if they were running away from me.

"See, baby?"

Everything became fuzzy. The pain in my head was excruciating.

"I love you," her strangled words vowed to me.

Suddenly, it all shifted again. The shades, the pain, the visions. It was too chaotic for me to comprehend. Yet, a part of me wanted so badly to understand. It meant something important—I could feel it.

"Wake up, dammit!" An irritated man shouted as an instant sting heated my cheek. "Get up." He smacked me, and it felt like he'd already done it a few times by the numbing sensation taking effect.

I attempted to gather enough wits to prevent the next slap I sensed coming, but my arms were too weak to raise. I peeked out through heavy eyelids, squinting at the bright lights beaming down on me. Archard's muscled torso hunched over me, glaring with a half-cocked brow, his golden hair framing a very angry face.

"What were you thinking?" he yelled. The boom of his voice echoed against the tender walls of my skull.

"Quiet, please," I begged.

"Why should I be quiet? This is serious, Nevaeh. You were going to kill someone."

His accusation was sobering. I started to remember the details of my failed attempt at taking Layla's life.

"I didn't though. Does that still count?" I wanted to retract my sarcasm the moment it reared its ugly head. Maybe this wasn't the time to be difficult.

"Only because I stopped you." His tone was more concerned than angry now. "Do you understand what would have happened if you had taken her life?" Fear flickered in his steel expression.

"Apparently not," I spat. "Why were you there anyway?" I sat up and froze once my feet touched the floor, holding as still as possible until my rolling insides settled. A dull throb pulsated in my shoulder, not the excruciating pain I felt before I blacked out. I assumed Archard had reduced my dislocation while I was unconscious.

"Apparently not?" he shouted back in disbelief, completely ignoring my question. "You would have been lost to us forever. Lost to me." His voice raised an octave.

He was worried.

"Who said I'm not already lost to you?" I sneered, narrowing my eyes. "Who said I was yours to lose?"

"Once you've killed in cold blood...," he turned his face away from my line of sight, "You're too vulnerable to do such a thing. It will take over you."

The angel strode over to a small table and poured water from a pitcher into a clear glass. I took the moment to study him. His feet were delightfully bare. Faded jeans were belted snugly to his waist, the bottom of his pant legs slightly frayed from dragging on the ground and constant wear. A plain, black tee shirt clung to his broad, lean chest. I trailed my eyes up the glittering flecks of gold nestled in cream and deep purple feathers that swayed with his movements and noticed two holes ripped in the fabric on his back, fitting tight around the bases of his wings. The edges of the holes were jagged and tattered as if his wings had shredded the material when they pushed through.

Did those things retract?

His steps portrayed confidence and unwavering strength as he made his way back to me, muscles straining against the bindings of his clothing. Such an awe-inspiring sight—and such an inappropriate time to be thinking this way. I had a hunch that feeling would always accompany him when we were close. However, his magnetism was measurably more faint than usual.

I realized I couldn't be around him without some part of me wanting to surrender to him though. I, also, realized it wasn't just because he was an angel.

I cleared my throat. "Taken over by what?" I asked, grabbing the cup he offered and lifting it to my lips. The cool water quenched my thirst while the embers of desire, which the water couldn't touch, prayed to be extinguished.

He studied me, his brows pinching together in disbelief. "Nevaeh, don't you understand what happened?"

"Not really. I just know I wanted to kill her. And, more than anything, I wanted to be with...whoever it was that was controlling me." I stared down at my feet, avoiding the judgment in his eyes.

"The Devil is trying to reach you, and you are leaving the door wide open," he growled.

"Sorry. It's just...it's all a little too hard to believe," I huffed.

"It shouldn't be so unbelievable. You've been seeing these types of things for a while now." He licked his lower lip and sighed. "Why won't you choose?" he breathed.

"I can't yet. Not with George being held captive. I can't leave him there."

I brushed some fallen hair from my face and looked to the ceiling, bating back the moisture welling in my eyes. "And I'm still undecided. I'm not sure I want to do this. It's so much responsibility." Warm tears spilled onto my cheeks.

"How can you still be undecided after all this?"

My eyes darted down from the ceiling and focused on his grimacing face. "It's not that simple for me, Archard. I only just accepted that there was a God recently, and I'm have some issues with how he likes to stay in the background. Besides that, I care about George too much to just let his soul rot in that fucking place." Needing desperately to escape his hard stare, I glanced at my feet again.

The conversation/dream I had about God lingered in the back of my mind, but I wasn't convinced it was a true message. I still hadn't figured out how to differentiate the crazy dreams I normally had from the ominous visions I was receiving as of late. Until I learned how to do that, there was no need to delve into that with Archard right now.

I stood up quickly, anxious to leave the room and his certain judgment, but my legs failed me. I fell clumsily back to the bed. "You just don't understand," I said under my breath.

In one surprisingly intense moment, Archard scooped me off the bed and gripped my arms, holding me upright. His hypnotizing, aqua eyes stared into mine, feverishly trying to relay some unsaid message.

I was fully aware of the yearning in my core, still faint but undeniable. There was a building ache between my thighs. I couldn't stop it. I didn't want to. My breath quickened, and my eyes shut tight. His touch was too much for my senses. That damn fragrance of honey and happiness.

I was fine until he touched me, dammit.

The longer he held me, the more I melted in his hands. "I do understand, Nevaeh." Pulling me closer, he exhaled softly against my ear, "Why do you think I'm here?"

His lips were like satin gliding over my earlobe. Energy fluxed between our bodies, heightening my awareness of how insufferably close I was to him. If I just turned my head a bit, I could taste him. I would taste Heaven once again.

"Why do you think I left my home to live in this unholy place, filled with people who care nothing about the beings that fight for them every day, never receiving acknowledgement or gratitude for our sacrifices?" His voice was thick with pain and love all at once.

"I don't know. Why would you do such a thing?" I breathed, entranced by his heat engulfing my body.

His face moved away from mine. I drank in his divine features, analyzing each crease and plane. He made hiding emotions seem effortless. Slowly, he let go of my arms and left me to support the dead weight of my body on my own.

"Won't you answer me?" I waited for him to give me a reason to surrender to this yearning — for him to convince me of his holiness and all he symbolized. "Why did you leave Heaven?"

"I just want you to see that you're not the only one risking someone's soul in this thing." A quick flare of emotion stirred in his expression. He wasn't as hard as he'd like me to believe. "Think about why you're doing it for George."

It wasn't the same. I love George. He'd taken care of me, so I should take care of him. It's my fault he's in Hell.

"Come on. I have some people I want you to meet."

Before I could reply, he turned and headed toward the door with his majestic wings sweeping behind him, the interwoven gold feathers gleaming under the bright overhead lights. I resisted the urge to reach out and touch the softness swaying before me as I followed him.

We walked in silence down a long, carpeted hallway of what looked like an abandoned factory. There were a few vacant offices lining the corridor, as well as four large rooms housing some kind of looming machines, each designated for producing different materials. He passed those rooms, leading me toward the solid, steel door marked Employees Only at the end.

As we moved closer, I noticed a familiar blend of an

undecipherable melody. It was lovely. Soon I realized, I was no longer following Archard but the angelic sounds reverberating into the hall.

"Brace yourself. They are not as subdued as I." He tugged down on the handle and pushed.

"Subdued?" My brow wrinkled as I looked up at Archard, confused, and slipped past him to enter the room beyond.

I was instantly compelled to weep at their magnificence.

My eyes perused over all fifteen of them, following every graceful movement. Some swooped through the room, some hovered above the ground, and others battled each other on the floor. They communicated in a heavenly language that sounded like orchestral harmony, each note weaving and overlapping another with unidentifiable precision. I'd never seen or heard anything so unearthly beautiful.

Every single being had their own uniquely decorated wings. Different hues of white lay soft against contrasting rainbows of colored tips. Glints of gold, silver, and coppery metals peeked through the whites, catching the light just right—like stars twinkling across the large room.

They weren't all men, but they were all ridiculously strong and agile. They fought one another, anticipating their battle partner's movements as if they had watched them do it a thousand times before. It was a *dance* of war, rather than the act of it.

My emotions betrayed me. Tears wet my cheeks, not because I was upset, but because the yearning was too great. The need to worship these creatures surpassed any other need. I wanted to love them, to do their bidding, and to surrender myself to each and every one of them.

I peered up at Archard and tried to ask for freedom from this overwhelming effect, but I couldn't speak. My skin tightened and puckered, my bra and panties becoming uncomfortably restricting.

Unable to fend off the urges any longer, my wobbly legs gave out, and I dropped to the ground. I crawled slowly across the dirty, cement floor, tugging at my abrasive clothes. I needed to show them what I had to offer, give them every bit of me I could.

I needed them to fix me. Love me. Want me. Bless me.

Archard belted a fragment of their language out from behind me somewhere. It sounded urgent, but I was too fixated on the angels in front of me to be concerned. I continued on my path and felt the cool air chill my skin when I finally broke free from the scratchy fabric of my shirt. The sensation made me ache for them even more. I wondered how tender and warm their touch would be against my hungry body.

When Archard finished speaking, there was a disruption in the atmosphere. All the angels turned toward us and stilled. Surprised expressions furrowed their glorious faces as they watched me slink across the floor like a cat in heat.

The vague sound of Archard's heavy steps pounded closer to me. I was suddenly lifted upright by the back of my pants, my belt cutting into my stomach as he jerked me to a stop. I looked back at him with wide eyes, not understanding his actions until he flung my shirt across my chest. The sneer on his face sobered my lustful drunkenness. I clung to the fabric draped over my breasts, embarrassed. I was very much aware of myself again as the intense desire subsided somewhat.

"I told you to brace yourself," Archard said angrily through gritted teeth.

The allure of the others retracted enough that I felt the comfortable heat of Archard's energy calling me back to him. "You didn't tell me what the hell I was up against." My cheeks flushed with shame and irritation as I hurriedly pulled my shirt back over my head. What did he think was going to happen? It's like throwing a hungry wolf into a flock of sheep and expecting it not to eat.

As curious faces stared at us—all of them smirking at the scene of Archard and me arguing—I realized that they were the wolves, and I was the lone lamb. Unfortunately, their collective pull had only stopped at a dull throb instead of continuing to fade completely away. I could handle that without taking my panties off, though.

"Nevaeh, these are my brothers and sisters. They are Earthbound as I am." With his temper slowly calming, he placed his hand at the small of my back and gently pushed me forward.

"So, you *are* fallen?" I asked, remembering what Malach had said about some of them taking a leave of absence.

"No." The corner of his mouth lifted in a half smile. "Not fallen, that would be those in Hell. We are bound to Earth because we've chosen to detach ourselves for the time being."

I shouted that lingering question in my mind, hoping he could hear me as I'd heard him before.

Are you my Guardian?

I felt the answer in my gut, but I needed validation.

No response crossed his lips, only a knowing gaze from his aqua eyes. He knew what I wanted to know. He just didn't want to answer.

"You must be The Clavis," a deep voice accused from the crowd of angels approaching us. The words rang harshly in my ears as I searched for the one who'd asked.

"No." The single defining word left my mouth before I knew it, and to my surprise it felt wrong. In my heart, I knew there was a nagging hope imploring that I say yes. But in the reality of things, how could someone with so little faith—in anything—carry such an important title? I refused to take claim of something that I may not be—may not want to be, for that matter. How could these beings have so much belief in someone who has so little?

"Yes," Archard corrected. "This is Nevaeh." He stood tall and stately beside me. Something was different about the vibe he put off, like he was sending a silent message to the others, requiring every bit of their attention and respect.

The energy he emitted was intimidating. I leaned away from him, barely enough for anyone to notice. Yet, he did. His disapproving eyes darted to me, lips in a thin, tight line. I marveled at the suddenly rigid stance of his body, all flexed muscle and fevered warning. His normally graceful wings stiffened, twitching in anticipation.

Archard saw me taking note of his posture and relaxed, but only a fraction. His gaze returned to the other angels. "She will be staying here. We need to instruct her."

"Wait! What?" I couldn't believe it. He was holding me hostage?

He didn't acknowledge my surprised reaction. "We will need to show her how to defend herself against them...and us." His eyes roamed the crowd of heavenly creatures and waited for arguments. No one spoke up, not even those with disapproving scowls.

I grabbed his arm, demanding his focus. "No. I never said I would stay with you. I want to go home. You can't keep me here."

Archard's fingers wrapped around my wrist and detached my hand from his forearm. He glowered down at me with a clear warning in his eyes as he spoke. "Seems to me, you don't have a home. And you obviously can't keep control of your wits." His words stung my pride.

"I can control myself just fine," I retorted, knowing that I couldn't. "Who do you think you are, anyway?" I poked a finger into his chest. "You don't seem like you want to help me, and I can take care—"

He grabbed the backside of my upper arm and yanked me closer, taking control of my temper-tantrum. "Dammit, girl. I *am* your Guardian." The admission erupted from his mouth.

My world stopped. Silence filled the air. I couldn't breathe. Suddenly, we were the only two in the gigantic room. The angels, and the enormous elephant, had all disappeared with that one phrase.

I knew the answer the whole time, but to hear him say it resulted in a very different reaction than I'd expected. My heart throbbed. His betrayal punched me in the gut. Rage climbed up the length of my body, begging to let loose.

He left my soul up for grabs.

"How could you?" I whispered, pulling my arm from his grip.

A glint of regret shined in his eyes. He looked back to the other angels and completely ignored me...again. All I could do was stare at the angel that abandoned me. He left my soul to be chased and influenced by all manner of otherworldly things.

"As I said, she will stay with me. While she is here, you all are to dampen your graces. She can't handle the intensity, yet."

"I thought The Clavis was half Celatum and half Demon. You'd think she could handle anything with that mix." A low rumble of chuckles broke out from the crowd. They were laughing at my weakness.

Go ahead. Stoke the fire, assholes.

Archard reluctantly responded with, "She has not yet chosen. Her powers are not fully developed." I could tell the statements were uncomfortable for him to admit. "We will have to keep her safe for now." His deceitfully handsome face turned to me and waited for an objection while begging me not to.

At that point, I was way too stunned to come up with any sarcastic responses that might relay my absolute unwillingness to obey him.

"We will begin practice tomorrow morning at sunrise," he said, returning his focus to the crowd.

The other angels nodded, accepting their orders. They followed him without question. No wonder he ignored confrontation. He wasn't used to someone challenging his authority.

Archard relaxed his stance and turned to walk away. The other angels muttered amongst each other and resumed their prior activities.

Still in shock, I held my place and watched as my angel left.

Even though I was totally enraged, I still couldn't deny the attraction that held me to him. I figured the fact that he's my Guardian would explain why I felt so differently towards him in comparison to other angels.

When he reached the door, he pushed on the handle, stopping mid-movement. "Are you coming?" he asked without looking back at me. Not waiting for my answer, he marched out of the room, letting the door slam hard behind him.

CHAPTER TWENTY-THREE

Teach Me A Lesson

I spent the rest of the night following Archard around in silence and learning the location of the factory's basic amenities. There wasn't much outside of some makeshift cots inside small offices, an employee bathroom with a tiny shower stall, and a small lounge void of any food.

I'd given Archard as much third-degree attitude as I could dish. I wasn't in the mood to find answers now. Maybe after a couple of days, I *might* forgive him enough to initiate some kind of interrogation. Until then, I decided to play along with his plan in order to survive while I figured out my next move. I would make damn sure he knew I was as mad as a hornet though.

The cafe wasn't even an option. Too much had happened, and I wasn't sure I could handle seeing Gavyn any time soon. No matter. I'd find somewhere to go. George taught me how to fend for myself, and I would do just that.

Today, I kept straying to the dream I had while conked out after we left Layla's. I shuddered to think that it was a link to my dead mother. The vision didn't offer any recognizable details that could help me identify the phantom as my mom. No precious clips of her combing my hair while she hummed me a song, or tickling me under a big fluffy blanket. Instead, it was a whirlwind of chaos and pain. The voice was vaguely familiar but far too morphed to say it was her for sure. Even if it *was* my mother, I was clueless about what she was trying to show me.

"Okay, your turn, cupcake." A ridiculously deep, angelic baritone, and his swift pat on my ass, quickly jerked me back to reality.

I spun and glared at Arkin. He was quite playful; more playful than I was in the mood for. Keeping my temper in check, I dismissed his childish gesture and settled into position on the center wrestling-mat.

Their training area was efficiently arranged. Large mats, weights, and an arsenal of unusual weaponry pinned along the factory wall filled the room. No guns or modern tools for these guys; they preferred mostly medieval looking objects like sais, katars, and flails.

"Hope you were paying attention." Arkin smirked as he circled the edge of the mat, eyeing me like prey. I made a mental note to listen closer when the angels were teaching before my attention honed onto the bare-chested, rippling body that was moving toward me in a predatory stance.

Sweat dripped from the wavy, copper hair that brushed his broad shoulders. His massive thighs flexed beneath blue jersey shorts as he continued to dance around me. My eyes traced the milky white, indigo-tipped wings stretching along either side of Arkin's fierce frame and then landed on his steady gaze.

"This is hardly fair," I griped. This was going to hurt.

"Who said it would be, kitten?" A shit-eating grin graced his gorgeous face. All his ripples contracted.

I recognized the sign to brace myself for a nasty blow, but as I watched the huge mass of angel barreling towards me at excessive speed, I wanted to charge him instead of bow down to him. My legs pushed forward before I knew what was happening and my feet pounded against the mat. He was the target at the end of my tunnel vision.

I smashed into his rigid torso, wrapping my arms around his waist. Sharp pains jabbed through my chest. Hitting Arkin was like smacking into concrete.

The angel engulfed me in his bulging arms and dragged me to the ground, trapping my much smaller body beneath his. My hands worked relentlessly, shoving at his shoulders and tugging at his elbows to get some space between us.

Arkin growled and grabbed my wrists, forcing them by my side, and then hooked his arms around mine. I wriggled under his weight, wincing at the restricting hold he had around my body. I could barely breathe. My confidence started to waver. He was too strong.

"We all have weak spots, kid," he assured me. This time he was attempting to help, not intimidate.

The first thing that came to mind was my knee striking his balls, but I couldn't get my leg loose either. His wing swept past my ear and the rustling sound of his feathers drew my focus. I struggled against his power as I considered the long, feathery limbs twitching above me. They seemed similar to a bird's, with the main bone of strength running across the top crest. His muscles and nerves were probably intertwined throughout the appendages, controlling their every movement.

I glowered at Arkin, exhausted and panting. His lips curled into a victorious smile, showing no intentions of slowing down or letting up. That pissed me off big time. I gathered what juice I had left and worked to free my arm from his grip. Finally, I wriggled a hand loose, yanking it from under the bend of his elbow. I wrapped my fingers around the soft arch of feathers behind his shoulder and squeezed.

A booming roar escaped his mouth. I jerked my hand away, afraid that I'd really caused him some damage. I didn't mean to. I thought that was what I was supposed to do. I thought the purpose of the lesson was to defeat him.

"Son of a...," he panted on my neck while curling his big body around me. The grumbling angel rolled off and pushed himself off the ground. "You learn fast," he said, stumbling to a nearby wall for support and hunching as if I *had* kneed him in the groin.

I scrambled to my feet then hurried to his side to examine his limp wing. "I'm so sorry! Are you okay?" I reached out to palpate the area I'd hurt.

"I'll be fine." He batted my hand away and took a few deep breaths. "How did you know?"

"I didn't. I just figured, if I were an angel, it would be a place of importance." I moved to place a comforting hand on his shoulder, but stopped when his wing cautiously flinched away from my gesture. "Did I do something wrong? Wasn't I supposed to defend myself?"

He snorted. "Yeah. Just didn't think you would figure our sweet spot out so soon." His caramel brown eyes peeked over at me forgivingly. "I'll be okay. Think my pride's hurt more than anything. Just wasn't expectin' it." He stretched out of his hunch and flapped his wings, stirring up a gust of wind that fluffed the stray hairs around my face. "Not so bad," he said, glancing at each massive appendage with satisfaction and then back at me. "It'll take a lot more than that to take me down, sweet cheeks." His hand reared back and smacked me on the ass again. "Besides, you pinch like a dame."

I ignored his incredibly inappropriate action and sexist remark. "So, that's how to hurt angels?"

"Yeah, one of the few ways, but keep it on the down-low." He leaned in close and placed a finger over my lips, then smirked. "Mm.

Soft lips, cupcake."

I rolled my eyes and swatted his finger.

"How do I defend myself from your...graces, is it?" Archard had mentioned something about dampening their graces around me. I assumed that was the mind-blowing need they invoked.

Arkin nodded as he pulled a ragged hand towel from the waistband of his shorts and blotted the sweat from his neck. "Well, we don't do it on purpose. It's just part of who we are." The angel shrugged and turned, leaning his back against the wall while his eyes roamed over the other angels sparring across the room from us.

"Human reactions are just a side effect." He smiled slyly, throwing me a sideways glance. "And not a bad one, I must say. I quite enjoy being adored."

I pursed my lips and shook my head disapprovingly. *What an arrogant asshole.* "I was told it's because we want to be linked to God and all that is heavenly so bad, we hunger for it?"

"Yeah, I guess you could put it like that. We symbolize the closeness to The Almighty that most of you were born with but have abandoned along your journey in life. We are a reminder of what you can have in the afterlife."

The buff angel sauntered over to a plastic office chair and snagged a water bottle sitting on the seat. He tilted his head back and squirted the liquid in his mouth like a pro football player, holding it inches from his face. He was cocky even when doing something as simple as taking a drink of water.

"How can I get past the overwhelming craving thing?" *And maybe past my inconvenient bond to Archard.*

"I'll handle this one, Arkin," a cool, low voice answered. We both turned to see a set of glimmering aqua eyes looking back at us.

Surprise, surprise.

"Our bond is the strongest. I should be the one to teach her." A smirk pulled at a corner of his divine lips, and I became curious about the pride dripping from his words.

If he was so proud of our connection, why did he leave me then?

"What if I don't want you to teach me?" I stiffened and crossed my arms over my chest in defiance.

"This could get very intense, Nevaeh. Would you rather Arkin see you at your worst, or someone who knows you better than you know yourself?"

The callousness I attempted to uphold crumbled like shattered glass. Not because I was afraid of what Arkin would think of me during what I figured would be a very degrading lesson, but because of the concerned pleading buried deep beneath Archard's expectant stare.

"I really don't think you want to do this with someone you barely know." My angel quietly advised.

"Wait a minute, bro. If she wants to be tested by my enticing moves, let her. She might enjoy it." Arkin's chest puffed up to demonstrate his masculinity. His all-too-famous conceited grin followed close behind.

"That's what I'm afraid of," Archard grumbled. He searched my face for a moment before locking his focus on the pumped up he-man snaking his arm around my waist. His eyes narrowed, measuring Arkin's gesture.

My insides fluttered to life with desire. Pure possessiveness glazed over his hardened features. A dangerous threat clouded his energy.

"You know what? I'm gonna go with him, Arkin." I smiled apologetically and shimmied out of his grip. He walked backwards, raising his hands in surrender, then joined a group of angels huddled on the far side of the room.

As we left the training room, I couldn't mistake the warmth

folding around me. That recurrent energy promising happiness, home, and sweet pleasures captured me inside its bubble. With its heat, my icy facade began to melt away, deeming me helpless against Archard's charm once again. He really had dampened his graces for me. I had not felt his sweet torture this strong since I asked him to leave me with Gavyn.

My heart skipped thinking about the deceived man I deserted at the café. I realized now that I should've spoken against Layla. I should've set things straight. He would've believed me, I'm sure of it. I feared it was too late though. Once trust is damaged, it's so hard to repair.

The heavy guilt and regret hanging on my shoulders lightened when a warm, smooth hand eased into mine. "Are you ready, Nevaeh?"

I nodded and surrendered to his beckoning graces as he led me farther down the hall. We passed one empty office after the next, making our way to the other end of the building; back to the room I woke in upon my arrival here, I assumed.

Anticipation fluttered in my stomach. The space between us was pleasantly charged. Delicious heat pulsed from his palm into mine. I inhaled a shaky breath, drawing in the alluring fragrance that was fast becoming my addiction. Each inhalation sprung to mind a new image pertaining to the aromas trailing behind him. At first, the smell of roses, homemade pies, and hugs; later, I smelled honey, bliss, and burning arousal.

It was vivid and intoxicating. I could've closed my eyes and needed only to follow his scent to know which direction to go. Oh, I was definitely in trouble. If I already wanted to give in to such a low hum of the graces that bound us, what was I going to do when he amped them up?

Archard opened the door to the room I remembered from the day before. He moved to the side and held an arm out, inviting me in. I angled myself sideways with my back pressed against the door jamb and squeezed past him through the sliver of space in the doorway. I absolutely refused to allow any part of me to brush against his hot, solid body, or those silky-soft wings. Being so close to him teased the straining passion inside me enough as it was.

Trying to ignore the yearning in my belly, I bit the inside of my cheek and concentrated on something less exciting. The room was simple and impersonal. The mattress and box spring rested on the floor against the north wall, piled high with a white, puffy comforter that mimicked clouds. My eyes skimmed over the small table I'd noticed yesterday, a gray office chair sitting in the corner, and a duffle bag half stuffed with clothes lying on the south wall.

Everything was pretty much the same as I remembered—except for one detail. A minor detail with a grand impact. The lighting. No harsh fluorescence buzzed from the ceiling. Instead, dozens of white candles flickered from all over the room. They lined the floors, throwing glowing halos against hard surfaces. It was wonderful. I watched the shadows leap across the walls like dancers in a ballet, completely amazed by the simple beauty of such a small change.

In one breath I was feeling warm fuzzies, and the very next I was thrown to my knees. A sudden blast of desire knocked the strength right out of me. This flood of emotion and physical craving caught me off guard and quickly grew to an intensity that dominated every function of my body. I groaned, rocking back and forth on my hands and knees, uncomfortable in my own skin. A hungry seed implanted itself in my heart and took root under my flesh. It was greedy for every last drop of love I could afford, which would never be enough.

Tears poured from my eyes. I kneeled on the floor, thirsting for approval, begging for love and forgiveness to feed the growing hunger within. The love and desire soon morphed into despair and sadness.

"What are you doing to me?" I cried.

Light fingertips traced from the crown of my head down to my neck, gently shifting my hair to one side. He lowered behind me and scooted in close. Archard wrapped his arms and legs around me, cocooning me within his grasp. The closer he got, the more I unraveled. "You have to feel the worst of it to comprehend," silky lips whispered in my ear, and then tenderly kissed my bare neck.

"Comprehend what? Why is this so different from what I normally feel around you? Why is there so much hurt and grief?" I buried my head into the crook of his elbow. My body trembled against his enveloping arms, legs, and chest.

Plush feathers encased us, pulling me tighter into him. "You have to remember your natural hunger for God and all that He is. What you were born with but have forgotten. You have to experience what it means to be without Him before you can appreciate the gift He's given you. You need to see what it's like for Him...being denied your love."

He nestled his face against my neck and held on relentlessly. "You have to feel what it's like to be completely severed from His embrace, so that you might understand that He's been *with* you all along." Sympathy seeped from his words. His tears trailed down my shoulder as Archard spoke. "So, you know that it is *you* who has abandoned *Him*."

Heart-wrenching sorrow filled me to the brim. Misery and anger swelled in my gut. There were so many emotions that I couldn't make sense of them all. "What does this have to do with your graces?" I hiccupped between cries, ready for the torture to end.

"The desire for us can't be overcome until you mend your rightful connection with Him. That can't be done if you fight Him." Archard's voice shook in my ear.

"I'm not fighting Him. I just can't be who you want me to be." I sucked in a lungful of air, trying to calm my unsteady breathing.

313

"Nevaeh, you fight Him, you fight yourself, and the goodness that He instilled in you every second that you choose not to take His side, every moment you distance yourself from what you were meant to be." He groaned harshly against my skin. "You are letting the demon in you run rampant through what you know is right." The agony emanating from him crushed mine in comparison.

"Why…why do you suffer with me now?" The question barely resonated from my mouth. My ability to think was becoming difficult.

"I do not suffer with you, Nevaeh. You are suffering with me. I'm merely letting you feel what I already know and feel every day since I've chosen to leave His loving arms for…." His speech slurred then ceased, the misery crippling him.

This was, by far, more destructive than the portals, than the other angels' graces, and the demons' threats. Even more shattering than George's wrongful ending. This was a demonstration of the poison running through my veins. It was humiliation.

The fleeting moments drove me closer to a cliff 's edge. I felt it coming closer, gaining speed. A dark nothing that would smother my light. An impending doom that would finally break me. Anticipation of the drop cut through the dreadful emotions racing in me. Archard's body grew rigid with mine, maybe to brace us against the fall—or perhaps to let me go one last time.

A rising humidity made the room almost unbearably hot. Bitter sweat dripped from our pores. The glowing halos flickered and shook, allowing black to fracture the light. Thick steam funneled around our bodies, searing my lungs as I struggled to control my erratic breathing. A hot gust of wind rushed through the room, thrashing our bodies back and forth.

Archard battled to keep his cocoon around me, squeezing me tighter, but his hands were slipping. His tormented yell deafened my ears, frightening me even more. I wiggled around to see anything other than flickering shadows writhing across the floorboards, but his grip was too tight. His massive wings sheltered me from the mayhem beyond.

"Archard! What's happening?" I screamed through gritted teeth.

The burden of his emotions drilled into my heart even deeper. Only guttural groans sounded from his heavenly mouth. Then my skin began to scorch. Fiery heat blistered my toes, climbing up my legs. I realized Archard was attempting to shield me from the igniting flames. He felt the burn long before I did, but continued to hold me.

The throbbing blaze took over. I begged for an ending, for the pain to vanish, for *his* pain to be relieved.

Just as I gave up, the candles blew out. Complete darkness prevailed. I gasped as my legs stretched out from under me, no longer supported by a floor, and the sensation of falling tickled my stomach. We were plunging into an eerily calm nothingness. The room had disappeared as if the whole world was swept away by a tornado.

I allowed my arms to relax and sail on the current of wind whizzing around us. I reveled in the cool breeze now blasting upwards against my charred skin, dulling the throbbing pain as we plummeted down.

"Archard?"

He didn't answer. His arms loosened from around me, and he drifted away. I panicked, swiping at the empty air, trying to find his unconscious body in the dark, but I only knocked him farther out of reach. The weight of his limp wings grazed my back, then he was gone.

"Archard! Wake up," I screamed.

The soundless repose of descent turned into a terrifying plunge into something unknown. The more I reached for Archard, the faster I fell.

Then, it came.

The severance.

It ripped through me, effortlessly, like a knife through butter. Quick but not painless. This pain was different from the aching loss of George. It was different from the heartbreaking sting of, once again, losing my angel. Even what I'd experienced minutes before, in the room, was too physical in comparison. This cut to an entirely new level. It snatched the life force from my body and left only a hollow shell.

Until this moment, I never realized the love that surrounded me. All the times I felt alone were nothing compared to the complete isolation I was experiencing now. I understood now that every kind act on earth was a sign of His love. The true love that I had forgotten and abandoned along the way.

The misery of this emptiness was debilitating. I couldn't force myself to move, to breathe, or even want to anymore. My very being was pointless now. My vacant soul *was* the nothingness that I'd felt rising to meet me at the cliff's edge. I had nothing left to reach for; not a single thing to latch onto in the silent darkness of my own personal hell. The light that I never knew was there snuffed out in a mere microsecond.

CHAPTER TWENTY-FOUR

Depths Of My Soul

I lay in the shadows of my emptiness, raw and alone, wondering if this would be how I spent my eternity. Futureless, without the hope of meeting George or my mother in a peaceful afterlife.

I had finally realized that the love of God was there the whole time. Traces of it wound into my everyday life; George's protective ways, Gavyn's comforting touch, and the friendly smiles of countless people around me.

I should've recognized those things as a blessing long ago. Instead, I was too stubborn to see it. Now I was on my own, static in this void.

Guilt of the life I led weighed upon me. My heart throbbed as much as my burnt flesh. I attempted to gather myself and search for Archard, but I couldn't force even a finger to flinch. It was as if the strings of Heaven, which kept me afloat through life, were snipped by a giant pair of scissors, leaving me as nothing more than a soulless rag doll. I didn't want to stay in this place. I didn't want to waste away as an empty, lonely husk.

There was too much silence. I couldn't even hear the incessant beating of my heart or my lungs deflating against labored breaths. I waited for Archard to call for me but knew if he did, I wouldn't be able to hear him either.

I sank into the desolate dark, pondering over the many gruesome ways that the demons would tortured George's soul, tearing his essence to shreds.

I failed him.

Lord, I know I haven't done anything that deserves your attention, but please save him somehow. He doesn't deserve that kind of punishment, I prayed.

No one answered, but in the quiet oblivion, I noticed a white glow approaching from the distance. My heart sped up.

"Archard." His name rushed across my dry lips.

The glowing orb jetted away. "No. Wait. Please come back," I begged.

I grunted, pressing my palms to the surface beneath me, and raised up. My arms gave out. My face hit the ground. I took a deep breath and pushed up again. This time I was able to stand; walking was another matter. It felt like I was dragging a car behind me, but I trudged along, chasing the only thing visible in this place, ignoring the sense of impending doom that was tying knots in my stomach. I had to find a way out. I had to find Archard.

As I advanced, nearly catching up with the orb, the muscles in my back stretched and stiffened, making it harder to move in fluid motions. My joints grinded. I was convinced my bones might give out, or even push through my skin, at any moment. I contemplated stopping, but what if Archard is alone too, waiting on me to find him? My eyes focused on the gliding sphere of light, and I forced myself to move forward. It found me for a reason. I needed to know what that reason was. I grunted and huffed, lurching myself down the unending path behind the glowing ball.

After miles and miles of following it through the endless dark, I slowed, panting and ready to quit. My feet stumbled, and I drifted to the side, gasping in shock when my hand slapped against a wall with sharp ridges roughening its surface. I looked up to see the orb's glow illuminating a doorway a few paces ahead. The light disappeared through the door, bathing me in pitch black once again.

My nerves tingled, warning me against following. I glanced over my shoulder into the black nothingness behind me and considered turning back. It was hard to ignore the caution signs screaming at me, but I refocused my attention in the direction of the doorway. I took a heavy step forward, then another.

As I crossed the threshold, the dim glow became visible again. The sudden sensation of cold metal chilled my hand. It took a moment for my vision to adjust before I saw the shiny, silver blade tucked comfortably within my grasp. I brushed away the intriguing question of how the blade mysteriously made its way into my hand and searched for the light.

I squinted my eyes and inspected the room I'd entered. It wasn't long before I realized where the floating orb led me. I cringed, wrapping my arms around my anxious midsection, and glanced back at the door — the large, iron slab — behind me, contemplating the urge to run.

My gaze wandered to the chair sitting in the center of the floor — a high-backed Victorian with paisley cushions. It was empty though. Memories of the pretty woman that occupied it before flashed through my mind. Air rushed in and out of my heaving chest. I closed my eyes and covered them with my empty hand, pressing my fingertips against my eyelids until the images left.

I spun in a circle, scanning the shadowy perimeter for signs of the demon that tortured the lady. No disturbing forms lurked in the corners, no shrill screams reverberated against the walls, and there was no woman waiting for her slashing. But still, the ominous feeling of evil hung grimly in the room.

The bubble of light began to glide in a slow circle around the edge of the room, drawing my attention to a large, silvery mirror on the wall to my right. As I lifted and lowered one unsteady foot and then the other, the pain in my weakening joints threatened to let me fall. I reached out for the wall, using it to support my body as I inched closer to the reflective surface with stiff, jerky movements.

I maneuvered myself in front of the glassy rectangle and pressed my hands on either side to keep myself upright. Puffs of labored breaths fogged up the area of mirror in front of my face. The orb drifted into the reflection, stilling just behind my right shoulder, distracting me from the tiny smudges of moisture that vanished and reappeared under my slowing breaths. I lifted my head and gaped at the reflection illuminated before me.

I jerked away in terror, choking on a gasp. The monster that haunted my memories of this prison from Hell stared back at me from the mirror. I wanted to run but could barely take one step.

I swallowed my fear and steadied myself, hoping it was only an illusion. We faced each other at close range, our gazes sliding over the other's image, memorizing every detail. Blood stained bones poked through wrinkled, charred skin. Dead eyes mindlessly bored into mine.

I'd expected the monster to jump through the mirror, but we stood there for the longest time, and it made no attempt to attack. I peered into its charcoal eyes, hoping to detect some hint of remorse or goodness, but I quickly became aware that there was no understanding this thing. The demon was now a vile product of the life it led before. How much evil must a person commit to turn into such a creature?

I raised a hand to touch the mirror, freezing in place when the demon did the same.

Is it playing games with me?

My curiosity got the upper hand. I had to know if the surface was solid. Would it keep the monster trapped behind the reflection, or was it another portal that would give way when the monster was ready to come after me? Even as horror lumped in my throat, I leaned toward the reflection and lightly traced a fingertip across it.

The real terror hit me like a brick wall. Every move I made, the demon mimicked perfectly; every stroke, every pause. My heart sank.

The stammered movements, the stiff, heavy limbs—I was morphing into this thing all along.

Bile worked its way up from my sour stomach. I hunched over and puked uncontrollably from my rotted mouth. The sound of my voice was harsh and screechy as I groaned against the urge to continue vomiting.

How did this happen?

I rubbed my eyes, attempting to scrub the image from my memory. I couldn't be the horrid thing in the mirror.

This had to be a dream.

I lowered my hands, holding them out in front of me. They were nearly black and charred to the bone with jagged, onyx-colored nails protruding from my fingers. My knobby knees collapsed to the floor. I peered over at the evolving form in the mirror as it lowered to the same position and continued its last transitions.

A blood-curdling scream erupted from my mouth as decrepit vertebrae sliced through the thin layer of flesh on my back. Strangely, the scream dwindled half-way through, and became a raspy moan. I was enjoying the delicious burning pain that ignited from the bones piercing my leathery skin. That frightened me more than anything. With my soul vacant, a yearning to succumb to this new evil form took flight like a phoenix.

Stunned from what was happening inside me, I didn't hear my name being called for some time. My demented gaze jumped from the reflection of myself to a figure behind me. It wriggled in the chair, violently pulling against restraints of some sort, yelling at me breathlessly.

I suddenly remembered the blade in my hand again. The cold metal bit into my broken, blistered flesh, begging me to drench it in blood. I glanced back at the glossy surface. The monster in the mirror's mouth curled into a disturbingly wicked smile.

The pleasure of the darkness rolled through my veins, filling me with renewed strength. Though my movements were still jerky and painful, I didn't hesitate to rise and stretch my much larger frame. The unnatural grinding and snapping of my new body yielded tears of anguish and freedom simultaneously.

I still couldn't understand how agony could bring so much pleasure. Really, I didn't care. I just knew I liked it, and I wanted more.

The persistent creature continued calling out to me from the chair. I snarled at the sound—too beautiful for my ears to tolerate. I shuddered over to the being, scrutinizing every disgusting detail of his existence.

"Nevaeh!" he screamed.

I roared to drown out the offensive righteousness of his voice.

The pureness of his white wings warned me to retreat into hiding. The very essence of this creature threatened to smite everything I was now, but the desire to bloody those pretty feathers was stronger than my urge to run.

As I shuffled around the prisoner, he tugged at the iron shackles holding him hostage. The ends of his bound wings twitched helplessly along the floor.

The instant I saw my clawed foot lift, a tiny voice in my head pleaded against it, but I ignored it. I stomped on the delicate, plum-tipped feathers and grinded them into the ground.

"Nevaeh!" he roared. "What are you doing?"

His voice assaulted my ears. My insides seethed with anger.

"Stop this. It's not who you are. You know that," the angel shrieked.

I lifted my foot from his wing, pleased with myself, and shuffled in front of him. He growled, and a blast of light shot out from his chest, blinding me as if a thousand laser beams had burned my eyes out. I crouched away, screeching, shielding my face in the crook of my elbow. From the corner of my eye, I saw the crimson blood trailing from his broken wing lying limply across the dirty ground.

Sight of the sticky blood captured my attention. I wanted more. I thirsted for velvety, red ribbons to stream against his pure skin, slow and steady. My lips pulled tight against sharp teeth. A delighted groan worked its way out of my throat, reverberating harshly through my heavy skull.

"Nevaeh, look at me!" He begged, tears spilling from his desperate eyes. Hints of defeat crept in and weakened the confidence in his expression. I sensed the notion of surrender crossing his mind, and that empowered me. I lifted my face to the ceiling and inhaled deeply. Fear. It oozed from his pores. Soon, I would make him beg for death.

I jerked my massive arm upwards, watching the shiny blade raise in my hand. The anticipation of bleeding the fucking angel until he was a lifeless heap at my feet excited me beyond measure.

In one stuttered motion, I slid the metal into the flesh of his face. I stumbled back in ecstasy, relishing in the metallic odor wafting through the air and the vision of an angel hemorrhaging from cheek to cheek.

He stopped his relentless begging but wasn't ready to ask for death—yet. Four more times, I sunk the blade into his flesh, violently shredding his repulsive beauty.

As the pleasure heightened with another strike, my vision suddenly blurred. I couldn't focus, couldn't revel in my work. Pictures of George splashed through my thoughts. His soul bound and broken just as the angel sitting before me. I shook my heavy head, but the offensive images kept coming.

My anguished screeches echoed off the walls, and I dropped clumsily to my boney knees. Memories flooded my sight, reminding me of a life beyond this place. The abrasive floor tore my burnt skin as I squirmed on the ground, trying to escape the visions.

"Nevaeh," the angel whispered, "this is not who you want to be. Listen to your gut. You are not evil. You can't let it take over." His words shook and slurred from the damage I had caused. "I didn't leave Heaven so you could become this monster, dammit."

A disembodied voice lingered inside me, barely audible. "He's right, ya know." I almost didn't recognize it. "Think of how you felt when you fell with Archard. Think of the emptiness. We don't want to become this!" Each word grew louder and louder, pushing to the forefront of my conscience. "We can't give up, knowing the things we know now. Knowing how much God loves us." I recognized the voice as the goodness I'd left behind when I surrendered to my inner monster—when I abandoned hope. "We can't let George's death be in vain."

Hot, tar-like tears flowed down my hideous face. I could feel the poison in my veins scrambling to desecrate every part of my inner conscience, but it was failing.

I couldn't continue in this path, it wasn't right. It *wasn't* who I wanted to be.

The changing images stopped on a single picture. It was a memory of George and I cuddled under a thin, shabby blanket, taking shelter under a bridge. I slept peacefully while he watched over me with unconditional love in his eyes.

I knew what needed to be done. The sharp claws of rage and evil retracted from my heart. Love and hope flooded me, washing away the evil within seconds.

My muscles relaxed. Loud pops and snaps rang in my ears as my bones relocated themselves back into their proper places. I rocked back and forth on my hands and knees, enduring the agony of transforming back to the being I was before. My eyes drifted to the hand bracing my weight off the floor and watched the wrinkled, burnt skin covering my fingers smooth out and lighten to its original color.

As the last of the transformation finished, I drew in a deep breath of relief and sat back on my feet, appreciating my very normal, very human looking hands. I felt whole again, spirit intact. "Thank you," I whispered to God, knowing he gave me the strength I needed to fight my haunting wickedness.

I didn't know what would happen from that point on, but if I made it out of here, I would find a way to release George. I had to learn to let my soul trust and have faith, especially if I was going to overcome the challenges I knew were ahead.

I eased down to the floor, suddenly too tired to hold myself upright.

"Nevaeh. Nevaeh?"

I heard Archard saying my name, but soon even that faded under the exhaustion that took over my body. The demonic transition and emotional roller-coaster took one hell of a toll on my body—and my mind.

One last thought fixed itself inside my skull before I shut down completely; the image of my angel bleeding, and the pain I'd caused him all along, etched into my memories. Somehow, I would tell him how sorry I was. I would make it up to him.

I retreated to a deep sleep, confident that someone watched over me.

CHAPTER TWENTY-FIVE

Lesson Learned

"Nevaeh."

I woke to the sweet whisper of my name and a strong hand smoothing the hair from my face. Every breath was full of his honeyed scent.

"Nevaeh, it's time to go," he coaxed. I felt safe and happy just to be near him—until I remembered where I was. My eyes flew open. I prayed to be out of the shadowy void, to see his face looking back at me.

"Archard?" There was only darkness, but I could feel him close to me. Relief came when I felt his warm skin under my fingertips.

"I'm here. Let's get you home." He slid his arms under my back and knees, lifting my limp body from the ground. I rested my head against his chest, enjoying the peaceful sound of his heart thumping in my ear. He hoisted us upward with one strong swoop of his wings. I had no idea where we were going, but it didn't matter because I was with him.

The cool breeze drifted across my skin as he pumped his massive wings beside us.

"Where are we going?" I asked.

"I told you. Home," he answered softly, his grip tightening around me.

"I thought I was stuck here." Tears filled my eyes, thankful to escape.

"Nevaeh, this place...it's not permanent. I brought you here so you could experience what you needed in order to help you understand the severity of your choices." The warmth of his sigh caressed my forehead. "You needed to see what could happen if you chose the other side, and how vulnerable you are if you don't make a choice at all." His thumb reached from its place on my shoulder and caressed my neck. "And most importantly, you needed to see what it was to lose something you didn't know you had."

"God's love." Tears trickled down my cheek. I felt ashamed as I replayed the awful journey in my mind. Haunting memories of Archard tied to the chair rushed in, filling me with guilt. "What did you mean when you said you didn't leave Heaven for me to become the monster I became?"

"Just rest. We can talk about it when we get back."

He still refused to give the answers I needed.

"How are we going to get back?"

"I have my own ways of opening the portals," he responded, and I could hear the hint of a smile behind his words.

I noticed, as we soared through the abyss, the urges I had towards Archard were different from before. There was still an unmistakable bond drawing me to him like a moth to a flame, but instead of the intense lust, I just...loved him. I could see that, even without his graces taking effect on me, whatever lingered between us was Heaven-made — ingrained in us when God kissed our souls to life. I wasn't sure that any amount of denying him would take away the emotions he invoked in me. And, after he'd shown me the misery he endured on Earth, I couldn't deny him if I wanted to.

The soothing air glided over our bodies as we flew upwards. Archard's wings began beating faster. We were still engulfed in darkness, but every once in a while, his shiny metal feathers reflected some far away light above us.

We traveled farther and farther through the black chasm of my soul, but finally, the light that I saw became brighter and clearer. My eyes focused on a watery surface, like Malach's portal. I remembered the way the rain halted, the wind thrashed at my face, and the walls buckled. The anticipation of experiencing that chaos again tightened my belly even though our dark atmosphere remained peaceful and undisturbed.

I wrapped my arms around Archard's neck and buried my head in his strong chest, bracing for the turbulence I feared was ahead. Sounds of crashing and whining penetrated the watery opening from the other side, but we remained in a bubble of serenity. The closer we got, the louder the sounds of wind and destruction became. Somewhere, there was a structure crumbling and hurricane force winds.

I peeked up at Archard's tired face. "Are we almost there?"

He held me tighter, his fingers digging into my skin. "Cover your ears," he commanded.

I did as he said, but in the end, it really didn't help. His chest vibrated against my arm so powerfully I thought he might explode. Sound emerged from his mouth, disrupting the silence with a gorgeous melody of orchestral notes. His face strained as he shouted out in his heavenly language.

We closed the distance to the portal at an alarming speed. The surface above us spiraled into a funnel of silver liquid. The music crossing Archard's lips echoed louder, seeming to break open the portal. The intensity of his voice stabbed at my ears like a million tiny needles; warm blood trickled between my fingers. I cupped my ears tighter, attempting to block out the sound.

Then, just as we were about to go through the portal, my angel came to an abrupt stop. His massive wings wrapped around me protectively, and we fell. Strangely, it wasn't a fall downward. We plummeted up into the opening—with a reversed gravity pulling toward it.

The air silenced once we broke the portal's veil. I pressed my frame into Archard's chest with anticipation. Cool liquid splashed against my skin and dried instantly. Time, and everything that made the world go around, seemed to stop on a dime.

Considering we flew up to get to the portal, I expected us to enter through the floor. I quickly realized I was wrong. Archard threw open his wings, once we were on the other side, and spanned them across the room, slowing our speed and controlling our shift in direction, as we dropped in through the ceiling and created an arch with our bodies. With barely enough space to accommodate Archard's massive appendages, let alone our dive-in landing, my butt grazed the floor just before he navigated us into an upright position. It was like that "Oh, shit" moment when you dive into a pool and realize you've misjudged the depth, then try not to break your neck on the bottom.

His breathing slowed, and he carefully set me on the ground. My eyes wandered over our surroundings, taking in the destruction that occurred from our arrival. We were back in Archard's room at the factory again. Hard, white puddles dotted the floor where the candles had melted. The fluffy blanket was shredded to bits and singed in some places. Cracks had formed along the ash-covered walls under the impact of our arrival.

Archard groaned behind me, and I instantly turned, focusing on his stumbling movement to the center of the room. Aside from looking worn-out, his skin was flawless; even his feathers were remarkably clean and neatly tucked against his back.

He fell to his knees with outstretched arms. His hands smacked into one another in front of him, creating a thunderous boom. I flinched, startle by the unexpected sound. He repeated this three more times, blasting a ripple of energy outward into the atmosphere that repaired the room. Everything moved in reverse like time rewinding around us; the candles pooled back into small pillars, the comforter seamlessly stitched itself together and renewed the burnt pieces, and the walls flattened and smoothed around us.

Within minutes, our surroundings looked as though we'd never left. Soft candle light played happily along the smooth walls, and the blanket invited us to crawl into bed. The only thing different was me.

I left this room with a damaged soul, denying myself the love God so freely gave, refusing to put my faith in anything. I returned mended and with an understanding I didn't have before.

"Are you okay, Nevaeh?"

"Yeah, I'm fine," I answered as Archard collapsed on the floor. I gasped and dropped by his side, frantically shaking his shoulders, but he didn't wake. His heavy body lay unresponsive at my knees. "Help! Someone help me!" I screamed, hoping that one of the other angels would hear. I scooted to his head and cradled it in my lap, praying for him to open his eyes.

Arkin barreled through the door seconds later, panting. "What's going on?"

"I don't know. He just crashed to the floor." My vision blurred as I fought to restrain my tears. "We came through the portal and he just...he fell." My voice shook uncontrollably. I worried that Archard was in more pain or harm because of me.

"You came through a portal?" Arkin stopped moving and stared at me with steel eyes, and then looked down at Archard. "Purgatory," he said.

"What? No...I don't know." I pondered the thought for a moment, growing more frustrated by the possibility that Archard might have taken me somewhere like Purgatory—not that I knew what that meant, but I sure-as-shit knew it wasn't somewhere I was supposed to go by the disappointed expression on Arkin's face. "Are you going to help him or not?" I snapped back, not caring to explain where we'd gone.

"No need to get feisty, kitten," he retorted. His surprised expression relaxed, and his lips tightened into a smirk. "I see he's taken care of your little issue of succumbing to our graces." Arkin stepped closer and kneeled beside Archard. He placed a hand on my angel's chest as I watched in hopeful silence. "He'll be peachy before you know it. He just needs some rest." Arkin smiled at me reassuringly and winked while making a clicking sound with his mouth.

I managed to calm myself enough that I didn't choke on my words. "What's wrong with him?"

He grabbed Archard's arms and pulled him upright. "It takes a lot out of us when we go through a portal, Nevaeh." Arkin hoisted the sleeping angel over his shoulder, then laid him on the bed. "We're not supposed to cross portals." He grunted, maneuvering Archard into a comfortable position. I was impressed with how gentle the strong, cocky angel was when handling his brother.

"I've seen an angel cross a portal before with no problem." Malach came to mind as I sat on the bed next to Archard.

"What angel have you seen?" Arkin asked, narrowing his eyes at me.

"An Archangel," I responded sheepishly.

"Hmm. And I was under the impression that we were the only angels that cared." He grinned.

"Maybe...maybe not." I dropped my gaze to the unconscious being beside me. The room filled with an awkward silence. Arkin waited for me to tell him what I knew, but I decided to ignore any further conversation on the topic for now.

"Ya know, he's not the only one that made sacrifices for you, Nevaeh," he added, sounding offended by my secrecy.

I looked into the hurt eyes staring at me from the other side of the bed. "I'm sorry," I whispered. "There are some people that were with me in the beginning of this mess...I'm not sure where I stand with them anymore, and I'm having a hard time knowing who to trust. Right now, I can barely trust myself. I'm working on it though."

"You can trust us."

"Arkin, it's not that easy. There is so much I don't know. So much that's kept from me." I nudged my chin towards Archard. "I just need someone to give me some straight answers." Tears welled in my eyes.

His eyes fixed on Archard as he mulled through something in his mind. "What do you want to know?" he asked after a few moments of what appeared to be some serious consideration.

"Why me?" I whimpered. "Why George?"

"George was sent to you for protection. He did what was asked of him, but I suspect the others found out what you are and saw an opportunity to persuade you. Unfortunately, he became another soul lost in the battle." His gaze darted to mine. "And you, cupcake...you are The Clavis. You *are* what God made you. You're gonna do great things in his name. There's no need for more explanation than that."

I didn't argue, but I still wasn't sure about my part in all this. "The demons said I only had a week to save George. Are we too late?" I choked out the words as I wiped my tears away with the back of my hand. "Can I still save him?"

"Nevaeh, by my count, you've only been gone one day, but I don't know how you plan on getting to him without giving yourself up in the process."

I knew what the right thing to do was—declare myself Light

Celatum—and I truly wanted to do the right thing, but I wasn't quite ready to commit, not until I could find a way to get George's soul where it belonged. Besides that, I still needed answers, and maybe holding off on my choice just a little longer would encourage the angels to give up information I was missing.

"Why was George sent to protect me? What happened to my family, Arkin?"

He sighed heavily, emotions torn again. "All I know is that your mom didn't die like you were told. She just sorta went away." He paused and glanced at Archard lying motionless on the bed, making sure he was still unconscious. "Your grandmother was your caretaker until the demons found you. Archard stayed too close, and they figured out that something was special about you. Once he drew their attention to you, they could smell the Celatum in your blood. He unintentionally led them straight to you, despite your family's efforts to keep you hidden."

"Wait. How could my mom just disappear? Don't guardians have some kind of tracking device on their people?"

He smiled slyly, "We do...until they opt for the other side. Her angel went rogue too. It's kinda hard to track when you don't have a lead or connection, sweet cheeks."

"So, she's Dark?" I buried the fear bubbling up as I thought about the person, or creature, she might be after all this time.

"We don't know for sure. It's just our best guess," he answered. "What about Archard? I thought Guardians were supposed to stay close to humans. How was he *too* close?" My eyes wandered to my angel's hand resting on the bed next to mine.

"We stay close, but invisible, to our charges. He appeared to you one day. You were hiding in a thicket. The demons were closing in on you from the branches. I'm sure you don't remember. You were so young." He shook his head and smiled sweetly at the memory of me as a child. "Archard grabbed you from the darkness and saved you. That was the demons' first clue. Most of us just help from the sidelines. We let you make your own choices, but gently nudge in times of danger." He moved his hands in a soft pushing motion.

"I do remember that. It was one of my few memories on the farm. Hell, it's one of the few memories I have period."

"Well, you held onto it for quite some time. A few years, actually. You knew you were different from the other kids. It became harder for Theora to keep you safe and hide what you were. The demons swarmed your house one night. She took you to a boat, miles away, and planned on running with you." Arkin lowered his gaze to the floor, his lips settling into a frown. "That's when something happened, and we lost track of you."

Flashes of one of my dreams replayed in my mind. The old lady with a young girl, it was her and me.

"What happened, Arkin?"

The palpable heaviness of heartache crept through the room, and I could see that the recollection was painful for him. "We were on the boat with you and Theora, trying to figure out how to keep you safe. The demons had followed us and clouded the air, trapping us from all sides. We fended them off, by using our holy powers. The first chance we got, we escaped. Archard and I steered the boat under a bridge far away from them. That's where the three of us decided to erase your memories. It was too dangerous for you to carry the knowledge of our world any longer; He should've never let you see. The more you knew, the easier they would find you." His eyes darkened with regret. "We knew you were special, too. We just didn't know why until much later."

Shocked and mad as hell, I glared at him, teeth grinding and nostrils flaring. "I can't believe you guys would do something like that. What about this free will you keep talking about?" They took my childhood away.

He ignored my outburst and continued. "That was when we gave up our Holiness for you, Nevaeh. Theora was old and knew she wasn't able to take care of you anymore. Not like you needed." A single tear rolled down his cheek. "Archard and I gave it up to stay here on Earth and look after you until the day you became a Celata."

"A lot of good that did," I spat, crossing my arms over my chest.

I couldn't look at either of them. I rose from the bed and paced to a lonely corner of the room, wanting so badly to leave. I should've known the information I was searching for might not have been what I actually wanted to hear.

Squeaking broke the silence when Arkin dragged the only chair in the room across the floor. I turned to find him sitting next to Archard, his elbows pressing firmly into his knees and his forehead resting on top of his clasped hands. He took a deep breath. "It weakened us when our Holiness ripped away from our souls. It was five minutes of torture that seemed like an eternity." A tear fell from between his hands and soaked into his jeans. "And in those five minutes, the demons caught back up with us. I remember lying on the floor of the boat next to Archard, paralyzed in unimaginable pain, while Theora tried to row us out of danger. Her failing body couldn't steer the boat. We capsized just as the demons were about to grab you."

He shuddered. Some of my anger toward them melted away. I could sympathize with what they experienced. The helplessness, the pain, even the feeling of my soul ripping away offered some insight to what they must have felt during those moments.

He sat back and wiped his glossy eyes with the palms of his massive hand. "We all went under. You were gone. Theora's body had washed up on a bank a few miles down when we found her." His stare grew distant, perhaps picturing what happened. He lost more than his Holiness that day.

"Arkin?" He jerked when the sound of my voice interrupted his thoughts. "Were you my grandmother's Guardian?"

He didn't nod, shrug, or even grimace. "She wanted to protect you above herself. She begged and begged despite my unwillingness. It was almost like she knew what you were to become." He shook his head slowly. "She loved you so much."

From the corner of my eye, I saw Archard's hand reach out and touch Arkin's leg. "Sorry, man, she needed to know," Arkin apologized.

Archard nodded his head in approval. The two brothers locked hands and stared at each other for a short moment, comforting the pain they had shared for so long.

"How long have you known about me? How long did it take you to find me?" I asked quietly, changing the subject.

Arkin glanced at Archard, silently asking for permission to continue answering my questions. Archard swiped his hand through the air, granting him consent. "Honestly, we've searched all these years for you. Found some other Celatum along the way, and other Guardians that had gone rogue for their own reasons. We just kinda joined forces, I guess, without even questioning it. We didn't find you until your angel here bumped into you on the steps of that cafe." He grinned and looked to Archard again, waiting for him to take over.

"The moment I touched you, I knew who you were. I'd expected us to find each other much sooner, but somehow, we didn't. Maybe I wasn't supposed to. George seemed to be doing a much better job than me." Archard smiled. "Ya know, he knew exactly what I was talking about when I asked him about you. He said another angel had shown him how important you were when he found you. He just didn't know what to call you." The angels snickered together and exchanged knowing glances. "The poor guy didn't know that in his drunken stupor he had met God himself."

I thought about the dream I had the day Margie was murdered. I recalled the vision of God leading George to me. "George took care of me, knowing what I am?" I assumed God just pushed him in my direction and asked him to look after me. I never knew that George had any clue about this side of me, or that he remembered the night he found me clearly enough to understand he'd met a supernatural being.

"Cupcake, he didn't just know, he accepted it. He agreed to keep you hidden." Arkin grinned proudly. "Even from yourself."

I snorted, remembering the recent events that led me to ask George for help. He knew I wasn't crazy the whole time, but he couldn't say anything without potentially putting me in danger with the demons.

Archard wriggled himself up in the bed and rested against the wall. "George said the angel told him you were different than the other Celatum. That you would be able to do things no one else could."

"So, that's why you think I'm The Clavis?"

Arkin's head bobbed, and he leaned forward, grinning from ear to ear. "We've known you were Celatum since you were very small, but —"

Archard cut the other angel off. "You are the only Celata we've known that can portal jump. That is a rare trait." His hand trembled from exhaustion while he patted the area of the bed next to him, inviting me to sit.

I hesitated, then walked towards him and lowered to the bed. Something told me he was withholding information again. I decided to let it go for now and trust that they would tell me when the time was right.

"What did you say to George before he died?" I asked Archard.

"I thanked him for guarding you in my place. I told him that he'd done a wonderful job and many angels would carry him to his place in Heaven." Regret furrowed his brow. "I told him that he could let go because you would continue to be protected. Unfortunately, not knowing your true gifts has made protecting you a little harder than I expected."

It was my turn to release some information. I took a deep breath and exhaled. "There's a book called 'The Clavis'. Do you know anything about it?"

The two angels tensed and looked at each other with worry on their faces. "We've heard that there was a book, yes. There are too many rumors about it though. We weren't sure what to believe. Some of the other guardians knew stories about The Clavis, but only bits and pieces. Nothing to give us any evidence that there was really a book or what might be written in it. We didn't even have a decent lead on how to find the origins of the rumors," Archard responded.

"Stories? There's more than one?"

"Yes. Some say you are a prophet. Others claim you to be a demon that will bring down the human race." The furrow deepened between Archard's brows.

"So, your guys don't know what is going to happen either." I was disappointed that not even the tales of The Clavis could show me some direction.

"Look here, cupcake, no one knows the truth because it hasn't happened, yet. It's all up to you how the real story ends. So, what if there is a book about The Clavis? That doesn't mean what's inside can't change." Arkin winked and smirked at me. "You are The Clavis as far as the angels here are concerned. We have faith that you will do what is best to fulfill God's plan for you. When the time comes, you alone will know what that is."

My shoulders suddenly felt pressured by the burden he placed on them. "How can you have so much faith in me? You guys barely know me."

Archard took my hand and encased it in his. "We have faith because we can feel it, and that's all we need." He squeezed my hand tighter and pulled it to his chest. "Besides, I know you better than you know yourself." His aqua eyes peered into mine. "I've been inside that head more times than you know."

Flashes of the mysterious being I had sensed in the bathroom at the Hall, and my first night at the café, appeared in my mind. Then, the whispering in the alley after I saw Archard watching me from the sidewalk. That was all him warning me and trying to get me to open up to him.

Shivers climbed up my spine, and I understood that what he said was completely true. I felt a deep and forbidden love pulsating from his body. The way he looked at me claimed my heart.

Arkin cleared his throat loudly, obviously trying to break the moment between Archard and me. "Man, it sure would help if we had some more leads, or maybe knew someone to interrogate for details." He raised a cocky eyebrow in my direction, eyeing me expectantly.

"Alright, alright. I may know someone that can help. I'll need to go to Gavyn's. I think he knows how to get in touch with the Archangel. That's if he'll talk to me." I hung my head in dread. I didn't want to talk to Gavyn. I didn't want to face the fact that I'd lied to him.

Archard grabbed my chin and forced me to look at him. "You'll feel better if you tell him the truth. I'm sure he has already forgiven you." He smiled, his face full of compassion.

Arkin clapped his hands and rubbed his palms together, beaming at me with eager eyes.

"So, which Archangel are we going to talk to?"

"Um, *I'll* be talking to Malach. You guys can stay here."

Both angels protested at once, heads shaking and arms waving in the air. "There is no fucking way," Archard argued.

Judging by the language he used, my angel would oversee every move I made from now on. I didn't know whether to be upset that they were arguing with me or flattered that they were looking out for me.

"Unless you're ready to make your choice right now, you won't be going anywhere alone. There's too much risk." His beautiful, ocean eyes lowered to the floor. "I will not leave you without a Guardian again."

"Okay then, tomorrow. We'll go see Gavyn and find out if he can contact Malach." I caressed Archard's twitching jaw and savored the roughness of his stubble against my thumb. "Tonight, we both need to rest."

CHAPTER TWENTY-SIX

A Minute Too Late

Archard walked by my side as close as he could without touching me, but it didn't take his touch to feel the sparks of power surging between us. He glanced at me warily from the corner of his eye, and I got the feeling he suspected I would run at any minute. I had no intention of it — right now.

I understood a little more about what he had given up for me. But there were still so many things left unsaid after our conversation last night. I continued to wonder about his love for me. Was it just a bond between a ward and his charge, or did he feel the "something more" that I experienced?

Arkin flanked my left, his floor-length, brown-leather jacket patting against his legs as he strutted along our route to Joe's. I noticed the graces that were now wasted on me worked more than efficiently on the poor schmucks rushing by us. He made it a point to lessen them before we left the factory, but they slowed their pace and intently watched him with pining in their eyes, even after we passed.

It was easy to pick out the troubled souls by the intensity of yearning they displayed. I sympathized with them, knowing what they felt when so close to the angels. It didn't help that an occasional flux of energy radiated around us, which I could only guess was Arkin teasing them. Luckily, he tested me in the process. I found I could resist the angels enough to function like a normal person among them.

Whatever realizations I'd come to while in Purgatory—more comfortably labeled as the void of my soul, since I knew nothing about it as of yet—with Archard seemed to have fixed something in me. My will was stronger. My faith was not perfect, but definitely more substantial.

We were now on day four of the seven I had left to save George's soul from Hell, and I had no idea how to even attempt that. My heart wanted to do the right thing, but so much depended on that one little decision. I wasn't ready to forfeit George, nor was I ready to step up to the plate and fulfill some prophecy.

My options were slim

If I declared myself Light Celatum, my gifts *might* develop enough to help the mission *and* save George. However, if I chose God's side over the other, I felt pretty confident it automatically damned George once the demons found out. Then there would be absolutely no chance of saving him. I couldn't take that chance, especially if I'm not as powerful as they think and I turned out being a dud. I needed a little more time.

When we approached Joe's Cafe, I noticed the change almost instantly. It *felt* different. The warm welcome had dissipated. Memories of pain, betrayal, and deceit oozed from the old bricks and mortar.

Goosebumps puckered my skin as we stood on the stairs peering inside. The lights were off. The staff and customers, which normally fluttered about at this time of the day, were nowhere around. Empty didn't begin to describe the cafe. This place wasn't the home I had considered mine anymore; it was a desolate vessel. A cruel reminder of the happiness that once resided within its walls.

I glanced at the angels, wondering if they detected the same negativity, or if it was just my personal reluctance about seeing Gavyn again. Both of their jaws were tensed, their bodies rigid like eager lions preparing to defend their territory.

I reached for the door. Now was as good a time as any.

"Nevaeh, wait," Arkin commanded as Archard grabbed my arm. Their eyes locked onto movement in the second story window.

Gavyn's apartment had a single light on, but we couldn't see who was inside. "Me first," Archard said, and then nudged his chin to the alley beside the cafe, motioning for Arkin to cover Joe's other exit. I felt out of my league with their smooth, military-style, secret conversation.

Once Arkin disappeared around the corner, Archard pulled me behind him protectively and opened the front door. It was all wrong. The air was bleak. Cold. Everything was in its place, yet something unseen was missing.

"Upstairs." Archard guided me down the hall toward Gavyn's apartment. "You stay behind me," he whispered sternly.

We moved, slow and measured, up the steps. The reflective sheen of Archard's eyes glancing over his shoulder to check on me was the only thing I could see in the black stairwell.

He stopped just a few steps from the top and eased the cracked door open farther, determining the culprit of the movement we'd seen outside. After an intense moment of holding my breath, Archard pushed off the second step and walked into the room.

When I entered behind him, I realized why he marched in so carelessly. Arkin was already inside, leaning his shoulder against the wall of Gavyn's hallway, his exposed wings casually framing his bare upper body. He clutched the fur-trimmed, leather jacket he had taken off—I assumed to fly up—in his right hand. His restless thumb repeatedly smoothed over the pelt while his eyes focused on the scene in front of him.

Archard sauntered to the kitchenette and rested his hip against the bar, cold gaze pointed toward the center of Gavyn's living room. I was both excited and worried about how easily we had accomplished our task.

Malach was circling the coffee table, grumbling to himself as he paced back and forth. His snow-white wings dragged behind him, scraping the edge of the table when he passed a corner too closely. My eyes skimmed over his feathers, noting how different they were from the last time I'd seen him; they were ruffled, distressed, like him. Occasionally, he'd stop and burst something out in his angelic language, otherwise he ignored our presence.

A sword hung heavily in his one hand, and a piece of paper in the other. Brooding eyebrows pinched together, emphasizing the worry lines on his face. It was alarming to see Malach so out of sorts. Even when he handled the demon that stole George's soul, he was calm and collected for the most part.

I glared at the Guardians, waiting for them to say something. Archard raised his eyebrows in my direction and shrugged. I huffed and rolled my eyes at them, knowing that they expected me to do the dirty work.

Archard's sarcastic words rang clearly in my head, *You wanted answers. Go get them.*

The staleness of the apartment set me on edge, but I ignored it. I nervously spun the ring on my thumb a few times and took a deep breath. "Malach, what happened here?" I asked softly, trying not to test his patience or spook him.

The Archangel froze and growled at me without looking up. "He left us."

"What?" I felt like I'd gotten the wind knocked out of me. "What do you mean?" I frantically began scouring the apartment. "Where is Gavyn, Malach?" I jogged down the hall and poked my head into his room, the bathroom, even in the closets, knowing he wouldn't be there.

"I. Said. He's. Gone." Malach's repeated in a rough, angry tone, and then continued making circles in the living room.

I searched every corner and found nothing more than a large crack in the wall and a wet spot on the ceiling. "I heard you the first time, you ass." I stomped over to the Archangel and snatched the paper from his hand.

He stopped in his tracks and stared at me with glossy eyes. So much sadness hid in the depths of those soft, peridot pools.

"What happened?" I whispered, almost hoping he couldn't hear me. I had a feeling I didn't want to know the truth about to slip from his lips.

"I felt the break and came as soon as I could." Malach's gaze moved to the crack in the wall. "It was too late, Nevaeh." He took two giant steps across the room and punched the crack so hard his fist went through the wall, and the apartment literally shook. His fierce hands broke apart clumps of plaster and threw them on the floor, determined to find the portal that wasn't there anymore.

I examined the paper in my hand, realizing I wouldn't be able to reason with Malach. Instantly, I recognized who wrote the letter by the shade of lipstick staining the page with a kiss.

Layla knew someone would come for Gavyn.

Dear High and Mighty Ones,

I had a feeling you would come to reclaim the goodness of Gavyn's soul. No need. It's right where it belongs — with me. Gav and I have huge plans together.

Read my words carefully, angels: He is mine. He's seen you unrighteous bastards for what you are. We've shown him the wrong of his ways, and he's decided to make things right. Consider this his formal resignation.

Don't worry. I will take good care of my lover. Oh, do me a favor. Tell Nevaeh and her little sex toy of a Guardian that I said thanks for the help convincing him!

Truly yours,
L.

Teardrops dripped from my chin and landed on the paper, smudging the ink. I barreled toward Archard and shoved the paper against his chest. "He's already forgiven me, huh?" I ran into Gavyn's room and slammed the door behind me before he could respond.

The familiar smell of his things smacked me in the face with the force of an atomic bomb. My heart shattered. He'd done this because of me, because of the pain I'd caused him. I should've come clean with everything from the beginning. He wouldn't have believed Layla if I had. I laid across his bed, hiding my face in my hands and crying for yet another person I had doomed.

I rolled onto my back and scowled, directing my anguish to the being that made me as I am. "If I'm supposed to be so great and do such important work in your name, how can I cause so much suffering and destruction?"

It was virtually too subtle to detect, but the voiceless words floated on a breeze around me with a gentleness that soothed my miserable soul.

You are strong enough to endure this, my child. They want you to doubt; that's how they win you over.

I sprang up, amazed that He heard me and actually responded.

Rising from Gavyn's bed, my attention drifted to something shiny laying on his dresser. The small pile of gold sparkled on the dark wood under a ray of light extending in from his window like a spot light. I scooped up the necklace and examined the simple, abandoned crucifix dangling from my hand.

Gavyn wouldn't want to be a slave to the demons. There is no way he willingly chose to go with Layla. I refused to believe it. I would find a way to fix this.

They told me, even if you choose to go Dark, you could come back from it. Gavyn's faith was strong, if anyone could return from Hell's clutch, it would be him, and I'd be the one to drag him out by the hair if I had to. It wouldn't be easy, but I didn't care. Determination drove me now. There had to be a way to bring him back, to bring both of the men I'd lost back. I was not going to lose anyone else to doubt.

I flung open the door and marched down the hall, ready to do some damage. I stepped into the living room, beaming confidence, and all eyes turned to me.

"Malach, I need to know exactly what you saw when you came in," I demanded.

The Archangel obviously didn't get demands very often. He pursed his lips and narrowed his eyes, seeming to struggle with whether or not to answer me. He widened his shoulders and placed his hands on his hips, then gave in to my command. "I came through the ceiling, same as before. The room was still red and hazy from her portal. Layla stopped with her body half inside already, winked, and threw the letter at me just before pulling herself through. I'm sorry, Nevaeh." He plopped down on the futon and dragged his hands down his face. "I couldn't get to the opening fast enough."

It was unsettling to see such a powerful creature so broken, but, at the same time, it was amazing to know that such heavenly beings cared for us so much. Each angel had built their own special relationship with those on Earth, and most humans had no clue.

"We will find them. If I'm The Clavis, then it is my responsibility to save everyone I can, right?" I glanced at Archard. Pride beamed from his sharp features.

"How did she get through the portal? I thought I was the only Celata able to do that?" A sour silence filled the room. No one wanted to answer, but I could tell they all knew.

"Hello?" I yelled, expecting someone to respond.

"She may have hit a new level in her demonic transformation. Her powers would get stronger if she's becoming full demon," Arkin answered casually while sifting through Gavyn's cabinets for food. "She probably won't have long before she's unable to turn back."

"So, there is a deadline on when you can change your mind?"

"Kind of, but it's different for everyone. The evil you let take over your heart, and how fast you give in to it, determines your change." Archard sighed and straightened from the bar, tensing as he shifted weight.

He was uncomfortable talking about this. Maybe he feared what might happen if I let my dark side out. I had a hunch the demons would make damn sure I was flooded with evil and that I didn't have much time to turn back.

I thought of Gavyn. His heart was full of love and warmth. I wondered how much time they would let him have before ripping his integrity to shreds. We had to move fast.

"Did you talk to Gavyn's Guardian?" I hoped his angel could offer some clues to what happened before he left with Layla.

Remorse consumed Malach's face. "I'm his Guardian," he whispered, his gaze never leaving the floor. "It's been me from the moment he made his decision."

"But...you're an Arch," I argued, stunned by his confession.

He nodded. "I asked to be assigned to him. I figured I could help him more than a Guardian angel. His powers were so out of control and so strong." The angel hung his head, shame contorting his strong features. "I guess I was wrong."

I didn't know what to say. No wonder Malach was so heartbroken about Gavyn. They were more than friends. They were bonded, like father and son. Like brothers. "Did Gavyn know?"

Malach shook his head. I couldn't see continuing the interrogation and bringing more misery to the Archangel. We needed to think about how to get Gavyn back.

I turned to Arkin and Archard. "Okay. We know that Layla is developing quickly. Gavyn is probably with her, but we have to remember Malach didn't see him enter the portal. So, we can't assume to know her game.

"We know that I can portal jump, but the risk is too great for me to do it safely." My brain was on fire, trying to filter through the facts. "And, if I make my choice now, there's no way of knowing what gifts I'll receive, or if the one I have will change?" I scanned the heavenly faces listening to me sort things out and waited for acknowledgement. Each one reluctantly agreed.

Archard stepped forward, facing me, and took my hands in his. The charge between us flared. It was strengthening. The faint hint of surprise in his eyes told me he felt it, too.

"If you declare yourself, your gifts might be the very thing that saves them."

I glanced down at his defined chest, afraid to see how he would react to my answer. "I can't. I can't take the chance of them knowing. I would lose George forever."

Relief sank into my heart as I heard his words swirl in my mind, *It's okay. I understand.*

When I returned my gaze to Archard face, his compassion and love shined back at me. "Just know, if it wasn't for that, I would have already declared myself. The moment we came back, last night, I knew what I wanted. I just can't do it right now. Saving my soul is not enough to convince me that it's okay to let George's go. Or Gavyn's."

"Then what's the plan, cupcake?" Arkin eyed me as he chomped on an apple.

"Malach, can you help us with manpower? We have a strong group of angels, but it would help to have some Archs on our side." Archard patiently gave the sad lump on the futon time to speak.

Malach reflected for a moment. "I can get a few...but why should I help rogue Guardians?"

For the first time since he sat on the couch, Malach's attention was entirely present with the rest of us. He wanted to get Gavyn back as badly as I did, but he was apparently too stubborn to offer help so easily.

"Malach, he's *my* Guardian. He had good reason for what he did," I argued in Archard's defense.

"I know who he is. I just don't like it." The Archangel glared at Archard and exhaled loudly. "What do you need us to do?"

"We're on day four. Only two more full days before she has to meet them with an answer. Let's make the most of it. We need to train her the best we can. Get your guys to find out any information about The Clavis, portal jumping, and if there's any loopholes into Hell. Then, just be there when I say."

"Be where exactly?" Malach raised a curious eyebrow.

"They want her? They'll have to fight for her." An arrogant grin curved Archard's flawless lips.

"Woo-hoo! Damn, straight!" Arkin cheered obnoxiously behind me.

I twisted around and giggled at the sight of Arkin dancing around the kitchenette as if he'd just won the lottery. From my peripheral, I noticed an envelope sitting on the bar in front of him. "Wait a sec."

I padded over to examine the unsealed sleeve, remembering that Layla left the note for Gavyn the day I went to the library. The side was neatly slit. I pinched the paper between my forefinger and thumb and removed it from the envelope. It was worn from opening and refolding it multiple times. He must have read it after I left that day.

"What's so important that you had to interrupt my happy dance, sweet cheeks?" Arkin leaned over the bar to look at the object in my hands while Archard and Malach gathered behind me.

I had to regain my wits with all three so close. I'd made progress with handling the angels' graces, but this was ridiculous. They were so close, and the energy swarming around me was so intense that I might combust. It wasn't lustful, just an overwhelming taste of bliss and passion. I wanted to throw my hands in the air, giving up on this world all together, and ride Malach's coattails through the portal back to Heaven.

Beads of sweat began to form on my forehead and neck. My slow, steady breathing was rapidly increasing to a pant. This situation was going to become dangerous if I couldn't gain control. The lines would soon blur again, between the growing faith I held prominent in my soul and the inherent evil lurking beneath it.

"Can you three back up just a smidge? I need some space." I forced the words out, not really wanting them to do as I requested.

They considered me for a moment with confused expressions on their faces, then realized what I was asking. Arkin and Malach both shifted to the opposite side of the bar and leaned against the far counter. Archard stood firm, refusing to leave my side. He scowled at the other angels, his jaw clenched and eyes narrowed.

"Hey, man, don't look at me. I've been keeping mine under wraps all day," Arkin protested.

My angel shook his head, dismissing Arkin's argument. Archard's inviting, aqua eyes darted to mine.

I want you to get accustomed to what little effect I still have on you. I need to be the one who levels you out in stressful times, he spoke in my mind.

Accepting his suggestion, I took a deep breath and relaxed into his presence. I noted that when the others stepped back, there was only the love and trust emitted by Archard; not the needful desire that threatened to conquer it. My bond with him dredged up the strength from my soul.

"So...what does it say?" Malach asked cautiously.

"It's another letter from Layla." My voice shook as I explained what the letter said. "She demanded he choose her over me, or I would die." Tears gathered in my eyes. "She *bullied* him into going with her." I sat the letter down on the counter, unable to look at her words any longer.

"What a bitch!" Arkin spat.

"So, he didn't choose willingly. That's good. There's still hope for him." Malach smiled with relief. "We just need to get to him before the evil consumes his heart."

"Oh, that's all? You make it sound so easy." The sarcasm in my words bit at him.

He held his tongue, acknowledging the difficulty in what he proposed.

After a few minutes of silence and brainstorming, it came to me. "What if I'm bait?" I don't know why I hadn't thought of it sooner. It could work.

"There's no way!" Archard objected.

"It's the only way." I touched his arm, trying to subdue the anger rumbling in his voice. "I won't have to go into a portal. We can bargain for them to bring George's soul and Gavyn to a meeting place. You guys can ambush the demons, and once we have sight of George and Gavyn, I can make my declaration and hope for the best."

"Hah...hope for the best?" he snorted. "That's how you're going to make it through this? Hope for the best?"

"Archard, she's right," Malach agreed.

"No, she's not!" my angel yelled, and then stomped to the other side of the room, eager to escape the argument.

"You know I'm right. What happened to having faith?" I followed

Archard until he stopped, but he wouldn't turn to face me. I smoothed my hand along the ridges of wings hidden beneath his duster. He shivered under my touch. "I have to do this. If I'm really The Clavis, God will be there to back me up, right?" My fingers barely wrapped halfway around his bicep as I tugged at his folded arms, urging him to turn around.

He finally grabbed my arm, dragged me in front of him, and locked his hands around my back. I smiled at the safety I found inside his protective hug.

"Ok," he whispered reluctantly.

HAVEN CAGE

CHAPTER TWENTY-SEVEN

Making Plans

The next night, after a day and a half of constant training, learning to move my body in ways I didn't even think were possible, I was thoroughly exhausted. I wound my arm around in a circle, stretching my sore shoulder as I wandered down a hallway of the factory. Arkin had made it his personal goal to have me trained to military status in just under forty hours. Unfortunately, my body was in total disagreement.

I tried to partner with a few of the other angels, but always ended up with him. I figured, after the first three times of asking another Guardian to show me a particular move and being directed back to Arkin, it was time to surrender. Archard and Arkin had probably conspired to take complete control of what I was doing—and with whom.

In the end, I enjoyed Arkin's methods of instruction. I'd gotten used to the sexist nicknames and crude gestures. Throughout my body's consistent beating, we formed our own special partnership. I found a friend in him. He would never hold back on me, never baby my feelings. Somehow, in the silence of our intense battles against one another, I learned I could trust him with my life and not think twice about it. We molded an unbreakable brother-sister relationship. Something I never had before.

Meanwhile, Archard and Malach worked on gathering what information they could. Half of the time, I saw them huddled in the manager's office at the factory, muttering about our situation; the other half, the two angels were nowhere to be found.

I finally spilled the beans about my experiences on the other side and everything I discussed with Gavyn. I told them about my debilitating visions, my demon encounters, and how I learned there was a book. There was too much happening and too many lives involved to keep secrets anymore.

The angels suggested that if we found whoever gave the book to Margie, they might bring us a little closer to the information inside. Now that we knew of a tangible resource about The Clavis, we figured the rumored stories had to contain some truths. Unfortunately, I couldn't get to it without risking myself.

I still felt like the vision of my mother, if that's who it was, held some profound answer that was lost in translation. It made more sense now that Arkin connected some of the dots for me. But how did she show me what happened? Why did she leave? Was she in Hell, too?

My heart sank with the idea that so many people in my life had ended up there. I couldn't help but think that maybe ending up in Hell was my true fate. It seemed the easiest end to all of this. I guess, if it's that easy though, it probably isn't the right answer.

I slowly shuffled back toward the room I now claimed as my own. The tight quarters, where Archard took me deep into my unknown, had sentimental value now. It didn't feel right sleeping anywhere else.

My muscles and bones hurt with even the slightest twitch. Several spots on my skin were beginning to turn a pretty shade of purple.

I laughed at the ridiculousness of me sparring with an angel. Who would've predicted it a few weeks ago?

The sting of a fresh cut on my lip forced me to stop laughing. I sucked air through my teeth and winced, recalling how Arkin had elbowed my mouth in defense when I yanked hard against his wing.

I entered my room and headed to the plush bed, peeling off my damp, sweaty clothes along the way. I grabbed the lighter lying on the small table and lit a few of the candles Archard left on the floor.

The mattress squeaked as I plopped down and settled onto the fluffy comforter. The chilly factory air drifted in through the door I left open, cooling the sweaty, bare skin not covered by my bra and panties. I was too tired and hot to care if someone walked in and saw me.

It was quiet at this end of the building. I welcomed the silence and centered myself. I shut everything out—except for Archard. His heavenly beauty was all I saw when I closed my eyes. So much worry and love laced the hard lines of his face when he looked at me lately.

Before we left Gavyn's apartment yesterday, I spoke to Archard alone. I replayed our conversation over and over in my mind, now. No one but George had ever been that concerned for me. He must've asked if I was sure about the plan I suggested fifty times, and every time I knew it was the only option.

A warm gust of wind ignited my spirit and distracted me. The sudden exhilaration was like breathing for the first time—like the first flicker of life.

I opened my eyelids to see my angel standing by the bed, staring at me with hunger in his eyes. I stayed still and quiet. I didn't want him to leave, but I didn't know if we were ready to address the undeniable connection between us, either.

Soft candlelight danced gloriously in the reflective sheen of his pupils, enhancing the mesmerizing shade of neon-blue glowing around them. His naked chest heaved in deep, heavy breaths as sweat dripped down his tight ridges of flesh. My eyes followed the droplets of moisture down to the dark jeans hanging low on his waist, leaving his incredible abs exposed for me to admire.

His magnificent wings flexed behind him, tightening in response to the increasing tension between us and pressing out against the thickening atmosphere. The sight of him rendered me completely defenseless to whatever intentions he had.

He shut his eyes and touched the top of my foot, tracing a slow path past my ankle, up my shin, and then stopping at my knee with his finger still pressing against my skin. His full lips pulled up into a satisfied grin. Archard shifted at my side, adjusting his weight and leaning over to reach me better. He let the rest of his hand settle on my inner thigh, just above my knee. Short, shallow respirations rushed in and out past his slick lips, while I quivered with anticipation for more.

"What are you doing?" I exhaled the words, not realizing I was holding my breath.

His grin widened. "Memorizing the feel of your skin," he whispered.

"Well, I have a lot more skin to memorize if that's the case." I slid my leg under his palm, desperate for more of his touch.

He shifted his weight, again. The scent filling the room changed from smooth honey to a spiced sweetness. I inhaled the aroma of need radiating from his pores and longed to taste his sugary essence.

A storm of emotions stirred in his eyes. Worry lines wrinkled his brow. He seemed to struggle with upholding his strong will and yielding to our attraction.

"Lay with me," I whispered. I needed to feel him beside me, at least.

He carefully lowered onto his side next to me, propping his head up with one hand. I searched for the hunger in his eyes and found it caged in their depths. The moment had passed. His better judgment had won.

That was unfortunate since my better judgment was very much

lacking. Our closeness electrified my cells. Sticky wetness dampened my panties. It was no longer a yearning to be close to Heaven, but a yearning to be his.

I rolled away from him. Maybe if I couldn't see him, I could trick my body into calming back down. As soon as I turned, though, he hooked his arm around my waist and tugged me into him. He leaned in and buried his face in my hair, inhaling deeply.

We lay, uncomfortably close, teasing ourselves with an undying fire.

He cupped my body, shielding me from the outside world while I melted into him, happily trapped in his love. As we drifted to sleep, the softness of his gallant wing dragged over my sensitive skin, blanketing me in warmth.

The next day, I woke to the flickering flame of the last candle illuminating the room. I was alone and tucked under the comforter — not Archard.

Pouting, I wiggled out of our bed, gathered the clean clothes I pilfered from an abandoned locker the day before, and headed down the hall to shower. I turned on the squeaky faucet, slipped off my underwear and bra, and stepped into the stall, ducking my head under the water. It was cold, but, hey, I would be clean.

After showering, I dried off with the rough, white, industrial towel I found under the sink, then hung it on the shower rod to dry. Keeping my head lowered and my eyes focused on the green line staining the bottom of the sink, I brushed my teeth in record time. I caught myself unintentionally snubbing the reflection in the mirror.

Seeing how much I had changed — my tired eyes, bruised body, and transformed soul—scared me to death. I couldn't see the familiar girl inside anymore, and the woman watching me from the glassy surface was too new for me to embrace.

I slid a worn, gray, Def Leppard t-shirt over my head and tied the excess fabric at the bottom into a small knot over my right hip, then tucked it under. Next, I tugged on black cargo pants that fit a little too snugly around my ass. I sucked in my gut, then freed it once the pants buttoned without too much coercion. I squatted then burst up into a jump a few times, testing the give of my attire. I even managed a high kick with little restriction.

After I shoved my feet into a pair of confiscated boots, I made my way towards the sparring room—clean and ready to get dirty again. I had some tension that begged for a much-needed release.

I stopped in front of an old Work Safety poster and used the dusty glass frame as a mirror. Pulling my hair into a damp pony-tail, I noticed voices chattering from the office next to me.

I pushed open the hollow, wooden door, and found Archard, Malach, and a stranger huddled around a long conference table. Judging by his outfit, the stranger was an Arch; his leather sandals, plated skirt, and jeweled sword screamed heavenly warrior.

"Hey, guys. What's up?" I greeted, interrupting their deep conversation.

"Hello, Nevaeh." Archard held out his hand, inviting me to join in the meeting. It was such a small gesture of inclusion, but one I was overly happy to accept. "This is Eyal. Malach located him this morning. He may have some useful information for us." Archard gently squeezed my hand and smiled.

"Hi." I smiled, attempting to be polite when I really just wanted to skip the formalities and get to the info.

Eyal dipped his head. "Nice to meet you."

This Arch had an unrecognizable accent. I bit the inside of my cheek and smirked, fighting to keep my laughter inside. The little sarcastic voice I kept confined to my brain was making fun of my ignorance and wondering why I assumed all angels were American.

Eyal moved to the edge of the table and perched an armed hip upon it, unfazed by my momentary lack of composure. He seemed friendly but still intimidating.

I gathered my focus and fidgeted impatiently. "Let's cut to the chase. What do you know about me?"

Bright white teeth contrasted greatly against his soot-black skin as the Arch grinned at my bluntness. "Well...I knew your mother's angel. He was a Guardian under my jurisdiction. His name was Rhett."

"Great! Where is he? We need to talk to him," I exclaimed.

"It's not that easy, Nevaeh," Archard answered, signaling Eyal to continue.

"He broke connection with us around the time you were born. We have no idea where he is or why he deserted us." His unsettled, sloe-colored eyes stared off into space for a moment before he began speaking again. "He was always very quiet and kindhearted over the centuries. We searched everywhere for him. His loss was great in our hearts." He raised off the table and rested a hand on the pommel of the sword dangling from his hip.

"Where is my mother?"

"We last knew Arianna's whereabouts the night she left you. She kept in touch with a few angels the first year after Rhett left, but it was getting harder for her to keep you safe with demons chasing her unsupervised soul. When she left you, she disconnected from us as well."

"So, she disappeared because of me?" My heart felt like it was at its breaking point once again.

"Arianna vanished to protect you, yes." He picked up a long, black jacket draped over the chair across from me. Eyal spun towards me and knocked a knuckle on the table to make a point, "For what it's worth, your mother was a fierce warrior. I have no doubt that she is still alive somewhere. There was nothing but goodness in her heart, and I refuse to believe she would betray us." The stranger reached over the table and offered his hand. I shook it and tightened my lips in a half-hearted smile. "Sorry I don't have more to give you." Eyal strolled confidently out the door.

"What am I supposed to do with this?" I whimpered to Archard, tears welling in my eyes. All that Eyal said only brought more confusion.

"We understand a little more about why she abandoned you. Chances are she is still on our side." Uncertainty hid behind Archard's hopeful expression.

"Please don't patronize me," I pleaded, losing control of my emotions. "So what if she *was* on our side then? Who's to say she didn't change her mind — that she hasn't crossed over since then?"

Malach stepped behind the chair across from me, gripping the back as he leaned over and stared into my eyes. "Look, Nevaeh, we'll figure this out. Right now, we need to focus on one dangerous situation at a time. We don't know much about the book, but we *will* find something in due time. We don't know where your mom is, or if she is even alive, so we'll keep searching for her," he said with a sure voice. He'd almost convinced me there was enough time to answer those questions. "At this moment, we need to save *you*. Unfortunately, you are literally Hell-bent on saving George's soul first. Not to mention the fact that we've now added Gavyn's soul to the pile of things to save." The Archangel paused in thought for a moment before continuing. "We have to proceed with our plan. Once we have George and Gavyn, you can declare sides. When your gifts develop, we can hypothesize about why the book is so special, and how to get it. Hopefully, that will lead us to your mom, too."

I needed the future that he promised.

"Archard and I discovered today that the book can only be used by The Clavis."

"That explains why they want me. They must think I'm The Clavis, too."

A psychotic breakdown was closing in on me. Tears trickled down my cheeks. This was all so frustrating. Little bits of information kept piling up, but nothing made enough sense to get very far.

Malach approached me cautiously. "Also...Hell portals can only be opened by demon blood." His tone lowered. "Nevaeh, we asked about your father, too. No one knows who he is."

"Fucking great." I huffed, glowering at my hands as I watched my fingers rotate George's ring.

Archard sat down beside me and rubbed small circles on my thigh with his thumb, patiently waiting for me to work through the craziness trampling my brain.

"What's the next move?" I asked, changing the subject.

Archard leaned forward in the chair and moved his hand to my cheek, pulling my attention back to him. "Malach and I found an abandoned location just south of here. There aren't any developments nearby for miles. The public will be safe if anything goes wrong. Malach managed to get a few Archangels to help, and there are sixteen of us Guardians." He searched my eyes for approval.

"Okay. What do we do when we get there? How do we make sure the demons come with George *and* Gavyn?" I restrained my building fear. I couldn't let Archard see how scared I really was. He would refuse to go through with the plan. "Do I try to contact them and offer my soul as a barter?"

"We've talked it over and decided it's too dangerous for you to speak with the demons anymore before tomorrow. We can't take the chance of them influencing you, again," Malach answered.

Archard squeezed my leg. "Malach and the other Archs are going to contact the demons and convince them we need Gavyn more than you, that we are willing to give you up for him and George. At the trade, we will hide you until they arrive. We'll take cover in the rafters, so they won't know how many of us there are, and we can catch them off guard."

Are you okay with this? Please tell me if you aren't, he begged in my thoughts.

I patted his hand reassuringly. "After they are surrounded, do I stay hidden, or do I come out to fight?"

The angels stiffened and glanced at each other. Archard lowered his gaze, nearly burning holes in the table with the anger in his eyes. "You will need to let them find you and engage first." His jaw twitched as he grinded his teeth. "If they fight a Celata, there will be just-cause to involve the others." Archard paused, regret clear in his gloomy expression.

Malach carried on eagerly. "We will be able to use the Celatum for more than mere tools in our war for the humans. We will be able to use them as actual soldiers. We've attempted this before, but none were strong enough to engage them. If you are The Clavis, you should be able to withstand the demons until we take them down."

Archard eyed Malach, then me. "Once you declare sides, our hope is that you can control portals to both sides, allowing us to move freely between all realms." He knew the chance I'd be taking could very well be beyond my capabilities.

"The Celatum could offer so much more than what they have in the past. We could finally put their gifts to full use," my angel explained.

"What if I'm not The Clavis?"

"If anything goes wrong, we will be there to save you. We will defeat the demons as we've done before," Malach assured.

"That's your plan B?" I scoffed, my eyes darting back and forth between the angels.

"Yes." Archard stood from his chair next to me, frustrated. "This is it, Nevaeh. If we can't save George and Gavyn tomorrow, there is no guarantee what will happen to them. But, no matter what, we will save you."

"I guess it's all or nothing." My voice shook as I thought about the two souls that may be lost to me in less than a day. Visions of them morphing into the demons I saw in Hell, as I had done in my own soulless void, made me cringe.

I shot out of my chair and slammed my hand on the table. "Let's do this." My nerves were fried, my emotions raw, but this was all I had to offer to them. I silently promised to give my everything to get them back.

I walked out of the room without saying another word, motivated to start training. My last day with Arkin was going to do me a lot of good.

CHAPTER TWENTY-EIGHT

Full Circle

Day seven.

This would be the day that would inevitably send my life into a tailspin unlike any before. Every cell in my body screamed *don't do this, there's gotta be another way.* Nervous acid churned in my gut, my eyelids weighed a ton, and I wasn't exactly positive I didn't have a concussion from our training session the night before.

I stayed awake for hours thinking of everything—anything—that might tip the scales. I'd be kidding myself if I thought there was really another way. This was the only chance we had. It started with me, and it would end with me—one way or another.

When I woke this morning, after a night of tossing and turning, the sight of my glorious angel lying on his stomach beside me calmed the chaos of my mind. His radiant warmth soothed my tired, achy muscles. Creamy, plum-tipped wings blanketed my bare legs.

Rubbing my legs back and forth, I cherished the silkiness of his down against my skin. I smiled at the sweet tinkling of his gold feathers shuffling against one another with my movements. The sound mimicked the jingling of coins dropping onto a pile of treasure.

His lazy groans startled me, and I stiffened, embarrassed that I was fondling him in his sleep.

He turned his head and gazed at me with sleepy eyes, then smiled. "Good morning, Nevaeh."

I giggled. My secret was safe. "Good morning."

Archard shifted, hugging my waist and pulling me under his body. With no intention of fighting him, I gladly scooted closer. Our legs tangled around one another like a pretzel. His wings readjusted and spread over the length of us both, shielding us from the cold.

I could've lost myself in that moment. The thought alone soured my euphoria, reminding me that this may be the last of my time with Archard. I wanted so badly to blurt out how I felt about him. I needed to tell him that I forgave him. I needed to ask for his forgiveness in return.

"Archard?"

"Yeah?" He looked into my eyes as if he knew what I was about to say. His aqua blues burrowed straight into my soul. The intensity stole my strength to speak.

Who was I to grant him forgiveness? Maybe he didn't think he'd done anything wrong.

Knock, knock.

Archard planted a quick kiss on my lips and grinned. "What?" he yelled.

Arkin cracked the door open and poked his head around the edge. "Hey, man, are you ready?"

"Yeah, we'll be right there." My angel's perfect smile disappeared, and apprehension lined his breath-taking features.

Arkin raked his eyes over our entwined bodies and smirked mischievously before vanishing behind the door. I rolled my eyes even though he was no longer there to see it.

"What are we ready for?" The chill of the factory rushed over my skin as Archard unwrapped himself from me and sluggishly lifted off the bed.

"To gather our gear and scout the place where we'll be meeting the demons. We need to make sure they aren't setting any traps." He slid his black leather boots on then shoved his arms and wings awkwardly through the holes of a heather-gray t-shirt. There was no denying the unease in his answer.

"Ok," I said, sitting up in the bed. "Are we flying or taking a vehicle?" I managed to sound eager, but truthfully, I was scared shitless.

"No. *You'll* stay here until dark. Rest. I can't take the chance of you running into a demon before we're ready. I have to be certain you're as safe as possible before I let you loose with the lions." He strolled toward me, kissed my forehead, and then turned to leave.

I gripped his wrist before he was able to walk away. "There is nothing safe about this. There never will be." I stood up on the mattress and cupped his face in my hands. My lips smashed into his, hunting for an escape from the growing dread attempting to devour me.

It lasted only a minute, but I would forever remember the freedom I found in his kiss. My entire existence—mind, body, and soul—reacted from the surge between us. Our tongues whirled against one another's, frantically trying to fuse our connection. I tasted an eternity of Heaven there.

He grabbed my hands, pulled them away from his cheeks, and held them between us. He grimaced as if in pain when his mouth disconnected from mine. He stared up into my eyes.

Did he not want me? Oh my God, what if he *didn't* feel the same as I did? Heat of embarrassment flushed my cheeks.

He reached a hand to the back of my head and gently pulled me closer again. This time it was a simple peck on my lips; not nearly enough to satisfy the hunger in my heart.

He spun and left me alone.

Hours passed as I waited for the angels to return. I felt so useless sitting around doing nothing. I'd already wasted time self-training, eating, napping, and finding shapes in the oil smudges on the walls as I paced back and forth from one end of the factory to the other. All of that activity took less than the blink of an eye compared to the hours I'd waited in anticipation.

The sun had risen and set since the angels left. They should've been back by now. What little bit of time I had left to save George and Gavyn was slipping away; yet, here I remained, useless, in this crappy building.

I didn't even know where to start hunting for them. My frustration grew when I realized the angels had probably concealed that little detail on purpose. I definitely would have followed them had I known where to go.

I slumped onto the beat-up office chair in our room, scrutinizing the leather outfit spread across the bed. I laughed, thinking how ridiculous it looked. Sighing, I yanked the pieces of tough clothing from the bed.

I held the small shirt out in front of me, wondering what Archard was thinking when he picked it out. It could have been worse, I guess. He could've given me one of the Archs' leather-plated skirts. At least he provided me some pants to wear.

After holding the material in my hands and examining it closer, I could see the purpose of his chosen attire. My fingers tightened and twisted around bunches of the heavy fabric. It was certainly sturdier than my thin, worn jeans.

I traded my baggy t-shirt for the leather top, feeling more appropriately dressed for our battle the moment I zipped the front of the skin-tight vest closed. I stuffed my legs into the leather pants and padded to the window, buttoning the top of them along the way.

The sky was deep purple, and the moon was already making its appearance. Memories of George and me naming the stars beneath the same moon sifted through my thoughts. It was many years ago, but I remember crouching next to him, imagining the most bizarre names until I fell asleep cuddled against his soft belly, like it was only nights ago.

"What are you thinking about?" Archard's enchanting warmth wrapped around me as soon as he stepped in the room.

I turned to look at him, not sure whether I should hug and kiss him, or slap him for taking so damn long. "Is everything okay?" I asked, shaking off his question. I couldn't bear to talk about George right now.

"Yes." He glided closer, staring past me into the evening sky. "Are you ready?"

"Yeah." I tugged his hardened face towards mine and softly kissed his chin. "It'll be fine."

His strong arms wrapped around me.

A cat-calling whistle sounded from the doorway. Arkin leaned against the door jamb, ogling me. "Wow, cupcake, you look hot in all that leather!"

A low growl rumbled from Archard's chest.

I slapped my angel's shoulder playfully. "Don't get upset. You're the one that gave me *all this leather*."

"I know, but did you have to fill it out so well?" A smirk pulled at the corner of his mouth.

My cheeks heated, and, again, I regretted having to wear the snug outfit. "I'm *so* sorry," I responded sarcastically to hide my chagrin. My forearms folded around my stomach, and I tugged the hem of my top down in an awkward attempt to hide the thin patch of exposed skin at my waist.

"Did you get it?" Archard strode toward Arkin with his hand out, ready to receive something.

Arkin retrieved a sword hidden behind his back. "You know it, brother." He held the blade out in front of him and slashed through the air ninja-style. "Hi-yah, yaw, wah," he joked, mimicking the corny noises that went along with any bad ninja movie.

Archard yanked the sword from Arkin's hand and punched his shoulder. The force knocked Arkin into a stumble, but he quickly righted himself while laughing at Archard's empty scorn. "You're welcome!"

"How did you get it?" Archard asked, scrutinizing every detail of the blade.

"Well, honestly, I had to steal it from an Arch." To my surprise, his words carried no remorse. Archard smiled graciously at Arkin, but refused to thank him.

"You stole it?" I squealed in disbelief. "But you're an angel."

"Yeah, I know." The egotistical, chauvinistic angel polished his nails on his chest proudly and then blew on them. He was completely okay, even happy, with his accomplishment. "I never said I was good at it." His mouth curled into an impish grin.

I shook my head at Arkin's idiocy and walked to Archard's side. The closer I got, the more I was drawn to the hunk of metal in his hand. It was gorgeous.

My curious gaze raked over the elegant sword. The end of the hilt secured a large, faceted amethyst within a bronze-tinted loop. The precious jewel gleamed under the stream of moonlight shining through the window, casting purple reflections on the floor. The sword-smith had slightly twisted the handle before the metal cooled, yielding the simplest element of decoration. My eyes moved down the blade, admiring the rich material, marbled with a strange patina that told of its ancient age.

"Do you like it?" Archard asked, resting the blade on his palms to present it to me.

"It's amazing."

He held the weapon out, urging me to take it.

I looked at Arkin with wide eyes. "You stole it for me?"

He nodded, watching me like a proud parent watching his kid opening a present on Christmas morning. "More like I procured it...if that makes you feel better."

I smiled graciously and lifted the antique sword from my angel's hands. From what I'd learned from the weapons portion of my training, the balance and weight were perfect. It seemed like it was fashioned for my hands alone. I swiped the sword through the air as Arkin had instructed me.

"We couldn't let you fight them with just those little fists of yours." Archard's body closed in around me from behind, encasing me in heat and power. He guided my arms outward and eased his knee into the back of my leg, adjusting my stance to fit against his. "Like this. You'll have more control," he whispered in my ear, searing my neck with his breath.

I swiped the blade back and forth, catching glints of light on the surface. "What's that?" I enquired, spotting a delicate scrolling pattern that stretched from hilt to tip.

"It's our language. It says, 'God will prevail with me as His humble weapon." He smiled down at me. "This sword is special, Nevaeh. It's one of very few that God blessed Himself. It has been around since He made us."

I was speechless. I detected a hum of energy buzzing from the sword into my hand the moment I'd taken it, but this was too much. I was not worthy enough to carry it. "I can't take this." I pushed the sword back at Archard.

"You have to." He nudged the blade away.

"Are we gonna sit here and debate this all day, or are we gonna use it to do some damage?" Arkin asked anxiously before strutting out of the room.

Archard and I glanced at each other, snickering, then followed him toward the training area.

When we entered the large room, I gasped at the power vibrating against the walls. Angels were scattered everywhere. They were all dressed for battle in leather like mine. Weapons were fastened to their backs, hips, thighs, and ankles. Their fierce statures would intimidate any creature that dared to get close to them.

"Listen up!" Arkin yelled at the chattering Archs and Guardians. They ceased talking the moment they heard his booming voice.

"Everyone up to speed? We go in, hide Nevaeh, and wait. The moment they find her, and we get eyes on George and Gavyn, we move. The demons have to initiate battle with her before we do anything. We can't let her fight for too long though. Everyone understand?"

The angels rumbled their agreement in unison.

I couldn't believe it. Reality hit me like a ton of bricks. This was really going to happen. It felt so surreal before, but now it was right in front of me.

This would end tonight.

I peered down at my feet. Anxiety tightened around my throat like a noose. I tried to relax the tension from my expression and gulp down a big dose of courage, but it was hard.

"Are you okay? We don't have to do this." Archard clasped his fingers with mine.

I shook my head. "We do have to." I shoved the fear down deep in my gut and numbed myself. "Let's get to it."

"Okay."

He looped the arm straps of a harness around my shoulders and secured it to my back. I adjusted the tension of the straps as he slid my sword into the sheath now fastened behind me. Waving my arms back and forth in front of me, I tested my ability to move, then reached for the blade, assuring that I could access it easily.

"Good?" Archard asked. I nodded.

Arkin clapped loudly, grabbing our attention as he marched in a circle around the soldiers. "Alright, angels, lets fly!"

I covered my ears to muffle the echoing thumps of beating wings and war calls. As the magnificent beings took flight, a gale force wind stirred up dust from the floor and slapped my pony-tail against my neck. I shrugged a shoulder up to shield my face from the wind, but kept my eyes drawn up toward the ceiling.

The sight above me was unbelievable. I studied the colorful blurs of feathers while they flapped in powerful movements against the air. Hues of reds, blues, and greens blended into the varying backgrounds of soft whites and precious metals as they soared into assembly. The angels looked like a huge spiral of exotic birds, rounding the room as one mass; their forms were precisely synchronized with one another as they joined in the dance of battle. The vibration of their roars and thrusting wings surged through the concrete floor below me, working its way up to a tingle in my toes.

Archard stepped in front of me, dipped down, and hoisted both my legs around his hips. Everything else disappeared. All I could focus on was how close we were and how good he felt between my thighs. Our invisible energy ignited, damn near setting the space between us on fire.

"You okay with riding like this?" He grinned. "You'll have a better grip on me." The playful gleam in his crystalline eyes betrayed his innocent reasoning. He knew exactly what he was doing, and it wasn't about safety.

"I think I can handle this." I squeezed my thighs tighter and pressed into him. I combed my fingers through his hair and twisted a curl at the base of his neck. Two can play that game.

He groaned and launched us into the air, thrusting his magnificent wings downward in a heavy swipe. We rose as high as the other angels and fell into formation, circling the cavernous room a couple more times. I never noticed before, I guess because I hadn't had this view, but there were large sliding windows lining the top of each wall. Archard yelled something in his heavenly language and then darted for one of the open windows. He pulled his wings in tight to his body and placed one hand gently on my head and one under the small of my back. We rocketed through the frame. A squeal escaped my mouth when we almost missed and hit the wall.

Archard laughed his deep, throaty laugh, gripping me tighter as he extended his wings and began flapping hard to keep us in flight. I decided it wasn't a good idea to watch where we were going while hanging upside down from his body. I burrowed my face comfortably into Archard's chest and enjoyed the cool night breeze against my skin with his heart pounding steady against my cheek.

I held on for dear life for about a half hour before I heard my angel whisper in my thoughts, *we are close*. My heart skipped a few beats. It was another reminder of what was about to go down, and I was scared to death.

For the first time since we were airborne, I peeked around Archard's arm to make sure the other angels hadn't succumbed to second thoughts and left me on my own. It was dark, but the view of the army of angels flanking us was glorious.

The moonlight shimmered off their metallic feathers as it did Archard's. Dozens of glittering wings twinkled like stars around us.

The silhouette of each soldier was ferocious and free in the night sky. They lined up perfectly, only breaking formation to enjoy a playful dive now and then. I felt overwhelmingly honored to fly with such unbelievable heavenly creatures.

We slowed, descending toward the ground moments later. A rush of adrenaline exploded inside me. Thankfully, it eliminated the edge of my anxiety — at least enough for me to breathe again.

Even if I wasn't The Clavis, I was certain of my place with the Celatum. I knew who had my back and trusted they would take care of me.

"Nevaeh, are you sure?" Archard asked in an uneven voice as he landed softly on the ground below us and eased me down from his body.

I stretched my cramped legs and adjusted my leather with trembling hands. "I'm sure. Let's get this over with." I grabbed his head, guiding it down to me, and kissed him softly on the lips.

As we broke away, I gazed at his perfect face and memorized every beautiful detail: his light, golden hair, slightly swollen, cherry lips, and the depths of his beckoning eyes. I pondered telling him what I felt, but decided it wasn't the right time. There would be a chance after. I wanted to tell him in a moment of happiness, not fear.

"Quit making googly eyes at one another so we can get this show on the road," Arkin teased, smacking my ass as he strolled by.

"Alright," Archard nodded. "There's a door just around this corner. Go in and wait there for my orders."

"Okay. What are you going to do?" I needed to know he would be near and that he was going to be safe.

"Make sure there aren't any demons already inside." He squeezed my shoulders lovingly and kissed my forehead. "Now go. It's almost time."

He flapped his wings and launched off the ground in a spiral upward, disappearing into the night. I'd aimed to get a layout of the building, but it was pitch black. I couldn't see much more than two feet in front of me. However, I could vaguely see the ornately designed facade next to me, and a huge window just beyond my reach.

I inched along the cold brick until my hand skimmed over a corner. Peeking around the edge of the wall, I made out the raised frame of the door Archard had mentioned. Rusty hinges whined in protest as I forced the slat of splintered wood open.

The inside was blacker than outside. I stilled as my eyes fought to adjust, but there was no light to take in. I fumbled around and found the walls were closer than I expected—not more than an arm's length away. One wall had some sort of screen window, and another wall framed a narrow entryway which I gathered led to the main part of the building. I slid my fingers along the door, tracing the etched wood to a handle notched out at waist-level.

The air was stuffy and stagnant. I was so tempted to leave the room, but Archard would have a shit-fit if I didn't listen. I pressed my ear to the door, listening for any signs of thumping wings or whispers from the angels.

Are you in? Archard's words entered my mind.

Yeah. Can you hear me?

Yes. Stay there. The demons aren't far. We are getting into position now. Stay hidden until I tell you, his troubled voice echoed against the walls of my head. Shit was about to get serious.

Where are you? I want to see you.

Wait a second.

Suddenly, thin rays of light seeped through the cracks around the door. A familiar aroma rolled into my little room.

What is that? What's going on?

An uneasy feeling rattled my nerves. My eyes jumped from dark wall to dark wall, seeking perspective. I'd never visited this place before, yet I somehow knew the smell and the feel, of this hallowed building. More than that, I was almost one hundred percent certain that in the deep crevices of my brain, I knew what was about to happen.

Earthy, sweet spices melded with the stale, moldy air. I scoured my memories to put a name with the odor roaming in from outside my small chamber; anything to spark a clear thought about my strange recognition.

We lit some lanterns and incense. It'll make it harder for them to detect us. Are you still ok?

A single drop of sweat slid down my face and stung the cut on my lip.

Everything tumbled into place like a domino reaction.

This can't be happening.

I rushed to look through a sliver of space in the doorframe. It was exactly how I remembered in the dream.

The broken, elaborately painted ceiling gave way to the glowing stars. The frayed, red velvet runner lay torn on the stone floor. Climbing ivy flourished around huge marble pillars. And, hiding in the rafters, I caught the neon glow of his eyes. He hid exactly where I knew he'd be.

I wiped the sweat from my mouth with the back of an unsteady hand and checked my sword to make sure it was there. I was going to need it.

Pieces of my dream continued to click into place, one scene at a time. This wasn't going to end well. The demons never intended to bring George and Gavyn for the trade.

At last, I recalled every terrible detail. I wasn't going to survive this, but what other option did I have? How could I save George and Gavyn if I didn't make it out alive?

There has to be another way. I raced frantically through different scenarios, pacing tight circles inside my confessional — a rat in a cage.

The spiced fragrance of incense flushed out of the room as another smell flooded in and violated my nostrils. Between the incoming putrid odor of sulfur and my frazzled nerves, I doubled over, unable to fight the vomit that spewed from my mouth.

Archard, I can't do this. I know how this ends, I screamed in my head.

What are you talking about, Nevaeh? Just stick to the plan. We'll keep you safe. I promise. Archard's assuring words attempted to save me from panic, but it wasn't enough.

There's another way. I have no choice. I'm so sorry, I answered.

Wait. What are you going to do? Nevaeh, don't do anything stupid, he pleaded.

I relayed every detail of my premonition into his mind and hoped that he was able to understand why I was doing what I was about to do.

NO! Nevaeh! Archard's energy surrounded me like a storm cloud, full of fury and speed. It clawed for a grip on my will, struggling to take control of my intentions and save me, but it failed.

I'm so sorry. I'll come back to you. Please forgive me. As I thought the words, I peeked through the door crack one last time. He was shuffling in the shadows, debating whether to come after me or not.

The demons lurked just outside my sinner's chamber. This is where I had belonged all along. Especially, for the choice I was about to make.

As I breathed the words, the burning on my forehead ignited. "I renounce God and relinquish my soul as a servant of Satan."

The harsh rush of bitterness flowed through my blood. Archard's mental shouting vanished. My insides felt as though they were tearing apart—a sure sign that my spirit was transitioning. The pain was excruciating and, yet, lovely to my newly poisoned heart.

I collapsed to the floor in agony, fire burning through my veins. Pushing past the agony, I crawled to the empty wall next to me.

A deluge of power exploded from my body. The ceiling quaked

and crumbled. The wood panels around me snapped and popped as the little room gave way. The door split in two, allowing low light from the lanterns in the church to seep into the small room.

My eyes focused beyond the broken door to the curious demons trampling toward me. Their screeches and clicks no longer bothered my ears. It was music to my darkening soul.

I had to move quickly. I couldn't let them get me, yet. My unsteady hand rose and pushed flat against the wall. I collected whatever power I might have gained by declaring myself and willed it to open a portal. There was no guarantee it would work, but it was my only chance to escape this trap.

Red-hot energy scalded my fingers and glowed beneath my skin as it flared out from my hand. I looked over my shoulder at the monsters scratching and scraping at the broken barriers separating them from me. Behind them, the angels dropped from the rafters, taking the demons out one by one.

The wall split beneath my hand and spread outward, dragging my focus away from the ruckus outside. It emitted the electric, glowing haze that I'd seen from the Hell portals before. It was working. If I could just speed it up a little more. I was so close.

A ripping pain crippled my leg. I glared back at the demon latched onto me, tugging me away from the portal. I kicked at it and lurched toward the wall, my scourging hand fluxing with power again.

Archard's form came into view just beyond the demon. He screamed my name over the chaos of battle. The ridges of his face deepened, and the endless sorrow in his eyes shattered what heart I had left. The last fleck of goodness in my withering soul yearned for him, and I regretted the choice I had made.

"I'll make it back to you. I'll make it back to you," I chanted as a reminder of my promise while surrendering the last of my freedom.

I kicked the demon's head as hard as I could, loosening its grip from my leg, and scrambled away from its bony hand.

I lunged myself upright, glancing back one last time. "See you in Hell," I spat at the monsters swarming my confessional. I succumbed, and the greedy hands of darkness jerked my body into the portal.

THE END

BOOKS BY HAVEN

The Faltering Souls Series

Falter

Nevaeh Richards thinks she has found a chance to leave her homeless life behind. When the spirit of the only father she knows is wrongfully taken to Hell, Nevaeh is hurled into a world haunted by monstrous demons, rogue Guardian angels, love that is beyond her control, and a soul-threatening choice between the inherent evil inside her and the faltering faith she is struggling to grasp.

Severance

Nevaeh has to face the overpowering gravity of her choice to save those she loves while striving for strength to fight her greatest threat—herself.

Contrition

Trial after trial, Nevaeh's loved-ones have struggled to save her from a dark destiny. The time has finally come for her to return home and join the Earth-bound angels in a war threatening to destroy the Human race. Is it really Nev who's walking the Earthly plane, though?

The Perilously Pretty Series

The Perilously Pretty Series is a compilation of wicked romance novels about badass women from all eras and walks of life.

Craving Love & Death

Most women in the '50s dream of a perfect life, pleasing their bread-winning husbands and raising happy families. Vivienne…well…she dreams of a life in which she doesn't succumb to the need to murder the men she sleeps with.

Coveting Love & Revenge

1871, high-society Savannah, Georgia.

Penniless and jaded governess, Synthia James, is trapped with her employer. When he bids their young housemaid to kill a man who threatens his business, Synthia's maternal instincts take over, and she commits the heinous deed herself.

ABOUT HAVEN CAGE

Haven Cage lives in the Carolinas with her husband and son. After many years of dabbling with drawing, painting, and working night shift in the medical field, she decided to try her hand at writing. Unfortunately, her love for books came later in life and proved to add a healthy challenging during her writing journey.

Determined to hone her craft, though, she soaks up as much information as she can, spends her free time tapping away in her favorite local coffee shop, and keeps a good book in hand whenever possible.

What began as a hobby has grown into a way of escape and the yearning to take her journey farther, her love for writing and reading deepening along the way.

Haven loves to socialize and hear from her fans. Connect with her at the following links:

Facebook.com/HavenCage/
Instagram: Haven Cage
Pinterest: Author Haven Cage
Twitter: @HavenCage

Look for Haven on Goodreads.com and add her to your bookshelf!

You can, also, visit her website at www.authorhavencage.com. While you're there, join Haven's Groupies to receive updates, exclusive sales info, and play Haven's Puzzlers for chances to win prizes.

If you enjoyed this book, please leave a review as it is how authors succeed in the publishing world. Without the reader's love, we would be nowhere.

nt.com/pod-product-compliance
.C

84